The
Sugar Cookie
Sweetheart Swap

ALSO BY BESTSELLING AUTHOR DONNA KAUFFMAN

Honey Pie

Babycakes

Sweet Stuff

Sugar Rush

Off Kilter

Some Like It Scot

Here Comes Trouble

A Great Kisser

Let Me In

The Great Scot

The Black Sheep and the English Rose

The Black Sheep and the Hidden Beauty

The Black Sheep and the Princess

Bad Boys in Kilts

Catch Me If You Can

Bad Boy's Next Exit

Jingle Bell Rock

Bad Boys on Board

I Love Bad Boys

READ MORE KATE ANGELL

Sweet Spot (Richmond Rogues)

No Tan Lines (Barefoot William)

Unwrapped (anthology)

The
Sugar Cookie
Sweetheart Swap

DONNA KAUFFMAN
KATE ANGELL
KIMBERLY KINCAID

KENSINGTON PUBLISHING CORP.
www.kensingtonbooks.com

KENSINGTON BOOKS are published by

Kensington Publishing Corp.
119 West 40th Street
New York, NY 10018

All Kensington titles, imprints, and distributed lines are available at special quantity discounts for bulk purchases for sales promotions, premiums, fund-raising, educational, or institutional use.

Special book excerpts or customized printings can also be created to fit specific needs. For details, write or phone the office of the Kensington special sales manager: Kensington Publishing Corp., 119 West 40th Street, New York, NY 10018, attn: Special Sales Department; phone 1-800-221-2647.

Kensington and the k logo are Reg. U.S. Pat. & TM Off.

ISBN-13: 978-0-7582-9088-5
ISBN-10: 0-7582-9088-8

First Kensington Trade Paperback Printing: October 2013

10 9 8 7 6 5 4 3 2 1

Printed in the United States of America

First Electronic Edition: October 2013

ISBN -13: 978-0-7582-9089-2
ISBN-10: 0-7582-9089-6

Contents

PROLOGUE

December 12

The evening air was crisp, with a light breeze whispering the promise of snow. The air inside the community center was significantly more heated. Every man, woman, child, and baked good in the little Blue Ridge town of Pine Mountain was jammed inside the big redbrick building for the annual Twelve Days of Christmas Cookie Swap and were excitedly bidding on tins filled with delicious holiday treats, all in the name of charity.

Normally Clara Parker looked forward to the event. She loved the holiday season, the town traditions, the decorations, and, most definitely, the cookies. Normally. This Christmas, however, the very idea of cookies was filling her with anxiety and dread.

Abby Denton, best friend and professional cookie baker, nudged her elbow. When Clara looked down—she had to look down to make eye contact with pretty much everyone—Abby was pushing a small box into her hands.

"Shh, secret cookie swap," she whispered.

Clara looked over Abby's head at her other best friend, Lily Callahan, who was also the recipient of a box of Abby's cookies. Which could only mean one thing.

Lily immediately shoved the box into her purse. "Oh

no, you did not smuggle your X-rated gingerbread men into the community center. The community center filled with families. With *children*." Lily looked over the red rims of her signature librarian-frame glasses, which looked fabulously smart with her smooth blond hair and neat-as-a-pin attire, and glared at their shorter friend. "We can't open these here!" she hissed under her breath.

Clara, on the other hand, picked open the little flap on the cutely decorated little brown box. "What did you do to them this time?" was all she wanted to know. She peeked under the lid at Abby's famous—or rather, infamous—anatomically correct gingerbread men. Her eyes went wide and stayed that way as she glanced at Abby, who tried—and epically failed—to keep her expression innocent and unknowing. "Peppermint sticks? Really?" Clara's giggle turned into a significant snort that had heads turning their direction, despite the noise level in the building.

Clara's pale skin warmed at the unwanted attention. With her narrow, six-foot frame and short cap of red curls, she liked to pretend she gave off a certain capricious, whimsical air, in the manner of, say, Katherine Hepburn. Only, in reality, it always seemed to play out a lot more like a really tall, awkward-looking Lucy Ricardo.

Lily leaned over and glanced in Clara's box, her mouth forming the shape of an O as her eyebrows lifted above the red frames, but she quickly smoothed her expression and pretended to have a sudden, significant level of fake interest in the auction. "Put those away. People are watching," she said out of the side of her mouth.

"They can look all they want, but they can't have mine," Clara said, her spirits significantly lifted. Or certainly more than she'd anticipated. To say it had been a rough week was the understatement of the year.

"Actually," Abby said, shifting her weight from one foot

to the other, her curvy frame tensing a little as her expression took on a brief, pensive look. Which immediately dissolved as a mischievous light set her warm brown eyes to twinkling. "Someone here can."

Clara looked from the little box in her hands to the tables that lined the walls around the community center's main recreation room. All of them had started the night loaded down with boxes and tins filled with homemade Christmas cookies, but were rapidly emptying as Marianna, the center director, auctioned them off to the highest bidder. Most of the festive parcels went for ten to fifteen dollars, some higher. No one was supposed to know whose tin was whose, and the contents were a surprise for the winner. But Clara had seen the distinctive mail-order cartons Abby had ordered for her brand-new online cookie business and she skimmed her gaze over the remaining goodies. "Where is your . . . there!" She zeroed in on a gaily decorated brown box printed with white icing trim. "You put your cookies in the swap."

"We all did," Abby reminded her.

"Yes, but you usually keep your gingerbread cookies G-rated for friends and neighbors," Clara pointed out. "No one is supposed to know about your little R-rated online enterprise." She grinned. "But I guess that's about to change. Go, you!"

Lily was forced to stop pretending she wasn't paying attention to their every word as she realized what Clara was getting at. She turned her full attention to their short friend, who, though also a blonde, looked nothing like Lily. Abby was a bit shorter, a lot softer, and dressed significantly more casually. Both women were bakers, though Lily was a trained chef, whereas Abby had learned the craft at her grandmother's side. Clara thought of Abby as soft hugs and warm cookies, whereas Lily was far more starched chef's jacket and meticulous career plan.

"You did not," Lily demanded of Abby. "Tell me you did not."

Abby sniffed and looked anywhere but at her two closest friends. "I don't know what you're talking about." But Clara saw the twinkle, and she applauded it. She wished she had half the confidence of either of her friends. And, with the recent sudden change in her job description, a fraction of their baking skills. She quashed the dread that curled right back into her gut and shamelessly kept the topic of conversation anywhere but on her. She'd been the center of enough of that in the past two days to last her a lifetime.

"Yes, Lily," Clara said, "Abby put gingerbread men with peppermint-stick peni—"

"Shh!" Lily whispered, so severely heads turned once again. "Don't you dare say that out loud." She pasted a serene, calm smile on her always carefully made-up face and nodded to some of their nearby neighbors as if to say, "nothing to see here, move along." Once folks had returned their attention back to the next item being auctioned off, she turned her severe expression right back to Abby. "I thought you'd decided to keep the nature of your online business a secret. At least from the folks in town."

Clara snorted again. "Like the town wasn't going to find out. Nothing stays a secret in Pine Mountain. Trust me, I know that better than anyone."

But Lily wasn't listening to her. *"What were you thinking?"*

Abby lifted a smooth shoulder, her shiny blond hair brushing the shoulders of her hand-knit, soft green sweater. "That this town could use some livening up? Come on, I was just trying to have a little fun. Lord knows we could all use a little of that. Which is why I gave you your own little treat boxes." Her expression softened as she looked at Lily. "We're all going through stuff right now.

You with this big cookie competition at the resort, me trying to get my online cookie business up and running, and Clara getting dumped right in the middle of Joe's Grocery."

Clara sucked in a breath. "You already heard?"

Abby rubbed Clara's arm. "Honey, the whole town has heard. Half of them were in the store when it happened."

Clara groaned, even as Lily said, "I didn't hear. What happened?" She turned to Clara. "Why didn't you tell me? Are you talking about Pete Mancuso?"

"Of course you didn't hear," Abby said. "Because you don't have a life. If we didn't drag you out to things like this, you'd never leave your kitchen."

"I'm trying to launch my career, you know that. You better than anyone, with your business starting up. The big resort cookie competition is going to be my ticket. I have to win it. And if I'm going to win it, that means I have to come up with the best, killer cookie recipes on the planet. The galaxy. This means everything."

"You put your business card in your cookie swap tin, didn't you?" Abby asked, though Clara might have said it sounded a bit more like an accusation. "That's the only reason you agreed to come tonight. You probably made test cookies for the contest and the ones in your swap tin are the rejects."

Now it was Lily's turn to pretend she didn't know what Abby was talking about, but she quickly relented. "It's not like they were horrible, they're wonderful. Just not up to competition greatness. And of course I put my card in the tin. That's just good business sense. Didn't you? Now that you're going public?"

Clara barely heard a word they were saying; the noise in the hall had turned into a buzzing inside her head. Everyone knew. Not just the folks in Joe's, which had been awful enough. Everyone. Dear God, she wanted to crawl under the nearest table. The only reason she'd agreed to come tonight was because Lily was looking for an excuse to duck the event and Abby had forced Clara into double-teaming with her to get their workaholic bestie out of the house and into the real world, at least for the evening.

If Clara had known just how much of a laughingstock she actually was at the moment, she'd have picked Lily's side and quite shamelessly hidden out in Lily's tiny apartment kitchen with her. Heck, maybe she'd have learned how to bake something. Which would come in real handy, given she was now in charge of a cookie-baking column for the local paper and she couldn't so much as boil water.

"She put a card in mine, too," Clara offered helpfully, then winced when Lily jabbed her with a pointy elbow. "What?" she said, rubbing the spot. "You did. And I was happy to help." She looked at Abby. "It is a smart idea. I'm surprised you didn't do it, too."

"Lily baked your swap cookies?"

Clara's face warmed again, and she knew, with her fair skin, that her freckles were now standing out like little beacons of guilt. "I didn't know you were going to put your gingerbread guys in the swap, I mean . . . Lily's are G-rated, and this is a family thing, so . . . I'm sorry."

"I didn't mean that," Abby said. "I'm not hurt that you got her to bake your cookies instead of me. I meant that it's tradition to make your own. Even the kids have to make their own."

"You of all people apparently know that I've had a hard enough week." Harder than even they knew. "The last thing I needed was to burn my house to the ground trying to make snickerdoodles. And given my run of luck, and my significant lack of baking skills, you know I would have."

"What did you enter last year? Or the year before that?" Abby eyed Lily. "Have you been covering for her all this time?"

Lily lifted her hands. "Boy, try to do a friend a favor."

"Refrigerator cookies, the store-bought ones," Clara said, ducking her chin as both of her friends swung their gazes to her. "Hey, not everyone is born knowing how to bake, okay?"

"It's not that hard. I'd have taught you," Abby said. "You should have asked me. You should have told us." She folded her arms and tried not to look hurt.

Clara immediately felt bad. She knew traditions were huge for Abby, and having just lost her grandmother, this season they probably were more poignant and meaningful than ever. And guilt piled on top of guilt, given there was more she hadn't told either of her friends.

"But that's not the point here," Abby said, regrouping and looking back to Lily. "I'm just saying that not everything has to be a business opportunity. Whatever happened to going out and mingling with your friends and neighbors for fun? You remember the word, right?" she said to Lily. "F-U-N?"

"Well, there's no rule that says you can't mix business with pleasure," Lily countered.

"Shh," Clara suddenly hissed, then excitedly grabbed Abby's arm. "Speaking of not mixing business with pleasure—liar, liar, pants on fire—I believe that's your little box of peppermint penises going up for grabs right now."

Abby couldn't keep the giggles from rolling out. "Grabs. Heh. I hope a woman wins it. I bet Catherine Carter wouldn't mind a few grins."

"Or maybe Tad Morgan," Clara offered, talking about their delightfully colorful hairdresser. "Did you see the picture of his new 'friend' he posted on his station? I swear, all the good ones are taken, and the better ones are gay."

"Tell me about it," Abby commiserated. "If I wasn't making anatomically correct gingerbread men, I might forget what that appendage looks like."

Clara snorted, clapped her hand over her mouth when the sound was a bit louder than she'd hoped—it always was—then snorted again when Abby made a little circular motion with her hands.

"Stop it, you two," Lily said, smiling benevolently through gritted teeth as several more heads turned in their direction. Then her face paled slightly. "Oh God. Oh . . . that's so not a good thing."

Clara gasped as her gaze followed Lily's. "Oh no. Did Reverend Hughes just bid on Abby's, uh, sticks-in-a-box?"

"He did," Lily said.

Even Abby had the grace to look abashed. "Oh, come on, given all the confessions he's heard in this town, surely he has a sense of humor, right?"

Then the mayor raised his hand, which got a friendly little bidding war going between him and the good reverend.

"Right?" Abby repeated, weakly. Even she groaned in defeat when the president of the school board—the same man who tried to get fish sticks and tater tots banned from the school lunch menu when he found out kids were making graphically suggestive arrangements with them—joined the fun. "I'm so going to hell."

"See, be careful what you wish for," Lily said. When Abby and Clara both looked confused, she added, "You were both just saying you were suffering from the lack of male attention. Well, looks like you'll have some men paying attention to you now, just not in the way you'd hoped. See, you criticize me for not having a life, but at least I

don't have to deal with guy drama. Speaking of which—"
she looked at Clara. "What happened with Pete? I thought
you guys were all hot and heavy after a few dates. You
were hoping for the 'big third date,' right?"

"What's the 'big third date'?" Abby asked, making air
quotes.

Lily looked at her. "The sex date? Come on, everyone
knows if the first two dates go well, by the third date,
someone is going to be clawing someone's clothes off before the night's over." She looked back at Clara, who was
a bit goggle-eyed. "Hey, just because I choose not to deal
with the hassle doesn't mean I don't miss the sex."

Heads were turning again, but even Lily was oblivious
this time. She took Clara's arm. "I am really sorry, whatever it was that happened. I know you really liked him."

"What's not to like," Abby said. "There is no peppermint stick that would do him justice. But men like that,
who look like him . . . I don't know, Clara. I think you
dodged a bullet there."

"Maybe," Clara admitted. "I just wished it hadn't been
shot at me while standing on line at Joe's."

"He broke up with you while you were buying groceries together? Wow, that's low." Lily's gaze skimmed
quickly over the crowded room. "Is he here? Because I'd
love to give him a bit of advice."

Clara winced at that, which brought Lily right back to
her. "Oh sweetie, no, I wasn't going to make another
scene. It just bugs me to no end when anyone can be so
cavalier and unthinking with someone else's emotions."

"I wasn't wincing about the scene, though I'm very glad
he's not here. I don't think I could have stayed otherwise."

"Well then, what is it?"

"Nothing, just—"

"Fran was in Joe's at the same time," Abby helpfully
provided, then patted Clara's arm when she turned

wounded eyes on her friend. "You should have told her. You should have told both of us."

"Yes, you should have. And you don't mean Fran—" Lily's eyes widened. "Fran Stinson? The editor at the paper, *your* editor?"

Clara nodded, steeped in the misery of that horrible memory all over again. "Apparently no one was all that surprised to hear Pete telling me about how his career was demanding all his time, and how I was a really sweet person, but . . ." She shook off the remembered humiliation of how excited she'd been to see Pete was calling her cell phone, and how she'd answered it, almost giddy to hear his plans for their next date. Their third date. Well, sort of, anyway. That's where she'd apparently, once again, read a whole lot more into his actions than he'd intended. "I was getting the supplies for you to bake my cookies, and I was trying to get them all on the counter and juggle the phone at the same time, and somehow I hit the speaker button just as he was regretfully telling me that he thought of me as a friend, and couldn't see me again—"

"Wait," Lily said, her dark blue eyes going downright stormy. "He broke up with you *over the phone*?"

Clara had to admit that maybe Abby had a point. Seeing the utter outrage on Lily's face did make her feel a little better. "Well, I'm not sure he thought of it that way. I think I might have overestimated—"

"That's just about the lowest thing ever. Lower than low. Of course, being God's gift to women, he probably didn't even bat an eye. You're right, Abby, men who look like him rarely ever think about women who—"

"Look like me," Clara finished.

Lily turned her fierce look on her friend. "Now that's not true, and not what I meant, and you know it. Guys like him, they go for the pretty, brainless sort, which you are most definitely not. Men like him aren't looking for an intellectual, emotional connection with someone well rounded and—"

"No, I think they're looking for someone with a byline in the local paper," Clara said, her misery complete.

Both Abby and Clara's mouths dropped open. "Oh no, he didn't," Abby said.

"Yeah, I'm pretty sure he did. I mean, thinking back over our lunch date, as soon as he heard I write a relationship advice column, he was a lot more casual. In fact, he made excuses to leave shortly after that, claiming some emergency at work. At the time I took it as a sincere thing, but now . . . I don't know. I think he was hoping I'd do some kind of story."

"Pig."

"Rat bastard," Abby added.

Clara smiled. "You guys really are good for the ego."

"How did it go with Fran?" Abby asked. "I mean, I heard she was there and you two had a little chat, but she can hardly hold your personal life against you."

"She can when my professional life is about writing advice for the relationship-challenged, and she witnessed, before her very eyes, that her advice columnist is perhaps the most challenged of all in that arena. I mean, everyone was all 'poor Clara-ing' me and not one person was dogging on Pete. You know? Like they all know about my abysmal record with men and didn't blame Pete in the least for moving on to greener pastures."

Lily and Abby wisely said not a single word to that.

But Clara knew what they were thinking. Clearly what the whole town of Pine Mountain had been thinking. Clara sucked at love, she sucked with men, and the very last thing she should be doing was offering advice when it was clear she needed a heaping helping of her own.

"So, are you saying Fran fired you?" Lily's eyes were filled with compassion. "Oh sweetie, you should have told us."

"She fired me from the column, but I did a sort of fast dance and tossed out a few other ideas for other columns. I mean, I was hoping if the column went well, I'd get promoted to features, but . . ."

"So, what did you settle on? What did she ask you to write?" Abby's eyes widened. "Oh, no, honey, did you get something awful, like obituaries, or the crime column or something?"

"Worse. She wants me to do a column on cookie baking. Between the huge resort cookie competition, and it being the Christmas season, she thought it would be a big hit. I don't know where it goes after the new year, but if I don't pull this off, I'm guessing the new year will have me hunting for a new job."

"Cookie baking column," Lily repeated. "But you can't bake."

"I know."

"So why would she even ask you to do that?" Abby asked.

"Because she saw all the ingredients on the counter, the ones I was buying for Lily to make my cookie swap cookies, and . . . well . . . she might have jumped to a conclusion. And I might have let her." She shrugged. "I was about to lose my job. In public. After being dumped. In public. I panicked. I said I could do it. She was so excited about it, you should have seen her. I mean, it was a good save, I thought." Clara looked at her two friends. "I know you guys are busy like crazy, and it's the holidays and all . . . but I thought, I don't know, maybe you could help a sister out?"

Before either could answer, there was a commotion at

the entryway. Everyone turned to see a man, tall, good-looking, his dark hair expensively cut, as was his long, exquisitely tailored cashmere coat, nudge his way through the crowd, apparently in a hurry to find someone, or something.

They weren't close enough to hear what he was asking, because the bidding war was hot and heavy now, and, to Clara's surprise, still on Abby's cookie box. Apparently while they'd chatted about the end of Clara's personal and professional life as she knew it, the male egos in the room had taken the innocent little bidding war into some kind of pissing contest.

"Who is that?" Lily asked.

"I don't know. Movie star looking for his remote set location?" Abby said with a deep, appreciative sigh.

Clara's gaze swung back to the entrance when Mr. Movie Star pushed further into the room, shoved his snow-dampened hair back with one hand, stuck his other one in the air, and shouted, "One hundred dollars."

The room went from noisy hubbub to pin-drop silence in the space of a breath.

Marianna, who was used to dealing with a gymnasium full of intractable teens, didn't bat an eye. She slammed her gavel down and said, "Sold! To the man in the nice coat."

"Thank you," the man said, his voice deep and commanding. "Now, while I have your attention, could someone here be so kind as to direct me to Philadelphia? I'd greatly appreciate it."

"I knew it," Abby said, her voice soft with female appreciation.

Someone stepped up and helped the guy, as someone else shoved his cookie swap prize under his arm.

Clara tugged on Abby's arm. "Oh my God, he just paid a hundred dollars for your gingerbread men!"

"I wonder if you could get him to give you a personal endorsement for your website," Lily pondered. "Guy who looks like him would get you some serious traffic."

"I'd like to give him a personal endorsement," Abby murmured, still starry-eyed, as the man left the building as swiftly as he'd come.

The rest of the evening was comparatively tame and by the time the three of them wedged their way out the front double doors onto the cement steps, the snow had begun.

"Wow, I guess it's a good thing this got done when it did. It's really coming down," Lily said.

Clara thought of her plans to head over to the neighboring town of Riverside, and the bookstore there. Specifically the baking section in the bookstore, where she'd hopefully find something so simplistic even she could follow the directions.

"I better get up the mountain," Abby said. "Before the roads slick over too badly."

"I've got two cookie recipes to tweak this evening," Lily said, then grinned at her friends. "I have a competition to win."

"I've got to figure out how to make cookies without causing a three-alarm fire."

"I just wish I could thank that guy for saving my cookie-baking bacon." When Clara and Lily looked at her blankly, she clarified, "I figure it's better some devastatingly handsome guy is out there eating my peppermint penis gingerbread men than the mayor or the reverend."

All three of them laughed, then Lily tugged them in. "Group hug."

Snow drifted down, dusting their heads, leaving melting crystals on the sleeves of their winter jackets as they all huddled for a quick embrace.

"Drive safe everyone, especially you, Abs," Lily said, as

they hurried down the community center steps toward their cars. "I worry about you all the way up the mountain."

"Driven that road my whole life," Abby called out as she made the dash for her car. "I'll be fine."

The snow was coming down more heavily now, but Clara didn't pick up her step. She loved the snow. She loved everything about winter. She waved at her friends as they dashed off, holding their swap winnings over their heads to protect their hair.

"I'll e-mail you some starter baking tips," Lily called out to Clara. "You'll do great. We'll all help."

"Thanks. You guys are the bestest besties," Clara called, making it to her little SUV as her friends made their way out of the packed lot. She sat in her car for a moment, gazing at the big brick building, reminding herself that they'd raised money for a good cause, she'd had a few laughs with her best friends . . . and, eventually, folks would stop looking at her with pity in their well-meaning eyes. She looked at the box of indecent gingerbread men sitting on the seat beside her. Right on top of the flier for the big ski resort cookie competition. She thought about her new job as cookie columnist and shook her head, smiling despite the knotted stomach. She'd been friends with Lily and Abby since grade school. They'd shared so many things over the years; teachers, parties, homework, sleepovers, bad dates, worse perms, even mono in the eleventh grade. "And now we're the three sugar-cookie-baking amigos," she murmured as she tried to decide what to do with Mrs. Teasdale's tin of fruitcake, which, of course, Clara had "won."

Poor woman was a dear, but she was in her eighties and didn't quite grasp the cookie swap concept. Every year she made a round fruitcake and wedged it into a cookie tin. And every year, everyone in Pine Mountain tried their best not to be the ones stuck with it at the swap. It was always easy to figure out which one was hers. Clara grunted as she hefted it to the back seat. Damn thing weighed a ton. Ignoring the fruitcake, she fished a gingerbread man out of the box and thought of her friends, of their immediate future, and lifted the stick man in a silent toast. "Here's to another new adventure."

Lily was right about one thing. No matter how challenging things got, they always had each other. But as Clara pulled out of the lot, the thought of heading to her cozy, quiet little house just didn't thrill her the same way as anticipating the sex date had.

Girlfriends might be forever . . . but finding a good man, and better yet, keeping him? She snapped the candy off with her teeth and sighed as she crunched it. "Well, it sure beats playing with a peppermint stick."

Where There's Smoke . . .

DONNA KAUFFMAN

Chapter 1

The snow was starting to come down thicker and faster as Clara Parker drove away from the cookie swap . . . and away from her warm, cozy little cottage off Main Street as well. She flipped her windshield wipers to high and clicked on the rear defrosters as she headed over the mountain toward Riverside instead.

A little snowstorm—or even a not-so-little one—wasn't going to keep her from her designated mission: Operation Find Cookie Cookbook. It sounded like a rather silly mission to risk life and limb for, but it was precisely her life she was intending to save. Her first Christmas cookie column was due in to her editor in less than forty-eight hours. Her first of twelve consecutive columns, one per day, every day, leading right up to Christmas. Twelve columns. Twelve cookie recipes, complete with handy baking tips. So, she figured it might be a good idea if she, you know, learned how to bake.

Clara prayed the Riverside bookstore had something with "for Dummies" in the title. "Okay, okay, 'Really Big Dummies,' " she murmured, navigating her way carefully through town on the snow-covered roads. She knew Abby and Lily would happily help her muddle her way through this sudden, unexpected career change, but they had their hands more than full with their own career-oriented baking endeavors at the moment. Besides, she'd gotten herself into her current situation and she needed to prove to her herself, not to mention her boss, that she could get herself back out of it.

It wasn't like being the relationship advice columnist for the *Pine Mountain Gazette* had been her dream job, anyway. It had simply been a means to an end—a stepping stone, she'd hoped, to the type of local-story journalism she'd always wanted to write. So, losing that job wasn't that big a blow. It was more like a relief, really.

"Yeah, that's what it was. A relief." Clara fished another one of Abby's anatomically correct gingerbread men cookies from the gift box on the passenger seat. "Who needs to earn money? Keeping a roof over my head and putting food on the table? Highly overrated." With the engine idling as she sat at the last traffic light before leaving Pine Mountain, Clara studied the perfectly piped white frosting that trimmed the perfect little gingerbread man's perfect little arms and perfect little legs. Cookies. What on earth had she been thinking, agreeing to write a column on Christmas cookies?

The only thing she knew less about than how to have a functional, long-term relationship, was how to bake. If her chance to springboard herself from advice columnist to a local features writer had been dicey, then making the same jump from a column about baking when she couldn't boil water? "Yeah. Awesome move, Clara. Awesome move."

Not that she'd had much of a choice. It had been writing a baking column or standing in the unemployment line. She sighed and snapped off a perfectly frosted leg, crunching as she waited for the light to turn green, trying not to panic. But there was no way around it, really. A columnist who wrote about baking would have to actually bake things. Which was really unfortunate, especially when one took into consideration that there should be a law preventing Clara Parker from ever being allowed, much less required, to voluntarily put herself in a position to be handling sharp objects around things that got really, really hot. Just ask the local fire department.

She finished off the cookie leg and was halfway through the other one as she left the twinkling lights of Pine Mountain behind her. If only eating cookies counted as research. She'd be golden, then. What she needed was a boost of optimism and confidence. She'd gotten away with being an advice columnist for almost three years, hadn't she? How hard could it be to get away with offering baking tips and recipes for the next ten days? So what if she couldn't even reheat Chinese take-out without involving the local PMFD? Besides, they'd probably already forgotten about that whole incident with the melted toaster oven.

Groaning, Clara snapped off a gingerbread arm, then munched her way through that, the other arm, and the head as she navigated the swirling snow and rapidly diminishing visibility down the other side of the mountain. *Why, oh why didn't you talk Fran into a column about something else? Anything else?* She spared a quick glare at the protruding peppermint stick remaining on the front of the little cookie man's torso, right before snapping it off with a decisive crunch. *Men.* It was all their fault, really, that she was in this predicament in the first place.

If Pete Mancuso hadn't been so charming when he'd rescued her runaway grocery cart that afternoon a week ago, offering to buy her a cup of coffee so she could catch her breath after almost being sideswiped by tiny Mrs. Teasdale in her mammoth Lincoln, she wouldn't have assumed he'd been interested in her. And when he'd bumped into her again later at the local café and invited her to an impromptu lunch where they'd spent the afternoon chatting away about their work and such—surely any woman would have been swept off her feet, right? She could hardly be blamed for thinking his intentions were romantic in nature. How was she supposed to know he was just hoping she'd do a human interest story about his star-on-the-rise career as a local chef made good?

But then, she of all people should have known better. She was astutely perceptive when it came to her friends, always aware of the things going on around her, even able to keep up or at least fake her way through most any conversational topic. All in all a pretty sharp, well . . . cookie. She also happened to be a too-tall, gawky woman who was a borderline klutz—and, okay, so maybe that line was invisible—with a shock of red hair, stick thin to the point that her curves ranked in the minus column, who possessed zero skill in knowing how to maximize any of it. And yet, there she'd sat, being all giddy date girl, while Pete had simply been networking. Of course he had. Because why in the world would a guy who looked like Pete Mancuso ever consider romancing klutzy Clara?

And, before Pete? Yeah, there had been Stuart Henry, the accountant at the firm in Riverside that did her taxes. He'd been so serious and goal oriented, so . . . focused. Some might have used the term nerd, but to her it had been more of a hot, professorial, bespectacled kind of thing. And he'd always been so intent, concentrating exclusively on her whenever they talked, oblivious to the world around him, making her feel special, as if she were the only woman in the room. So, no one could blame her if it had taken a few dates—all right, maybe a few months' worth of dates—to realize that he was, in fact, oblivious to the world around him, and that she really was the only woman in the room. The only woman in the room willing to listen to his endless soliloquies on tax law, his utter fascination regarding corporate withholdings, and the excitement of debating the relative merits of resort property ownership versus group timeshares.

Even more mortifying? She hadn't been the one to break up with him. Turns out Stuart's mother didn't really approve of him dating a redhead. She claimed they were all no-good homewreckers. Which, since Stuart was single, was somewhat confusing, until he explained that his father had run off with a redheaded actuary. All of which meant Clara really wasn't the only woman in the room after all. Stuart's mother was also in the room. In fact, Stuart's mother owned the room. And she wasn't about to sublet any of it to Clara.

Before Stuart, it had been Willard Blickensderfer, the newly imported Swiss ski instructor at the Pine Mountain resort. Clara smiled briefly as the peppermint candy slowly dissolved on her tongue. Willard had been a good half foot shorter than she, but there were certain perks to that. They'd aligned well in other ways. Especially when they were both horizontal. In fact, he'd been great in bed, very energetic, very . . . attentive. Turns out, unlike Stuart's mother, Willard had quite a thing for natural redheads. A very good, very enthusiastic thing. He'd also made her feel like the only woman in the room. Which, she'd learned— in a quite mortifying manner on a late-night surprise visit to his little mountain A-frame—was actually a rare thing for him. To his credit, he'd been equally enthusiastic about having her join the two other redheads he'd already been . . . entertaining. So he hadn't, technically, broken up with her. But even Clara had her standards. And though she'd been raised to play well with others, there were some things she simply did not share.

And before Willard . . . gah. She really didn't want to think about it. She had thirty all but staring her in the face and the most meaningful relationship she'd ever had was her freshman year in college. And that hadn't even really been a relationship. What it had been was a solid friendship that seemed headed toward something more serious, or maybe that had only been in her mind, but she had definitely been falling, and falling hard. Only he'd had to leave school suddenly right before the end of their first year for a family emergency, and . . . that had been that. But of all the guys she'd ever spent any appreciable time with, Will Mason had been the only . . . well, the only real one. No artifice, no pretense, no game playing.

Of course, they hadn't really dated. They'd never even kissed. She'd been even more insecure about her height, about her hair, her awkwardness, her . . . well, everything, back then. So not sexy.

But Will . . . well, maybe he hadn't made her feel beautiful exactly, or even like the only woman in the room, but what he had done was even better. He'd made her feel good, happy. Normal. And desirable, even if just as a friend. There had been no other goal than that, no other agenda. He wasn't angling to get her to do his homework, or give him her cuter best friend's phone number. He'd sincerely seemed to like hanging out with her, just . . . for her.

They'd been initially partnered in a study lab for a science class, but had ended up spending hours talking while pretending to do their lab work, much of that time sprinkled liberally with laughter. He'd gotten her dry humor, even thought her always too-loud laugh-snort was cute, or at least not mortifying, and she'd gotten that underneath his laid-back, easy-going style he was a guy with goals, with determination. He was smart, and driven in his own way. He just wasn't obvious about it.

She fished out another cookie, then shoved it back in the box as she slowed down to enter Riverside proper.

More sugar wasn't helping her still-thumping pulse, nor was thinking about her first crush. Like her, he'd been away from home for the first time, and they'd bonded over that. He was originally from Bealetown, which was on the other side of Pine Mountain, so they'd had a lot of the local landmarks in common, if not the same hometown, exactly. As far as she was concerned, if men were more like Will, she'd probably still have her old job at the *Gazette*.

"Actually if there were more men out there like Will Mason, they probably wouldn't need an advice columnist in the first place." *So, either way, you lose.* Clara snorted as she slowly eased into the bookstore parking lot, careful to keep her tires from slipping or sliding in the snow that was starting to mount up on the pavement. It looked like she'd be using four-wheel drive to get home. Maybe even put on the tire chains she kept in the back.

Honestly, it's just as well you're not dishing out advice any longer, she thought as she jockeyed into the first available space she could find. A woman could only take so much rejection before her naturally rose-colored optimism turned into a tell-it-like-it-is reality check, tinged with barely concealed cynicism. For that matter, Will could have grown up to be a self-absorbed, commitment phobic, womanizing jerk, for all she knew.

Memories of how his thatch of wheat-blond hair had always looked like he'd just climbed out of bed, those puppy dog brown eyes of his, the ridiculously sweet dimples that only popped out when he smiled like he meant it . . . yeah, so, okay it was hard to imagine him being a jerk of any kind. But still, she wouldn't be surprised by anything anymore.

"See? You're jaded." She debated on indulging in one more crunchable man cookie, then firmly tucked the flap closed on the box. "No more cookie-shaped men. No more real men, either. And, definitely, no more whining. Be thankful you have a job. Be thankful it's your very favorite time of year. Now, go forth and learn to bake!"

She climbed out and flipped up the hood of her winter coat, then made her way carefully across the parking lot, trying not to pull a face plant, or butt plant for that matter, before making it to the curb. She should have thought to bring weather-appropriate footwear, but she'd come straight from the community center and the forecasters hadn't been really calling for the snowfall to amount to anything. Of course, that had been in Pine Mountain. Riverside was in the valley and often got dumped on in the winter.

Despite her now half-numb toes, once she made it to the sidewalk in front of the bookstore, she didn't hurry toward the big double wooden doors. Instead, she took her own advice and took a moment to enjoy the thick, fat flakes as they tumbled through the crisp night air, twirling all around her. She truly loved the winter, loved the snow, loved all the traditions of the holidays. She wasn't going to let some minor personal setback—okay, even a not-so-minor one—interfere with enjoying her favorite time of year. Her own private little rebellion against the reality check life was handing her. Again. To that end, she stuck her tongue out and let a few flakes melt on her tongue.

"Take that, life," she said, a resolute smile on her face as she pulled open the big wooden doors with an enthusiastic, rebellion-fueled tug . . . and slipped, almost falling flat on the snow-covered pavement as her feet went out from under her. She managed at the last second to grip the oversized door handle, barely preserving her clothes and her butt, if not her pride.

When she finally managed to right herself, she was relieved to find not a single person had noticed her less-than-graceful entrance. Not because the place was empty.

Far from it. The shop was jam-packed. Body-to-body packed. But everyone was facing toward the back of the store. Now that she thought about it, the parking lot had been rather full. Of course, it was only two weeks to Christmas, so every parking lot was an endless sea of jockeying cars these days . . . but this was a little nuts, even for this time of year.

It took her a moment as she tipped her hood off—which crumpled and promptly sent a sheaf of snow down the back of her neck and under her collar, making her squeal—to realize some kind of event was going on.

"I know, honey," a woman in front of Clara said, when her squeal and wriggling to keep more snow from going inside her coat drew attention. "It is pretty exciting, right?"

"Right," Clara agreed, dancing a little jig to make the snow melt faster, even though she hadn't a clue what the woman was talking about. If there were signs posted outside, she'd missed them while having her defiant snowflake moment, and the place was too jammed full inside to see any signs. Her height did come in handy on occasion, however, and she could look over most of the sea of heads to where some kind of table was set up near the back of the store. Ah, a book signing. There were too many people crowded in front of the table to see who the guest author was, but she was guessing, since the entire line snaking up and down almost every aisle was comprised entirely of women, that it was probably a children's author. Which made perfect sense at Christmastime.

She'd shopped in the bookstore many times over the years, but had to dodge elbows and shopping bags as she tried to figure out where the cookbook aisle was. That part of the store format was foreign to her. She managed to only partially knock over a spinner rack and clear a corner off of a huge display table before mercifully spying

Paula Deen smiling benevolently like Clara's own personal savior from an endcap cookbook display. Sighing in relief, Clara dodged around another cluster of excitedly chattering women—whoever this author was, these women sure were excited, bordering on downright giddy—and escaped into the otherwise mercifully abandoned cookbook aisle. Apparently no one in the store was shopping for anything other than whatever the guest author was selling.

Clara tuned out the hubbub and refocused on the mission at hand. Tilting her head, she started a slow scan of the shelves crammed full of cookbooks. *My God, there are so many.* Was she the only person in the world who didn't cook? And just how many recipes did any one person actually need? She kept skimming titles, trying to be bolstered rather than intimidated by the sheer numbers of spines she had to scan through. Surely with that kind of inventory, there would be something that would get her through the rudimentary steps without burning her little cottage to the ground. She made a mental note to contact her insurance agent to see about upping her coverage. And another note to put the PMFD on speed dial. She kept skimming.

"I still can't believe he's actually right here, in the flesh."

"And have you seen the flesh? My, my, he sure grew up fine, didn't he?"

"Oh, that's better than fine. That's prime, grade-A man meat right there."

A gurgle of shocked laughter followed that proclamation, then, "When you're right, you're right."

Clara looked up over the top of the bookshelf to find two middle-aged women standing in the line snaking along on the other side. *The children's author was a guy?* She supposed, if she thought about it, that probably wasn't so odd. And if he was "grade-A man meat," well, that explained the enthusiasm a little more. She craned her neck to try and get a peek behind the table again, but it was hopeless. Not that she cared, really. She was giving up men. Okay, so she was temporarily giving up men. Eventually she'd want sex again, so she'd have to get over her newly jaded and cynical outlook. But that was next time. And not until next year, or at least until twelve cookie columns from now. For the time being, she was single, celibate, and focused on her career. Such as it was.

"I read a story in the paper about him. Said he's from Bealetown, born and raised. Came home from college to help his mom after his dad passed. Joined the fire department, just like his dad, his granddad, too. Well respected from what I read."

"Makes you wonder what the family thinks about him being part of something like this, doesn't it?"

"Well, I don't know. I mean, it's a charity thing, right? Doesn't the money from the sales go to that children's hospital? I bet they're real proud of him."

"Well, I'm not sure how proud I'd feel if my Jimmy shucked his clothes to pose on the front of some calendar, women drooling all over him."

"No offense, honey, but nobody is going to pay money to see your husband naked on the front of anything. Billy Mason, on the other hand . . . well, we're here, and we're drooling, aren't we?" The woman laughed, and, to her credit, her friend laughed right along with her.

"Like you said," her friend added, "it's for charity. We're here just being civic minded is all."

"Exactly. If that makes you feel better." They both snickered again.

But Clara wasn't really listening any longer. Her attention had been derailed when they'd mentioned the name Billy Mason. *Couldn't be.* It was just that she'd been thinking about Will for the first time in eons—her memories had made her take that mental leap. Because what would the odds of it be, anyway? Except, she remembered, all too clearly, his telling her one night about how everyone called him Billy back home, and when he'd left for college, he'd decided he wanted to be known as Will, something more adult sounding.

Clara had followed along, though, privately, she'd thought Billy really suited him better. It was cute, and sexy. When he smiled, he had those sweet dimples and a hint of a cleft in his chin, plus there had still been a few freckles sprinkled across the bridge of his nose. He hadn't been classically handsome, more a hybrid between cute, towheaded kid and burgeoning adult. He'd been taller than she by a fair amount, which she'd also privately liked, and though he was a lot less gawky than she was, he was more geek than jock. Rawboned, her grandfather would have termed it—as she'd once overheard him describing her. "Only, you know, a girl," he'd added at the time, but, after looking up the word, Clara hadn't thought the qualification made it all that much better.

She remembered that though Will still had a bit of that adolescent baby face, his jaw was angular and his beard, though also blond, was more whiskery looking than peach fuzzy. His neck was a little on the long side, his Adam's apple a wee bit too pronounced, but she remembered him having broad shoulders, and big, capable hands, helping her by always automatically carrying her books, or ushering her, steady palm on her back as they navigated through crowded hallways and along rows of seats in packed lecture halls. Something about that broad hand always made her feel steadier, less klutzy. Yep, steady, reliable, always with a grin and a funny aside . . . that was the Will Mason she knew. Or had known, nine, almost ten years ago.

But . . . Will Mason, studly fireman calendar guy?

Clara had to have it wrong. And yet, with her mind still

sifting through yesteryear and all those long nights she'd spent in the library with him, or grabbing pizza, or walking the quad, suddenly she was nudging herself through the crowd, working her way toward the back of the store. Not to butt in line. She just needed to see, needed to know for sure, whether it was him. It would bug her and keep her up wondering if she didn't find out. At least, that was her excuse.

Every step closer she got, the more she tried to convince herself it wasn't him . . . the more she knew it couldn't be anyone else. When Will had left a week before the end of their freshman year, right during finals, she hadn't known what the emergency was, just that it was something to do with his family. When he hadn't come back, or contacted her, even to say good-bye, she'd asked around and found out his dad had died of a heart attack. She knew he had four younger sisters, who would have also become suddenly fatherless, and that he came from a long line of firemen. So, the story lined up.

Of course, he'd been pretty emphatic that he wasn't going to end up being another one in that long line. He'd been the first Mason in his entire family tree to go to college. And, from what he'd told her, they'd all been very proud of him, supported him and his choice. She wondered if he had ever gone back, gotten his degree.

Of course, she thought, as she excuse-me-pardon-me'd her way up another row, if he was here signing some kind of hot fireman calendar . . . she had to guess probably not.

Hot, hunky fireman calendar guy. Will Mason. She smiled to herself, just not able to picture those two things in the same sentence. Unless calendar guys had gotten less bulky muscle mass and more . . . well, refined sounded better than skinny. Will had been strong, and able-bodied, but though she'd never seen him without a shirt, she re-

ally couldn't imagine his body being the kind that someone would want to spray tan, oil up, and put on the cover
of a calendar.

"Hey, no butting in line." The woman next to her
shoved her shopping bag in front of Clara to block her
way.

Clara grunted as the heavy bag connected with her
stomach and hips. "I'm not—I don't want a calendar," she
managed through a pained wheeze. "I'm just—"

"We all waited," the woman persisted. "You have to
wait." She shoved her bag again.

"Mel, come on, she's just trying to shop here—" Someone tried to pull the woman back in line and Clara took
the opportunity to squeeze by before being thumped
again.

"No cheaters," the woman—Mel—erupted, and yanked
her arm free just as Clara was edging past, which had the
unfortunate result of sending a sharp elbow, backed up by
the full force of the weighted-down book bag, directly
into Clara's hip.

The woman in front of Clara turned at the commotion,
and instinctively reached out to help, which was very kind
of her, except by turning, she'd created a gap in the line,
which Clara careened straight through as she tried and
failed to regain her balance. She barely missed barreling
into the woman standing just beyond that, saved only
when the person next to her quickly tugged the woman
out of the way . . . which gave the still wheeling Clara a
direct opening straight to the front of the line. Which was
where she landed, half sprawled across the heavy wooden
table that had been set up for the signing.

Breath knocked out of her, sounding like a gasping fish
as she tried to wheeze out an apology, she managed to de-
molish the rest of the neatly organized table display as she
scrambled off and tried to push herself upright. Which

would have worked, except her free hand was on a slick, shiny calendar, which slid when she pushed upward, sending her right back across the thigh high table. "Unh, oof! Gah!" was what came out instead.

A pair of strong, very capable hands clamped on her upper arms, lifting her up just enough to get her feet under her. Her rescuer stood, as Clara's feet found purchase on the carpeting, but he kept those wonderfully steady, strong hands on her as she tried to stop wobbling on her feet.

She sucked in a deep breath as the air rushed back in, and finally looked up to apologize once again, and thank him for keeping her from doing any further damage, to herself or his nice table display. Only whatever words she might have said died as her throat closed right back over again. She stared into a pair of oh-so-familiar puppy dog brown eyes. A quick scan over the rest of him, however, proved that was the only part of Will Mason that was familiar.

Holy . . . moley. Late bloomer didn't even begin to describe the—what had that woman called it? Man meat? Dear Lord, he had plenty of that. And none of it needed a spray tan or any other fake enhancements to help sell it, because it was pretty damn fine in all its chiseled magnificence, all on its own.

He had on a pair of canvas turn-out fireman pants and red suspenders. That was it. In between was an expanse of gorgeously perfect pecs and six-pack abs, framed by big, broad shoulders and arms with that nice pump of bicep and hard, curving triceps. It was honestly just . . . what the hell had he been eating for the past nine years?

"Wow. Will," she finally managed. "Uh, long time." *Brilliant opener, Clara.* And here she thought nothing could be more mortifying than Pete dumping her in front of God and everyone while standing on line at Joe's Grocery two days ago. Not true, as it turned out. Because it immediately became quite clear that the recognition did not go both ways. Of course, what with the family tragedy, he'd probably forgotten her five minutes after leaving campus. And that had been almost a full decade ago.

Then his handsome smile faltered as his gaze focused and he really looked at her. Instantly, his face split wide in a sexy smile that made her insides go a little flippy. Okay, a lot flippy.

"Parker? Is that really you?"

Clara couldn't stem the flush of embarrassment that had already flooded her cheeks, and likely turned her neck into a lovely, splotchy mess as well. Only one person had ever called her Parker. It was silly, because he'd probably meant it in a buddy kind of way, but . . . well, it had always made her feel special. She tried to ignore the splotchy neck and did her best to channel her inner Lauren Bacall as she pasted on a smile and went for the throaty voice. "How many ever-so-graceful, redheaded bombshells do you know?" Her smile twisted wryly. "Emphasis, of course, on the bomb part."

He laughed, and those dimples flickered to life. The tiny cleft made an appearance, too . . . which brought back so many memories, all of them so very good, that she found herself laughing as well. Which helped her to ignore the utterly adult reaction that other certain tingly parts of her body were having. "Nice save, by the way," she added. "I owe you."

Brown eyes twinkled. "Well, how about I collect the debt with a cup of coffee later. When this . . ." He gestured vaguely to the line behind her. " . . . is over. It might be a little bit," he added, looking sheepish. "It's for charity."

Yes, Will, she wanted to say, that was why all those women had crowded into narrow aisles, in an overheated bookstore, in the middle of an impending snowstorm. For charity.

And how on earth he managed to look all adorably humble, much less naïve, when he was sitting behind a table in a public bookstore in all of his half-naked, chiseled glory, signing calendars that featured . . . Her gaze drifted downward and her eyebrows climbed as she looked back at him. "You're on the cover."

"Yeah. No accounting for taste, right?"

She could have sworn his cheeks darkened, just a fraction.

"Hey, you gonna stand there all day?" came a disgruntled voice behind her. "Because we waited *in line.*"

Clara didn't miss the emphasis on the last part, and she quickly straightened away from the table.

"I meant it, about the coffee. Would you wait around a bit?" he asked, looking and sounding quite sincere.

Clara reminded herself that she'd thought Pete Mancuso had sounded sweetly sincere, too. But she knew Will. And he'd never been anything but honest and open. His entire outward appearance might have undergone an almost unbelievable transformation, but those eyes, that voice . . . the way he looked at her . . . all of that made her want to believe that underneath his now Adonis-like frame, he was still the same tall, skinny, geeky kid who'd carried her book bag for her.

Acutely aware now of a multitude of gazes drilling her in the back, Clara clutched her purse and the cookbook she just now realized she was also carrying to her chest. "Yeah. I mean yes, sure. I'd—I'd like that."

Two ladies behind her more or less bodily shoved her to the side. Will kept his hand on her arm until she'd moved around the side of the table, then sent her an apologetic look before turning back to his adoring fans.

Clara was certain it was just her imagination, but his smile didn't seem quite as sincere when he asked the pushy woman how she wanted her calendar signed. No dimples.

Bumping and wedging her way around another spinning display rack, she finally reached the edge of the store, intending to head to the cashier. Good thing she looked down at the cookbook in her hand. "Red Hot Meat." She tried to suppress the laughter, but couldn't, or the loud snort that followed, either. Her gaze shifted immediately to the back of the room, and somehow—because her karma was like that—the seas parted and Will looked right at her. And grinned.

Suddenly she didn't feel so awkward, or dorky. Okay, so that wasn't at all true. Her neck splotches now reached all the way down the front of her chest and probably across her entire torso. But she found that it didn't matter as much.

Old friends, she reminded herself as she fumbled the cookbook back on the shelf. That's all they were. She was giving up on romance. At least through the holidays. And, after that, she was just going to date men for sex. The sex part she could manage. She had needs, after all. It was just the relationship part she sucked at. And it had been her experience that men didn't really want a relationship with her anyway. She should have figured out the sex solution earlier. Could have saved herself a lot of trouble, not to mention public humiliation.

Right now, however, there would be no sex, either. She had cookies to bake. Columns to write. A career to save.

Her gaze drifted to the back of the store again. "And that's one fireman who won't—can't—be on your speed dial."

Chapter 2

Will pushed open the door of the twenty-four hour coffee shop conveniently located two doors down from the bookstore, and gestured for Parker—Clara—to go in ahead of him. "You know, if you'd given me a head's up that you were coming, I'd have made sure you got a calendar." His smile deepened when she glanced at him. "No need for the grand entrance."

"Yes, well, embarrassing myself in local retail establishments seems to be a trend with me this week," she said, brushing the snow off her sleeves as she turned to look at him. Which had the unfortunate effect of fluffing a frosty pile of flakes right into his eyes. "Oh! Sorry."

He laughed and wiped his hand down his face. "That's okay. The bookstore was pretty warm with all those people. I could use a little cooling off. So, what other events have you been crashing this week?"

He'd forgotten how easily she blushed . . . and how cute she was when she tried to brazen it out.

"Actually, I didn't know about the signing. I came to pick up a cookbook." She lifted the bag in her hands, then tried to pull it away when he reached for it.

He just laughed and slipped it from her fingers before she clobbered an unsuspecting patron with it. "So, you've learned to cook then?"

She was even cuter when the blush crept down to her neck, making her all flustered and nervous. The Parker he remembered wasn't at all shy or self-conscious, at least she hadn't been with him. He'd noticed it often enough when they were in groups of people, though. Something about the way she'd so readily opened up to him, laughed with him, shared her thoughts, had always made him feel good, confident, strong. Things he hadn't been so sure of back then. And, perhaps, not always these days, either. He knew how much he'd missed that—missed her—nine years ago, when life had forced a new path on him. Seeing her hazel-green eyes light up and her lips twist in that self-deprecating way she had made him realize how much he still missed it now.

"What do you know about my cooking prowess or lack thereof?" she asked, still trying to bluff her way out.

He stepped behind her and helped slide off her coat. He'd forgotten how nice it could be, standing close to a woman near his own height. He recalled the countless times he'd wanted to step in closer, lean in, kiss the side of her neck, wondering what it would taste like, and if she'd drop her head back on his shoulder, and invite him to discover even more.

In your dreams, maybe. Back then, he'd had less than no game with the opposite sex. He was too tall, too skinny, too quiet, without a single sports uniform hanging in his locker. The lack of which had also been a deep disappointment to his basketball-playing father, who'd looked forward to sharing that bonding experience with his only son. But it just hadn't been Will's thing. And his father hadn't been all that excited to talk with him about things like science or technology, either. His mom had been too busy dealing with her own issues, as well as his four younger sisters, to really be there for him, though he knew she would have if she'd been able.

So, lacking that home-based foundation of confidence, he'd always felt a bit out of step with his peer group. Not that the opposite sex hadn't come on to him anyway from time to time. He just never expected it, always got so tongue-tied, always blew it. But not with Parker. Never with Parker. Which was why he'd never risked pushing it. She'd become too important to him to blow it by making some dork move.

But he wasn't an inexperienced college freshman now. And she smelled sweet and inviting. Her hair, damp from the snow, clung to her neck, and he had an almost over-whelming urge to lean in, nudge it aside, and finally find out the answer to that burning question. She was no col-lege freshman now, either. Would she move back against him? Invite him in? Turn into his arms and offer up more than a taste of her slim neck? He wasn't sure if it was the close proximity, the bombardment of unexpected memo-ries, or the fact that he hadn't eaten anything since the bagel he'd had for breakfast . . . but his body surged to life. And he didn't do a damn thing to stop it from happening.

"Well," he said, still standing close behind her, neither of them taking their seats. "Perhaps you've forgotten that little incident with the microwave and exploding popcorn bag."

"As I recall, I explained how we didn't have a mi-crowave in my house growing up. How was I supposed to know you couldn't put that aluminum popcorn shaker thing in there?" She turned around, but rather than step back to give her space, he stayed where he was, which crowded her between the edge of the table . . . and him. Her pupils expanded as she held his gaze. His smile grew as his gaze drifted down to her mouth.

He'd also forgotten her habit of biting the corner of her bottom lip when she was nervous. Mostly because he'd never been the one to make her nervous. He wished he'd known back then that making a girl a little nervous wasn't always a bad thing.

Without taking his gaze from hers, he hung her coat on the peg by the booth next to them, and let his gear bag slide from his shoulder to the bench seat. He was a heartbeat away from tossing the bag with the cookbook in it to the table too, and pulling her into his arms, but something in the way her gaze flickered away from his held him in place at the last second. It was insane, anyway, to think they could not only just pick up where they'd left off, but that they'd move immediately forward into something they'd never been to each other. But that didn't stop him from wanting to, from wanting her.

He slid the book out of the store bag instead, and broke eye contact to look at the title. *"Cookie Baking for Children,"* he read aloud, then immediately took a respectful step back. It had been almost ten years. And he was an idiot. "A mommy-daughter project?" he asked, surprised by the thick note in his voice, and even more by just how disappointing it was to realize she was married, with kids. *Of course she is, dumbass!* "Or son," he quickly added, then forged a smile. "If my mom had taught me how to bake as a kid, maybe I would have a menu that included more than grilled cheese sandwiches and spaghetti."

"Didn't your sisters teach you? I figured with the size of your family, you'd have learned by osmosis."

It didn't escape him that she hadn't answered the question. "Five women in our tiny kitchen? I did my best to be just about anywhere else when that was going on."

She smiled at that, and quickly snatched the book back. "It's a gift," she said, only she looked away as she said it.

Clearly not the truth, then. But why hedge? "So, not for you and your kids."

"I don't have any kids."

He tried not to be obvious with his sigh of relief. Especially when he wasn't even sure why it mattered in the first place. Sure, she'd been important to him once, very much so, but that had been a long, long time ago.

"How about you?" she asked, and he noticed her gaze had dropped to his hands.

"No kids. Not yet, anyway." He couldn't help it, he glanced at her hands, too. No ring. Which was when he quickly added, "Not married, either."

She laughed. "Not for lack of offers, I'm guessing."

He frowned, raised one eyebrow. "Why would you say that?"

"What, you don't have any mirrors where you live?" She laughed as he felt his own face and neck warm up a little. "I mean, come on, you were just sitting next door, half naked, signing hundreds of photos of yourself. You've really, uh . . . blossomed since I last saw you. Not that you weren't good-looking back in college," she hurried to add, looking suddenly embarrassed. "I mean, we were just friends, I know, but, I noticed. Then. And now. It was kind of hard not to, what with your shirt off and all those muscles, I mean . . . look at you. And . . . oh boy." She started to turn away, but he put his hand on her arm.

"I noticed you, too." The words were out before he'd had a chance to figure out what he should be saying, or not saying. But, now that they were, he had to admit, he was curious about her response. "Then . . . and now."

To his surprise, she laughed, making her eyes spark more green than brown, even as her fair skin stayed delightfully pink. "What, that I was an ungainly, awkward giraffe? Hard not to, I know." Her smile turned wry. "Only in my case, given my ever-so-graceful entrance, clearly I didn't grow out of it."

He reached up and pushed a damp, dark red curl from her forehead. He'd also forgotten how nice it was to look into a woman's eyes when they were almost level with his own. "That's not what I remember. To me, you were like this wonderful, exotic creature. So tall, with hair the most brilliant color, a laugh that could light up a room—or me, anyway—and the most amazing ability to just come out and say whatever was on your mind. I was both intimidated by you and inspired."

Her mouth dropped open, stunned surprise clear in her eyes . . . but his gaze had drifted to, and stayed on her mouth. "I used to wonder," he said, hearing the husky note in his own voice. "God, you have no idea how much time I spent wondering what it would be like to kiss you."

He saw her throat work, watched as her lips parted again, heard the soft intake of breath. "Why . . . uh . . . why didn't you?" Her voice was barely more than a whisper.

He stroked a finger along the side of her face and felt an almost palpable sizzle of awareness that leapt from his fingertip straight to his pulse. "You were the best friend I'd ever had . . . the only girl I'd ever known that way. I had buddies back home, good ones, but you were . . . we were really friends. True friends. I didn't want to mess that up. And I probably would have. I wasn't all that confident back then. I was the awkward one."

"I never saw that."

"Because I wasn't when I was with you. I was just . . . myself."

"Me, too," she said, sounding in utter awe that he might have felt the same. "I never felt stupid or dorky with you. I mean, I was anyway, but somehow, when I was with you, well, okay, it was still embarrassing, but it didn't cripple me socially like it usually did. It was funny and just . . . well, me. And that was okay."

"It was totally okay." His lips curved. "You made me feel all manly and capable. I mean, if you'd been a total Amazon warrior, I'd have never been able to string two words together around you. I liked that you were both goddess and dork. It made you more real."

"Dork, for sure. But goddess?" Her lips quirked. "Now I know you've mistaken me for someone else."

He shook his head. "There's only one Parker."

Her smile warmed, as did her eyes. "I forgot how much I liked it that you called me Parker. Why did you?"

"To keep the boundaries established, so you'd know I just wanted to be friends, buddies. Give me a shot, anyway." Now his grin turned self-deprecating. "Epic failure, just so you know. You were a friend, a buddy even, but I was never, not for one second, anything but completely and fully aware that you were all girl." He let his hand drop away. "Probably a good thing I had to leave school the end of our first year. I'm sure I'd have eventually screwed it all up anyway."

"I'm sorry," she said, her gaze deepening as she looked at him. "About your dad. I—I asked, after you left."

"I should have told you, should have contacted you, said good-bye at least," he said. "They didn't tell me—I didn't know, until I got home. And then it was . . . well, it was overwhelming, really. In more ways than I'd ever had to deal with before. I knew immediately that college wasn't going to be in the cards for me after all and so I just, well, I shut it all out. It was the only way I could deal with everything. I'm sorry. I shouldn't have shut you out along with everything else."

"No, no. Don't be. I mean, I was worried, and I felt so bad. About all of it. But I completely understood. I can't even imagine what that must have been like for you."

"You didn't have a father, either. Or a mother."

"But I don't remember my parents. I was too young when they died. You can't mourn what you never had. I thought about you losing your dad, and tried to imagine what it would be like to suddenly lose my grandmother.

And I didn't have siblings and everything else you had to deal with."

"Is your grandmother—"

"She passed three years ago, but it wasn't sudden, and, in the end, it was a blessing for her. Hard, and sad, but still, nothing like what you went through. My life wasn't utterly changed because of it. Anyway, I didn't mean to bring up a painful subject. I was just, well, I'm sorry, that's all."

"Thank you," he said. "It wasn't easy then, and I still miss him, we all do, but it was a long time ago now. I'm fine. We're all fine." He held her gaze. "Man, I missed you when I left. So much."

"Yeah," she said, softly. "I did, too."

"So many times I just needed someone to talk to, to help me get a handle on everything. I—a hundred times, more than that, I wanted to call you."

"You could have. You should have."

He shook his head. "It was all too complicated. My life was upside down, and you were still back at school, where I wanted to be." He shook his head again, but this time to clear the lingering memories. "It was partly because I didn't want to burden you, but mostly, I think now it was selfish. I just—"

"Didn't need to be reminded that you weren't going to get what you wanted so badly."

He caught her gaze again. "Yes," he said, knowing she meant a college degree . . . and also knowing it had been that and so much more. He started to lift his hand to her face again, to move in closer, but the barista chose that moment to stop by their table.

"Peppermint mocha lattes?" he asked brightly, seemingly unaware he was interrupting a moment. "It's our holiday special."

Parker stepped back, banged her hip against the table, then, that twisty-lip smile on her face, stumbled as she awkwardly angled her long frame into the narrow confines of the booth bench in a half sprawl, before righting herself and propping her elbow on the table, chin in hand, as if she'd been nothing but graceful.

"You okay?" Will asked, unable to keep from grinning.

"What? Why do you ask?" she asked with fake innocence.

He chuckled. "I'll just have a regular hot chocolate, Lonzo," he told the barista, reading his nametag. He glanced at their booth. "Parker?"

"Same for me."

"Extra whipped cream on both," he told the young man, who took the order, then headed toward the front counter. "Hey, do you have sandwiches, anything like that?"

Lonzo turned back, smiling. "We've got an ahi tuna sprout wrap. Assortment of cookies and pastries. And we do a breakfast panini after eleven p.m."

The sound of that breakfast thing made Will's stomach growl, but it was only a little after ten. He looked at Parker. "Do you want anything else?" She shook her head, so he turned back to the barista. "I'll take the wrap, two if you have them, a few cookies—any kind—and a bottle of water, too."

The young man's smile spread to a grin. "Long day?"

Will chuckled. "You have no idea."

Lonzo gave him a quick onceover, then, eyes twinkling, he added, "Yeah. I wanted a calendar, but that line was crazy long."

Will heard a quickly stifled snort from Parker and felt his face warm just a little, but he smiled at the younger man. "I signed stock before I left. You can probably grab one tomorrow. It's a good cause."

Lonzo's grin broadened. "Yeah, that's totally what I was thinking. Doing it for the cause." He whistled as he headed back to the front counter.

Parker wiggled her eyebrows at Will when he turned back toward the booth. "He's a cutie. I could get his number for you."

"Thanks, but I prefer tall redheads with a cooking impediment." He grinned when her cheeks went pink all over again. Yep, he'd definitely underestimated the pleasure of flustering a pretty girl. He debated on whether to slide in next to her like he wanted to, but ended up shoving his gear bag over and sliding in across from her.

"You have quite the adoring public." She nudged his feet under the table with her toes. "Now who's the god?"

The heat crawled down to his neck. He'd forgotten that flustering thing went both ways. "It's for a good cause," he said, which had become his go-to, standard reply for any comment made to him about his current fifteen minutes of cover model fame.

"How did the whole thing come about?"

"Good friend of mine, a guy on the squad, his mother-in-law works for a publishing house that does this kind of thing. And he has a daughter who's pretty sick. It's not good."

"Oh, I'm so sorry."

"Yeah, it's—he feels really helpless. So his wife's mother pitched the idea to her bosses, about doing a charity calendar featuring firemen from Philly and surrounding areas, with the proceeds going to the children's research hospital where his daughter, and a lot of other kids, are being treated."

"Is your friend in the calendar?"

Will laughed. "Marvin? No. He's not . . . well, let's just say he was happy to recruit me, but even happier not to step in front of the camera himself."

Parker smiled. "It's a good thing, you helping him. Are you glad you did it?"

"Oh, of course. It's . . . I won't lie. It's turned into something I couldn't—I had no idea, about any of this kind of thing." He waved his hand in the general direction of the bookstore. "Much less what it would become."

"But it's bringing more money to the cause, right?"

"Absolutely. Which is the only reason on God's green earth I'd have sat behind that table half dressed in turn-out gear for nine straight hours, trust me," he said, chuckling.

"You made more than just the kids at that research hospital happy." She grinned. "Those women were downright giddy."

He dipped his chin, willing the heat to leave his face. "It's . . . crazy. That's all I can say."

"You didn't know you'd be on the cover?"

He shook his head. "Found out when the calendars arrived four weeks ago. We started selling them a week or so before Thanksgiving. It's . . . well, it's certainly turned out to be a way bigger deal than I anticipated. Newspaper interviews, photos, signings. A couple of us even did this morning show for a regional network in Philly. Crazy. But it's almost over, thank God, so . . ." He shrugged.

Parker just kept grinning at him. And when Lonzo came over bearing a large tray filled with their order, leaving him an extra cookie "on the house" under which Will found a note with the young man's cell number scrawled on it, her grin turned into a snort of laughter.

"Come on," she goaded. "You have to kind of love it. I mean, at the very least, you probably got a few hot dates out of the deal."

"I'm not a piece of meat," he said. "I'm sensitive, I have feelings," he added, with faux seriousness, which lasted for about a split second. Then they both busted out laughing.

"Yeah, that's what I thought. Men," Parker said, snatching one of his cookies.

Will's eyebrows lifted at that parting shot. "Ouch. Sounds like someone isn't all that enchanted with my gender at the moment."

"Like I said, it's been an interesting week. Month. Okay, years. Years, Will." She waved her cookie before he could respond. "But that's all in the past."

"It is?"

"Yep." She took a decisive bite of the thick, chewy chocolate chip cookie and his entire body surged right back to life when a melted piece of chip glazed the corner of her mouth. He'd never wanted to lick anything more in his entire life.

"I've sworn off men. Except for sex, of course."

Will had just taken a sip of water to cool himself off and almost choked on it. He managed to get it down, barely, then said, "Excuse me? Did you just say—?"

"I did. I mean, I'm not dead, right? And we're all adults. Besides, it turns out I completely suck at relationships."

"But not at sex."

Her neck got a little splotchy, but she brazened it out. He didn't feel the least bit responsible, either. After all, she'd started it.

"I'd like to think not," she said, somewhat primly. "No complaints, anyway."

"I'd bet not."

Her gaze narrowed. "What does that mean?"

He lifted his hands off the table, palms out. "Nothing. Compliment."

"Oh. Well . . . thank you. You'd probably agree with me, too, right? About just having sex, I mean. Not about me being good at it, since you wouldn't know that, but wouldn't it just be easier all around if that's all we did? Have sex?"

"I—" Will was pretty sure the combination of his body going rock hard and his brain firing off multiple synapses as he pictured doing with her exactly what she was saying she wanted to do—have sex and only sex, all the time— had left him completely incapable of speaking anything intelligible.

"I just think it would be a lot easier if we were direct and up front about wanting what we want, without all the emotional entanglements, right?"

He made some kind of strangled noise in his throat that she apparently took for agreement.

"Men have always taken the caveman approach. I think it's time we women wised up and did the same thing. You man, me woman, we mate like bunnies. Then you leave cave and me with big smile on my face. Win-win."

It took several sips of water before he could will his brain to stop the bombardment of images, from picturing her in an admittedly politically incorrect, skimpy little animal-fur cavewoman getup, to him dragging her back to his cave by her . . . her pelt, so they could have wild, Jurassic sex—all the time, her words—giving him an entirely new appreciation for the hunter-gatherer work ethic.

"I, uh—" He paused to clear his throat, but even so the words still came out a bit strained. "I might have thought so," he managed. "Once upon a time."

She looked surprised. "But not now? Oh." Her smile faded as comprehension dawned. "Are you . . . you're in a relationship then? A good one." She hadn't made that last part a question. And he tried to figure out if her expression was disappointment, resignation, or indifference. For once, he couldn't quite tell.

"I'm—"

She cut off his reply. "That's good, though. I mean, I do realize that there are people who have good relationships, great ones, even. In fact, it's a relief to hear from some-one—anyone—who's in one. In my former line of work . . . well, let's just say, my current viewpoint would have probably received a very favorable response, but it wouldn't have helped anyone."

"Your . . . former line of work?" His lips quirked. "I'm almost afraid to ask."

She kicked his ankle under the table, and he chuckled even as he winced. She wore very pointy shoes.

"I wrote an advice column for the *Pine Mountain Gazette*." She lifted a hand. "Don't say it, I know. It's not exactly the journalism career I'd dreamed of."

"I bet it was challenging though, dealing with a con-stant stream of everyone else's problems. Is that why you left?"

"Oh, I didn't quit. I was fired. Because of a very public relationship failure that happened right in front of my ed-itor at our local grocery store earlier this week."

"Ah. So . . . that would be the other retail establishment scene you referred to before." He reached across the table, covered her hand with his own. "I'm sorry, Parker. For the job loss. Not so much for the loser of a guy. You're better off without him."

"You don't know anything about him. He's actually a nice guy."

"Nice guys don't dump their girlfriends in a grocery store, in public."

"Well, to his credit, he didn't know it was in public, he was on speakerphone—don't ask—and . . . well, full dis-closure, he didn't think of me as his girlfriend. So, tech-nically, he wasn't dumping me, but I—" She broke off, ducked her chin and picked at the lid on her hot choco-late. With a short sigh, she added, "I misread things. I—I do that. And losing the job . . . well, that was probably a mercy killing, too."

He tugged her hand back across the table and kept it trapped under his. "Aw, come on, Parker. That can't be true. You're just upset, and understandably so, especially with it happening this time of year. I remember how much you loved the holidays. So . . . don't be so hard on yourself."

She peered up through her lashes and met his gaze across the table. Then, to his surprise, she smiled. "You are a sensitive guy. With feelings. Not just another hunky piece of meat."

He barked out a laugh at that, and squeezed her hand more tightly under his. "Hunky, huh?"

"Sweet, sensitive guys don't fish." But her smile grew. "I forgot how good you were at making me feel like less of a complete loser." The corners of her mouth twisted a little. "But just like then, you can't make it any less true."

He smiled with her, then leaned forward to dab the chocolate from the corner of her mouth. With his gaze still on hers, he put his fingertip in his mouth and savored the taste of the only sweet thing he could have at the moment. "Not true. Not to me. Never with me."

Her eyes went a bit rounder, and her lips parted. . . . He had to fight the very grown-up urge to drag her right across the table.

Yeah. They definitely weren't kids any longer.

Chapter 3

Will wove his fingers through hers, and everything in-side of Clara said *yes*. Yes to finding each other again, yes to sharing fond memories, yes to picking up where they'd left off . . . and yes to finding out what would have happened next if he'd stayed, what would happen next now that he was back.

"Will, would you like to—"

"Parker, I really want—"

"Excuse me—I'm *so* sorry to interrupt."

Hands still clasped, both Clara and Will broke off speak-ing, but found it harder to break eye contact and look at Lonzo, who was once again standing beside their table.

"My manager just called and told me to go ahead and close up if I didn't have anybody here."

Clara blinked, as if coming out of a fog, which wasn't far from being accurate. A hormone fog. A quick glance at the small café showed they were, indeed, the only ones there.

"I thought you stayed open twenty-four hours?" Will asked.

"Normally we do. But the snowstorm is picking up and now they're calling for it to potentially dump a pretty heavy load in the valley. My manager thought it would be a good idea to clean up and get everything shut down properly before we lose power. Last time this happened we didn't and we ended up losing a lot of product. Were you—do you live nearby?"

Clara thought perhaps there was possibly a hint of a personal inquiry in that, but then she saw Lonzo notice their clasped hands, and his expression shifted a bit. "Will you be able to get wherever it is you're going, I mean? We have a few motels local, if that helps. I have a list—"

"That's okay, I have a truck with a plow," Will told him. "We'll be fine."

There was a bit of a wistful note in Lonzo's sigh as he gave them the check and carry-out containers for what was left of Will's food.

Clara reached for her purse, but Will tugged her hand and reached in his back pocket for his wallet. "I got it."

"I thought this was payback for—"

"I'm the one who did all the eating." He handed over some cash and thanked Lonzo with the full dimples-out grin, telling him to keep the change. The young man blushed straight to his roots, stammered out a "Thanks for coming in," then headed to the back and started closing up.

"Guess we've officially been kicked out," Will said, shifting those dimples back in her direction.

She could have told him that from the moment he'd put his hand on hers and licked that dab of chocolate off his fingertip, she was pretty sure her knees weren't going to support her weight, much less balance her upright. But when he lifted her hand and brushed his lips across the back of her knuckles, snagging a bit of whipped cream foam she hadn't realized she'd splashed there, she all but swallowed her own tongue, so she just gurgled a little as they both slid out of their respective sides of the booth. Fortunately he kept her hand in his, keeping her upright, if not entirely steady.

"I haven't looked out there since we came in, so I don't know how bad it is over the mountain. You still live in Pine Mountain?"

"I inherited my grandma's place." Clara was very aware of how warm his palm was now that he'd slid his hand around to hold hers. "You're still in Bealetown, right? I— I overheard ladies in line saying you're with the fire department there."

"I am. Well, I was. But I should probably check in. I left my radio in the truck. If this storm is turning into something nasty, they might need any help they can get."

"Was? Is—is the calendar thing taking the place of work for now?"

He let her hand go and she tried not to sigh at the loss of contact, but then he slipped her coat off the peg and nudged her around so he could help her on with it.

"Actually, I'm not technically working at the moment. I'm changing jobs shortly, and using the time in between to promote the calendar and get things set up in the new office."

Clara turned to face him before he could help her put her coat on. "You're leaving the fire department?"

"No. I'm still going to be working with them, just in a different capacity. It's taken way too long, but I did finally finish my degree, taking classes as I've been able."

"You did?" Clara spontaneously hugged him. "That's great. I always felt bad that your family circumstances forced you back home again. I mean, I know you had to do what you had to do, and I'm sure your family was beyond grateful for it, but I also knew how much you wanted your science degree. Wait—what will you be doing with that and the fire department?"

"Well, I went in a bit of a different direction, which is also why it took longer. I lost most of the credits I'd gotten that first year. Technology has really advanced with forensic investigations, both in the law enforcement field, and with our departments, too. So much so that they established a new tri-county forensic fire unit to work with the local fire marshals on their investigations."

"Wow, that's fantastic. So, you'll be part of that department?"

He nodded, smiled, and she could see both the excitement and the pride in his eyes. "Actually, I'll be heading up the department office for our county, which will be located conveniently in Bealetown. We're setting it up in a newly dedicated space between the police academy and the county courthouse offices. We officially open the beginning of the new year. So I took the rest of my annual leave to help get it set up—well, and now to deal with this calendar craziness, too."

"That's—wow." Clara beamed, thrilled for him. "I'm so happy for you, and proud of you. That had to be really hard, with . . . well, with everything you've had to deal with. I bet your whole family is just beside themselves."

"It's just my sisters now, but yes, they are. And they've been amazingly supportive. Wonderful, truly."

Clara belatedly realized she was still standing in his arms when she instinctively tightened her grip at the news update on his family. "Your mom . . . ? I'm sorry. I know you said she was facing a lot of health issues, even back when we were in college."

"She passed about four years ago now. That's why I stayed after dad's funeral. She was in far worse shape than she'd let on to any of us, but once dad was gone, she couldn't hide it any longer, and, well . . ." He shook his head. "It was sad, but, as you said about your grandmother, merciful, as there wasn't anything that could be done by then. We all miss her like crazy, especially this time of year, but . . . it's kept us all close, and I know that would have made her happy."

"Oh, Will, I'm still so sorry." Clara instinctively hugged him again, purely as a friend, offering solace. But when his arms came around her and held her close, tightened, briefly, as he pressed his face to her hair . . . she couldn't deny that while her heart was offering sympathy, her body was responding on a whole bunch of other levels.

He set her back, pushed the hair from her forehead as he looked into her eyes, smiling at her with those oh-so-familiar brown eyes, swamping her again with long-forgotten memories.

"I'm really glad you crashed my calendar signing," he said, his dimples flickering briefly as he added, "literally."

She laughed, which unfortunately included a snort. His dimples came out in full force with his grin, and she rolled her eyes and flushed at the same time.

"You're still cute when you do that."

"I'm a dork when I do that."

"Yeah," he said, dropping a light kiss on her nose. "But a really cute dork."

Even the playful kiss sent shivers of awareness through her, causing her to speak without thinking. "For the first time, I'm really glad I suck at baking."

"Ah. So the children's cookbook . . . a gift to yourself, then?" His teasing grin brought out that slight cleft in the chin.

She wanted to lick it. "Uh—" she paused to clear her throat of the sudden dryness she found there. Which was pretty much the only dry thing on her at the moment. "I got a new job. The same day I lost my old job. I'm the *Gazette*'s new Christmas cookie food columnist."

"Congratulations," he said, then immediately added, "Oh."

"Exactly. A cookie columnist who can't bake. Not much of an improvement over a relationship advice columnist who sucks at relationships." She gave him a wry grin.

"Let's just say that you've ultimately been a lot more successful in your career trajectory than I have."

Just then the lights went off in the other half of the coffee shop, reminding them they were on borrowed time.

"I have faith in you," he said, smiling, then turned her around so he could help her on with her coat.

Quite honestly, she hadn't really recovered from when he'd taken it off of her. He was just the right height to make her feel girly rather than gangly. He definitely had the body now to make her feel entirely and utterly female. She shivered a little when his fingertips brushed the sides of her neck as he eased the jacket up and over her shoulders.

"Jacket still damp?"

His mouth was much closer to her ear than she'd realized, making the proximity feel somehow far more intimate than when they'd been hugging each other just moments ago. So much so, she found it really tempting to lean back the tiniest bit into him.

No men, remember? Hugging an old friend is fine, but there will be no leaning. And no kissing. Kissing leads to sex. You have a career to save first. Focus.

She wasted another second debating on whether or not it really mattered if she started the celibacy thing a measly one day later, but given she'd already used up five or six hours of the forty-eight she had to her deadline, she really couldn't afford to lose any more.

And then there was the fact that despite their long absence from each other's lives, just during the short time of their reunion she already knew there was no way she'd be able to keep anything she did with Will Mason in the no-strings-attached column.

"Um, no—no. I'm fine. The hot chocolate is wearing off I guess."

He helped her settle the coat on her shoulders, but

didn't immediately step back once she'd wriggled it on straight. She fumbled with the zipper, all thumbs, and he turned her to face him again. "I've got it." His voice sounded even deeper . . . huskier as he brushed her fingers aside and took the corners of her jacket in his hands. He bent his head to fit the metal tab into the slot, and she almost—almost—leaned in to nuzzle a little in that thick, wheat blonde hair. Only now, with the way he'd matured, his face all angular and ridiculously handsome, and his body all big and rugged . . . it did something a lot more mature to her body, too.

He lifted his gaze to hers, saving her from caving in to the urge, then held it as he pulled the zipper tab slowly upward. She'd just been in his arms a moment ago, but this didn't feel friendly. He was all crowded up against her, so the backs of his knuckles brushed along the full length of her torso as he closed the front of her coat.

She could feel the edge of the table pressing into the backs of her thighs, and she might have moaned a little when he eased the zipper tab past the slight-to-almost-nonexistent curve that might have been her breasts, if she had any to speak of. She did have nipples, though, and they stood right up at the drive-by bit of almost-attention. God, even her nipples were desperate for him. She was really in trouble here. She cleared her throat and had every intention of stepping back when he reached the top, only he let go of the tab and took hold of either side of her hood, keeping her right where she stood. Deep in his personal space. Where it was getting all foggy again. A thick, steamy bog of needy hormones that she could so easily slide into, sink under, and take him with her.

"You should probably put this up." He slid her hood up, then gently tugged the ties that dangled from either side, his fingers now directly brushing the bare skin of her chin and neck.

Honest to God, there was no way putting *on* clothes could possibly be this erotically charged. Once again, she had to be making more of a situation than what it really was. This was all some kind of wild, overblown scenario that only she was living in. He was just helping her on with her coat. Like Pete had just been a nice guy buying her a cup of coffee after a near-death experience.

She closed her eyes and let out the breath she realized she was holding. *What's happening here is a run-in with an old acquaintance. Nothing more.* He'd been a very good friend to her years ago, but that was all he'd been. They'd relived some past memories, caught up on current events, and, yes, some of those memories had been quite . . . revelatory. But she didn't trust herself enough at the moment to make a judgment call on whether or not any of it meant anything in the here and now.

In a lot of ways, important ways, attractive ways, he was still the same Will Mason, her Will Mason. But he was also, quite clearly, and very magnificently, a whole lot more. And she hadn't been around while that had been happening for him, so she didn't know how it might have changed him. Plus, it had to be said, that kind of transformation clearly hadn't happened for her. So . . . she didn't know the rules that went along with who they were now.

He'd grown up to become some kind of Adonis that women drooled over. In public. Standing in long lines, even, just for the privilege of saying hello. She, on the other hand, was only good at getting dumped, in public, while standing in line at the grocery store.

"Hey."

She realized her eyes were still closed. Possibly scrunched a little. "Hey, what?" she asked, not opening them. Mortification was already starting to seep in. He was her friend. Her now very hot friend. Who probably flirted as easily as he breathed. But that was it. She was pretty sure, that was it.

"What's going on in there, under that hood?" He still had his hands on either side of it, holding the ties, knuckles still brushing under her ducked chin. His hands were so warm. And potentially serial flirter or not, he was every bit as comforting a presence now as he'd been then. More so even, admittedly, given his added physical dimensions.

"I'm just trying really hard not to go three for three in a single week," she finally murmured.

His knuckles pressed upward, until her face was lifted to his. "Look at me."

She opened her eyes. And drowned, effortlessly, helplessly, in the sea of warm, decadent brown staring back at her.

"Three for what three?" To his credit, while his eyes were inviting, he'd been serious with the question, not teasing.

"Grocery store. Book store." She paused, tried like crazy to see if she could find answers in all that warm, inviting brown. "Coffee shop."

His lips lifted a little. "I won't let you destroy anything between here and the door. Promise."

To her surprise, especially given her now-thundering heart, she smiled. "Thanks."

"But?" He searched her eyes. "That's not what you meant."

She gave a short shake of her head, which had the unfortunate result of causing his fingers to brush along the side of her jaw. She might have shivered a little. Her knees definitely went a bit wobbly. She closed her eyes for the second time, partly in familiar embarrassment, partly to try and regain her equilibrium. Which she wasn't going to be able to do while staring into his eyes.

"Parker."

Just that one word, that silly, boundary-setting, best-friends-only pet name . . . well, it did all kinds of things, sentimental things, lust-fueled things, to her insides. But it was that note, that rough little note that she'd never heard before, that had her opening her eyes again.

"You didn't misread anything this time." And then he tugged her that spare inch closer, and her breath caught, her racing heart stuttered, as he lowered his mouth to hers.

"Will," she breathed against his lips. "I—I don't want to screw anything up. With us."

He lifted his head just enough to look into her eyes. "There hasn't been an us to screw up for nine years."

"True. But now—"

"Now I get a second chance. I don't want regrets. And if I don't kiss you, and find out what kind of us there might yet be . . . I always would."

She hadn't thought her heart could beat any harder, or that her pulse could race any faster. She'd been wrong. Her gaze drifted to his mouth.

This time she was pretty sure that low guttural groan came from him.

"Parker . . . what do *you* want?"

Her breath caught. And she realized that every time she'd started something with someone—even if it turned out it was only in her own head—her only concern had been figuring out what they wanted, and trying to give that, be that. No one had ever, not once, asked her what she wanted. "I want . . . time."

He started to lift his head, with the intent of moving back entirely, and her heart tilted even farther in his direction, because he'd just given her proof that he'd put her needs, her wants, above his own. But that wasn't why she'd said it . . . or what she'd meant.

"Your new job. No men." His voice was deep now, barely a rough whisper. "Right. I'd say I was sorry I pushed, but I'm not. But I will step back. If that's what you want. For now."

"No," she said. "I mean, yes, I said that, about the job, about no men, and I meant it, mostly . . . but that's not—" She broke off, knowing she should think this through more clearly, but nothing was clear at the moment. That fog between them was so drenched with sexual tension, now that she knew he was right there in the fog with her, she had to press her thighs together to keep her legs from shaking.

She traced her fingertips along his jaw, barely able to believe she was really doing this. So she said the words before she could chicken out . . . or wise up. "A lot of time has passed without you. I can't get that back. So, that's what I want. I want time now." She looked into his eyes. "Time with you. That's what I meant. I want that time."

"Wow."

Clara's eyes had already started drifting shut as she slid her hand around the back of Will's neck, her lips parting as she anticipated the feel of his mouth on hers . . . only to freeze and blink her eyes right back open again when she realized that neither she nor Will had said that. They both turned to look at Lonzo, who stood only a few feet away, gulping, and looking more than a little flushed.

"I'm . . . *so* sorry. Really. *Very* . . . sorry. But—"

"Right," Will said, then cleared the gravel from his throat. "Sorry. We're heading out." With a sheepish grin, Will gave Clara a quick, sexy wink, then flipped up the hood of his sweatshirt, grabbed his gear bag from the booth, and took her hand. "Come on."

They stepped outside into a swirling snowstorm. This time, she was the one to say it. "Wow."

"I should have checked in." He smiled at her as flakes frosted both of their hoods. "I guess I got a little distracted."

Clara smiled back, and captured a snowflake on her tongue out of habit. Her body was still clamoring for what it had been about to get back in the coffee shop. A little cooling off was in order. *Probably for the best, anyway.* Which . . . she knew that was true, but that didn't mean she had to like it. She opened her mouth to tell him she was going to head home before it got any worse—not sure whether she meant the road conditions, or the condition of her aching, lusting body—but she lost all of her words and her breath when he spun her neatly up against him.

"I forgot you used to do that."

"Do what?"

"Capture snowflakes on your tongue. Did you know that I was not a fan of our mountain winters until I met you?"

God, but he said the damnedest things. Just when she needed her defenses to hold firm . . . not melt away as easily as . . . well, a snowflake.

"Snowflakes always made you happy," he said. "I couldn't help but wonder if yours just somehow tasted better." And then his hand was sliding inside her hoodie, his warm palm cupping her neck as he tipped her face upward. She closed her eyes and spluttered out a laugh as the flakes landed rapidly here, there, and everywhere, on her heated skin. She opened her mouth to protest, only to lose that ability—again—when she felt his lips on her cheek. And then on her chin. Her temple. The tip of her nose. The corner of her eyebrow. She sighed . . . and let him taste her snowflakes.

Then he was urging her chin upward, bringing her wet, damp lips straight up against his warm, hard, inviting ones. He groaned, deep in his throat, as he took her mouth. And it was nothing less than that. And everything she'd always wanted.

She slid her hands to his shoulders, more to hang on

than with any intent of her own. He teased her lips open, then mated warmth with warmth, playing, taking, giving, until she was so worked up she wouldn't have known if they were in the middle of a blizzard, or on a hot, tropical beach.

"Snowflakes are pretty good. But you taste even better," he murmured against her lips. "And I should let you get out of this snowstorm."

"Mmm-hmm," was all she was capable of. And then, with a strong arm around her shoulders and a hand on her arm, he was shepherding her across the parking lot, steadying her from slipping in the rapidly accumulating snow.

She squealed as the ankle-deep drifts soaked her shoes, and found herself immediately aloft in his arms.

"Oh! Will! No! I'm way too—you really shouldn't—"

"Hey, pipe down, short stuff. I do this for a living, remember? Normally it would be over my shoulder and we'd be climbing down a ladder outside of a burning building, so just hold on and enjoy your snowflakes, okay?"

She held on . . . but for once, snowflakes ran a distant second in terms of sensory pleasures. Never, not once in her entire life, past toddlerhood anyway, had anyone carried her. Anywhere. Ever. And given it might be that long before it ever happened again, she looped her arms around his neck and did as he asked. She enjoyed it. The feel of his arms holding her, being braced against his chest, feeling his warm breath puff little crystalline clouds with every snowy step. She only wished she'd parked farther away. *And short stuff?* It was like she'd entered some kind of parallel universe. She felt almost . . . delicate.

"Keys?" he asked.

She just blinked at him, still steeping in the moment.

"So I can unlock your car and not put your feet in the snow again."

"Oh." She fumbled for her purse, fumbled some more for her keys, and did her very best to not ask him what happened next. She produced the keys and pointed to her small SUV. "Thank you."

He smiled down at her, snowflakes frosting the tips of his eyelashes. "My pleasure."

Seriously, it was such a fairytale moment. Clearly, she'd fallen and hit her head earlier when she'd first arrived and this whole episode was some kind of concussive dream, from which she'd wake up any moment. So she closed her eyes and willed herself to stay unconscious. Just a little bit longer.

She pretended not to hear the locks click open, and she shamelessly didn't even try to stand on her own two feet as he opened the door.

"Watch your head."

And then she was being gently tucked into her freezing cold car and he was standing in the open door, blocking the wind and the snow. "I want you to follow me over the mountain. I can use the plow on the front of my truck to get us through any tricky spots. I'm guessing I'll be heading in to the station for the rest of the night, but I'll make sure you get home safely. If it gets too bad, we'll park your SUV and I'll get you home."

Clara could have told him she'd happily let him get her wherever he desired. Right here on the freezing cold front seat of her SUV was sounding pretty good at the moment. He was big, he'd keep her warm.

His smile faded. "Are you uncomfortable driving in this? Why don't we leave your vehicle here, then, and—"

Clara sadly let the last tingling moments of her twinkling little fairytale moment sparkle out. "No, no, I'm fine. I've driven in this my whole adult life and certainly in a lot worse. I have four-wheel drive, so with your plow, we'll be fine." She shivered as the cold really started to seep in past the layers of her clothing. "Thank you, Will. For . . . everything."

Then he leaned in, cupped her cheek, and kissed her. Gentle, teasing, sweet . . . with just a promise of carnal. She sighed when he lifted his head.

"I can't believe I waited ten years to do that. I'm such an idiot." He stroked her cheek, then lifted a snowflake from the edge of her hood and licked it off his fingertip. "Yep. You're way better. Drive safe."

Don't go. "You, too." She'd meant about the safe driving, but was thinking about snowflakes versus the taste of pure, unadulterated Will Mason. Will won that contest without even trying.

He closed the door, brushing the snow off the window and knocking it off where it had piled up on the side view mirror. Then he stood there, wearing little more than a few layers of sweatshirt, gear bag slung over his back, not even shivering. He made a circular motion with his finger, making her realize she was just sitting there, dazed, staring at him. But, honestly, would anyone blame her?

She managed to stab the key in the ignition on the third try, and sighed when the engine started right up. Relief, she told herself. It was a sigh of relief. She smiled at him through the rapidly fogging window and he saluted before jogging off across the lot toward an oversized diesel pickup with a big plow strapped to the front.

Dear Lord, even his truck made her think about sex. She rolled her eyes at herself and followed him out of the lot.

Clara followed him over the mountain out of Riverside and up the next one into Pine Mountain proper. It had taken far too long, giving her way too much time to overthink pretty much every minute of her evening with him. Should she invite him in? He'd said he'd probably be going on to the fire station in Bealetown, but should she at least ask, so he'd offer some other kind of plan to see her again? Or should she just take tonight as a few hours of unexpected joy and quit while she was ahead?

She knew she should put off thinking about starting up anything until after finishing her cookie column commitment ... and figuring out how to parlay that into a job that would carry her into the new year and beyond. But that didn't stop her from visualizing every possible scenario on how the night might end. It was a miracle she hadn't gone off the road into a snowdrift multiple times. Oh ... multiple, multiple times.

Once they got into town, he pulled over and motioned her up alongside him. She rolled down her window as did he.

"I have to get going," he called out, having to pretty much yell to be heard over the loud thrum of his engine and the now howling wind. "Big pileup at the top of the mountain between here and Bealetown. Looks like the streets here in town aren't too bad. Can you make it okay to your place?"

She nodded. "I'm just around the corner, on Oak. I'll be fine. Thanks for getting me home safe." *And thanks for making me feel desirable and feminine, even a little bit sexy. And thanks for kissing me like* . . . Well, like she'd always wanted to be kissed. Like she mattered. But she didn't know how to say any of that, or even if she should. She didn't know what to say, to prolong the moment, to prolong ... everything.

"Get inside. Stay warm." He grinned, then started to put his window up.

"Okay, I will." Disappointment washed through her in a heavy wave, so much so, she knew it was better that it had ended before anything had really begun. She hit the button to put her window up. At least this time she knew she wouldn't get dumped in some new public display of humiliation. Can't get dumped when you've never officially been picked up.

A sudden rapping on her window made her jump and let out a little scream. She jerked her head and saw Will standing next to her car. Heart pounding in her throat, she quickly groped for the button to put the window down. "Is everything okay?" she asked, looking up at him as he ducked down, his hood back up over his head. "What's wrong?"

"Nothing. Absolutely nothing. It's just . . . it's going to be a long night." With her window all the way down now and snow swirling into her car, he pushed his hood off and ducked his head inside. His hands were still warm when he cupped her face. "And I miss you already. Crazy, right?"

She could only shake her head.

He kissed her again, only there was nothing teasing and tender about this one. It was hot, commanding . . . definitely laying claim.

They were both huffing out clouds of crystalline air when he finally lifted his head. "How the hell did I not do this ten years ago?" He shook his head, sounding truly mystified.

This time he captured a snowflake and pressed it on her lips.

And then he was gone.

Chapter 4

"**O**h no! *No, no, no*. This can't be happening." Clara watched in horror as her kitchen curtains caught fire anyway. "This is so much worse than the toaster oven." She'd inadvertently caught her oven mitt on fire when trying to fish out the cookies now burning on the bottom of her oven, and had flung the flaming mitt into the sink. Or had meant to. Only she'd flung with a bit more force, perhaps, than absolutely necessary—but her hand was on fire, or almost on fire, so could you blame her?—and it hit the curtains instead. Which went right up in flames. "Crap, crap, crap." She hadn't gotten the fire extinguisher replaced or refilled or whatever it was one did with them after using them, following the toaster oven incident. So she wasn't sure what, exactly, to do.

She tried to remember the feed-a-fire/starve-a-fire rules from when she'd been a Girl Scout but that had been way too long ago and she was too freaked out at the moment to really think clearly anyway. "Water. Water has to kill fire, right?" She couldn't get to the sink because it was directly under the burning curtains and sparks were flying. She didn't think the spray bottle she used to mist her plants would be particularly practical, so she started flinging open cupboards, looking for something—"Ah ha!" She grabbed her grandmother's big stock pot and raced down the hall to the guest bathroom, only the pot was too deep to fit under the faucet in the small sink. So she raced upstairs to the full bathroom on the second floor and filled it in the tub, sloshing water all the way back down again as she hurried back before the cupboards caught on—"Shit. *Shit, shit, shit.*"

The cupboard next to the curtains was already glowing embers. She flung the pot of water at it anyway. As it turns out, flinging water out of a big pot straight at something, really doesn't work all that well. Most of it landed at her feet. "Hose. I need a hose." She dashed back down the hall to the front door, thinking she'd just drag the damn garden hose down the hall. Only she opened the door to about a foot of fresh snow that had drifted onto her porch overnight . . . which was now in her foyer. *Frozen. The damn hose would be frozen.* "Of course it would."

She grabbed the foyer throw rug off the floor and raced back up the stairs and got it wet in the tub—*God, that made it heavy*—and dragged it back downstairs, thinking she'd just beat at the flames with it. Only it was so damn heavy she couldn't really lift it all that well, much less wield it effectively, and ended up almost swinging herself right back out of the kitchen.

She had to call the fire department, she knew that, but she couldn't just stand there and watch her grandmother's cottage burn to the ground while she waited for them to show up. She dropped the sodden rug and looked around for her phone. Panic gave way to tears, which she blinked furiously away as she tried to punch in 911 in the thickening smoke.

Which was how Will found her. Coughing, crying, with soot streaking her face and her sweatpants, her T-shirt and bunny slippers soaked from the stock pot and the wet rug. So much for the end of the mortification section of her relationship attempts.

"Are you okay?" he asked, or rather demanded, turning her to face him.

She coughed in his face, then made a rather inelegant snorting sound as she tried to get air in past her now stuffed up nose. So she nodded, when really, she was anything but okay.

He didn't bother asking her anything else, and a second later she was once again airborne, clinging to him with arms around his neck as he carried her outdoors through drifts of snow, to the front seat of his still-running truck. Only it wasn't nearly as romantic as the last time.

"Stay here," he ordered.

She nodded, unable to do anything else, feeling beyond pathetic and stupid. And she hadn't even had the chance to call her insurance guy.

Will dragged a gear bag from the half bench seat behind the driver's seat and tossed it next to her. "There's a sweatshirt, sweatpants, jacket. Get them out. Take off the wet stuff. Put them on." Then he grabbed a huge, real-sized fire extinguisher and a spare tank from behind the same seat and took off back toward the open door of the house.

Clara followed directions, chattering now in her wet clothes, despite the heater blasting in the cab of the running truck. She didn't even bother looking around first to see if anyone who happened to be out shoveling was paying attention, just numbly dragged her wet clothes off and pulled on Will's dry and wonderfully soft sweats, then his jacket, too, not even caring that they swam on her. She dug around, found socks, and put those on, too, then pulled on a second pair. The whole time all she could think about was that she was going to lose the only thing that meant anything to her, the only thing of value she had. And not simply monetary value, but sentimental, emotional, lifelong value.

Clara had mostly grown up in the tiny two-bedroom

bungalow, at least all the lifetime she could remember anyway, and cherished her only remaining connection to family. It had been paid off long before it came into Clara's
possession, which was the only thing that had made following her journalism dream, such as it was, even possible. As long as she had the house, and her grandmother's
now-aging SUV, she could afford to make next to nothing
as a Pine Mountain columnist while working toward her
actual journalistic goals.

"Oh, God," she whispered against the hands she'd fisted
in the sleeves of Will's sweatshirt and pressed against her
mouth. "What have I done? *I'm so sorry, Grammy Jo.*" She
started to shake in earnest, the combination of damp skin
and shock too much to will away.

She dazedly wondered why she wasn't hearing the
sirens. Where were the fire trucks? They should be here
by now. Will couldn't fight that blaze alone. She even put a
shaky hand on the door handle, though what she thought
she was going to do to help, she had no idea.

And then he was back. All big and rugged and soot
streaked and frowning. One thing was for sure, he looked
a hell of a lot sexier post-fire combat than she did. He
opened the door and shoved both spent tanks behind the
seat, then climbed in and shut the door against the cold.

"I—I dialed 911," she said, teeth chattering so hard she
added a few one's on the end. "Wh-where are they?"

"I radioed in, told them to hold off. I got it. It's out.
Fire marshal is coming, though, so we'll need to wait for
him, answer questions for his report."

"It's . . . out? Really?"

Will's expression softened and he reached out and
cupped a warm, sooty palm to her cheek. "Yes, really. I
know it was scary and seemed larger than life. Fire is like
that. But compared to how bad it could have been—"

"I'm not g-going to l-lose the house?"

"I'm not going to lie, it's going to take some work, but no, it's not a loss. Not even close. No major structural damage that I could see. But your kitchen is—"

"Toaster oven'd."

He lifted his soot-caked brows. "Well, toast, anyway. I'm afraid so."

She nodded, trying to take in the good news, but she was still struggling to assimilate that she'd come so close to burning her house down. Sure, she'd made jokes about the fire department being on her speed dial after the toaster oven thing, but all that had done was leave a huge scorch mark on her counter. And, well, it had taken her grass a while to grow back when she'd pitched the thing out the window into the backyard.

Will pushed her hair back, stroked her cheek. "You okay? We should go get you checked out for smoke inhalation. A little pure O2 would help with the shock, too."

"I'm o—" She paused at his raised eyebrow. "Fine. I've been better. But I don't need . . ." She stopped, dipped her chin when the tears threatened again, closing her throat. Now that the immediate danger was over, it was all just too much to even think about.

"Come here." Will pulled her across the bench seat, into his lap. He smiled into her eyes, even as he ran his wide palms down her arms and up her back, warming her, soothing her, calming her. "We're quite the pair here." He reached up and dabbed a smudge of charcoal off the tip of her nose.

"Yeah," she said, hearing the watery tone of her words; tears were still brimming at the corners of her eyes. "Carbon is the new black."

"Or the really, really old black." He smiled, a look of such affection in his eyes she almost lost it.

She sniffled, then gave up completely when he tucked

her against his chest and held her tightly, pressing his soot-streaked cheek to her hair.

To his credit, he just let her cry it out, rubbing her back, pressing soft kisses to the crown of her head. When she'd finally spent herself and was down to inelegant gurgling, he carefully shifted her off his lap and back into her seat, handing her a stash of napkins from the floor console. He leaned across and buckled her in, then pulled his own seatbelt on before backing the truck out of the driveway.

"What about the fire marshal?"

"He's a friend. I'll have him come talk to you after he does his preliminary report."

"I know I've looked better, but I really don't need to go to the hospital."

"We're not going to the hospital."

"Then where—"

"You can't stay in your house, it's not safe."

"I can go to a motel, but I need—"

"You need a kitchen."

Oh God. Her column. "I—I'll call my friend Lily. She can probably put me up." Clara's mind was still reeling about almost losing her house, and even thinking about her deadline was almost too much at the moment, but she was clearheaded enough to know that Lily was in the throes of trying to win that cookie contest at the resort. The last thing she needed was a displaced houseguest. Much less one who needed to borrow her kitchen.

He glanced over at her. "I have a kitchen."

Her eyebrows climbed. "Will, that's—you don't have to—"

"I have a kitchen. One I rarely use for more than heating up leftovers. I also have a spare room." He shot her a fast grin. "No men, no sex while you rescue your career. I haven't forgotten."

"I—are you sure?" She was so startled by the offer, and

the possible solution to one of now several very big problems topping her to-do list, that she couldn't even deal with the whole possible sexual repercussions of what staying under his roof would do to her. And frankly, being sexually frustrated and in close proximity to the solution to that frustration was the very least of those big problems.

He idled at the stop sign at the end of her street. "I'm sure. We'll clean up, talk with the marshal, then come back over later and get whatever you need from the house. Or, better yet, make me a list and I'll take care of it."

"Will—"

His smile shifted, and that look, the one that reflected the connection they had, the friendship bond, came into his eyes again. "It'll be okay. Like you said, we're grown adults. We should just be able to say what we want, right? I want to help you. I have the space."

"How was it that you found me when you did?"

"I've been up all night helping the crews with some pretty bad road accidents that happened last night and ended up bunking in with the guys at the firehouse here. I was actually heading to your place—they gave me your address, hope that's okay. They knew I followed you back last night from Riverside. Anyway, I was going to stop by before going back to Bealetown because . . ."

He let the sentence die off. "Because?" she echoed.

"Because I wanted to see you, maybe make sure last night wasn't some kind of food-deprived, sleep-deprived hallucination." His smile faltered. "Then I saw the black smoke rolling up. I have to tell you, it definitely gave me my second wind, but if that's what I'd been looking for, there are a few other far more pleasurable ways to go about it."

"So . . . that's not what you were looking for?"

"I just wanted to see you."

Despite the chaos of the last hour or so, and still being

more than a little rattled, Clara could recall, in stunning and very explicit detail, what his kisses had felt like, tasted like, how they had made her feel. "Maybe my coming to your place isn't such a good idea," she said, forcing her thoughts to her deadline, and the added burden of dealing with her burned-out kitchen. "The holidays are almost here and I'm sure you don't need—"

"Parker, I'm not angling for anything. Promise. If you feel you need to make other arrangements, that's fine, but for right now, let's start with this plan, okay?"

"Okay. And thank you. For . . . everything."

"What are friends for?" He turned onto the main road, then headed out of Pine Mountain on the road toward Bealetown.

What are friends for, indeed. As if she needed a reminder with all she had going on that that was all they could be. And maybe she did need it. He'd teased her a little, sure, and he'd kissed her all but senseless, but that didn't mean he was interested in anything serious. He'd gotten answers to some long-ago questions, and he'd made it clear that he still saw her as a friend. Possibly a friend he'd like a few benefits with, but with all he had going on, she doubted he was looking for more. He'd jumped in pretty easily, after all, so perhaps that kind of thing was just a casual choice for him. With the way he looked, she doubted he'd have a problem finding whatever kind of partner he wanted, for whatever duration he wanted.

She couldn't do the casual, no-strings thing with him, though. Now, after the new year, or ever. But that wasn't stopping her from thinking about being in his house while he got cleaned up. In his shower. Alone. And naked. Friends shouldn't picture friends naked, right? Of course, one look at herself in a mirror would probably kill any fantasies she had about him wanting her to maybe join him, help him wash his back . . .

"I just have one question," she blurted out, fervently shutting down any and all images of a naked Will doing anything. With or without her.

"And what would that be?"

She smiled at him. "Are you paid up on your fire insurance?"

Chapter 5

"Thanks for coming by, Eric. I really appreciate it." Will gave a short wave to his EMT pal as Eric lugged his equipment back to the squad truck then closed the front door and returned to his kitchen.

Clara, soot-free now and clothed in yet another set of his sweats, sat on a stool beside the heavy butcher block counter that doubled as a prep table and dining room table. "You really didn't need to do that."

"It's my training. Indulge me." He leaned a hip against the stove. "I'm glad you're okay."

"You're glad someone other than me has now pronounced me okay." She waved off her own comment. "I'm sorry. You're doing more than your job, you're being my friend. And I couldn't be more grateful."

She'd already talked to the marshal, so he knew the whole story about how the fire had started. Will had sat in on their session, so he also knew she was facing her first column deadline, which was now less than a full day away.

"I got the fire marshal to bring me something of yours."

She instantly brightened. "My laptop?"

"Uh, no. We still have to go pick up clothes and whatever, so we can grab it then. I have one you can borrow in the meantime. I have wifi, so you shouldn't have any

problems getting or sending mail, doing research, whatever."

"We could go now. That is, if you have the time. I can
drive my own car back."

"Don't you want to see what the fire marshal brought?"

"Oh, right. Sure." She held up a hand. "Wait. Is it
something tragic? Like a singed teddy bear, rescued from
the ruins of my one and only baking attempt?"

"Why would you have a teddy bear in the kitchen?"

She stuck her tongue out at him, and he immediately
felt better. It was good to see her start to return to her regular self. Listening and watching while she spoke to Nick,
he had marveled both at how much she was the same
Parker he'd known and how far she'd come since then. She
had downplayed her journalistic history to him, but Nick
had asked a few questions about her job, mostly as it per-
tained to the reason for the fire. She'd been quite the professional, detailing everything, which had included a bit
more of her history with the *Gazette*. Before writing the
advice column, she'd written the column with all the news
and events happening at the ski resort, and there was no
missing her enthusiasm when talking about her town, her
people.

And, though she'd deny it, she was more graceful, more
polished, more at ease with her long-limbed body. A body,
even swimming in his sweatpants and sweatshirt, that was
doing things to him he was having a hard time controlling.

No men, no sex. Friends only. Damn it. "Not a teddy bear."
He hefted the grocery sack onto the kitchen counter. "I
called Nick while he was still at your place and he managed to rescue this from the kitchen carnage." He slid out
the children's cookie cookbook and put it on the counter.
One look at her expression and his smile faded. "Okay, so
maybe I misjudged the tragic part. I thought you needed

this to make your deadline. And it would save time not having to replace it."

She looked at the sooty book with a mixture of trepidation and disgust. "I've been thinking that maybe I'm not cut out to do this job. I need to call Fran—my editor—and tell her to find another cookie columnist. I mean, as signs go, almost burning down my grandmother's house is a pretty unmistakable one. I'm not only oh-for-two in the baking column, I'm two-for-two in the requiring-fire-department-intervention-when-baking column. We're talking the Vegas of neon signs here."

"The fire was an accident. It didn't have anything to do with the actual baking."

"I inadvertently dumped the cookies off the sheet trying to slide the tray out and they were burning on the bottom of the oven. It was saving the burning cookies that caused me to catch the mitt on fire."

"But if they hadn't slid off the pan, they might have tasted awesome."

She just gave him a look that said *nice try.*

"Don't you want to know? I mean, aren't you a little bit curious? You never even got to taste one."

"Bold words from a guy with a very nice kitchen. A very nice kitchen with a gas stove. A gas stove he's presently blocking with his formidable body. Subconscious stance, maybe. A smart stance, I say."

"I'll help."

Her eyebrows climbed halfway up her forehead. Well, one of them did. The other one had been partially singed off. She hadn't mentioned it after taking her shower, so neither had he. Actually, he thought it was kind of cute. In a classic Parker kind of way. Something he doubted she'd appreciate his saying.

"I thought you said you steered clear of the kitchen growing up."

"I did. I'm not going to help you with the mixing part, but I figure I can put my training to use with the baking part. I can man the stove and handle the cookie sheets."

She laughed. "Well, I had thought it would be a good idea to keep the fire department on speed dial, but I guess having a fireman actually posted on duty is even better. Possibly a requirement once Nick files his report."

"Hey, we made good lab partners once, right?"

She flushed a little, smiled. "You're right. We did."

He liked seeing the color come back to her cheeks. "It's settled then." He pushed the book across the counter. "Pick a few recipes and make a shopping list."

"I wasn't getting fancy. It was just the basic stuff. Flour, sugar, eggs, butter, you know."

"Eggs I have. The rest would be on the list." He lifted his hands in self defense. "Like I said, I don't cook. You should probably put cookie sheets on the list, too. And a mixer thingie."

"A mixer thingie." She slowly lowered her forehead to the counter. "I'm so doomed."

He came around the table and put his hands on her shoulders, easing the tension with a gentle massage.

"You have exactly the rest of your life to stop doing that." She groaned, and went boneless under his ministrations.

He, on the other hand, went hard as stone. The idea of her all pliant and soft and moaning like that, under him . . . Deciding it was smarter to stay on the other side of the kitchen, he gave her a little pat and walked over to the pantry, willing his body to subside before he had to turn and face her again.

"Before we do the grocery store run, can we go back to my place so I can get some clothes?"

"What, you don't like my fashionable fire department sweats?"

"I'm thinking you won't like them when the sleeves droop in the batter, or worse, over a stove-top flame."

"Point taken." He hadn't wanted to tell her earlier, when she'd still been pretty shocky, that even though her clothes hadn't been anywhere near the fire, everything in the house likely smelled like burned curtains and cabinets. And that generally that smell wasn't something a quick run in the washing machine would fix. She had enough on her plate to deal with. They could always make a quick run into one of the local chain stores and pick up a few items to tide her over until she got her clothes professionally cleaned.

He turned to find her still cradling her head on her arms and decided now was not the time to go into that. He walked to her side and put his hand on her hair, stroking, touching her cheek. "Maybe you should go lie down for a bit. We're pushing things a bit too hard, too fast here. You need to rest, regroup. I can pick up the groceries and grab a few things for you. We can start the cookie thing later today or this evening."

He figured he'd check her closet for sizes and pick up a few pairs of sweats and tees at the sporting goods store. With four sisters and countless Christmases and birthdays behind him, he knew better than to set foot in a woman's clothing store.

"I'm fine, I probably just need to eat something. All I've had since yesterday is some cookie dough batter and a few anatomically correct gingerbread men."

He'd been making a rudimentary list on the back of an envelope, but paused to look up. "What kind of ginger-bread men?"

She laughed, but kept her face buried in her arms. "Never mind."

He leaned his elbows on the table. "Seriously. Who

makes—wait, not you. Is that what you were baking? Isn't the *Gazette* like a family paper?"

She snort-giggled. "Not me. A friend of mine. She sells them, actually. I was at the charity cookie swap in Pine Mountain last night before coming to the bookstore. Abby made a box up for me and another friend of mine. Lily, I mentioned her before. Who also bakes for a living. Which, when you think about it, makes it even more hilarious that I'm the one doing a cookie column. I mean, they've never had to call the fire department even once. And I'm angling to be on the Pine Mountain Fire Department's next Christmas card list as a frequent caller."

"Pine Mountain? I thought when you said two-for-two, you meant the popcorn incident at school as the first time."

She lifted her head and gave him that wry, crooked smile. "I'm not counting the popcorn incident. You didn't exactly stop me from putting the thing in the microwave as I recall. So I only claim collateral responsibility for that one."

He tapped her right back. "I didn't even notice you'd put it in there, or I would have. As I recall, I was . . . distracted."

"By what? Certainly not the invertebrate lab we were working on. It's a miracle we made it through the first half of that semester without flunking out of that class. Professor Cannalis was insane. And possibly also an invertebrate."

"I was distracted because it was the first time you'd invited me to study in your dorm room instead of the lab or study hall. You were wearing that green fleece thing and black sweatpants."

She groaned. "Yes, guaranteed to make men drool." She lifted her head and gave him a baleful look. "I can't believe you remember what I was wearing." She laughed then, and pushed back up to a sitting position, ruffling her hand through her now-dry curls. "Except it was that awful, wasn't it? I can't believe I wore that outfit in front of you. It's what I wore to study in. I never left the dorm in that."

"Awful isn't the word I'd have used. And I'm glad you never wore it outside the dorm. I liked that you wore it for me."

She looked at him as if he'd sprouted two heads. "You're kidding. It was hideous."

"You always dressed so . . . well, not primly, but . . . neatly, I guess."

"I dressed in whatever pants I could find that didn't stop above my ankles and shirts that had sleeves that went all the way to my wrists. Trust me, wasn't easy. Still isn't."

"All I remember is it was soft and fuzzy and clung to your body like a second skin. You were like some green-fleeced feline goddess in that thing."

She stared at him, open mouthed, for a full ten seconds, then barked out a laugh. "And you had clearly suffered from some serious burned-popcorn fumes, my friend, because there was nothing feline about me in or out of that outfit."

He merely smiled at her. "You have your memories, I have mine."

She eyed him warily, but stretched and slid off the stool. "We should probably get going before it gets dark and the roads turn icy. Are you sure you don't have to go be a fireman somewhere? I still don't know if this is the right thing. I should call Fran, tell her what happened, which will take care of my having a job anyway—"

He'd rounded the table and took her by the elbows, shuffling her right in front of him. "You have to at least try, right? Or else the burned kitchen is for nothing. Just . . . let's go for the first column and if we can't pull it off by your deadline, then you can figure out what comes next."

She held his gaze for a long beat, then another. "Why are you doing this? I mean, lending me your spare room, your kitchen, that's one thing. But you said yourself you're getting prepped for your new job and you must have a million other things you should be doing."

"I don't know if you've noticed, but we had a blizzard out there last night. Or parts of the area did, anyway, depending on which side of the mountain you were on. My new office? Is in the blizzard part. I'm not doing anything today. I put in an all-night shift as a volunteer, so I'm off that rotation, too. I—"

"Should probably get some sleep. You're the one who needs to rest. I can call Lily and—"

"Parker."

She stopped, and took a breath.

"I want to help. I can help. And we're wasting deadline time talking about it. Adults speaking clearly about what they want, remember?"

"Right. Fine. Okay. I'm just not used to . . . I'm not good at reading situations like this."

He tilted her chin up. "There's nothing to read." Though, even as he said it, he knew it wasn't quite true. Even recently soot covered, exhausted, and hungry, there were undercurrents in the undercurrents that were running between them. But there would be time to explore those once they'd met her first deadline. Then he'd decide if he wanted to try and breach her no-men rule. Which, given it was taking pretty much all his willpower not to pull her into his arms and kiss some more life back into her cheeks, was likely to be a brief inner debate.

"Come on," he said, possibly a bit more gruffly than he meant to. "Let's get out of here. We'll stop and grab a bite to eat on the way."

Chapter 6

"**O**h my God, those actually look . . . edible!" Clara stepped back as Will slid the two brand-new cookie sheets from the oven and juggled them on the equally brand-new cooling racks. "Well, they're not on fire, anyway."

Clara was still marveling over Will's mountain cabin and how beautifully he'd remodeled it. The timber structure was over seventy years old, but everything inside had been gutted and reworked to suit more modern needs. The dining room space had been incorporated into the kitchen space, with the big, heavy wood slab providing plenty of room for food prep on the side facing the oven, sink, and fridge, with room to eat while seated on one of the padded café chairs lined up on the other side.

From there, the room opened up to the living area, which featured the original stone fireplace. But the main draw was the huge picture window that dominated the back wall of the cabin, with a view over the mountainside. The cabin was isolated, yet it was a pretty straight shot down the mountain road into town. With the leaves off the trees, she could see the valley below, and the vista of the mountains framing the other side. It was breathtaking. And with the snow on the rear deck railing and the bare tree limbs, almost magical.

Completing the room was an oversized old couch with a thick quilted throw piled at one end, fronted by a heavy wood coffee table that looked like it had seen its fair share of heavy boot heels resting on it. There was a wooden cabinet on the wall opposite the fireplace, which she assumed held his television or stereo or whatever electronic gadgets he enjoyed.

She noted right off the books and periodicals stacked on the floor at the end of the couch, and smiled at the idea that though he'd left school, he hadn't left his love of reading behind. She remembered him complaining that the thing he hated most about the heavy class load was that it left little time or inclination to read for pleasure. They'd shared more books in common than movies, which had been a first for her. It had been another thing that had sealed their friendship bond.

The other room on the main floor was the master bedroom and adjoining bath, which he'd added on to the original structure. Otherwise, there were just the two small guest rooms on the second floor which shared a bathroom. The one she was staying in had been tastefully if neutrally furnished with a basic double bed, restored antique wooden dresser, and small desk positioned under the dormer window that looked out the front of the house. The one interesting piece was the wardrobe, which appeared too big to have been brought into the room through the narrow doorway, but there it stood. There was no closet built into the room, so it made sense, and she thought it was a rather charming addition. Since the door to the other room was open, she'd noted that it had been turned into a small office of sorts, but she hadn't really nosed around. She hadn't seen his bedroom or master bath, either.

And it was going to stay that way.

"Wait," she said, when she saw Will picking up the spatula to slide the cookies off the sheet. She grabbed the cookbook. "It says they need to cool five minutes first."

Will lifted his still oven mitted hands up, palms out. "Yes, Chef."

"If only." She edged in front of him and bent over the cookie sheets. "The chocolate chips melted! And they look golden brown, just like the picture." She straightened. "Mostly I'm just happy they're not little death balls like the last batch. Or little bricks like the batch before that. I wish I knew what I did different this time to make them turn out right. Or right-looking anyway."

"I think the key was discovering there's a difference between baking powder and baking soda."

"Maybe. Who knew, right? Why name them so similarly and give them similar jobs, but make them not interchangeable," she said as she turned around, only to find he was still right behind her. As in *right* behind her.

He smiled. And didn't move. "Like you said, it is a miracle we didn't flunk that first semester of science."

"You mean me flunking. I think you were just humoring me so I didn't feel so ridiculous. Then and now. You knew about the baking soda powder thing, didn't you, science guy?"

His dimples peeked out. "Maybe." He talked over her rebuttal. "But one thing I've learned in science is that it's better to learn by figuring it out yourself than simply by observing others. You tend to remember those lessons better. And it can help illuminate other mysteries as well."

"Fancy talk for saying 'told you so' but I appreciate the thought." It was too easy to get caught up in those wonderfully deep brown eyes of his, especially when he was smiling at her and they had that affectionate twinkle in them. As if he alone understood how her brain worked . . . and he liked it.

She cleared her throat and turned back to the cookies. "I think it's been five minutes."

He reached past her and popped one of the cookies off the sheet. "Try one."

Feeling him behind her brought back memories of the night before in the coffee shop, when he'd put her coat on . . . and taken it off. "They're probably still hot."

He nudged her around with his other hand, free now of the oven mitt, until she found herself between him and the edge of the work table. He broke the cookie in half, and she could see the melted chocolate string, all glossy and melty, between the two halves. She opened her mouth to say something, anything, to get her perspective back, but he took advantage of the moment and tucked her half of the cookie between her teeth, while he simultaneously bit into the other half.

They both groaned and she saw his eyes close just before hers did the same. "Oh my God," she said, around a mouth full of cookie. "These are—"

"Incredible."

"I never knew chocolate chip cookies could taste like this."

"My sister says it's the oatmeal mixed in."

Clara enjoyed every last bit of her bite of cookie, reveling in all the buttery, chocolaty flavors, her eyes still closed. "Your sister is a genius."

"This is no kids' recipe, I can tell you that," he said, sounding equally entranced. "These things are probably illegal in several states."

Clara opened her eyes at the same time he did. Their gazes connected, held, then he slowly fed her another bite. She thought he might have groaned when she sank her teeth into the warm, crumbly cookie, but she was too busy making her own little happy noises as more of the delectable chocolate melted on her tongue. "Seriously illegal," she said, eyes shut again, her body humming on a chocolate buzz . . . and a Will buzz. "State. Federal. Possibly international."

She opened her eyes to find his gaze had gone as deep and chocolaty as the cookies, all but devouring her as she licked the last bit of chocolate from the corner of her mouth.

His voice was rough, and deep, when he spoke. "I don't know if I want to thank my sister right now, or kill her for giving us this recipe."

"I want to erect a statue in her honor in the town square. She just single-handedly rescued my first column. Won't she like having her recipe featured in the cookie column?"

"Probably. Definitely. But that's not what I'm talking about."

Clara could feel the heat rising between them, and it had nothing to do with oven temperatures or hot cookie sheets. "Right."

"How committed are you to that whole no-men thing?"

She felt her throat close over. While every inch of the rest of her stood up and cheered. Loudly. "It seemed like the smart thing at the time."

"And now?"

And now she wanted him to clear the work table with one big strong arm and take her right in the middle of his sister's awesome chocolate chip cookies. "My job," she managed. "Deadlines."

"We've got the first one covered."

"True." Her gaze might have drifted to his mouth. And she swore she could feel his grip tighten on the counter where he'd braced his hands on either side of her hips.

"I have three more sisters. They all bake. You have two friends who bake. That's five more columns."

"It sounds so easy when you put it like that."

"It could be easy, Parker. In fact, I think it could be the easiest thing I've ever done." He lifted one hand and brushed at a smudge of flour on her cheek. "What's hard is not doing anything. Really, really hard."

She swallowed past the tightness in her throat and forced her gaze to stay on his face, and not travel down the front of his body, looking for proof of that statement. Every part of her all but jumped up and down and begged her to just let go, go with the moment, let him do . . . whatever he wanted to do. For as long as he wanted to do it.

But she made herself remember standing in Joe's Grocery, and that moment when she'd entered Willard's cabin to find an orgy in progress, and listening to Stuart's mother say awful things while he just stood by and looked helpless to intervene. She didn't want to add Will to that list. Will could never be on that list. He was the one good thing, her one relationship success, even if that relationship was just friendship. Will was gorgeous and confident now, wanted what he wanted and didn't seem at all shy about going after it . . . but how long would he want it? Want her?

"I—I can't be an easy thing," she whispered. "I—I don't want to be that. Ever again. Especially with you." She started to raise a shaky hand to his face, but thought better of touching him and curled her fingers into her palm. "You matter to me, Will. You did back then, and you already do now. So, I just . . . I need to matter, too."

He looked honestly stunned, which didn't help her in the clear-thinking department at all. "What makes you think you don't?"

"Look at you," she whispered. "You're . . . amazing. And I'm, I'm still gawky and awkward. I have one eyebrow, for God's sake, and I should be declared my own personal disaster site. You're accomplishing your goals and I'm trying not to lose my second job in a week's time. I know you're caught up in memories of our past friendship, and it was a good time in our lives. I'm a little caught up, too. I just . . . don't want this to be some retro, second chance fling. It would be—"

"The third thing," he finished. "Grocery store, book store . . ."

"Will's kitchen," she finished. "Only, this one would be so much worse, you know? I'm trying to be smart this time."

"Okay."

She blinked, and hated—hated—how hard and fast her heart sank when he didn't put up even a token fight for her. Even as she realized that was what she'd just asked him to do, and should be happy, relieved, that he'd respected her enough not to push harder. Or that she'd been right, and it ultimately hadn't been that big a deal to begin with. Just . . . convenient. Easy. She ducked her chin, not wanting him to see any of that in her expression. He was being a good guy. She was the one being ridiculous.

But there was to be no easy escape. He tipped her chin up until she was forced to look into his eyes. "You're right. It shouldn't be easy. It shouldn't be something jumped into without taking the time to make it mean something first." He cupped her face. "You do mean something. You did then and if anything, it feels like more now. Or like it could be more. But just because we're not kids anymore, and the things I want to do to you, and with you, are decidedly adult, doesn't mean we should leapfrog past all the other important things and go straight to the adult things."

"Will—"

"Parker." He framed her face now. "When I take you to bed, I want there to be absolutely no doubt in your mind that you matter. I want you to know, I want us both to know, that sex isn't just something we're doing because it's easy and available, but because we mean to go on like we began. Friends first. And always. Out of bed . . . and in."

Tears burned at the corners of her eyes. No one had ever said anything like that to her. And no one, except for Will, had ever known her well enough to mean it.

His mouth turned downward and he thumbed away her tears. "I'm not trying to upset you. I won't push." At her arch look, even as her lips trembled, he smiled. "Okay, I won't push anymore. You've had a hell of a day and I know you're under the gun with this new column stint. I think your idea of handling it honestly, as a non-baker, with the 'If I can do it, anyone can' approach, bringing humor and your own missteps to the project, is brilliant. I know your editor will love it."

"I hope so. It's the only way I can hope to pull it off."

"So, let's get through launching your new career as the Lucy Ricardo of baking, and get to know each other better while you're at it. Do you trust me?"

She nodded. It was all she was capable of.

"Then that's where we start." He slid one tear off her cheek on the side of his thumb, then leaned in and very gently kissed away the matching one on her other cheek. "It's been a really long day for us both. You've got the first column nailed. A good night's sleep followed by my famous firehouse breakfast—the only other meal I can cook, by the way—and we'll both get a fresh start on the rest tomorrow. Deal?"

She nodded again, knowing if she even tried to tell him what he meant to her in that moment, she'd fall apart much as she had in the cab of his truck after the fire. Which was almost impossible to believe had happened earlier that very day. He was right. Again. It had been a really long day. Brutal, in many ways. And beautiful in others.

"I'll take kitchen cleanup duty this time," he said. "Your turn next time. Why don't you go on up. Take my laptop, climb into bed, work there in peace and quiet, then get some sleep. Do you need anything? Hot tea?" He smiled. "Some awesome chocolate chip cookies and milk?"

Just you. It was only the fresh tears clogging her throat that mercifully kept her from blurting the words out loud. She could only imagine how wonderfully comforting it would feel to crawl into his bed instead and say the hell with the column, to be pulled into his arms, to feel the warmth and strength of him comforting her all night long. Sometimes being an adult about things sucked. "I'm good." She pushed away from the work table and he stepped back so she could slide out. She paused at the door to the foyer and stairs leading to the second floor. "Thank you."

He grinned, and it was so honest, so open, so . . . Will. Her Will. And just like that, all the tension, all the worry, all the bad things, and even all the frustrating things, simply fell away. At least for that moment. She did trust him, and that was exactly the right place to start. So she clung to it, and in that way, clung to him, and everything he'd promised.

"Anytime," he said. Then that grin deepened, and the dimples winked, the cleft appeared, and she hurried up the stairs before she changed her mind.

Chapter 7

Being a good guy was pretty much going to kill him. Not that he'd ever considered himself a bad guy in the past. But if Santa did in fact keep a naughty-or-nice list, the thoughts he'd been having about Parker for the past two days would definitely put him with the first group.

He watched from the doorway as she sat curled on his couch, feet tucked up under his mother's old quilt, which she'd thrown over her legs. A pile of notes, index cards, and a book on baking basics littered the coffee table in front of her. She had two pens on top of the pile and a pencil tucked behind one ear, but wasn't using any of them as far as he could tell. The ever present, oversized glass of ice and Coke—her go-to deadline beverage in college and now—fought for space amongst the writer's coffee-table detritus. It was empty, he noted, once again, making a mental note to switch from cans to two-liter bottles.

Tiny little gold-rimmed half glasses, which were a new addition since college, had been pushed up on her head, making her short red curls stick out at odd angles. She wore no makeup other than the Chapstick she was always rubbing over her lips . . . so she could bite it right back off again, as she was doing now while typing away, then pausing, staring, studying, thinking, occasionally swearing, then typing some more. It was probably wrong to be jealous of a tube of Chapstick for its constant lip contact with her, but there it was.

They'd gone back by her house later that first day, but, as he'd predicted, her clothes would require professional cleaning. They'd even left her laptop behind, stuffed in a sealed plastic bag with a bunch of scrunched up newspapers to try and detoxify it. Her SUV had been buried under snowdrifts and piles from the street plows, so that had been left behind as well. She'd fallen asleep as they'd made their way back to Bealetown, the exhaustion and shock finally catching up with her, so he hadn't stopped anywhere on the trek back. He'd intended to make a quick run out to pick up a few things for her, but he'd put it off with various excuses, which he realized now was because he liked her just the way she was.

Swallowed up in the navy blue sweats and BCFD hoodie he'd given her, she should have looked shapeless and less desirable, but it hadn't had that effect at all. Quite the opposite. The dark color made her pale skin look even creamier, softer, all but begging him to put some color into those cheeks of hers. And he knew exactly how her body felt now, so his imagination had no problem putting forth a scenario that had him joining her on the couch, sliding his laptop to the floor, then plucking her glasses from her head, and the pencil from behind her ear . . . and taking off whatever was left of that Chapstick with his mouth on hers, as he slid her down and under him . . .

He cleared his throat, and his mind, causing her to look up as he walked through the kitchen to the living room.

She blinked once and he could almost see her disconnect from whatever she'd been writing, as she shifted her attention outward, to him. "You're back."

"I am. Roads are pretty clear in town now, so things are looking up. You look like you could use a refill."

"I'll get it. I need to get up, stretch my legs."

"Column number four going okay?"

"That's just it. It's flying. It's going so okay that I'm pretty sure I must be doing something terribly wrong."

"This is one of your friend Lily's recipes?"

She nodded. "I was going to use one of Abby's grandma's recipes. She had a whole stash that she doesn't make for sale, and I thought it might bring some attention to her business. But I couldn't get a hold of her. Power is probably out on her mountain from the storm. I swear, it goes out on her in a stiff wind."

"Do you want me to get someone from her local fire department to do a quick check, make sure she's okay?"

Her expression immediately softened. "That's so nice of you. But I heard from Lily earlier and she got a text from Abby saying she'd made it home fine. She's used to the power going out, so I'm sure she's okay. Oh, and Lily's neck-deep in that cookie competition at the resort, apparently in some kind of tangle with the guy who dumped me at the grocery store."

Will's eyebrows lifted. "Wow."

"I know, right? He's a pretty good chef, too, so it's looking like she's got some serious competition. I didn't want to bug her about my dinky little column when she has all that going on."

"But she came through?"

"She tested about a hundred different recipes trying to find the ones she wanted to use in the competition. So she gave me one of her rejects—"

"You're writing about a recipe reject?"

"It wasn't a bad recipe when she got done with it, just not contest worthy. But perfection isn't what I'm making the column about. It's about how even a seasoned chef has to work with a recipe to get it just right. Even they have cookie rejects. She let me use some of the backstory on how she got it just right and some of the rejects that happened to her along the way. It's not exactly Lucille Ball Bakes, but it still follows the theme of the column that everybody starts somewhere and nobody is the perfect baker."

"Sounds great. I think you're on a roll. Have you heard from Fran yet with any feedback on your bumbling baker concept?"

"Actually, yes." She smiled and looked a bit petrified at the same time.

"Good? Bad?"

"Terrifying, mostly."

He sat down next to her on the couch and smiled. "So, pretty damn good then, I take it. What's the scary part?"

"Where do I begin?"

He reached under the quilt and pulled her sock-covered feet out from where she'd tucked them under her thighs and stretched them across his lap, gently kneading up and down the soles.

She groaned and let her head tip back against the couch. It was all he could do not to growl and drag her right on top of him, but he'd wanted—no, needed—to put his hands on her, and this had seemed the safest, friends-first way he could do that. Stupid, stupid man.

After a deep, appreciative sigh, she continued the conversation, head still back, eyes still closed. "Seems like I'm not the only bumbling baker out there. My 'humorous but eventually victorious take on baking,' as Fran calls it, has apparently struck a chord with a number of readers."

"That doesn't sound scary, it sounds fantastic."

"It's very gratifying and hugely relieving. The scary part is, well, it's twofold. First, she included an e-mail account for the column that went directly to the paper, to help them gauge the response to the first few columns. Fran has now transferred that account to me."

"But you said they liked the column."

"They do. And they have questions. Lots of them." She rolled her head to the side and looked at him meaningfully. "That they somehow think I can answer."

"Well, that sounds like the idea for a continuation of the column. You can tackle some of their baking or cooking questions and find the answers that work. Keep the whole column thing rolling."

"See, that's the thing. That was Fran's immediate response, too."

"That's great! But you don't look excited. Listen, I know it pushed you to step outside your comfort zone, but it looks like taking that chance is paying off."

"Will, I don't want to be the bumbling baker forever. I don't even want to be one for the next—however many days are left. I mean, I'm thrilled that I found a way to make this thing work, and I can't thank your sisters enough for coming through with some recipes, but it's not something I wanted to start, much less continue. It was just a means to an end, and the only way I could keep working at the paper at that moment. I don't have a love for cooking or baking. What I do have is a healthy respect for not burning anything else to the ground. I mean, I do see now why Lily and Abby love it and I get the challenge, the reward. But it works for them because they had a natural love of the process. I have a natural fear of it. Funny for a few columns, but—"

"Not the future you'd imagined for yourself."

She shook her head and let it tip back on the couch again. "Even less than being an advice columnist. What I want to write are stories about people, about what's going on in our town and beyond. Nothing hard-hitting or gritty, we're a little mountain town, we don't really have hard-hitting and the only grit is the stuff on the roads after the snowstorms. But we do have people with amazing everyday life stories to tell and I'd love to be the one to tell them. Some cautionary, some motivating, some inspiring, rewarding, covering life's ups and downs. And definitely not in a question-and-answer format."

"So, have you pitched that to Fran?"

"I did when I was first hired on, but she had an urgent need to fill some slots and I was willing to be a team player, thinking it would earn me respect and I'd eventually win her trust and get to where I wanted to be. Instead I ended up getting moved from writing about resort events to giving advice, then getting fired from that and clinging on by a skinny string of Christmas cookie sprinkles."

"The positive reaction to the column has to help put points back in your column, though, right?"

"It should, but I know Fran and she isn't about to walk away from something that has readers already excited. She sees advertising dollar signs. And I see . . . I see being thankful I have a job—and I am—but I also see a future doing something I'm not cut out for. Again."

"Have you thought about quitting? About relocating?"

She lifted her head, honestly surprised. "To where? The *Gazette* is our only paper. I don't want to do big-city journalism, I want small town."

"Bealetown is a small town. So is Riverside. I know they're not *your* small town, but they're still local to the area and to your background. At the very least, maybe the idea that you're willing to walk might make Fran sit up and pay attention."

She started to say something, then paused, then just looked at him, something close to wonder in her eyes. "You know, that also terrifies me. But kind of in a good way."

He grinned, surprised by how much pleasure it gave him to see her light up . . . and see the wheels start to spin. He focused on her foot massage.

Still smiling, she tipped her head back again and closed her eyes.

"I remember the first time you did that."

He took in the dreamy look of pleasure on her face, how relaxed she was, comfortable with him, trusting him. And, he couldn't help it, it made him wonder what she would look like when she climaxed while under him, which immediately had him shifting a bit so her feet were a little further away from the bulge growing in his jeans.

"It was that all-nighter for the chem lab final, remember? We were sitting in the library on those godawful wooden chairs. My feet fell asleep for like the third time in an hour and you pulled them up in your lap and used those magic hands. God, it was like the best thing ever." She sighed. "Still is."

Santa shouldn't put him on the naughty list. *Santa should give me a freaking medal is what Santa should do.* He wished he'd never sat on the couch. Wished he'd never promised friends first. Because they were already friends. Yes, a lot had happened to both of them since college, but the core things, the essence of who they were and why they'd connected, hadn't changed at all. At least not as far as he could tell. In some ways it was as if they'd just picked up right where they'd left off.

Rationally he knew that wasn't really possible, and that she was right. They didn't really know each other in the sense of how they'd gotten from where they'd left off, to where they were today. But how much of that mattered? He wanted to know everything, every day of those gap years, all the ones that mattered anyway . . . but just how much of that did he have to know before he could kiss her again?

He'd thought about it a lot while driving to and from town. Hell, he'd thought about little else while he was supposed to be getting his office set up, too. He'd decided that it wasn't really about the things that had happened in between. Clearly they were still interested in each other, still retained whatever goodwill they'd created as friends, still felt that unshakable bond. They were still attracted to each other, and, from what he could tell, Parker was just as interested as he in shifting their friendship to something more serious, or certainly more adult. He understood she didn't want to make another relationship mistake. He wasn't looking to add to her list, either.

But, to him, what mattered was what was happening now. What they shared now. What they learned about each other now. For lack of a better way of stating it, they had to do what other people did when figuring out a new relationship. They needed to date. To do the things couples did when they were first starting out.

Which seemed silly, in some respects, because they weren't strangers to each other. But how else were they going to figure things out? How else to build the kind of trust needed for the kind of intimacy that friends didn't share . . . but lovers did? He wasn't even sure when it had happened. That first day in science lab? The night of the burned popcorn in her dorm? Or right that very second, sitting on the couch in his cabin, feeling so right and natural together, he couldn't imagine coming home to an empty cabin now.

All he knew was that his heart was thumping and his palms were sweating. He wanted a lot more than sex with Clara Parker. He wanted it all.

But how did he ask his old college buddy who happened to be living with him out on a date?

"So, are you going to bake Lily's cookies today? Do we have what you need? You should have called, I could have picked up—"

"I was going to, and realized I don't have your cell phone number."

"Sure you do—uh . . . no, wow. Now that I think about it, I guess we never did that." It was another little reality check on where they were on the getting-to-know-you spectrum. Hell, even folks who were just dating for the first time had each other's damn phone numbers. He picked up her phone from the coffee table and punched in his number. "Now you have it." He pushed the number he'd just set, making his own phone ring. He dug it out and silenced it, then saved her incoming number. "And now I have yours. Sorry, should have done that when you got here."

"We were a little deadline distracted."

We were a lot of things distracted, he wanted to say. "I did bring you a little something else from town."

"You did? I love little somethings." She sat up straighter and slid her feet from his lap.

He should have been relieved, but he already missed the contact. "Well, you might not be as in love with this as I thought you would, but I had Nick pick up the issues of the *Gazette* with your cookie column in them when he was over there doing some work today."

She instantly broke out in a wide smile. "That's the nicest thing. Despite my less-than-gracious comments on my future as a food columnist, I would like to see how Fran laid the thing out and where she positioned it."

Will reached inside his jacket and slid out the papers he'd folded and tucked in the inside pocket. "I only kept the pages with the column, sorry, but I'm guessing you can get a pretty good idea."

She shifted closer and took them, sliding her glasses down as she unfolded the sheaf and read through them. He had to curl his fingers into his palm to keep from tucking her next to him and reading them over her shoulder with her. It felt like the most natural thing in the world to do . . . and yet . . .

"I like it." She flipped to the second one. "I really do. Good placement, and I like how she set it up, more like an article with a recipe attached than the standard Dear Abby kind of thing."

He grinned. "They used the photo. Cute."

She smacked him with the paper, but was smiling. "It's ridiculous, but sadly accurate. Thanks for taking that, by the way. You should have gotten photo credit. I told Fran."

He slipped one of the papers away from her and looked more closely. "Hey, I did." He shot her a wink. "I have my first published photographer credit. If I ever get tired of taking forensic photos of burned stuff, I'll have a fall back."

"Well, actually, that's not far off. I am missing an eyebrow."

He squinted. "The photo is too small to tell." He glanced at her. "The dusting of flour on your cheek and smear of chocolate on your chin is sexy."

She slid off her glasses. "Here. You clearly need these more than I do."

He took them and perched the tiny lenses on his nose. "How do you see out of these things? Maybe that's the baking problem right there. You're only seeing half the recipe."

She laughed and reached for her glasses, which he lifted out of reach, causing her to fall hands first in his lap. With fists landing in a very unfortunate place. His eyes might have crossed as he let out a little squeak of pain. Her efforts to scramble off of him only made the situation worse. So much worse. Until he lifted her off him and plopped her at the other end of the couch, then tried to take the throbbing pain like a man.

"Will, I'm so sorry!"

He merely nodded and gritted his teeth in what he

hoped passed for a natural smile. "Fine," he managed. "It's all fine." Or would be. Someday. If he never wanted kids.

"Maybe I should go to the store, get the stuff I need," she offered. "You've been running around and taking care of me like some housebound invalid, but I've driven in this weather my whole life—"

Will cut her off with a shake of his head. It took a few more moments to form actual words, then sentences. "The roads in town are clear." He shifted in his seat, winced again, then shook it off, or pretended to. "But living up here above town, the wind keeps blowing the roads shut with all the snow. With the plow it's no big deal, but with that weight on the front, it doesn't drive like a regular truck. I don't want you out there."

One partially singed red eyebrow lifted, but rather than the "I am woman, hear me roar" lecture he'd half expected, she said, "Yeah, you're probably right. I almost burned down one house. We don't need me on snowy mountain roads operating heavy machinery. Would it be too much of an imposition to ask you to drive me down for a little grocery store excursion? You can just drop me off if you have things you need to do at your new office or wherever." She picked up her phone and smiled. "I could text you when I'm done."

He smiled. "That's a date." Not exactly what he'd had in mind, but it was a start.

Chapter 8

Clara scowled as the little incoming mail alert chimed again. She shouldn't have synced her new cookie column e-mail account to her cell phone. It had been dinging every other second since she'd stepped inside the grocery store. It was a miracle she didn't have hive splotches all over her body by now just thinking about how she was going to respond to all of them. Or any of them. She'd thought a lot about Will's idea while wandering the aisles. The more she considered it, the more she liked it. And only partly because it would give her an escape from having to play the bumbling baker one day longer than absolutely necessary. It wasn't that she minded being the proverbial butt of the joke. In fact, that was the easiest part. She could just be herself.

She just wished she could be herself, writing about something that mattered to her.

As soon as she got home, she'd have to log in and start reading through them. Home. Will's home, not her home. Although, admittedly, the cabin was where her mind had automatically gone. "Home base," she corrected. And it was home base. Until she got contractors into her cottage, which she'd found out wasn't going to happen until after the holidays. She'd gotten one of the local guys to go over and tarp, tape, and otherwise secure the back wall behind the cabinets where the fire had gone through the plaster and insulation, stopping just shy of going all the way through. But it wasn't stable, and with the weather being unpredictable, Stan the contractor guy had recommended she cover it all up until it could be looked at by the insurance inspector, who also wasn't coming until after Christmas. Which was yet a week away.

"Home base," she repeated as she unloaded her cart onto the conveyor belt, her thoughts drifting to Will's little cabin, tucked away up in the woods on the side of the mountain. It felt like more than simply a base, a rest stop. "Feels like home." The check out girl gave her a questioning look, and Clara covered with a quick smile. "Talking to myself. Lists, always making lists."

The young girl gave her the kind of half smile people did when they were pretty sure they were talking to a loony person, but figured it was better to play it safe and be nice. Clara was also pretty sure the girl was checking out her missing eyebrow. She tugged Will's wool cap down a bit lower on her forehead, and stowed the filled grocery totes in her cart. She had bigger things to worry about. Like her e-mail.

Her phone buzzed in her pocket. She pulled it out enough to see who was calling, then let out an embarrassingly loud laugh-snort when she saw the name on the screen. She answered the call, ignoring the grocery girl's expression of pity. "Rescue Ranger? Really?"

"Well, you knew who it was, right?" Will's deep chuckle warmed her right down to her previously numb toes.

She even grinned at the clerk before wheeling her cart toward the sliding front doors. "I'm just now getting done, are you close?"

"Very."

She barely stopped short of running the cart right into him. "Cute," she said into the phone.

"No, you are," he said into his phone.

The familiar childhood tease shouldn't have made her blush. Maybe it was the dimples. Maybe it was the fact that she'd been living for three straight days now with a guy who posed half naked for firemen calendars and was so sexually frustrated that it was a miracle she could walk straight. Whatever it was, she felt her skin go hot and her legs get a bit wobbly. Something about being outside the cabin, in the real world, changed things, made it seem somehow less safe, less predictable. Which made no sense given at least now there weren't two beds and a very comfortable leather couch within close proximity.

She hung up her phone and pushed the cart so it rolled forward and bumped against his legs. "Good timing. You can steer."

Still dimpled, tousled, and sexy as hell, he tucked his phone away and easily commandeered the cart. His smile faltered momentarily when he noted the number of grocery totes lining the inside of the cart. "I thought you said you just needed a few things. What are we baking?"

The "we" shouldn't affect her like that, either. He used it so easily. So casually. At least that's what she kept telling herself. In the three days she'd been living under his roof, he'd been gone for large chunks of time, doing whatever it was he needed to be doing to get his new office set up. But since that first day when he'd manned the oven and anything having to do with potential fire hazards, he'd always been there when it came time to do the hands-on baking research part of her new job. And as much as she wished she could say otherwise, she was really going to hate it when the time came that she'd be doing it by herself. Yet another reason to think hard and fast about his idea of reaching for the job she wanted at another paper.

It was more than that, though. She liked working with him and it wasn't lost on her how quickly and naturally they'd seemed to find a perfect rhythm. It was sort of like being chem lab partners again, only this time they got to eat the results of their experiments. Well, most of them.

"I've been cooped up in the house for two straight days now, with all that snow outside," she said. *And wanting to jump your bones for pretty much every single second of it.* "I might have overcompensated a little with some additional comfort food." Not that comfort food was any real substitute for sex, but it was better than nothing. Or it had felt that way when she was loading her cart.

"You should have said something, I'd—"

"No, it's okay, really." She sucked in her breath as they stepped outside into the bitter cold. "I should have eaten something before going shopping, but I also got things to restock your pantry and fridge. You've been kind enough to house me under unfortunate circumstances; the least I can do is contribute to the grocery bill. Speaking of which—" She turned, only to find he was a lot closer behind her than she'd thought. He'd parked the cart under one of the metal sidewalk barricades and was pulling his keys out when she more or less smacked right into him.

"Whoa there," he said, smiling automatically, taking her arm and steadying her as if it was second nature. And, sadly, with her, it pretty much had to be. But he was always that. Right there for her.

"Sorry."

"I was going to pull the truck around rather than try to jockey the stuff over an icy parking lot."

"You mean jockey the stuff and me across an icy parking lot." She smiled. "Smart."

He was still holding her arm, and she was still tucked between him and the grocery cart. She told herself she didn't move because his big body was mercifully blocking the brisk, bone-chilling wind. It sounded plausible, anyway.

"So . . . speaking of which, what?" he asked.

It took her a moment to recapture the conversational thread. "I heard back from the insurance agent and my contractor. They can't get started on anything until after Christmas, and, to be honest, the way it sounded, I'm thinking they won't get started before the new year. At least with the contractor. My agent said he'd be able to come out on the twenty-ninth. You've already been so great, and I don't want to overstay my welcome, so—"

He pulled off a glove and cupped her cheek, the warmth of his palm radiating heat all the way through her. "So you'll stay with me. Parker," he said, talking right over her attempt to explain her plan, "I like having you there. When I first moved in, I remember how much I loved the peace and quiet." He grinned. "After life with four sisters, it was a really welcome change. Then I guess I just got used to it. I don't know that I ever thought about it feeling lonely or too quiet." He rubbed his thumb over her cheek. "But it would be both of those things now."

She tried to ignore the rush of pleasure his words gave her and shot him a wry smile instead. "So, you're saying I'm noisy and cramping your style then?"

He tugged her closer. "I'm saying I want you to stay as long as you need to." There was that pure, honest, unguarded affection in his eyes again.

And it occurred to Clara that that was the one thing she'd never seen before in the men she'd dated. Sure, they'd looked at her with desire, or interest, but not . . . not like Will looked at her.

And while his body might make her pulse jump, that look did funny things to parts of her insides she'd never felt before. Perversely, and maybe out of a latent sense of self-preservation, she wondered if he'd ever looked at anyone else like that. Maybe he looked at all the women he'd dated that way. "Will, I—"

"Please. Stay." Then he leaned in and kissed her. It was short, sweet, barely a peck on the lips. The kind of kiss a friend gave to a friend.

Which did nothing to explain the sudden hormonal inferno it set off inside of her. He could have taken her right there on the icy sidewalk and she wouldn't have done a thing to stop him.

"Wait here," he said, somewhat abruptly. "I'll be right back."

Without his body blocking the chill, all the heat and arousal from being so deep in his personal space again should have instantly evaporated. Only she was still standing there, basking in the afterglow, when he reemerged from the grocery store with a big zipper bag cooler and a bag of ice.

"How much of this stuff requires refrigeration?" he asked, while she was still staring at the cooler bag.

"I don't know, not much. Why?"

"Well, you said before, how we don't really know each other, in regards to who we are today, what we're about."

"Okay."

"I want you to know me. So, I thought I'd show you what I'm about these days. My new offices aren't that far from here."

Surprised and touched by the offer, she smiled. "I would like that. But, do we really need a cooler with ice for that detour? How big is the place?"

"Not very, but, uh . . ."

It surprised her to see him stumble over his words. She didn't know if it was simply a manifestation of being ten years older, or perhaps the combination of training his body into the workhorse machine it was now, so he could run into burning buildings and do whatever had to be done, but the main difference in the Will Mason of today was his innate confidence. The man standing in front of her now, however, reminded her more of the skinny, geeky college freshman. And something about that made the flutter inside her belly grow even stronger.

"But?" she prodded.

"I want to take you out. On a date."

Of all the things he could have said, she hadn't expected that. And he'd blurted it out, like a wet-behind-the-ears kid who'd have to borrow his dad's car keys. Completely at odds with the rugged, handsome guy who had a bit of a swagger and came on to her like it was the most natural thing in the world. It was incredibly endearing, and connected so directly to the part of her that still felt dorky and awkward as she tried to find her way in the big bad real world, that she realized no amount of rules and restrictions was going to keep him from finding his way into her heart.

She also realized that one of the real reasons she'd put him at arm's length was that she hadn't thought she was worthy of this new, improved Will. Like he'd moved into some other realm with his godlike body and innate confidence, and she was still left behind in Dorksville. And that was a combination she'd tried before, with dismal, painful results.

But, in that moment, it was just her and the guy who'd been her trusted friend and confidant, who'd shared with her the challenges and tribulations of stepping out of a somewhat sheltered, small-town life into the endless possibilities that could be their future. It was a lot harder to say no to that guy. In fact, it was impossible.

"I'd like that. Both the office tour . . . and the date."

She was surprised and secretly thrilled to see the flush of relief on his face. Like he couldn't get a date with any woman on the planet. She could think of a few hundred women at that calendar signing alone who'd have eagerly accepted. And yet he'd been almost . . . nervous, it seemed, waiting for her response. "Why don't we just go by the cabin and drop this stuff off and I can change clothes." She gestured to the oversized hoodie and sweatpants she was wearing, tucked into too-big snow boots. "Or not. I keep forgetting that my current wardrobe is all pretty much just like this." She smiled sweetly. "I don't suppose the date is me going clothes shopping?"

"You look fine. And we're already here in town, so no point in going up and down the mountain. Between the cooler and the cold weather, there isn't anything that won't hold up for at least an hour or two."

Clara could have told him that his idea of her looking date-ready and her idea of the same were light years apart, but since everything else she owned smelled like pit bar-beque, she could only smile, nod, and pray she didn't feel awkwardly underdressed wherever it was he was taking her. Which, frankly, was pretty much a given. The fact that he was dressed casually in jeans, hoodie, and leather bomber jacket meant nothing. She was certain he could turn up in canvas fireman pants and nothing else and be happily welcomed in pretty much any establishment, any-where.

He loaded the cooler, then pulled the truck around. Cooler and totes were tucked on the bench seat behind the front truck seat in short order, then he was helping her up into the passenger side. "You're not going to tell me where we're going?"

"My new office."

"I meant on our date." But he'd already closed the door and headed around the back of the truck to the driver's side. Clara didn't know whether to be thrilled or scared that he was trying to find a way to grow their friendship into something she could trust as the basis of a fully real-ized relationship. She wanted to be thrilled. She wanted the promise of what they might have together. But fear was taking the leading edge. She might not have had him in her life for quite some time, but the memory of him, of their friendship, had been one of the best things she'd had to look back on. If she took that irreversible step forward with him, gave in to her growing desire to explore every part of what might be between them . . . and it failed, then she'd lose all of that. Failure now would taint everything good that had come before, erasing what little confidence she had with men along with it. And she honestly didn't know how she'd go on from there, with nothing left to build on.

"Ready?" He smiled at her as he hooked his seatbelt and adjusted the heat.

The flutter became a full out heart palpitation. *Well, crap.* It was too late to think about it and decide. She already knew, or her heart did. She wanted him. All of him. The past, the present, the future. All of it. And if she couldn't find a way to be ready now . . . she never would be.

Chapter 9

Will pulled into the parking lot of his firehouse. His now former firehouse.

"I thought you said the new offices were between the police academy and the county courthouse?"

"They are. This is my station, or was, where I used to work. And will still volunteer when I can."

"Oh. Cool." She looked at him, her expression unreadable. "Did you need something from here for the office?"

"No. I wanted to show you what I've been doing for the past nine years, or at least where I've been doing it. And—you still love the holidays, right?"

Now she looked completely confused. "Yes, I do. But what—"

"Well, we have an empty lot around back where we sell Christmas trees as a station fundraiser every year. They've got mulled cider and usually some music playing. And . . . I thought maybe we'd pick one out." It was silly to feel so flustered, only now that he was explaining it all, he wondered how lame she must think he was to take her Christmas tree shopping on their first date. "You, uh, may have noticed that I don't have a tree up. All four of my sisters usually go overboard with their decorating, and since I make the rounds, I generally just enjoy the fruits of their labors."

"You've never put up your own tree?"

"We have one at the firehouse every year."

"That's not the same thing."

"I know, but it was enough for me."

"Well, please don't feel like you need to put up a tree for me, I really don't need—"

"I do."

That made her blink. "You suddenly need a tree? Why?"

"Because it would be fun to put one up with you." There. He'd said it.

She stared at him and he still wasn't sure what was going through her mind. "Do you have decorations? No, you couldn't, you never put a tree up. Will, you can't just throw any old thing on them. Part of what makes a tree special is decorating it with things that matter, or have some history or tradition."

"Well, every tree has to start somewhere, right? I'll call my sisters and have them put aside a few of the ornaments from our family. We had so many they each have a batch, which they've added to, so I know they can spare a few." He grinned. "I'm sure they'll be more than happy to show you every one of my childhood ornament creations made in school or Boy Scouts."

"You were a Boy Scout?"

"You say that like you're surprised."

"Well, not meaning you're not Boy Scout material, but just that I guess I think of them as doing camping and outdoor stuff like that and—"

"Just because I had four sisters and was good at math does not mean I didn't know how to pitch a tent or tell a good campfire ghost story."

She grinned at that. "You told ghost stories?"

"I told great ghost stories. Actually, to be honest, my grandpa told awesome ghost stories, so most of mine were lifted from him, but I held my own pretty well."

She just sat there, smiling at him. Then she kind of abruptly said, "I need to know something."

"I won't tell ghost stories in bed—assuming we share one someday—unless, of course, you ask me to."

She laughed. "Good to know. But that wasn't it."

His smile remained steady, but something more serious was flickering in her eyes and he felt his palms get a little sweaty. "Ask me anything."

"I've told you about my dating past, well the general gist of it, anyway. Just take the grocery store incident and multiply by . . . a bigger number than it should be."

"You want to know about my dating past?"

She nodded. "Not invasive, private details, or names or how many, or anything like that. It's just . . ." She paused, sighed. "I feel stupid for even asking, especially after you're being so great and understanding about everything, and you're trying to do things the way I asked. But . . . I told you how I'm not good at judging things. Relationship things. And you've also been great about listening to all of my ridiculous insecurities and—"

"They're not ridiculous. They're honest. And I appreciate, more than you know, that you've been so honest and up front with me. Because while I did listen, and I think I kind of got it . . ." Now it was his turn to sigh. "If I'm being completely honest, I have to admit that it went in one ear, and my reaction was more or less, well, I'll figure out what it will take for Parker to be happy so I can have what I want. Which isn't really the same thing as listening and truly understanding what you meant."

"But you think you do now?"

"More than I did, yes. That's why I thought we should go out and do something a normal couple would do as they start to get to know each other."

"Buy a Christmas tree together? To decorate back at the house we're sharing?" She laughed.

He laughed too. "See, that's just it. I want to figure it out, but . . . well, we can't turn back time and date like two people who just met, because we didn't just meet. We share a past, and even though a lot of time has passed, it's clear to me, and I think you, that it meant something then, and that it still does now."

"Will—"

"No, let me get this out while I'm thinking somewhat clearly on the subject." He shot her a fast grin. "Or as clear as I can anyway. I realized when we didn't even have each other's phone numbers, despite sharing a house, and a past, and a bond that appears to have withstood the test of time and distance, that you were right. We really aren't currently connected. Not even like newly dating couples would be. So I figured I'd start with showing you where I'm from, where I'm going. I've gotten a little peek into that with you this week, from listening to you talk to Nick, and working on your new column with you. I don't know how else to go about convincing you that I'm worth taking a chance on. And not just as your best friend."

"That's just it. You don't need to convince me, Will. I want all the same things you do. In fact, the more perspective I try to retain, the more I realize I can't do any of that, because you're right. We know each other. We know we want each other. What I don't know is why me? I mean, is it because I'm here and this is just something interesting to pursue? Old friend, second chances? Easy come, easy go? Have you been serious about anyone before? Do you want to be serious about anyone? I mean, you've changed so much. Not on the inside, not who you are, but . . . let's just say I'm thinking you don't have as hard a time finding potential serious dates as I do." She stopped, looked away. "I'm sounding like pathetic, insecure girl. I realize that. And, you know, I'm not. Not really. Normally I'd just go for it and figure what happens happens and that's life. Which, possibly, hasn't been the best strategy."

"Parker."

"I can't do that with you. You matter. Or you did once. And now you do again. It's not easy come, easy go where you're concerned." She lifted a shoulder, still keeping her gaze out the passenger window. "And . . . I guess I need to know if that's how you view your relationships. If that's how you view me."

"Parker, turn around."

She didn't. "You look at me and I see there is honest affection there, true friendship. And I know you want more. But that's already more than I've had, and if you're not thinking about this in a big picture kind of way, if that's not where your life is, I totally get that. But then I really, really can't just jump and—"

He flipped his seatbelt off, then hers, in short order, and pulled her across the bench seat until she was facing him, half in his lap. He hadn't known what to expect, but the intense, almost fierce feeling he had, to make things right, to make her happy, to be happy with her, shook him like nothing ever had. "When I kissed you outside the bookstore, it was curiosity. And second chances. And . . . who the hell knows. When we bake together in the kitchen, when I watch you work, all curled up on my couch, wearing my sweats, chewing your bottom lip and wearing those ridiculous glasses and I still get hard . . . When you laugh at my jokes and make me laugh just as hard and I realize that nobody ever got me like you did. Like you still do." His voice gentled a bit, but that only revealed an even rougher edge. "When I'm at work and you're on my mind, I can't wait to get back home again, because now you're there . . . God, Parker, you're home and hearth . . . and my best friend is back and it feels so fucking incredible and

I feel so damn lucky. I don't even know exactly how it happened, or why, but I know I don't want to screw it up. And I'm right back there, in college, afraid to kiss you, afraid to do or say something that will end it."

"Will—" Her voice cracked and he saw the tears built up behind her eyes and he thought his own heart might crack right along with it.

He was laying himself open for her, every shred, every insecurity, taking the kind of risks he hadn't dared take, not since the day he'd gotten that phone call at school. Maybe even longer.

"You don't have to—"

"Yes, I do. For you, and for me." He ran his fingers over her cheeks, skimmed her ears, pushed the cap off her head and wove his fingers into her hair. "So, the answer is yes. I'm thinking big picture, and no, there is nothing remotely casual about this for me. I have never, not once, felt this way." He could see the real worry, the real fear in her eyes, feel the light tremor in her skin. "I've been falling in love with you since that first day in science lab. Fate stepped in, cruelly, and I thought it just wasn't meant to be. But here you are. And I am the luckiest bastard alive because I get a second chance. And maybe that was all the better master plan, maybe we both needed to grow up and figure things out on our own first, so we'd be ready now, so we'd know what it is we have, and how special it is. I have no idea. But one thing I do know is that I'm in this. Fully, one hundred percent, all in. Until we either figure out forever, or that there isn't meant to be one. But I can't—won't— let fear of losing what we had in the past keep us from finding out what we could have in the future."

She kept searching his eyes, but the fear was gone from hers now, replaced by a kind of stunned joy. He drank that in as if he needed it to live, and maybe he did.

"So, let's go buy a Christmas tree," he said, trying and

epically failing to reel it in. Because he swore what he felt was mirrored in her eyes, and he knew that he would never forget every single crystalline second of this moment. "And when you're ready, I want to introduce you to the guys on my squad. We're close and that won't change despite my new job title, so you'll be seeing them around. My sisters are dying—and I mean that in as scary and overwhelming a way as it sounds—to meet you. But they're going to love you, so it's not something you have to worry about. And we can go back and get your Christmas ornaments out and find some way to fumigate them so they can go on the tree, too." He stopped, took a breath, shook his head, then grinned, full out. He thought his heart might leap straight out through his chest. "And this isn't supposed to be all about me. I just . . . it can't be not about you. Not anymore."

She looked dazed, and more than a little overwhelmed. But the brilliant smile that slowly slid across her face told him it was in the very best of ways.

"Parker—Clara—"

She kissed him. His face in her hands, full on, no stopping, full steam ahead kissed him. And, for a moment, he simply let her.

She let one hand drop to his chest, and pressed her fingertips against his thundering heart. "Yes," she said against his lips.

He lifted his head just a fraction. "Yes?"

"Yes. I'll buy a Christmas tree with you." She kissed him again. "And yes, I'll meet your squad guys." Another kiss. "And your sisters. Which you'd better be right, because it's four against one and I was an only child, so I'm already terrified." Then she pulled his head down and met his gaze deeply, fully . . . and he watched as she fell all the way in. No guard, no walls. And his heart went tumbling right after.

"And yes," she said, more quietly this time, "to home. To hearth. To laughing together." Her smile twisted a little. "Although maybe not so much with baking."

He chuckled, her eyes twinkled, and that warm buzz, that intimate connection they had, brought every part of him to aching attention.

She dropped a single kiss on his lips. "Yes, to you," she whispered. "To us."

He groaned, and felt the tension ease from his body as he pulled her fully onto his lap, and sank into a kiss so deep, so carnal, so . . . committed, he didn't care that they were parked in front of his station house, or that any moment the fire alarms could go off—which would so be Parker's luck—and every guy he'd ever worked with would see him making out in the cab of his truck.

Because he was her guy. And she was his girl. That's all that mattered.

"Can I ask you a favor?" she said, breathless as he worked his way along her jaw.

"Anything."

"Can we do the tree thing later?"

It thrilled him to hear that same need in her voice. He lifted his head and grinned at her.

"Wow. That is one wicked grin you have there."

"Tree?" he said, taking in her own eyes, glittering now with a need that matched his own. "What tree?" His voice was rough, dark, but she wasn't put off by it. If he was any judge, quite the opposite. He'd be the gentle lover perhaps. Someday. But not today.

"I think we need to be somewhere a little more private," she murmured.

"We can be home in fifteen minutes."

"Home sounds good. Really good."

Home. The idea that they were both talking about the same place, and that it didn't seem to scare her, in fact, it sounded like it thrilled her, only amped things up further. And the idea that she wasn't going to be sleeping in the guest room any longer—"You know, I think I can get us there in ten."

Chapter 10

He'd broken numerous safety and traffic laws and probably cashed every karmic chip he had, but they made it back to the cabin in one piece. Which was a miracle when you considered he'd barely been able to keep his eyes on the road. *Thank God for muscle memory.*

He slid out of the truck, then slipped his arms around Parker and pulled her out through his open door, keeping her tucked next to his chest.

"I know I should be all independent woman and demand that you let me walk on my own two feet." She looped her arms around his neck and rested her cheek on his jacket. "But I have to say this whole being carried thing is the only time I've felt, well, okay, not petite, exactly, but . . ." She snuggled closer and let that speak for her.

He leaned down so his lips were next to her ear as he carried her to the front door. "I've got you. I've always got you."

In their frenzied tear up the mountain, he'd envisioned them racing into the cabin, clawing off clothes and boots as they went, and falling into his bed, pretty much like the wild animal he'd become when he'd backed his truck out of the station house lot.

But having her in his arms, the feel of her cheek pressed

to his heart, slowed everything down, way down, until it was like he could feel each individual beat. And they were tapping out the words "don't screw this up, don't screw this up."

He'd convinced her to risk moving forward, he'd pretty much bared his soul, and there she was, happily snuggled against his chest as he made it up the front stone steps and across the wide, snow-blown porch. That should have been the hard part, the big hurdle. Getting her to agree to try.

So why, as he unlocked the door and carried her over the proverbial threshold, did it feel like that hardest part hadn't even begun yet? It wasn't about the sex, or whether they'd be a good fit, or if he'd find out how to please her. He'd quite happily make that his mission in life.

It was more than that, bigger than that. He hadn't laid himself bare just to get her in bed. And, for the first time, he felt a little of the terror she must have felt. Okay, maybe a lot. She'd tried and failed at past relationships. He hadn't even tried.

He stepped into his house with her in his arms, and he felt his stomach drop like he'd just stepped out on a crumbling ledge. Because along with the absolute and utter confidence that she was *the one* came the kind of fear and vulnerability he had only felt one other time in his life. When he'd come home after his father's sudden death, looking at a whole new life plan, one that included helping his four sisters find their way, both through their grief and onward from there, as well as helping his mother find her way to the end of her own path. He'd been terrified pretty much all of the time back then.

Some would think running into burning buildings was scary, but after facing that, fighting fires was easy by comparison. That was science, physics, a world he understood.

He realized now that with his mother gone and his sisters launched, he'd grown comfortable living in that world. The idea of letting someone in, letting someone matter? Other than his sisters, his teammates on the squad? Yeah, that was a place he now realized he'd spent the past nine years avoiding at all costs. Until Parker had strolled into the bookstore and changed everything with a single klutzy stumble.

He'd used the obligation of family, and then the danger of his job, as his excuses to keep new relationships at arm's length—all valid, rational reasons to his mind. He knew at some point he'd have to consider what else he wanted from life. Did he want a partner, did he want children, did he want to risk loving, which meant possibly losing again? He just . . . never had.

Only now, as he slid Parker from his arms, keeping her close as her feet touched the floor, keeping his gaze steadily on hers . . . he couldn't think about anything but that.

He wondered for the first time if maybe she'd been right to worry. He'd never even considered it, so certain exploring their relationship was the right thing to do. Was he following his heart . . . or following the path of least resistance? He wouldn't have to think, wouldn't have to consider . . . he could simply pick up where he'd left off with her. He knew her, trusted her . . . felt safe with her. Yet another comfortable world for him to inhabit.

So, was it fair for him to wade into the deep end for the first time ever and risk taking her under with him if he couldn't manage it after all?

"Will? What's wrong? Oh God, you're having second thoughts."

"Yes. I mean no! No. Not about you."

"But about something."

Mind still racing, heart racing, he braced for the hysterics, knowing he'd deserve every last shriek and curse.

Instead he felt her chilly palm brace his cheek as she turned his gaze back to hers. To his surprise, she smiled. "You look . . . poleaxed. Which is kind of how I feel. So if we need to take a step back, go buy a tree, have a dinner or two out, then—"

"That's not it."

He was trying not to hurt her, that was the whole point of taking a moment, and yet, from the devastated look that flashed through her eyes just then, he'd managed to do just that. "No, no, Parker, listen. I just—I realized that I'm promising you the moon, wanting my cake, the icing, and half the bakery, all of which I'd give willingly to you. The thing is, I was telling the truth when I said I haven't done this before. But, unlike you, I've never even tried." He pulled her into his arms, needing the closeness, needing . . . her. "I don't want to promise you anything that I can't deliver."

"Do you want to? Keep the promise?"

"More than I knew I could want anything."

She smiled and tipped up on her toes just enough to kiss him. "Then that's all that matters. I know there aren't any guarantees. Life has taught both of us that hard lesson. But that's not what I was worried about. It was intention, and thoughtfulness, and wanting the same things, small picture and big."

"That we have."

"Then that's where we start."

And just like that, his heart settled. Everything settled, as if that last empty, known hole in his orbit had been filled. She'd stumbled into his life . . . and set everything back on the right path.

He slid a wide palm behind her slender neck, tipping her mouth up to his. "How did you get so smart?"

"Well, there was this guy I met in college . . . he taught

me everything I needed to know about what a real relationship should be. It just took me a little while to figure that out."

This time, when he took her mouth, it wasn't simply the thrill of discovering the long awaited answer to a young man's fantasy . . . it was the beginning of a whole new journey. "Parker—Clara—"

"Parker's good."

He grinned against her mouth, then gently nipped her bottom lip. "Why yes, Parker certainly is. Question is, can Parker also be a little bad?"

She giggled, and there might have been a little snort in there. "What, and risk ticking Santa off this close to the big day?"

"Honey, I'm pretty sure that list is about a whole different kind of naughty."

"Pretty sure?"

He lifted his head enough to look into her eyes. "Do you trust me?"

Her smile was slow, her nod even slower, the twinkle in her eyes revealing a whole new shade of wicked that turned him on and maybe even scared him a little. In the best of ways.

"You'll save me if you're wrong, right? Rescue Ranger?"

He barked out a laugh even as he was pretty sure he might split the zipper on the front of his jeans. He hauled her up and over his shoulder, making her splutter in laughter and maybe a little indignation. "What are you—"

"This is how we rangers rescue damsels in distress, ma'am." He crossed the living room on the way to the master bedroom, and ran a wide palm up the back of one of her legs, pausing with his fingertips just stroking her inner thigh. He felt her quiver, heard her soft moan. "Would you be in distress, ma'am?"

"Oh—yes. Indeed, I believe I am, kind sir. Deep, *deep,* distress." Her voice had gone all throaty, with just a hint of southern belle.

Note to self: be careful playing games with Parker. She's pretty damn good at it.

Her hand snaked down his back and tucked around his buttocks, which she squeezed . . . then stretched to reach even further.

Correction: very damn good.

He laid her across his bed and followed her down, propping elbows on either side of her shoulders. "See? Soft landing. You're safe."

She eyed him and that wicked glint hadn't eased up a bit. "Really?"

"Any distress you may still be experiencing . . . well, I will make it my personal mission to see that all your suffering is . . . eased."

She ruffled her fingers in his hair. "Just . . . promise me one thing."

"Done."

She nudged him, smiled. "You haven't heard it yet."

He just smiled.

"Mmm. Did I mention confidence is very sexy on you?" she asked.

It was on her, too. Damn sexy. "What's the one thing?"

She cupped his cheek, and, on closer inspection, behind that devilish twinkle, was a hint of vulnerability that tugged at him, hard. Painfully hard. He didn't ever want to do anything to earn that look.

"Promise me that if you feel yourself looking for a way out, for any reason . . . just tell me. Straight out, okay?"

"Okay."

Her smile was soft, sweet, and he hated that she still felt worried about him. Except he knew it was smart, and right, to be that way. Then the corner crooked up a little, and she added, "I mean, sure, it will still crush me to poor, pathetic smithereens, but at least I'll know I can trust that you'll always be honest with me. About everything."

He dipped in and kissed the tender place on her lip where she nibbled when worried. Soothed it a little, as he'd been aching to do for days now. "I'll always take very good care of every last one of your smithereens. I promise." He kissed along the side of her jaw. "But I think I'd be better prepared to take care of said smithereens if I actually had a chance to, you know, inspect them." He dropped a kiss on the pulse in her neck, nipped her earlobe. "Catalog them." He traced his tongue along the sensitive rim of her ear, earning a shiver and a provocative hip wriggle underneath him. "Inventory every—" He tugged his hoodie off over her head and tossed it aside, then leaned in and kissed her collarbone, before running his hands down her torso and pulling up the white tee she wore underneath. He pulled that up, too, then slid down to kiss the soft spot next to her navel. "Last—" He slid the T-shirt up higher, slowly revealing her bare breasts. "One."

Chapter 11

"**G**ood idea," Clara gasped, her hips lifting of their own volition. "Wouldn't want you to—" She sucked in a breath as he ran his hands up her torso and rubbed his thumbs over her nipples. Her still oh-so-desperate nipples. "—miss a smither."

He shifted up so her legs parted and he could settle between them, then leaned his mouth down next to her ear. "I'm a scientist," he whispered roughly. "I'm trained never to miss a smither."

"Oh, thank God."

He started to work his way back down her body, tugging the tee up and off. "Will—" Usually at the first "unveiling" Clara always made some hopefully pithy comment about her nonexistent breasts, mostly to beat her partner to the punch. But whatever she might have said to him was lost on a short gasp, then a very long, heartfelt moan. Will had bypassed her utter lack of cup-size and gone right to what she did have: nipples. Oh so very needy nipples. And, as proclaimed, he didn't miss a single smither.

She was writhing under him as he worked his way down her torso, clever fingers still keeping her nipples aching and wanting as his mouth and tongue found new territory to explore. She'd spent an inordinate amount of time the past week imagining what getting naked with

Will would be like. She wished she hadn't spent most of it worrying about how not to make it awkward or weird, having sex with someone who had been a good friend . . . because there was nothing at all awkward about this. It was . . . perfect. Precisely because it *was* Will.

And it was already the most erotic lovemaking she'd ever experienced. Splayed across his old quilt, in his big, baggie sweats and—*oh . . . no*. Desperate nipples was one thing, not even a bad thing, by sex standards. But . . . there were some buzzkills that even Will's already proven mastery of the smither couldn't overcome.

She wove her fingers through that thick thatch of blonde hair and none-too-gently tugged his head up, just as his tongue was about to dip past the drawstring waist-band. "Will."

He chuckled against the soft skin of her stomach, the sound so rough and sexy she almost pushed his head right back down again and to hell with awkward underwear.

"No patience," he murmured, dropping hot little kisses around her navel.

She urged him upward, but he was having none of that.

"Ten years, Parker. Don't I get to explore a little?"

There was something about the way he said her name, about it being a name only he called her, that drove her a little closer to that sweet edge. And in the moment it took to think that, he dipped under the waistband of her sweat-pants, and . . . laughed.

"Well," he said, devilish glee clear in his voice. "Hello, Kitty." He looked up at her, brown eyes dancing. "Some-what appropriate when you think about it."

She swatted at his head, but had to stifle a snicker. "It was in your guest room dresser in a plastic-wrapped three pack. And the fact that I didn't ask you about it shows enormous restraint on my part, I think."

"Left behind by my baby sister, Meggie, no doubt,

though that's something I honestly don't want to think about at the moment." He dipped his chin down again and refocused his attention. "I am, however, very interested in finding out just how welcoming Kitty might be."

If Hello Kitty panties weren't a buzz kill, snort-laughing during first-time sex should have been, but his amused chuckle, all low and deep and sexy in his throat, even as he began the most torturous exploration with his tongue, somehow made it not just okay, but added to the erotic charge of the moment.

He slid the sweats slowly down trembling legs, tugging off boots, socks, and everything but her panties.

"Aren't you . . . a little overdressed," she managed, as he slid back on the bed, between her legs. She surprised him—and herself—by pushing him to his back and straddling him.

He'd dropped his jacket to the floor already. Now he pulled off shirt and hoodie in one fluid display of perfect, chiseled muscle and tossed them in the same direction.

"Show off," she said, but she might have been drooling. Just a little. Then he propped his hands behind his head and everything flexed, and she sent up a private little thank you to Santa. Who had apparently decided to reward her with pretty much the most fantastic present ever, despite almost burning down her grandmother's cottage.

And she wasn't one not to appreciate a well-wrapped gift. She smiled and toyed with the button to his jeans.

"That's not going to be as easy as a drawstring," he said.

She heard the strain in his voice . . . and marveled at it. Her confidence grew. "Do you trust me?"

His immediate grin made her shudder in pleasure, and instinctively push down a little bit on his thighs.

He groaned. She popped the button free. Slowly, carefully, she drew the zipper tab down over the bulge straining against the row of silver tabs.

"You know," he said, his voice a hard rasp, "I've spent several very long days wanting to kiss that spot on your lip."

"Spot?" she said, distracted by her work in progress.

He reached up, lifted just a little, flexing every part of those delicious abs, and touched the corner of her mouth . . . where she was presently biting her lip.

"It got so bad, I got hard every time you did that. You're so damn sexy when you concentrate."

She gave him a look indicating he was clearly addled, probably from blood loss to the brain. But, privately, enjoyed the hell out of knowing she hadn't been the only one completely distracted by imagining them in various sexual entanglements. All over the cabin.

"Briefs," she said, revealing tight black cotton, inch by torturous inch. "Boxer briefs." Zipper done, she reached for the belt loops on his hips and tugged. "Very . . . snug boxer briefs."

"No patience," he said again, only he wasn't doing a damn thing to stop her this time. He kicked his boots off and she slid off jeans and everything else, except the briefs. Fair being fair and all. Besides, the snug fit around his well muscled thighs was just, well, it was damn sexy.

She toyed with the waistband, and felt him twitch . . . grow.

"Danger, danger," he murmured, and a hot thrill raced straight through to her core.

She started to pull the elastic band, but his hand came around her wrist like a velvet vise. "My turn again."

An instant later, she was flat on her back, and any resistance she might have shown died swiftly as he found her nipples with his fingers . . . and the inside of her thigh with his tongue. "Fair is fair," she gasped, as the elastic band on her hips gave way in a tight little *snap*. A moment later she was arching tightly off the bed as the tip of his tongue found the exact right spot . . . and stayed there. And stayed there. His fingers stroked her nipples until she thought she'd scream from the intensity of the pleasure that rippled down through her.

"Thank you for trusting me, Parker," he murmured against her, the vibration of the words alone tripping her right along the edge. "Come," he whispered, and with one gentle flick, took her hurtling over.

Everything clenched, then expanded, all soft and accepting, then clenched more tightly again as he continued, taking her, keeping her there, until she was clutching at him. "Will . . . Will."

She tugged his hair, reached fingers toward his shoulders. "Will."

And he must have heard something in that final, desperate plea, because he moved up her body and between her still trembling legs, naked now, and impressively ready. He settled his weight and she felt the length of him press into her belly. Then he slid down until he nudged between her legs, making her shake with need as he pulled her thighs up tight to his hips. "Hold on to me."

She didn't have to be told twice. She sank fingertips into thick shoulder muscles. Her hips were already half off the bed as he pressed, slowly and oh-so incredibly, perfectly, into her.

"Jesus," he whispered, holding completely still once he was fully inside of her. "Parker." He turned his face into the side of her neck, and slowly began to move.

She wrapped legs and arms around him . . . and moved with him. Slowly, rhythmically . . . perfectly. She wanted it to go on forever . . . and she wanted to take him where he'd taken her, feel what she'd felt, when she'd utterly shattered.

She turned and pressed a kiss to the thrumming pulse point on the side of his neck, just below his ear, as they moved together, their slow-motion erotic dance in perfect sync. He was taking her higher, and deeper, with every thrust. And the climax this time was coming from some other place, deep within her, so strong, so mighty, she wasn't sure she'd survive it. And was pretty sure she didn't care.

She kissed him again, then nudged him until he lifted his head to look at her. She lifted into him, squeezed him more tightly, held him there for a beat longer, then another one. "I was just waiting for you. All this time . . . it was you."

That fierce light returned to his eyes and he took her mouth, and her, driving her straight to the edge and hurtling past it, flinging himself over it right after her.

It was long moments before they could even begin to control their breathing. He did finally manage to prop his weight on his elbows, bury his face in the now-damp curls clinging to her neck. "It was always you," he said, when he finally found enough breath to get the words out.

He kissed the side of her neck, then rolled to his side, pulling her with him. Legs entwined, she nestled against his chest as easily and naturally as every moment leading up to that one. He stroked her hair. She listened to his thudding heartbeat. And lost track of time as she drifted and simply let herself feel.

"Can this be our first holiday tradition?" she said, as the enormity of the new direction her life would be taking began to sink in. She pressed a kiss, directly over his heart.

She felt his amused chuckle rumble under her lips, then, quite suddenly, she was on her back again, and he was smiling down at her, dimples flashing, those brown eyes she knew now she'd always loved, always trusted, shining with amusement, affection, and, quite clearly, love. "Well, to get it right, I'll have to buy you a new pair of Kitty panties."

She laughed. "It was a three pack. So we're covered, at least for a few years." She traced the slight cleft in his chin with her fingertip, and finally, fully let herself love him right back.

He kissed the corner of her mouth, pulled her close, then kissed her again, as if he had all the time in the world. And, she supposed, he did.

"Merry Christmas to us," she murmured, as she let him take her under all over again.

He moved on top of her, grinned. "And to all a good life."

Clara Parker might not be a natural in the kitchen—okay, so she's downright dangerous. Good thing she fell in love with a fireman!—but even she could make Mama Mason's famous chocolate chip cookies. (The secret is in the ground oatmeal!) This recipe is perfect for the holidays as it makes nine dozen. I know! Some of them might even have a chance of making it into those cute tins you bought to give to other people. (And hey, everyone should make at least one test batch, right?)

Happy baking, and happy holidays!

MAMA MASON'S MEGASIZED CHOCOLATE CHIP COOKIES

2 cups butter
2 cups sugar
2 cups brown sugar
4 eggs
2 teaspoons vanilla
5 cups oatmeal (not instant)
4 cups flour
1 teaspoon salt
2 teaspoons baking powder
2 teaspoons baking soda
1 Hershey's bar (8 ounces), grated
24 ounces chocolate chips
3 cups nuts (optional)

Preheat oven to 375°F.

Mix butter and both sugars together until smooth. Add in eggs, one at a time, mixing in until assimilated. Stir in vanilla. Use a food processor to grind the oatmeal to powder, then whisk together with flour, salt, baking power, and baking soda. Add in the flour mixture in several increments, blending just until mixed. Grate the Hershey's bar, then stir in grated Hershey's and chocolate chips. Stir in nuts if desired. (Chopped pecans or chopped walnuts are ideal.) Scoop 2 inches apart onto ungreased cookie sheets in golf-ball-sized drops. (A melon scoop or ice cream scoop with the squeeze handle works great.) Bake for 6 to 8 minutes, or until golden brown. Let cool on sheets for 5 minutes, then transfer to racks to complete cooling.

Makes approximately 9 dozen cookies.

The Gingerbread Man

Kate Angell

Chapter 1

"**W**hat's your name?" Abby Denton asked the man who slouched on the gray flannel sofa in her living room. "Lander," he managed with effort.

Her heart went out to him. He was all banged up. His dark hair was mussed and his blue eyes were dazed. A bump stood out on his forehead. "I'm Abby," she said slowly, making sure he understood her. "What's the last thing you remember prior to your car accident?" she pressed. It was important to keep him conscious.

"A peppermint-stick penis."

Abby blushed. This couldn't be good. She'd seen the man at the Pine Mountain Community Center earlier that evening. How could she forget him? He'd blown inside, tall and compelling in a black cashmere coat with a blustery winter wind at his back just as the snow began to fall. He'd glanced around, then taken part in the town's annual Christmas Cookie Swap. That surprised her. He didn't look like the sweet-tooth type. More like a man on a mission.

Dozens of decorative boxes and tins were displayed on long tables, then auctioned off to the highest bidder. No one knew which container belonged to which baker. The contents were a surprise to the winner.

Lander had shouted out a one hundred dollar bid for the brown box decorated with a white icing border. Abby was concerned at first, wondering why this stranger was so quick to outbid everyone else. That was half the fun, she thought, watching the bids climb higher and higher.

Not this time. He'd won the cookies, then gone on to ask for directions to Philadelphia. Abby assumed his GPS wasn't working. Cell phone services were hit and miss here in the Blue Ridge Mountains.

Why was he in such a hurry? she'd wondered. The holidays were a time of joy and fun. Not mad dashes through the hills. Somehow she doubted he was on his way to Grandma's house.

After receiving his instructions, he'd tucked the box under his arm, turned, and left without a backward glance. His shoulders had been squared; his strides, long and purposeful. He was a man in a hurry. Abby had smiled to herself. He had no idea what type of holiday cookies he'd won. Chances were he'd expected sugar cookies or snickerdoodles. Perhaps even shortbread, spice, or raspberry-filled thumbprints.

Instead he'd gotten her erotic gingerbread men.

She sat across from him now, perched on the edge of a plaid overstuffed chair. She couldn't help but stare at this man who'd caused her so much panic and worry. Thank goodness he was coherent. He'd been out cold for close to two hours. It had taken Abby that long to catch her breath after saving him from frostbite.

His body had been cold, so cold it scared the hell out of her when she touched his cheeks. His lips had turned blue. Snow had drifted through the broken glass on the driver's window. His dark eyelashes spiked like icicles.

She watched closely as he removed one black leather driving glove, and then carefully touched the bump on his forehead. His skin was pale. A bruise colored his left cheek. A cut marred his chin.

"The accident," he muttered. His tone was deep, flat, questioning.

She nodded, encouraging him to speak. "You were headed north on Rural Route Four. It was snowing. Hard. Visibility must have been close to zero."

His eyebrows drew together as he searched his memory. "There was thick fog and, what that didn't cover, the snow did," he said, recalling the drive.

She knew that to be true. The twisting two-lane road could be treacherous in bad weather, slick and icy. Abby usually crept along, sticking to the speed limit. "What caused you to swerve?" she gently prodded him. "A deer? Drifting snow?"

His answer came slowly. "My stomach growled," he recalled. "I'd missed lunch, but couldn't find a place to grab a meal anywhere in Pine Mountain. The place was a ghost town when I arrived. Even the gas station convenience store was closed up tight."

"Everyone was at the community center for the cookie swap," she explained. "We gather there once a year. The proceeds support a local charity."

"It was the cookies." He pressed his palms to his eyes, as if pushing back the image. "I was several miles down the road when I remembered the box lying on the seat beside me. I cracked the lid and found a dozen gingerbread men with candy-cane erections."

He lowered his hands and gave her a look of frustration and disbelief. "I took my eyes off the road and stared at the gingerbread men a moment too long. I couldn't believe what I was seeing."

He doesn't look pleased, Abby thought, digging her hands into the pockets of her jacket. She'd worked so hard to get her G-men to stand at attention.

"My Mercedes hit an icy patch and started to slide," he

added. "Whichever way I turned the steering wheel, I couldn't correct the skid."

"A vehicle out of control on an icy road is scary," she agreed.

His jaw worked, and his words were as disjointed as his memory. "Steep slope. Pine trees. Crashed." He paused, rolled his shoulders. "I must've blacked out."

Abby had wondered what put him in the ditch.

She now knew. *Her* cookies had caused *his* accident.

She felt awful and suddenly cold. So cold, in fact, that her hooded down jacket, wool mittens, and Caribou Pac Boots no longer warmed her. She shivered.

Lander straightened on the sofa, glanced around her living room. "Where am I?" He blinked, trying to focus. "How'd I get here?"

"You're at my cabin," she said. "I was driving home from the community center when I noticed the taillights on your car lit up in the ravine. I parked on the shoulder, set my flashers, and tried to call for emergency assistance, but my call didn't go through. I ended up hiking down the slope to the spot where your car had crashed through the pine trees."

Hiking wasn't the operative word, Abby realized. More like a rescue mission. A blanket of snow had covered the ground. Night shadows snuck along the slope. Worse yet, the batteries on her flashlight were low and her visibility was limited.

She'd tripped, fallen, then slid on her bottom, slamming feetfirst into the front tire on the driver's side. A sharp pain shot through her foot. She swore she'd broken her big toe. It still throbbed. She had no doubt she'd find it red and swollen when she took her boot off.

"I tugged and pulled until I got your car door open," she further said. She'd nearly wrenched her shoulder out of the socket doing so. "You were slouched over the steering wheel. I shook you, but you didn't respond. I had to get you out of the vehicle. I couldn't leave you there to freeze."

She didn't add how frightened she'd been when she thought he wasn't breathing. She'd leaned over him; her cheek was so close to his, she'd felt the ice cold brush of his skin. A small puff of frosty air had escaped his lips, whispering over her mouth. She'd never been so relieved in her life. He was alive.

"How'd you get me out of the car and up the hill?" he wanted to know.

With great difficulty, she thought. Her heart had raced and panic pushed her hard. "I unfastened your seat belt then tried to grip you under the arms. Your shoulders were too wide. I went with your leather belt," she said. "I tugged, dragged, and prayed you up the slope. It was slow going, but you were able to stand enough to lean on me. It took us nearly an hour to reach the road. You don't re-member any of that?"

Her arms had ached and her stomach had cramped. Her hands had started to go numb from the cold. She was a strong woman, but Lander was a big man. And almost dead weight on top of it all.

She'd hoped another vehicle would pass their way, but no one was on the road. Not unusual. Anyone with any sense was already home, warm and cozy, waiting out the snowstorm.

Lander shook his head. "You dragged me," he repeated, disbelievingly. "I recall so little. So that's why my rib cage and abdomen are sore."

He pushed back the sides on his coat and looked down at his belt. His gaze widened when he saw his white dress shirt was untucked, wrinkled, and several buttons were missing. The back pocket on his black trousers was torn; the front zipper was halfway down. He zipped it back up.

Bruises formed a darkened band about his waist where she'd struggled with his belt. The buckle had cut a deep imprint at his navel. There were claw marks over his ribs where her fingers encased in the wool mittens had dug into his flesh. Imprints from her palms marked his hips.

She bit down on her bottom lip. "I'm sorry if I hurt you."

"Hurt me?" He shook his head. "You saved my life."

My cookies caused your accident. She kept that information to herself, for the moment anyway.

"Your coat is ruined," she noted. The depth of snow and the damp ground had smudged the black cashmere. A few dead leaves and twigs were stuck to his collar.

"I can always purchase another coat," he said. "I can't buy another life." His tone was gravelly, but grateful.

"I'm betting you'll need a new car, too," she said, honestly. Best he knew the truth. "The hood appeared totaled from what I could tell."

She tugged off her mittens, noticing a hole over her little finger. Her fingernails had turned blue. She shook out her hands to restore their circulation. "I couldn't reach emergency services, but I did manage to leave a text message with our local mechanic before I lost all cell communication. His name is Shane Griffin and he works at Grady's Garage. He has a tow truck and can dig out your Mercedes once the storm passes."

His brow creased. "How long will the blizzard last?" he asked, concerned.

"A day or two, possibly three," she said, feeling confident. "I thought about driving you back to town to a hotel, but the road south was impassable. I live up here on the mountain. It was the closest place to bring you so you could thaw out, since we're already snowed in. Plows clear the main streets first. I'm the last to be dug out."

He frowned in frustration. "I wanted to be home tonight."

"Home is where?"

"Philadelphia."

"I'm afraid you're stuck here for the duration of the snowstorm," she said.

His expression darkened. "I hate breaking promises," he said, more to himself than to her. "Especially when someone needs me."

Abby wondered who needed him. His family? A girlfriend? His wife? He wasn't wearing a wedding band, she noticed, but men didn't always follow tradition. He could well be married.

He squinted. "Why is it so dark in here?'

"The electricity's out," she said. "I was about to light a fire when you came to again."

"A fire . . ." He clutched his coat to his chest, trying to get warm. There was no warmth in the damp cashmere. Dry clothes were a necessity. She didn't want him getting sick.

She rose and shrugged out of her jacket. What could she offer him to wear? "You're freezing," she said. "I have a pair of sweats you can borrow, but the sweatshirt will be tight across your shoulders and the pants too short. I've got extra thick socks."

He nodded. "That works for me, but what about you?"

"Long underwear, a fresh sweater and jeans, UGG slippers, and I'll be fine, too," she told him. She winced. And a bandage for her big toe.

He slowly stood, drawing in a deep breath to steady himself. He emptied his coat pockets, tossed his wallet and cell phone on the coffee table. "Where can I change?" he asked.

"The bathroom is down the hall, third door on the

right," she told him. Rising, she crossed the room to a bookshelf with knickknacks, novels, and lanterns. She stepped only on the heel of her right foot in an attempt to keep the pressure off her toes. Standing before the shelf, she selected two Coleman camping lanterns.

She returned to him. "Battery-operated," she said, flicking both switches, then handing him one. They soon stood within a circle of light as bright as a Christmas star.

"This way." She motioned to him. "You'll find towels in the cupboard. I'll get your sweats and pass them to you. Then we can hang up your clothes. They'll dry quickly by the fire."

He followed her down the hall. "You're limping," he said at her back. "What's wrong?"

The man was observant. "I stubbed my toe," she told him, appreciating his concern. She didn't mention that she'd fallen, slid, and slammed feetfirst into the tire on his car. What he didn't know only hurt her. "I'll be fine."

She didn't look fine, Lander thought. The hallway was narrow and dark and he wished he could see her better. His angel of mercy. He held his lantern high, the light catching her in profile. A deep crease cut across her forehead and her eyebrows were drawn tightly together. She tried to hide her pain, but he'd seen her wince. Twice.

Abby came to a stop before the bathroom; she pushed the door open. The hinges creaked. No doubt the cabin was as old as the mountain.

"I'll be right back," she said, continuing down the hallway.

Lander crossed the threshold. He set his lantern on the polished wood vanity and took a quick look around. The bathroom was small, clean, and tidy with handicap bars by the toilet and the tub. He wondered if Abby needed the bars for a chronic foot problem.

He took off his coat. The accident had beaten him up.

His face was cut and bruised. His skin was clammy and his head hurt where he'd hit the steering wheel. Not to mention that his body ached all over when he moved too fast. He'd never been so cold.

He'd unbuttoned his shirt and pulled his belt through the pant loops by the time Abby returned. She wasn't kidding when she said he was in bad shape when she'd found him. His chest was covered with bruises. It hurt to take a deep breath. It was quite possible he'd cracked or broken a rib.

Seconds later, she knocked on the door frame. "Your socks and sweats," she said, handing him a neatly folded pile of clothes in a pastel hue that had him raising one eyebrow.

"Lavender?" he asked, wishing they were gray.

"It was that or hot pink." Her expression was apologetic.

"The color's fine." At least he had something dry to wear. "The socks have matching purple butterflies," he noted.

"They're the warmest pair I own."

He held up one hand. "No complaints here."

"I'll meet you back in the living room when you're dressed," she said, and closed the door behind her.

He bent, untied, and slipped off his Italian wingtips. His shoes were ruined. He peeled down his ice-cold socks. His feet looked blue in the lantern light.

His shirt came next, followed by his pants. He wore no underwear. His testicles had retracted and his penis had shrunk. He needed to warm up and fast.

He crossed to the cupboard. Inside, he found a stack of towels and a folded-up walker. The walker was old and used. One roller was twisted out of alignment. Now he was puzzled. He hoped Abby didn't have a serious physical ailment.

Selecting a fluffy blue towel, he briskly dried himself off. That was better, *much* better. His circulation began to return, in most parts of his body. His penis still felt like an icicle. Not surprising. He was drained and his emotions were spent. He felt numb inside. It was doubtful he'd thaw out anytime soon.

He hung the towel on a wooden bar, then tugged on the sweatpants. The drawstring stretched to fit around his waist. The length hit him just below the knee.

The sweatshirt came next. It hurt to raise his arms too high, and he had difficulty slipping it over his head. The neck hole was small and he felt strangled. The top fit as tightly as a straitjacket. He could barely move his arms without stretching the material. He'd manage for the time being. His own clothes would dry quickly by the fire.

He tugged on the wool socks. His toes were scrunched, and the tops rose to mid-calf. He glanced in the mirror over the sink. Purple matched his bruises. He could live with the sweats until his clothes dried.

He combed his hair with his fingers. His mouth felt gritty. A tube of toothpaste lay on the counter. He unscrewed the cap and squeezed a small amount on to his forefinger. He scrubbed his teeth, careful of his swollen lower lip. He turned the handle for the cold water, and a trickle came from the spout. He cupped his palm, caught the remaining drips, and rinsed his mouth. He assumed this was the last of the water until the electricity was restored and the pump kicked on.

He wondered if Abby kept a supply of bottled water in case of bad weather. He hoped so. A low-flow toilet could be manually flushed by adding water.

He picked up his clothes, shoes, and lantern, then returned to the living room. His gaze widened at the transformation. Abby had been busy. She'd changed clothes in record time, and then set about adjusting the lighting and warming the room.

A dozen camp lanterns illuminated his path back to the sofa. It looked so inviting to his aching body. The couch was draped with warm wool blankets and a homemade quilt. He watched as she set the iron grate aside, then struck and dropped the long stick match on rolled newspaper. The stacked logs immediately caught fire in the stone fireplace. Light blazed and danced. In that moment, he got his first real look at the woman and her home.

Abby was blond, full-figured, and curvy. Having shaken off the snowflakes, she was now bundled in a blue knit sweater, worn jeans, and shearling slippers. She was pretty and desirable. In another time, another place, she was the type of woman every guy would like to cuddle up next to by the fire.

Their eyes met, and her smile was tentative. "Warming up?" she asked, coming toward him.

The burning logs had heated the room in a short time. He rubbed his hands together. "I'm feeling much better."

She took his coat and clothes and laid them over a makeshift indoor clothesline near the fire. She cocked her head, as if counting the items of clothing. He noticed her cheeks reddened. She now knew he didn't wear underwear.

She released a soft breath that sounded like a sigh, then turned back to him. "How's your head?" Her concern was evident in the furrowing of her brow.

"I could use an aspirin," he said, feeling the bump on his forehead. His head continued to throb.

She nodded, then crossed to the kitchen, opened two separate cupboards, and returned with a small bottle of water and an unopened container of Extra Strength Tylenol. He broke the seal on the box, popped two

Tylenol onto his palm, then into his mouth. He drank deeply of the water.

"Thanks," he said, lowering himself onto the sofa.

She lightly touched his brow, and he couldn't hold back a low, painful moan. "Let me get you an ice bag," she said. "That bump looks bad."

She walked back to the kitchen, located the bag in a drawer, and filled it with ice. She threaded the stopper, then brought it to him. He gently pressed it to his brow and felt immediate relief course through him. His entire body relaxed.

"Are you hungry?" she asked next.

On cue, his stomach growled.

They both laughed. He had to admit she was even prettier when she laughed. Still, he hadn't thought of food since he'd opened the box of erotic gingerbread men. "I could eat, but don't go to any trouble."

"I'm ready for dinner myself," she said. "I have a pantry filled with canned goods, but we need to start with the food in the refrigerator so it doesn't spoil. How about grilled cheese sandwiches and hot dogs?"

"Fine by me," he agreed. When was the last time he'd had real comfort food? He couldn't remember. "How will you manage the sandwiches without a stove?"

"I have utensils for hearth cooking," she told him. "A long-handled skewer for the hot dogs and a cast iron skillet for the grilled cheese. It's like we're camping out."

That piqued Lander's interest. He'd never spent time in the woods as a kid. He'd preferred the country club pool and tennis courts to tents and hiking. "What can I do?" he offered.

"Sit and relax," said Abby. "I've got it covered."

"What about your toe?" he asked, concerned. "Should you be standing?"

She wiggled her foot. "It feels better since I took off my boots. My slippers are comfy."

Then why was she still limping? He caught her walking on her right heel on her way to the kitchen. He wasn't used to a woman taking charge and caring for him. The ladies in his life depended on his direction and guidance. They were often needy. Much of the time he did their thinking for them.

Abby was self-sufficient. She moved amid the shadows, her presence like the soft glow of a candle in the darkness, collecting the items for their dinner. She then made several trips from the kitchen to the fireplace, carrying food, plates, and cooking utensils. She drew a wide wooden side table close to the stone hearth and set up a workstation.

He watched, curious, as she slipped on a pair of black, elbow-length oven mitts before placing the large round skillet onto the logs. She buttered the pan and the grilled cheese sandwiches soon sizzled. Next, she skewered four hot dogs and held them over the fire. She laughed when one fell off the stick and the flames ate it.

Lander leaned more deeply into the sofa and smiled, too. He liked her laugh; it was deep, yet feminine. He didn't know one thing about this woman who had pulled him from his car, then driven him up the mountain to her home. Yet he felt close to her in a way he didn't understand. Oftentimes invisible bonds were formed in tragic situations. She had saved his life.

She'd also mentioned being at the community center when he'd stopped for directions. All he could recall from his quick stop was that the main room had been packed with people. He was a man who favored blondes, but he hadn't noticed her in the crowd. He'd been short on time and running late.

Rolling his shoulders, he reached for a quilt, one patterned with colorful squares. Two of the borders were raw-edged, unfinished. That didn't matter to him. He draped it across his lap. His groin remained chilled. It was a slow thaw for his boys. They still pulled tight against his body.

He took a moment and studied his surroundings. The rustic A-frame log cabin was cozy. He liked the open-beam cathedral ceiling. Snow pelted the large triangular-shaped window and ribbons of frost patterned the glass pane. The furniture was solid and overstuffed. Braided rugs covered the hardwood floor. A big wicker basket cornered the couch, filled with skeins of yarn and knitting needles.

"Folk architecture?" he asked her over the crackle of the fire.

She seemed surprised he recognized the design. "My great-great-grandfather Alden rescued and restored the cabin. The logs are eastern white pine."

"Hand-hewn with dovetail corners," he noted, observing them with a keen eye. The logs were two feet in diameter and flat on the sides. Alden had taken his time and given great care to the restoration. Lander valued fine craftsmanship.

"How long have you lived here?" he asked, curious.

There was a softening at the corners of her eyes. "I'm from Pine Mountain," she said.

"Do you live alone?"

She shook her head. "I have . . . someone."

He wondered *who* that someone might be, but didn't push the subject. She was entitled to her privacy, though he was a bit perplexed the person hadn't made an appearance.

"Dinner's served," she said a moment later. She crossed to him, only to slow her steps when she spotted the quilt across his lap. She stared at his groin overly long, a wistful look in her eyes. Under normal circumstances he'd get a hard-on. Not now. He sensed that whatever she saw, whatever she was thinking, had nothing to do with him as a man, and everything to do with the quilt.

"You okay?" he asked, meaning it.

She blinked, but a hint of sadness lingered in her eyes. "I'm fine," she assured him. She leaned closer, and he felt her body heat. Her cheeks were flushed from standing so near the fire. Her oven mitts warmed his hands as she passed him his dinner. She took his ice bag and set it on a worn dish towel to absorb the condensation.

She looked pretty, he thought. The bright blaze at her back cast her in a halo of light. The scents of wool, pine logs, and woman collected around him. If he had to be snowbound, here was as good a place as any. The cabin was homey. Abby made him feel comfortable.

He looked down on his plate. The grilled cheese sandwich was perfectly toasted. The two hot dogs were slightly charred at one end. He didn't care. He was starving. While his manners dictated he wait for her to take the first bite, his stomach demanded he dig in. The sandwich melted in his mouth.

"This tastes good, Abby."

She smiled, pleased with his compliment. She returned to the overstuffed chair across from him and set her plate down on the coffee table between them. "What would you like to drink?" she asked. "I have water, milk, or apple juice."

Lander didn't drink a lot of milk, but neither did he want it to spoil. He had no idea how long they'd be snowed in here without electricity. "Small glass of milk," he decided.

She went to the refrigerator, poured out two paper cups, then returned. She was a little wobbly on her feet, which worried him. She sighed heavily when she settled in her chair. He'd like to take a look at her toe after dinner, if she'd let him. To see how badly she was hurt.

They ate in silence with the crackle of the fire a perfect accompaniment to the meal. He stole the occasional glance at Abby. She'd cut up her hot dog with a plastic fork and took small bites. She looked vibrant, healthy, and her physical strength still amazed him. He couldn't fathom how she'd managed to drag him up a snowy ravine. He was six-two and weighed two-ten. Not only was she strong, but good-hearted. She'd given him a change of clothes and cooked his dinner. She was generous and kind. And had saved his life.

He had no misconceptions about his fate following the accident.

He would've frozen to death in his car overnight if she hadn't found him.

"Would you care for another sandwich or hot dog?" Abby asked, taking her last bite of grilled cheese. She flicked her tongue and licked a bit of melted cheese from one finger. Her innocent gesture caught him off guard. Her *flick* caused his dick to stir. Heat collared his neck. He was as embarrassed as he was relieved. His penis had returned to the living. He shifted the quilt to better cover the slight tenting in his sweatpants.

He debated having seconds. He was a big man and could have easily eaten another sandwich, but he passed. He didn't want Abby standing on her foot any longer than was absolutely necessary. Instead, he patted his stomach. "I'm full, thanks."

She raised an eyebrow, not believing him. "Dessert then?" she suggested.

It was the holidays. He enjoyed the occasional sweet. He nodded. "What do you have?"

"Several friends have dropped off holiday goodies," she said. "We have pecan squares, red velvet brownies, eggnog pound cake, or vanilla malted ice cream cake."

"What's your favorite?" he asked.

"My good friend Lily Callahan is a self-taught cake and pastry caterer. She makes the best ice cream cake. Each slice is orgas—" She blushed, and changed her description. "To die for."

Orgasmic cake, Lander read between the lines. Definitely worth a try. "Cake it is," he said, agreeing with her choice. "Can I cut it for you?"

She shook her head. "Thanks, but I'm getting around better now."

He watched as she picked up the paper plates and hobbled to the kitchen. The lady lied—she wasn't moving well. The corners of her mouth pinched as she walked on the side of her right foot, taking all the pressure off her big toe. He'd eat dessert, then take a look at her injury. She might need a bandage or a splint.

She returned in a matter of seconds and served him a plate with a large slice of cake. Triple-layer angel food cake with stripes of vanilla ice cream and topped with a whipped white frosting. "Hot chocolate with a peppermint stick to drink?" she proposed.

The memory of the erotic gingerbread men had him shaking his head. He might never eat peppermint again.

"More milk, then?" she asked. "We should finish off the carton."

He nodded. That sounded far better.

He rubbed his forehead and realized his headache was almost gone. His rib cage and abdomen remained sore. It hurt to take a deep breath. Hopefully he would recover in a day or two.

Outside, the blizzard worsened. He listened to the creaks of the cabin and the howl of the wind. The logs in the fireplace popped and sparked and the scent of pine was strong. The camp lanterns kept a steady glow.

He had a question for Abby when she returned with his dessert. "Why don't you have a generator?" he asked her.

She lowered herself to her chair, then said, "My grandma Ada was afraid of them. She thought we'd get asphyxiated."

He glanced down the hallway, wondering if Ada slept through the storm. "Where is your grandmother now?"

"She passed away in October." Her voice was barely above a whisper.

He wasn't a stranger to loss. "I'm sorry, Abby."

"Me, too." Her shoulders slumped.

Her pain was recent. He knew if she raised her head, he'd see wetness on her cheeks. He felt bad for her.

"Gram was eighty-eight," she said. "She had arthritis and needed a walker to get around. She loved poetry, crossword puzzles, board games, and photography. She remained as sharp as a tack up until her final night."

"This is your first Christmas without her then."

"I'm not feeling very merry," she admitted on a sigh. "Especially since it's December twelfth."

He couldn't let that go by without an explanation. "Why is that?"

"We always had our tree up by today, all decorated and sparkling. It was a family tradition since it was also Gram's birthday."

The air lay heavy between them. Lander didn't have a clue what to say next. He needn't have worried. Abby opened up to him, grateful for the opportunity to talk to someone.

"Our annual cut tree was delivered three days ago. I forgot to cancel the order this year," she said. "Now the six-foot evergreen is in the garage, ready to be placed in its stand. I just don't have the heart or energy to drag out the decorations and ornaments."

"Too many memories?" he guessed.

"It was my grandma and me for as long as I can remember, and now it's just me." Her voice sounded sad. "Ada raised me. My parents were from Pine Mountain, but moved to Raleigh when I was in the sixth grade. Their new jobs included a lot of traveling. My mother didn't want to uproot me every few months, so my grandmother opened her door and I moved in. Her husband had died the previous year. She welcomed my company. We were both family and friends."

"My dad and I were close, too," he reflected, surprised he'd spoken his thoughts out loud. There was an intimacy to the cabin; somehow sharing their losses gave them a bond. "He died of a heart attack a year ago . . . tomorrow."

"Were you close?" she asked.

"We had a solid father-son relationship. He worked long hours, but always found time for his family."

His father's death right before Christmas had hit his family hard. Especially his mother. That had disturbed him greatly. She'd made it through the funeral, and then withdrawn from the world. She'd spent her days in the master-bedroom suite, staring out the window or, on occasion, pacing the carpet. The light in his mother's eyes had vanished with her husband's passing.

It had taken Lander and his sister, Angela, six months to get his mom to venture outside their home so she could return to the living. Not until a week ago had she fully appeared her old self. He and Angela had purposely planned numerous projects and festivities for these two weeks prior to Christmas. They wanted to keep their mother busy and to continue with their time-honored traditions. His father would've wanted it that way.

It was unfortunate that Lander wasn't around to participate in the merriment. He was snowbound. He wasn't certain his sister could motivate their mom to grab on to the Christmas spirit and move forward with their plans. Angela wasn't strong enough to put her foot down when their mother wanted to slip back to her bedroom and let the holidays pass her by. He needed to be home with them, but there was no way off the mountain right now.

"Your slice of ice cream cake is melting," Abby said, breaking into his thoughts.

He looked down on his lap. His plate had tipped and a stream of vanilla ice cream was sliding toward the edge. Toward his groin. He scooped a bite with his plastic spoon. The dessert tasted like Christmas on his tongue. Holiday decadence, he mused. The angel food cake was moist; the heavy-cream frosting reminded him of a soda-fountain vanilla malt.

"Delicious," he said after he'd taken his last bite.

"There's nothing like a rich dessert to finish a meal."

She looked satisfied, Lander thought. The corners of her eyes crinkled, as if she were smiling to herself. Her lips curved slightly. Shadows fell across the arches of her cheek bones, deepening the hollows in her cheeks. She slouched on her chair, her legs stretched before her.

Here was a woman comfortable in her own skin, he thought. She wasn't trying to impress him with small talk and flirty smiles. She'd felt a great loss with her grandmother's passing. Should the blizzard continue, perhaps he could draw her into the holiday spirit. He'd think of something. Setting up the Christmas tree might help.

"It's early yet, but it's so dark outside, it seems much later," Abby said. "Let me clean up, and, if you're up to the challenge, we can play cards or a board game."

He had his standing monthly poker night with his banking colleagues, but he couldn't remember the last time he'd played a board game. He glanced at his watch. It was only seven p.m. "Works for me," he agreed.

She stood, and he rose, too. She motioned him to sit back down. "I've got it under control," she insisted.

"The two of us will get the job done quicker."

She nodded, relenting. She tossed their paper plates and cups into the trash can, while he crossed to the fireplace and collected the cast-iron pans. The ironware had cooled on a brick shelf by the hearth. He carried them to the sink. There, Abby cleaned them with salt and water, scrubbing each with a steel brush. She carefully dried the cookware, then rubbed in a bit of cooking oil to keep them seasoned.

"Appreciate your help," she thanked him. "It's game time. Follow me." She crooked her finger. "I have a closet filled with board games."

She attempted to step around him, only to trip over her own feet. A groan escaped her lips as she gritted her teeth. Lander grimaced. There was no doubt that her toe still hurt her.

"Take my arm," he offered.

She backed up against the counter, released a breath. "Give me a second," she said. "I can make it to the closet." Her words were brave, but her expression was pained.

"There'll be no games until I take a look at your foot," he said firmly.

She looked up at him. "You're pretty bossy for a man stranded in my cabin."

He stared down at her. "Not bossy, but concerned."

Taking her by the hand, he led her back to her chair. She sighed, but went willingly. Her hand was small and soft within his grasp. Her fingernails were cut short and glossed with a clear polish.

She sat down, frowned, as he knelt before her. He placed her foot on his thigh and gently removed her right shearling slipper. Her foot was narrow and her big toe was largely swollen. Adding to her discomfort, her toenail had turned black. It looked extremely painful.

He looked up, met her gaze. "Your toe looks worse than my forehead," he said. "I'm not a doctor, so I honestly don't know if it's broken. But I can make you feel better by taping your big toe to the one next to it for support. You'll find it easier to walk. Ice would help, too."

He moved her foot from his thigh, then rose. "Do you have gauze and adhesive tape?"

"There's a first aid kit under the sink in the bathroom," she told him. "I'm not sure how much tape is left on the roll. We can always use masking tape if necessary."

He lifted a lantern off the coffee table and headed down the hallway. Abby was organized; he quickly found what he needed. Returning, he hunkered down before her once again. Cupping her heel, he positioned her foot on his knee this time.

He tentatively touched her toe and she inhaled sharply. She clutched the arms of the chair until her knuckles turned white. The last thing he wanted was to cause her further pain. He looked over at the fireplace. "Do you want a piece of wood to bite down on while I bandage your toe?"

She gave him a small smile and said, "I could use an entire log if you can drag it over here." She drew a deep breath. "I had no idea an injured toe could hurt so much."

"You just told me it didn't hurt."

"I lied."

He shook his head, but couldn't stay mad at her. He'd guessed as much. He gently squeezed her ankle to gauge how much pressure she could stand. Not much, by the way she bit down on her bottom lip. "I'll be careful," he promised.

She didn't wince or say another word as he placed a gauze pad around and between her two toes. He then ripped off strips of adhesive tape and wrapped them together. Afterward, he took the ice pack she'd given him earlier and refilled it with cubes from the freezer. He then pulled the coffee table flush against her chair.

"Elevate your foot," he said as he adjusted the ice bag over her toes. She pulled back slightly from the weight of the bag until she found a comfortable position. "Try and relax," he said. "Once your toe's numb, it won't hurt quite so much."

He remained by her side, waiting for the ice to take effect. Minutes passed before she finally said, "There's little feeling now." She eyed him thoughtfully. "Thanks, Lander. I'm used to doing the doctoring, not having someone take care of me."

"What caused your injury?" he asked, returning to the sofa.

She dipped her head, reluctant to tell him.

"Abby?" he nudged her further. "This has to be a recent accident."

She folded her hands in her lap and admitted, "It happened today actually."

"When today?" he pressed. "Were you hurt at the community center?"

She shook her head.

His stomach slowly sank. "Afterward, then, helping me?"

"It wasn't your fault in any way," she tried to reassure him. "The ravine was snowy and slippery and I lost my balance. I slid down the slope on my bottom, and slammed into your front tire."

She winced again, just thinking about it.

He exhaled sharply. "You could've broken your ankle, your leg."

"But I didn't, Lander, it's just a toe."

A toe was a toe. She was hurt and he felt awful. "I owe you, Abby."

She looked uneasy. "I did what anyone would do in a similar situation."

"This situation involved me," he said. "Don't downplay the risk you took. You could've been killed if you'd slipped down the mountain slope. It was damn steep. I'll always be grateful."

She tilted her head; a hint of a grin tipped the corners of her lips. "So grateful you'd let me win at Scrabble?" she asked.

"I'll give you a fifty-point advantage," he said, getting into the spirit of the game. "After that, choose your words wisely."

Chapter 2

Abby beat Lander at Scrabble. Cleaned his clock, actually, winning by one hundred and fifteen points. Their game ended when she added her final letters for "bread" to his well-placed "ginger." He stared at the word "gingerbread" for several seconds. A scowl crossed his brow.

What was he thinking? she wondered. Was he remembering her erotic cookies?

Scratching his chin, he said, "Double word and triple letter scores." He exhaled loudly. "Gingerbread isn't my favorite word at the moment, but nice going, Abby."

She understood his aversion. "I left the box of cookies in your car." She figured he should know.

His lip curled. "I hope the gingerbread men freeze their peppermint sticks off."

"Could happen," she said. "The temperature overnight will drop below zero."

She looked away and clasped her hands together. She was in a fine predicament. She had no idea how Lander would react when he learned that she was the erotic gingerbread maker. Would he shrug and laugh it off? It seemed doubtful. His angry silence would hurt her more. Her baking ego was already flatter than a burned cookie. Defeated, she sighed, capturing a yawn behind her hand.

"Are you tired?" he asked, concerned.

She collected the tiles and stored them in the cloth bag, then folded the game board. "It's been a long day, wouldn't you say?" A second yawn escaped from her lips.

"Don't let me keep you up."

Abby leaned forward in her chair, lifted two lanterns off the coffee table, then stood. Not easy. She'd grown stiff and sore from sitting too long. She ached all over. She'd exercised muscles today she hadn't used in a very long time. Fortunately, her toe remained numb from the ice bag.

"I'll show you to the guest room before I call it a night," she offered.

"Don't go to any trouble," he was quick to say. He stretched out on the sofa, his feet hanging over the end. "I can sleep on the couch."

"You're too tall," she insisted. "You'd wake up with a crick in your neck. I have far better accommodations. The loft will give you more privacy."

She nodded toward the fireplace. "Select two small logs, a sheet of newspaper, and a couple of matchsticks. The upstairs fireplace will keep you warm."

She watched as he collected the necessary items, his profile catching the light just right. Noble and fine, she thought. Despite her ill-fitting sweats, he carried authority and dignity on his broad shoulders. He seemed a man who would take charge, one people would listen to.

Abby liked strong men. She became lost looking at him, at his long shadow, splashed on the wall larger than life. Just like the man. He was a daydream that would feed her soul long after he'd gone.

He moved carefully and cautiously, as if his body wasn't functioning at full capacity. She imagined the worst of the aches and pains from the accident would sneak up on both of them tomorrow.

Crossing to the kitchen, she located a gallon jug of water. Lander faced a long night ahead, and might enjoy a midnight snack. She cracked the refrigerator door, check-ing on the contents. The inside remained cold. She chose a pecan square and a slice of eggnog pound cake, then sealed them in a zip-lock bag. "Some goodies in case you get hungry," she told him.

"You don't mind me eating in bed?" he asked as he ap-proached her, his arms laden with the materials to build a fire.

She inhaled the raw scent of pine and man. Earthy and arousing. Her heart quickened and her belly warmed. She stared at him. "You don't look like a man who'd leave crumbs on the sheets."

"You're right." He grinned, the corners of his eyes crin-kling. "I prefer not to roll over and hear the crunch of crackers under my back."

Abby had a fantasy moment, one where he was in bed, his hair mussed, naked, all warm and sexually hungry. She surprised herself by being so daring with her thoughts over a man she'd just met. He was so handsome; he could melt her resistance like the hot flame of a candle licking an ici-cle. Her image of him was so potent and lustful that heat tipped her nipples and snuck between her thighs. She was suddenly burning up.

Embarrassment walked her down the hall.

She felt Lander's eyes on the back of her head the entire way. He made her feel nervous and excited. Expectant. For no reason other than he was a man and she was a woman and they were snowbound together.

The loft was built above the den, and was her favorite room in the cabin. A second triangular window show-cased snowflakes being whipped by the wind. The icy coldness from the glass seeped inside. They climbed twelve wide steps to the second floor. The stairs proved difficult, but she was determined not to show her discomfort. She put as little weight as possible on her sore toe.

Lander stopped on the top step and looked around. "Very nice, Abby."

She agreed. Gazing about the room, she allowed the memories of youthful slumber parties with her good friends Clara and Lily to touch her heart. Here had been their hideaway. They'd giggled, played games, discussed boys, and eaten her grandmother's freshly baked gingerbread men.

No one baked gingerbread like Gram. The scent was disarming, the taste was soothing. Spicy, but sweet. Abby could be having the worst day of her life, and all it took was one bite of gingerbread to turn her day around.

After Ada had passed away, Abby decided to take the recipe to a whole new level, one with erotic appeal. There'd been no man in her life, so, on a whim, she'd created an anatomically correct G-man. She knew her grandma would've shaken her head, and yet hidden her smile. Gram had always encouraged Abby in whatever she'd chosen to do, even if her entrepreneurial debut included peppermint-stick penises.

Abby had shown the cookies to her two best friends, who'd laughed out loud and loved them. An Internet business had been born in November. To her surprise and delight, the Gingerbread Man website had taken off slowly, but steadily. Which presented a new problem. Pine Mountain was moderately conservative, so she kept her company private. Ordering was discreet and confidential. Only Lily and Clara were aware that Abby was behind the erotic creations.

She had filled all but one order to date. That particular request was for a holiday bachelorette party in Las Vegas. Thirty-six erect gingerbread men needed to be baked, decorated, boxed, and mailed before the upcoming weekend.

Abby tapped her taped toe on the hardwood floor, thinking. A stab of pain added to her woes, but she ignored it. She had bigger problems than sticking penises on cookies. She hoped the blizzard wouldn't hover too long. She didn't want to bake with Lander at the cabin. She preferred to keep him in the dark about her carnal G-men for a while yet.

Still favoring her big toe, she carried the gallon of water and lantern across the room, placing them on a golden oak nightstand. She watched as Lander moved between the light and shadows. He showed interest in the furniture. His gaze was appreciative.

"I like the sleigh bed," he said, running his hand over the curving headboard.

"It's been in the family for a hundred years," Abby said proudly. The ornate Victorian design spoke of elegant times gone by. And the couples who'd slept in the bed.

She watched as he crossed to the sturdy knotty pine rocking chair with the red tufted corduroy cushions. He set it in motion. The chair moaned. One corner of his mouth tipped in a half smile. "I guessed it would creak."

He next took interest in the framed seasonal photographs on the wall. "Great gallery," he said.

"My grandmother took those photos," Abby shared with him. "Winter can be rough on mountain animals. Gram photographed a deer standing in a snowdrift in the backyard, eating acorns from an outdoor feeder. Ada fed the doe all year long. Our resident red fox liked fruit."

Lander took in the next photograph. The melting snow announced the arrival of spring. Abby's favorite season. The landscape held the promise of new life, green and vibrant. Wildflowers covered the mountainside. A cardinal perched on a tree branch and stared into the camera.

The beauty of a summer sunrise was captured in the third shot. Abby was a morning person. She often hiked at dawn. The air was still and clear and the view was spectacular. She valued time spent alone with her thoughts.

The final photograph brought to mind autumn's crispness and changing leaves, when coats and boots emerged from the closet. The sound of dry leaves crunching underfoot always made Abby smile. The picture on the wall was a close-up of the cabin's front porch. Inviting porches were a Pine Mountain cabin staple, welcoming all who passed by. A dozen fat pumpkins huddled on the wooden planks and a straw scarecrow decorated the door. Two Adirondack chairs counted down the days to the first snow. They would then be stored in the garage.

Lander stepped toward the three-shelf bookcase. He thumbed through the titles. "Someone likes mysteries," he noted with approval.

"My grandmother was a fan of Agatha Christie, M. C. Beaton, Ellery Queen, and Erle Stanley Gardner," said Abby. "She'd often read the same book over and over again, even though she knew the ending."

He studied the magazines on the bottom shelf. "These *National Geographics, Reader's Digest,* and *Life* magazines date back to the 1950s."

"Collectibles, and Gram's favorite issues," she said, feeling nostalgic. "I haven't the heart to throw them away."

"I wouldn't either," he said.

He looked at her then, his expression thoughtful. "What was once important to someone in your family should be important to you, too."

"Speaking from experience?" she asked.

He nodded. "My father had an antique revolving world globe on a floor stand in his office. The continents were hand cut and raised with parchment-colored oceans. There was a small crack in the globe over Australia. I used to spin it as a kid, over and over again, driving my father crazy. My dad was pretty smart. He'd let me turn the sphere, but only if I stopped it with my finger. I then had to research the city and continent. Needless to say, I scored high in geography in school after that."

He looked off into the distance, as if spinning the world again in his mind. Finally, he said, "I kept the globe after he passed away. It's a good memory for me."

They stood in silence for several minutes, staring at one another. Abby felt an inexplicable draw toward this man. The feeling stretched beyond his good looks and solid build and had everything to do with his compassion for family. He cared. He had no problem talking about his feelings. She liked that about him. It actually made him more masculine. He had a strong sense of self.

Her heart began to warm for the first time since her grandmother's passing. She'd hidden her sadness from her friends. She'd attended town functions with forced smiles and appropriate small talk. Everyone had his own holiday agenda. No one realized her pain. She had felt very much alone, even in a crowd of people. Her loneliness now eased.

Abby knew herself well. She was a logical woman. Practical in a patched quilt kind of way. Pieces of her life stitched together in a wayward pattern. She realized that Lander was only passing through Pine Mountain. His stay with her would be short, but somehow had a purpose. He'd shown up at a time when she needed more than her own company.

A soft, wanting sigh escaped her lips. She liked his being there. Although a part of her hated the fact her erotic gingerbread men were the reason for his accident in the first place.

The wild whirling of the wind echoed down the chimney of the stone fireplace, making her shiver. The temperature in the loft was cool, but not uncomfortably cold. A fire would drive away the midnight chill.

"Can you start a fire?" she asked him.

He nodded easily. "Not a problem."

She kept her eye on him as he eased the iron grate aside, crouched down, and laid out the logs. Then set the fire to burning. The man had confidence and skills. Abby had the distinct feeling he'd built many fires before tonight. She wondered about his home and if he had his own fireplace. Did he have a woman to share its mesmerizing warmth?

She watched as he splayed his hands toward the low flames, flexing his fingers and wrists before pushing to his feet. He reset the grate, then turned and faced her. His smile was slow and self-assured. And very sexy.

Abby stared at his mouth overly long. "Nice fire," she finally managed.

"I'll sleep well tonight." He stretched his arms over his head, gave a low groan. She imagined his muscles were tight and bruised.

"Sheets and blankets are in the hope chest," she said, rounding the foot of the bed. She lifted the lid and released the rich scent of cedar. It filled the loft with a holiday feel. All the room needed was a string of Christmas lights and steaming mugs of hot chocolate with marshmallows to make it the perfect Santa retreat. With that in mind, she chose a black pine-embroidered bedding set, two wool blankets, and a pillow. She moved to one side of the queen-sized bed and placed the bedding on a padded bench against the wall.

"Let me help you," Lander offered, standing opposite her across the bed.

She smiled to herself. He could make both a fire and a bed. Lander was capable and competent. There was a certainty to his presence she'd never felt with another man. She felt comfortable with him.

Intimacy lay on the mattress between them as they spread the sheets and tucked in the corners. Abby took her time smoothing the blanket. She wanted it to be perfect. She slipped on the pillowcase, centered the pillow against the headboard. The bed looked inviting.

Too inviting. She was so bone tired; she nearly slid down on the blanket and closed her eyes. Instead, she forced herself back to being the good hostess, even if it killed her. And her big toe. Which was now starting to throb from all her standing.

"There's a half-bath," she said, pointing to the door in the far corner. "A guest toothbrush and paste should be in the cupboard. The gallon of water—"

"Used for the brush and flush," he finished for her.

He understood, and that pleased her. What other surprises about him would she discover before the blizzard passed?

There was nothing left for her to do or to say, so she picked up her lantern and walked toward the stairs. She winced, but it wasn't from her hurt toe. She'd taken two steps, glanced down into the den where she happened to spot a straw broom. A silver string of holly berries decorated the wooden handle and the lower shaft was scented with cinnamon oil. The delightful Christmasy sight and smell brought heaviness to her heart. She'd purchased the holiday broom for her grandmother a few days before she'd passed away. Ada had been so excited over Abby's gift that she'd "hugged the stuffing right out of her," as Gram used to say.

It took Abby a moment to catch her breath. Her emotions were unpredictable. She couldn't control how she felt. Her sadness came and went, and, at times, crushed her completely. Now was such a moment. She gripped the handrail to steady herself.

Inhaling slowly, she spoke around the lump in her throat. "Holler if you need anything," she said to Lander. "I sleep light. I always heard my grandma whenever she called."

"Abby?" She hadn't heard him come up behind her. His voice was low, deep, and sincere.

He placed his hands on her shoulders, squeezed lightly. "I'm certain you took good care of Ada," he said. "It must have been a great comfort for her to know you were close by."

She leaned back, and their bodies brushed. She felt his strength and compassion. She didn't dare turn around. Tears now filled her eyes, and the loft blurred around her. She swallowed, sniffed, and felt vulnerable for breaking down in front of him.

"It's doubtful I'll call you in the middle of the night," he continued, "but I appreciate your offer."

She could do no more than nod, afraid if she tried to speak that her voice would crack. While she could dry her tears, her heart still cried.

Lander released her, saying, " 'Night, Abby."

She slowly took the stairs.

One step at a time.

Her heart and her big toe aching all the way.

"Abby!" A man's deep voice jarred her awake.

It was Lander, she realized, sitting up on the sofa with a start. She blinked, focusing. She'd fallen asleep in her clothes, choosing the living room, lulled by the warmth of the fire.

"Abby!" he called a second time.

Panic hit her, a feeling she hadn't expected. For whatever reason, he needed her. She hadn't felt that since her grandmother's passing. Most likely he'd tripped in the dark. Or perhaps he'd eaten his midnight snacks and wanted seconds. She'd find out soon enough.

With a hurried movement, she tossed back the unfinished quilt that covered her. The square-patterned throw was her grandmother's last project. Yellows and reds, greens and golds. Edged with earthy brown. Like nature's garden, Gram often said. Ada had passed away before trimming the excess batting and binding the corners. Still, it was Abby's favorite.

She hadn't iced her toe for several hours; the dull ache had her hobbling down the hallway toward the loft. She did a one-legged hop up the stairs. Pushing back her hair with her hand, she stared at the bare-chested man propped against the headboard.

He'd turned on his lantern. He had bed-head, but his eyes were bright. She was surprised to see him without her sweatshirt, but he looked good in his skin. The blanket was tucked in around his waist, exposing wide shoulders, sinewy biceps and a strong chest. A hint of his navel.

Hot, sexy, and masculine came to mind. She was suddenly wide-awake and openly staring at him. Her heart beat faster. He was all male.

"What is it, Lander?" she asked, her voice breathy. She had the sudden urge to touch him. She fisted her hands instead.

"Did you lose a cat?" he asked. An honest question but there was an undertone to his words, amused yet perturbed.

"Ah, Tennyson." She couldn't help but smile. "He's never lost, but he seldom lets me find him."

"He found me," Lander said, looking down the wool blanket toward his toes. "He crawled into bed and used my calf as a scratching post."

"I'm sorry he bothered you." She set her lantern on the bookcase and crossed to his bed. "I'll take him back downstairs with me."

Lifting the bottom corner on the blanket, she reached for the male calico. Tenn batted at her hand, not wanting to be removed from the man or his bed. She finally captured the cat around his middle and, in doing so, her knuckles brushed Lander's leg. His very bare leg.

Apparently he'd taken off his sweatpants, too. His body heat was warmer than the fireplace. Her whole hand tingled.

She quickly released the blanket as she drew Tennyson close to her chest. The cat curled comfortably in her arms. His purr ruffled the silence.

Lander looked at the cat closely. "Tennyson appears to have lived eight lives," he said, the concern in his voice for her pet touching that soft spot in her heart she rarely showed anyone.

Abby stroked the cat. True, Tenn was scruffy. Although he ate well, he'd lost weight as he'd grown older. "My boy showed up at the cabin eighteen years ago during a blizzard much like the one tonight," she told Lander. "Gram was reading poetry and heard an animal crying outside the back door. She got up and found the kitten nearly buried beneath a mound of snow; shivering and half-frozen. We never discovered how he got there. He was smaller than my palm.

"We wrapped him in a blanket and fed him warm milk from a doll's bottle. We weren't sure he was going to make it, but he did. Unfortunately, he lost half an ear and the end of his tail. His fur has always been spiky." She hugged the calico closer, letting Tenn know how important he was to her, and not just because male calicos were so rare. "I think that gives him character. We named him Alfred, Lord Tennyson, after Gram's favorite poet."

The cat fussed in her arms, wanting to get down. Abby set him on the floor. "He should follow me downstairs," she said, turning.

Tenn had a mind of his own. He didn't move.

What was he up to?

She bent to scoop him up again, but he got away from her. An awkward leap and his old bones landed back on Lander's bed. The cat padded straight toward the headboard where he lay down beside their houseguest's pillow. Seemed he had picked his place to sleep on this cold night and no one was going to cajole him out of it.

Abby shook her head, frowned. Tennyson gave her little alternative. She'd have to kneel on the bed to reach him. Perhaps even climb across a naked Lander. Heaven help her if she accidentally grabbed *his* peppermint stick. While the idea was appealing, her body ached and her toe hurt too much to play kitty-cat games. Tenn could be stubborn.

"Tennyson," she said sternly. "Come here."

The calico yawned in her face and closed his eyes. There was nothing worse than being ignored by a cat.

Lander scratched Tenn's ears. "He can stay, Abby. I'm more a dog kind of guy, but I don't mind cats. My sister has two."

She breathed easier. "You're certain?"

"I'm fine with his company now that I know who he is," Lander reassured her.

Tennyson gave her the cat's-eye of satisfaction. As if he understood every word. He'd won this round. "Tenn snores," she warned, retrieving her lantern and taking her leave.

"So do I on occasion," Lander said, "especially when I'm tired, as I am tonight."

She glanced over her shoulder at the top stair. She wished she had a camera. The calico had snuggled even closer to Lander. The man slept on his back, and the cat now curled in the crook of his arm.

Lucky cat, Abby thought, as she followed the glow of light back to the living room. She wouldn't have minded snuggling with the two of them. Not that it would ever happen, but the thought of it provided an image of everything important to her. Her love of animals—and her desire for a man of her own.

She once again returned to the sofa and stretched out, covering up with the quilt. Frost curtained the front window in wide swags. Snowdrifts climbed the side of the cabin. The heat of the fire chased the chill from the air.

All was well in her world atop Pine Mountain.

She fell asleep, feeling safe and secure in a blizzard that might not blow over for several days.

Thud, thud, thump, crunch.

Damn, Lander hated the fact he was making so much noise at such an early hour. He had slept soundly, but rose religiously at six a.m. A habit he intended to put to good use on this cold, frosty morning. Tennyson had no such compulsion. The cat took over his spot under the covers the second he left the bed.

Abby hadn't been kidding about Tenn's snoring. The calico snored so deeply, so loudly, his entire body rumbled. He'd wakened Lander twice. The cat had kneaded his arm while sleeping, his claws extended. Lander had pinpricks on his left elbow. A small price to pay after the previous exhausting day, he decided. He was damn glad to be alive.

The sleigh bed was comfortable. The blankets and heat from the fire had kept him warm. Had he not been a man on a mission, he might have slept an extra hour. Simply because there was nowhere to go and little to accomplish until the snowstorm passed. But he'd been hit with an idea at first light. His plan would cause him some effort. He hoped his body would hold up long enough for him to accomplish it.

What he was about to do, he did for Abby.

He'd gotten dressed, washed his face, and brushed his teeth. There'd been no sign of a razor, so he'd worn his morning stubble. His whiskers helped cover the cut on his lip and several of the bruises on his chin. Rigidly sore from the accident, he walked like an eighty-year-old man.

Clutching the handrail, he'd slowly descended the stairs to the den.

The picture window revealed a darkly overcast and blustery day. Snowflakes whipped wildly. The blizzard showed no mercy. He'd searched along the hallway for the outside door. In the process, he'd discovered a second bedroom and a fully stocked pantry before stepping into the two-car garage.

His socks had stuck to the cold cement floor as he circled the hood of a silver Ford Escape, looking for the Christmas tree. He'd finally found it propped against a small snow blower. The tree needed to be rescued from its chilly fate. He had nearly frozen his balls while dragging it inside.

It was one big evergreen. Already set in a red metal stand. The tree was wrapped in thick twine, yet the branches were damn prickly. The tree needed water. Every movement he made proved awkward. He didn't let that stop him. He was jabbed in the forehead and poked near his eye as he maneuvered it down the hallway. He had no idea where Abby slept, but he tried hard not to disturb her. Still, he made enough noise to start an avalanche.

He shoved the tree into the living room, and stopped. That's when he saw her, seated on the sofa, wide-awake, and eyeing him warily. "I heard you coming down the hall," she said, her tone tentative. "You have a very distinctive *thump*."

"My shoulders are stiff," he admitted, hating the fact he'd made such a noisy entrance. "I couldn't lift and carry it quietly."

"So you wrestled it." Flat, no humor in her voice.

"The tree almost won," he said ruefully. "The door to the garage is narrow. There are pine needles all over the floor. I'll sweep them up later."

Facing him, she appeared pale and not all that pleased. "Why did you bring it indoors?" she asked.

He heard the slight tremor in her voice and tried to lighten the moment. "The blizzard hasn't let up," he said. "Decorating the tree will give us something to do."

"I'd have been fine with nothing at all." She tossed back the quilt and rose. Her jaw was set, and she looked determined not to pursue the matter any further. He watched as she hobbled to the kitchen; one slipper was on and the other off. It disturbed him that her toe still hurt her.

She'd changed clothes during the night, he noted. Her curves fit nicely in a red waffle pullover and black jeans. Her face was free of makeup and her hair was in free flight.

He saw her glance at the tree, only to turn away. He understood what she was feeling. Her heart hurt. Abby was about to face her first Christmas without her grandmother.

A dull ache creased his brow, eating away at him. He knew that whatever he did, it would be an uphill battle to make her feel better. He was determined to try. Holiday perfect it wouldn't be. Hopefully decorating the tree was the first step. He wanted to make her smile.

She now stood at the kitchen counter, her back to him. "Add a log to the fireplace," she softly requested, "and I'll cook us breakfast, pumpkin-bread French toast."

Something he'd never eaten, but it sounded good.

The tree could wait, he decided, as he leaned it against the wall. He crossed the room and readied the fire. He watched from the corner of his eye as she opened the refrigerator. "Good, it's still cold inside." She sounded relieved. Removing the needed items, she cracked eggs and poured milk into a mixing bowl. Sprinkled in vanilla and nutmeg. Then selected a whisk and stirred like crazy. The delicious scent woke his appetite.

He made a trip to the kitchen for her cookware and paper goods. She followed him back to the fireplace, carrying a loaf of pumpkin bread, the ceramic bowl, a jug of maple syrup, and a container of instant coffee.

"Where are the Christmas decorations?" he asked her. He could wrap some garlands on the tree and hang a few shiny ornaments with the best of them.

She hesitated. "They're boxed in the storeroom in the garage."

"Is the room locked?" he asked.

She narrowed her gaze on him. Her brown eyes held more sadness than annoyance. "You're persistent, Lander," she said on a sigh. "It's very easy access once you shove the ladder and paint cans aside."

He placed the cast-iron pot and skillet on the side table near the fireplace, then went on to say, "Loss is painful, Abby. I'm here to help you have a nice Christmas."

Her shoulders sagged. "It's hard to be happy. Everywhere I look I see Gram: in the kitchen fixing breakfast, sitting on the sofa knitting, fussing over a jigsaw puzzle. Always smiling."

"The grieving process can be long and painful," he said. "You need to focus on the good times, on the strength of the memories she left you," he said, drawing on his own pain to help her through hers.

There had been nights he'd been so angry with his father for leaving him that he pounded his fist against the wall. He'd cursed, pushed through the pain, and remained strong for his mother and sister. He now wanted Abby to feel the spirit and cheer she'd once shared with Ada.

"I made it through Christmas without my father just one year ago," he said. "You'll manage, too. Believe me."

He surprised himself by putting his arm around her and drawing her close. She fit nicely against him, a woman warm from sleep and softly curved. "Wouldn't your grandmother want you to continue your special traditions?" he asked.

She rested her cheek against his chest, an unconscious gesture as she sought his comfort. He liked that. "I suppose so," she agreed.

"I'll deal with the tree after we eat," he said. "You can sit, elevate your foot, and watch while I do the work if you prefer not to help." There, he'd given her the option. He'd let her make up her own mind.

"Thanks, Lander." Her body relaxed against his, and her acceptance came on a deep sigh. "I always looked forward to decorating the tree. It's my favorite part of the season."

He hugged her tighter. What a surprising shift of events for him. His accident was turning into something very different with this kind, generous woman. Something he'd never imagined when he woke up in her cabin. Warm, intimate. Sharing memories with her.

He would've turned her toward him then, had she not been holding the mixing bowl. Instead, he lightly kissed her on the forehead. The static electricity of her hair tickled his lips. "Christmas centers around the tree at my house as well," he told her.

Peering up at him, she said, "We've always stood the evergreen in the corner by the front window. There, it catches the natural light during the day and, at night, the Christmas lights reflect off the glass. It looks like we have two trees instead of one. It's amazing."

"I can do that," he assured her. It made him feel good to see her eyes bright, her pretty smile coming back.

She stepped away from him then. In spite of himself, he frowned. He felt the physical gap between them keenly. A strange emptiness filled him. He missed her standing next to him.

He had the urge to pull her back, but didn't act on it. Human contact in a stressful situation was comforting. Abby needed that comfort. She wasn't looking for anything else from him, he knew. He was a man she'd found in a wrecked car. Nothing more. The problem was, he had different ideas. He found he liked holding her. A little too much.

He could've hovered around her while she cooked, but instead chose to change into his own clothes. He removed his shirt and slacks from the makeshift line and headed toward the bathroom.

Abby's sweatshirt was binding, and it felt good to stretch out his arms in his long-sleeved shirt. His slacks had a hundred wrinkles and a missing back pocket. He didn't care. He decided to keep on the wool socks she'd given him. They were warmer than his wingtips. The leather had cracked over the toe. He'd lost one shoelace.

He folded the sweats on the countertop, then returned to the living room. The scent of pumpkin-bread French toast drew him like a crooked finger. His mouth watered. He was one hungry man.

"Have a seat." She gestured toward the sofa.

"I can boil water for the coffee," he offered.

She shook her head, smiling. "It's easier to serve you than have two cooks at the fireplace."

He understood. She didn't want them bumping into each other standing so near the flames. But hot sparks from the fire were the least of his worries, he thought. He was attracted to Abby.

Stepping back and out of her way, he took a moment to appreciate her body. He admired the gentle slope of her shoulders, the fullness of her breasts, and the curve of her hips. The firm tone of her thighs. He stared so long, he soon sported an erection. One he needed to hide.

Crossing to the couch, he settled deep. He swallowed a low moan of momentary comfort. The cushions were soft. His body relaxed. He covered his groin with the quilt.

Moments later, Abby came to him, a little wobbly on her feet. He figured her big toe continued to bother her.

He'd insist she sit in her chair while he positioned the tree, then carried in the ornaments from the garage.

"Instant coffee?" she offered him, once the water in the pot had boiled. "Santa's Helper was Gram's favorite blend. We drank it black. I have sugar, if you like."

"I'm sure it will be fine."

"It can be a little strong."

She watched, her expression tentative, as he took his first sip. He tried not to make a face, but his lips puckered. *Strong* was a mild word for the dark roasted brew. It had kick. The morning espresso he'd once ordered while on vacation in Mexico had been easier to swallow.

Abby laughed at him, a teasing sound that warmed her brown eyes. "I figured the coffee might be a little strong for you, but I took a chance. It's an acquired taste."

He took a second sip. For her, he'd brave it. "Give me some time, I'll get used to it."

"You won't be around long enough to learn to appreciate the flavor," she said, glancing toward the front window. "The blizzard will pass and the snow plows will begin clearing the main streets in town. The crews will work their way up the mountain. Then you'll be free to leave." Her voice trailed off, as if she left a lingering thought or wish unsaid.

He sank down deeper into the sofa. He would return to Philadelphia, Lander thought. His chest tightened, for no conceivable reason. He'd known Abby for less than a day, yet he felt he'd known her for years. The sensation was strange; the moment, poignant. He felt a significant shift in his life, but wasn't yet certain as to the outcome. He liked this woman and wanted to know her better. Time, however, was not on his side.

She returned to the fireplace, then came back and served him a paper plate stacked with pumpkin-bread French toast. Four thick pieces. She handed him a paper cup of warm maple syrup.

He'd eaten in five-star restaurants much of his life, but, at that moment, nothing could compare to this delicious, hot breakfast. Being snowbound provided the atmosphere. Abby was the perfect companion. Spiky-haired Tennyson now made an appearance. The cat entered the living room as if he owned the place. He took a few steps, then stretched his skinny body. He walked a bit farther, and proceeded to groom himself.

"Eat?" Abby asked the calico as she set her plate of food on the coffee table.

Tenn didn't have to be asked twice. He headed toward the kitchen. Lander heard the creak of a cabinet door, then the pop of a lid. The scent of tuna reached him.

Abby returned a moment later, settling on her chair. "Tennyson doesn't have many teeth," she said. "He eats very slowly, savoring each bite. He'll be at his bowl for at least twenty minutes."

"Savoring is good," Lander agreed as he poured syrup on his French toast, sliced off a corner, and dug in. He continued to eat and didn't look up until he'd almost cleared his plate.

When he did glance at Abby, he found her staring at him. Questioning, yet amused. All it had taken was one bite of breakfast, and his manners eluded him. He hadn't made any attempt at conversation. He'd eaten like a man who hadn't seen food for a week. His neck heated.

"Abby, I—" he started.

She cut him off. One corner of her mouth curved into a smile. "You were hungry," she noted.

"Starving," he admitted, sliding his hand over his stomach. "Even though I've done nothing to work up an appetite."

"Your body's beat-up and you're healing," she explained. "You need the extra nutrition."

She had a point, he realized. He finished his breakfast, but passed on a second cup of coffee. Santa's Helper had given him a buzz. He felt energized. He took the initiative and insisted Abby stay seated while he cleaned up. Tennyson had licked his plate clean by the time Lander seasoned the cast-iron cookware.

He was ready to push forward with their day. He crossed to the evergreen, tugged it toward the designated corner. He secured the red metal stand, then untied and unwound the heavy twine. He shook the tree, and the branches began to unfold like an upside down umbrella. Shades of green contoured the branches, the inner ones darker than the outer tips. The tree stretched and groaned and its prickly needles quivered. The fullness forced him to take a step back. The evergreen was majestic.

"It's bigger than we had last year," Abby said, taking it all in. She'd angled her chair to face the window and propped up her foot on a small, round ottoman.

Lander saw what he knew she preferred he not see. Her shoulders were squared and she had a stiff upper lip. This time it wasn't her big toe that caused her pain. She gripped the arms of the chair as if holding on for dear life. She was desperately afraid to let go; afraid to succumb to her memories and heavy heart.

Tennyson sensed her mood. He hopped up and curled on her lap, demanding her attention. Abby's hand shook slightly as she stroked him. Lander could see how much the cat meant to her. The calico was a link to her grandmother. He heard Tenn purring clear across the room.

"The tree is dry," he said, clearing his throat. "I'll add water to the stand, and then bring in the boxes from the garage."

She swallowed, nodded, and continued to pet her cat.

In a very short time, he had located the ornaments. The storeroom was neat and the cardboard boxes were marked. There were three total. He hefted the first, and his muscles strained. He swore it was filled with bricks, not shiny Christmas decorations.

Back inside, he set the box down by Abby's chair. "What do you have in here?" he asked her, exhaling sharply.

"I should've warned you," she said, looking guilty. "You'll find solid lead figurines: a vintage Santa, his sleigh, and eight reindeer. Gram and I display them before the hearth."

Solid lead. That explained the weight of the box. At any other time it wouldn't have mattered. He was a strong guy. At that moment pain radiated from his ribs, but he refused to complain. The tree was more important. He'd manage somehow.

He hunkered down beside her and unpacked the box. Each figurine was preserved in bubble wrap. He took his time, admiring the unique set. The pieces bore the same image on both the front and the back of the figure.

"These are amazing, Abby," he said, meaning it. The holiday figurines rolled back the years to his own youth and the Lionel train set he'd owned as a kid. Fitting each railroad car and caboose on the track, rearranging the miniature houses each day, then letting out a holler when the whistling locomotive set off on its circular trip around the tracks. Those were good times.

"The figures have been handed down over generations," Abby told him. "They were cast in Germany."

He rose and, one by one, arranged the figures to the left of the fireplace, leaving Abby room to cook their meals.

"How's that look?" he asked her.

She scrunched her nose and said, "We always lined up the reindeer in pairs."

He matched them up. "Better?"

"Separate the sleigh from the reindeer by an inch or two."

He did so. "Okay, now?"

"I'd like Santa nearer to the sleigh."

He complied.

She shook her head. "Santa's too close now."

He backed Santa up.

"Could you tilt the sleigh on one runner, so it looks like it's flying through the sky?"

Flying through the sky? He was about to make the adjustment, when he heard her chuckle. A muffled chuckle, but a chuckle nonetheless.

She was playing him.

He straightened and crossed his arms over his chest. He gave her a hard stare, which didn't faze her in the least. She actually laughed at him.

"Your laughter is at my expense," he said, walking toward her. He pretended to be upset. He wasn't. He was glad to see her happy.

"I'm sorry, Lander," she said, trying to make amends. "Really I am. No more teasing. Swear."

Reaching her, he rested his hip on the arm of her chair and leaned in, sexually close. "Should you break your word and make fun of me again, I will settle the score."

Her eyes rounded. "You'd get even with me?"

"You've been warned." He breathed against her mouth.

Awareness slipped between them, warm and potent. Inviting. Tempting. Stimulating. She licked her lips; her mouth was full and lush. And kissable.

He wanted to kiss her, but he intentionally held back. Instead he decided he would tease her on his terms. A hot look, a subtle touch, a suggestive word. Endless foreplay throughout the day.

Let it snow, let it snow, let it snow.

Chapter 3

Abby held her breath and waited for Lander to kiss her. She waited and waited, and waited some more. He was so close, the stubble on his jaw scraped her cheek. He stared deeply into her eyes, and his blue gaze darkened. Dilated. His masculine heat embraced her. He carried the scent of bayberry soap. Fresh, clean, and woodsy.

Calmness failed her. Anticipation gave her goose bumps. Her whole body tightened. She was afraid he could hear the pounding of her heart.

She could've kissed him, but she didn't want to initiate what he had no desire to finish. She hadn't a clue how he felt about her. There was nothing worse than a woman kissing a man who didn't want her to kiss him.

Caught between her lap and Lander's hip, Tennyson chose that moment to let them both know he felt crowded. The cat gave a low growl that sounded old and rusty as he pressed his paw to Lander's stomach and gave him a push. A big push for such an elderly cat. Tenn was protecting his territory. Abby belonged to him.

Lander took the hint and eased back an inch. A slight tip to his lips, and he straightened his shoulders and stood. "Sorry, big guy," he said to Tennyson as he scratched the calico's ears. The cat purred. He again looked at Abby. "I'll bring in the rest of the Christmas ornaments now."

She managed a nod, but it was difficult. A minute ago she was ready to fall into his arms and kiss him. Now she was in the throes of what she'd been avoiding for a week. Decorating the tree.

She watched from the corner of her eye as he left the living room. He walked with purpose, and looked damn fine from the back. The man was solid and strong and she loved the square set of his shoulders. He had a tight butt and long legs. Very nice indeed.

Her hand shook as she petted Tenn. That surprised her. Even though she considered herself grounded in the real world, Lander's nearness had left her nervous. She wondered what she should do next. The daring side of her personality—the part that came up with her erotic cookies—couldn't resist wanting to take the next step.

He'd warned her against teasing him a second time. If she did, what would he do? Playfully chuck her under the chin? Gently shake her by the shoulders? Possibly even kiss her? The kiss appealed to her the most.

She'd dated over the years, but had never gotten serious over any man. Her mood became thoughtful. She knew why. When osteoporosis bent her grandmother's shoulders and arthritis buckled her knees, Abby had chosen to stick close to the cabin. To be there when Gram needed her. Whether it was helping her with her medication or arranging her favorite pillow to make her comfy, she wanted to be the caregiver for the woman who'd raised her.

Now, her grandmother was no longer with her, except perhaps in spirit. Gram's presence was strong inside Abby, but a different set of emotions made her tingle. It was Lander staying with her until the blizzard blew itself out. A subtle heat made her wiggle on the chair cushion as her nipples hardened. He was a man she wanted to know better. They weren't going anywhere, anytime soon.

"Here's the next box of decorations," he said, joining her once again. "Not quite so heavy, but I did hear bells."

Bending down, he set it by her chair. Abby breathed him in. Crisp air from the garage clung to him. Winter and man. A romantic combination.

"Sleigh bells," she told him, smiling. "Gram would take me into town for a winter sleigh ride when I was younger." How could she ever forget her grandma helping her pull on her red mittens with the finely stitched snowmen on them? Or kissing her cold red nose?

"When the owner of the sleigh and team closed down his business, she bought one of the leather reins as a decoration," she continued. "We'd wrap it around the front door. The bells would announce visitors."

Lander rubbed his chin. "Does that include Santa?" he asked.

She gave him a small smile. "And Rudolph," she said, her voice soft.

She ran her hand along the taped cardboard. Tears welled in her eyes but she willed them back. This wasn't going to be easy. She wasn't certain she was ready to recall her holiday memories. She drew a deep breath. Gram would want her to move forward. She would do her best. "I'll unwrap the bells," she managed.

"I'll grab the last box." He took off again, leaving her alone.

Abby couldn't turn back now. She clutched Tennyson close as she scooted to the edge of her chair. The cat flicked his one ear, his full attention on her fingers as she slowly stripped the masking tape. He meowed, pawed at the tape, and it stuck to his pad. He was suddenly a kitten again, rolling around on her lap, trying to shake off the stickiness. His playfulness eased her pain.

The calico had tired of the game by the time Lander returned. Abby gently removed the tape from Tennyson's paw. The cat then hopped off her lap and took off to stalk the evergreen. He circled the tree with interest, sniffing, then used the trunk as a scratching post.

Lander lowered the box next to the one Abby had begun to open. He looked concerned. "Will Tenn climb the tree?" he asked her, watching as the cat now batted a bottom branch.

"Tennyson is more a looker than a climber," she said. "He's knocked decorations off the lower limbs, so Gram and I would only hang the smaller wooden ornaments within his reach. That way nothing got broken."

Lander looked around. "What's next, Abs?" he asked.

Abs. The shortening of her name slowed her heart, and her breath stilled. Her grandmother had affectionately called her Abs, but no one else ever had.

She clasped her hands in her lap and awaited her grief. Surprisingly, she didn't flinch, didn't feel overly sad, and didn't request he call her Abby. She had survived the moment. She breathed again.

"Are you feeling all right?" He bent slightly, tipped her chin up with his finger. He ran his thumb over her lower lip, and then traced the curve of her upper. "You look pale."

From pale to pink, her cheeks heated. Her mouth was sensitive to his touch. Pleasure warmed her. Her eyelids felt heavy. The edges of the room blurred around her.

Tennyson's hiss brought her back to reality. The branch he batted had swung back and smacked him on the nose. He was ticked. His ear flattened and he crouched near the Christmas tree base. He appeared ready to leap and take down the evergreen.

Lander stepped back as Abby clapped her hands and called to her cat. "Tenn, come here." The calico didn't pay her one bit of attention. Why should he? Her voice wasn't her own; she sounded breathy and aroused.

She cleared her throat, patted her thigh, and tried again. "Tennyson, lap?" she coaxed, hoping he'd return to her and she wouldn't have to get up and go after him. Her toe still hurt; she'd wanted to stay off her foot today as much as was possible.

The calico looked from the tree to her, and eventually found her lap more inviting. A final slap at the branch and he came to her. His first attempt at jumping onto her lap fell short, so she bent and scooped him into her arms. There wasn't much room between her left leg and the side of the chair, but that's where he chose to settle in. He stretched out his skinny body and rested his head on her knee. He then nipped her hand, wanting to be petted.

Abby could multitask. She stroked Tennyson's shoulders with one hand, and opened the boxes of Christmas decorations with the other. She found herself humming as she unrolled the long, leather strip of bells. They jingled all the way.

"I'll hang these if you like," Lander said from beside her.

She passed him the rein, appreciating his enthusiasm and assistance. Had he not been here, the tree would never have left the garage and the decorations would've remained packed. He gave her the courage to look back, to remember, so she could move forward. However slowly.

"There are curl hooks around the door frame," she told him. "Gram tacked them to the wood and never removed them. They were reusable year after year."

Lander walked to the door, located the hooks, and hung the bells. Any slip of a breeze sneaking inside would have them ringing. Abby loved the holiday sound.

Pulling the cardboard box closer to her, she slowly and carefully began to unwrap the ornaments protected in bubble wrap. Each one had a childhood story behind it. She opened her heart to their memories. Each decoration reminded her of happier times. She spotted the Mrs. Claus doll that she'd loved and remembered countless tea parties shared with Gram, sipping hot chocolate from tiny cups, and the first time she'd made sprinkle cookies when she was ten.

She drew out her memories and embraced her feelings.

"How do the bells look?" Lander asked, returning to her chair.

"Perfect," she said. The long leather rein curved over the entire wooden rim. "You can help unpack ornaments, if you like."

He smiled. "I like."

He lowered himself onto the ottoman, sharing space with her elevated foot. He glanced at her toe, then asked, "How's it feel?"

She made a face. "I know it's there."

He ran his hand down his side. "My ribs are sore, too," he admitted. "No sudden moves and I should be fine."

Abby couldn't take her eyes off Lander as he dug into the box closest to him. She admired the slight roll of his shoulders and the easy flex of his biceps as he collected the next ornament.

"Spiky," he said as he peeled off the wrap. He studied the sphere in his hand. "Handmade?" he guessed, grinning at her.

Abby blushed. "A fourth grade art project. I made it for my grandmother."

"Very creative," he said, holding the ornament by its string. "You have hidden talents."

Hidden and erotic, she thought wryly, recalling that her naughty gingerbread men were the cause of his accident and the reason for his being here in the first place.

But that wasn't what tugged at her heart. Her grandmother had thought her creative, too. Ada had praised her
arts and crafts; especially the Styrofoam ball covered in
paste and rolled in red glitter. Red-and-white straws had
been cut at different lengths and inserted around the ball.
The decoration had hung on the tree for eighteen years.
Only a smudge of glitter had worn off. And two of the
straws were slightly bent now.

Lander pushed to his feet and asked, "Where do you
want the ornament hung on the tree?"

"Upper half works best," she suggested, "just in case
Tennyson gets curious."

Lander placed the Styrofoam ball on the tree, taking
care to make sure the ornament was secure and placed at
the right angle. He then stood back and looked at her. "I
have decorating skills," he said, tongue in cheek.

"You could get a job as a window decorator at a fancy
retail store," Abby agreed.

"Job options are good." He grinned.

She wondered what he did for a living. Asking him,
however, would only put her in a position of telling him
what she did. She wasn't a doctor or a lawyer. She was an
erotic-gingerbread maker. She'd keep her secret a while
longer.

"Can you string lights?" she asked him next.

He crossed back to her. "With the best of them."

She passed him the neatly rolled strands. Their fingers
brushed, and the warmth of his hand lingered with intimacy and expectation. She felt his light touch spread over
her entire body. Her cotton panties felt too tight.

Her lips parted in surprise.

His smile tipped knowingly before he checked out the
lights. "No tangles," he said, sounding relieved.

She rolled her hips, shifted her bottom on the overstuffed chair. Tennyson adjusted his position beside her, too. "Gram was a stickler when it came to taking the lights off the tree," she told him. "She liked everything neat and organized."

"I agree with Ada," he said. "You're looking at a guy who learned that the hard way."

She raised one brow. "How so?"

"My family was taking down the tree when I was nine, and I didn't want any part of it. My father insisted I participate. I broke several ornaments in my hurry to get back to my computer games. My mother quickly directed me to take off the lights. I unwound the strands, balled them up, and tossed them in a box. My father let me get away with it."

He paused, rubbed the back of his neck, remembering. "The next year my dad gave me the job of stringing the lights. You can guess what happened. Needless to say, they were one tangled mess, which was my fault," he said ruefully. "It took me hours to straighten them. Lesson learned."

"I would've liked your father," she said, meaning it.

Lander looked at her then, a deep, searching, considering look, which touched her. "He would've liked you, too, Abby," he said sincerely.

His words meant a lot to her. Family was so very important. Even when loved ones were gone, they left their imprint everywhere. Even if you couldn't see it, you felt it. More so this time of year, Abby thought, suddenly getting all sentimental. "Thank you," she said around the lump in her throat.

Lander was a considerate man. Glancing away, he gave her time to collect herself. Shortly thereafter, he held up the candle-shaped decorative lights and said, "Antique bubble lights. I haven't seen these for years."

"They were Gram's favorite," she said. "As a kid, I would plug them in, then stand before the tree and stare at the candles, waiting for them to warm up and bubble. One strand is clear liquid and the other glitter-filled."

Lander moved to the tree and secured the lights over the branches. "Wish we had electricity," he said as he stretched toward the upper limbs. "Guess the bubbling will have to wait."

"You'll see them bubble," Abby assured him.

He bent, plugged in the strand, and then stepped back. "We'll know the electricity is back on when the tree lights up."

He would depart when the candles came on.

The thought made her stomach hurt. She wasn't ready for him to leave.

But the weather was turning in his favor, she noted. She pointed toward the window. "The storm's letting up. The wind remains strong, but the snowfall has lessened."

He jammed his hands into his pants pockets as he contemplated the drifting snowflakes. She wished she could read his mind. He appeared conflicted. His brow creased. His eyes narrowed. His jaw worked. A release of his breath and his expression relaxed.

Having grown tired of sitting, Abby rolled her shoulders, stretched out her arms, then quickly returned to the cardboard box. Not wanting him to catch her watching him.

"Stiff shoulders?" he asked her on his return.

Apparently he'd seen her shifting on her chair. Perhaps had even felt her stare. There was nothing she could do about it now. She drew a steadying breath.

The scent of evergreen surrounded Lander. Several pine needles stuck to the cuff of his shirt. Casually, as if they were a couple and he'd touched her for years, he curved his hand over her shoulder, then brushed his thumb across the back of her neck beneath her hair. He drew slow circles just above the collar of her shirt. Changing gradually from friendly to intimate, the pressure moved beyond a massage. His touch was warm, stroking and caressing. Gratifying her senses.

The man had great hands. His kneading fingers felt so good that she closed her eyes, only to blink them open when he slid his hand from her shoulder to her spine. Her heat index spiked. He rubbed her back thoroughly, as if he were her lover and touched her often.

His massage stirred every nerve and sensitive point throughout her body. Her mouth was suddenly dry. Her nipples peaked. Her pulse quickened. Her panties dampened. Her toes curled inside her wool socks. Her big toe stopped hurting for several seconds.

She was so into his massage, all thought fled. She needed to say something, anything, while she could still move her lips. He'd asked for an additional ornament for the tree moments ago. She had one unwrapped and ready for him. Her hand shook as she held up a colorfully hand-painted, blown-glass Santa by its metal hook.

"Inherited from my great-great-grandmother," she said, sounding short of breath. "It was made in Germany."

He gave her shoulder a final squeeze before he took the small Santa from her. "You have an incredible collection of vintage ornaments," he complimented, taking a corner of his shirttail and wiping off a bit of dust from Saint Nick's beard.

"Not too old-fashioned?" she hesitantly asked. Did she mean the ornaments or her?

He shook his head. "I find them unique and charming, especially those ornaments made by a sweet fourth grader."

His answer warmed her from the inside out. "There are a few more by me at the bottom of the box," she said, hunting through the bubble wrap and newspaper. Anything to take her mind off him touching her.

She became very quiet, intent on her quest. From

snowmen and pinecones to children on a toboggan and a horse-drawn sleigh, she uncovered a dozen more blown-glass designs. The Dresden Christmas ornaments came next.

Lander held up a very thin embossed cardboard cardinal. "It looks like celluloid," he said, amazed by his find. "So detailed, you can actually see the feathers."

The man knew his ornaments, Abby thought. Present-day ornaments were shiny, glossy, and mass produced. She'd never known anyone outside her grandmother who could identify and appreciate the aged patina of celluloid. She was impressed.

"What do you think, Abs?" Lander sought her approval as he placed each ornament on the tree.

"The tree is coming to life," she said.

A wooden nutcracker came next. He placed it low on the tree. Her grandfather had whittled a train and a drum. The two rounded out the bottom branches.

A crystal star followed. She noted he winced when stretching toward the higher branches. The top foot of the tree remained bare of any decoration. His ribs apparently still hurt.

"Care to take a break and ice your side?" she asked him.

He looked at her over his shoulder. "Hasn't the ice in the freezer compartment melted by now?"

"We're on a mountain in the winter," she reminded him, pushing off her chair. She picked up the ice bag from the coffee table. "I can crack open the front door and scoop snow off the porch." She grabbed her mittens off the coat rack, slipped them on.

"What about putting on your jacket?" he asked, coming toward her.

"I'll make it fast."

She cracked the door and tried to be quick, only to have a gust of wind blow snow in her face. The icy flakes stung her cheeks. The force shoved her back a step. The door nearly slammed on her bum toe.

Son of a snowman. The cold air sliced bone deep. She shivered. Being the gentleman that he was, Lander retrieved her hooded down jacket and joined her at the door. "The storm's getting the better of you," he said, looking worried.

He gently brushed the snowflakes from her hair and off her shoulders. Then ran his thumb over her cheekbones and lips. His touch heated her faster than the fireplace. Hotter, too.

"The wind caught me," she said. "I had trouble opening the door."

He held her coat for her, standing so close that his breath warmed the back of her neck. "Put this on." His tone brooked no argument. "We'll do this together. I'll hold the door and you scoop snow."

She looked up at him. His hair was mussed, his forehead was darkly bruised. His mouth pulled tight. His concern for her touched her deeply.

Between the two of them, it took only a few seconds to accomplish their task. Lander clutched his side, and then put his weight behind opening the door that the wind wanted to close. Abby was quick. She filled the ice bag with four handfuls of snow, then capped off the top.

Once back inside, she passed the bag to Lander. She'd only been outside a few seconds, yet her hands felt stiff, frozen. She quickly tugged off her mittens, blew on her fingertips, then rubbed her hands together.

Lander surprised her. He set the ice bag on the three-legged catchall table for keys and mail located to the left of the door. He took her hands and pressed them between his own. Things took a turn she didn't see coming when her fingers didn't warm as fast as he would've liked.

Without a word, he drew them under his white shirt. Held them there. Her hands splayed against the solid heat of his chest. Her palms caught fire.

Their gazes locked, held.

His stare was interested and intense, and as blue as a flame. Beneath her palm his heart beat rhythmic and steady.

Her own pulse was off the charts. She felt winded. She couldn't stand still.

Her fingers fisted and her nails scored his ribs.

His abdomen flexed. Muscles rippled.

Her feelings were strong for this man. Forged quickly, but as true as if she'd known him for a long time. They'd talked, shared, bonded. She had the urge to wrap her arms around him. To sink into his body. To hold him in her life until she was ready to let him go.

As if she ever could.

Lander liked having her hands on him. Cold as they were, they soon warmed against his abdomen. He wrapped his arms about her shoulders and tucked her to him. Her bulky jacket flattened against his chest. She had no idea how she affected him. He inhaled sharply then let it out. The thick down fiber couldn't hide her curves. Abby was a beautiful woman.

He rested his chin on the top of her head. A few snow-flakes still clung to her hair. The silky strands felt as cold as the outdoors against his skin. Damp, too, as the snow melted.

He hugged her tighter, and she didn't resist. She slid her hands from his belly to his back, stroking lightly. Gentle was a turn-on for him.

Sure, he'd had urgent and ridiculously wild sex in his lifetime. Where clothes were ripped off and partners climaxed in the heat of the moment. That wasn't on his mind now. In his experience with women, he preferred sensual kisses and slow foreplay which aroused emotion.

He wanted a woman to desire him long after her orgasm.

His feelings for Abby were undefined, yet real. She'd saved his life after the accident. Being snowbound had brought them closer together. She was kind and genuine. Wholesome. He'd never met anyone quite like her.

In his mind, he knew he could walk away tomorrow; he'd helped her cope with her memories of her grandmother. She would now make it through Christmas, even if she were alone. But his heart pounded out a different message. For some reason the thought of leaving her tore at him. They had something special, he was sure of it. He wanted to see where it might lead. Time, however, dictated that he could not stay.

He knew his family needed him, too. Their holiday traditions stretched out over the next two weeks. He was expected to take part in the festivities. Even though it had been a year since his father's passing, he wanted to stand by his mother's side when she got really quiet. When she remembered Christmases past with his dad. Lander's responsibilities were many, he knew, and he wasn't a man to take them lightly.

He decided not to worry about his departure. Instead, he continued to hold Abby as if they had all the time in the world. In truth, this moment seemed unending. He couldn't control the weather. The sky remained gunmetal gray. Snowdrifts banked the windows. The cabin was without electricity. It was just the two of them.

He had no idea how long they stood together, just holding each other. He kissed her forehead, and she squeezed him tighter. Eventually, she was the first to move. She cleared her throat, trying to make light of what could've turned into a very sexy situation. It almost did when she ran her hand along his bare side, making him want her. Tipping back her head, she said, "You need the ice bag."

He did and he didn't. He'd rather hug Abby.

She had other ideas, however. Stepping back, she retrieved the bag from the three-legged table. Passed it to him. She then shrugged off her jacket and hung it up. Her cheeks were still pink from the cold. She swung her arms at her sides, unsure as to what should come next.

"We have a few more ornaments and tinsel to put on the tree," she finally said.

"No problem, Abs, I'll do it," he said, holding his ribs.

She shook her head, wiggled her foot. "My toe feels fine. You sit and ice your side and I'll hang the rest."

He let her do so. He was pleased she'd made the offer. Her willingness to take part in decorating the tree was a positive step forward. He crossed to the couch, where he immediately noticed that Tennyson had moved from the chair to take over the center cushion, king-of-the-hill style. Tenn curled in a ball beneath the unfinished quilt. Lander lowered himself at the far end. The tip of the cat's tail twitched, but he didn't come out and visit.

Lander watched as Abby bent over one of the boxes, going shoulders deep, her bottom raised. Didn't she know what she was doing to him? She had a very sweet ass, he thought. Round and firm. Her face was flushed when she straightened. She held up a small, brown-painted Dixie cup with googly eyes, white antlers, and whiskers.

"My reindeer," she said, smiling.

Lander narrowed his eyes on the decoration. "Whiskers, Abs?" he asked.

"My teacher, Mrs. Cleary, instructed the class to make reindeer ornaments, but I wanted to do a cat for Tennyson," she explained. "We compromised."

Lander shook his head, chuckled. "You're such a rebel, Abby."

"Not so much a rebel, but I can be stubborn at times."

He nodded. A somber thought hit him. If it wasn't for her stubbornness, he wouldn't be sitting here now by a warm fire. He could just as easily have frozen, possibly died, in his crashed car. Thank God she'd found him.

He watched as she set the ornament on the coffee table between them then dived back into the box. She soon showed off two more elementary school projects. "My snowflakes have seen better days," she noted, disappointed.

The construction paper had yellowed and there were several tears along the edges. "Perhaps using some Scotch tape would hold them together for another year," he suggested.

She crossed to the three-legged table, pulled out a drawer, and located a tape dispenser. She worked quietly for several minutes. She then turned back to him, seemingly pleased by the results. "Flakes for one more year," she said.

Back at the box, she drew out a handful of pipe-cleaner candy canes. Red ones were twisted with white and an assortment of small shiny beads decorated the crook at the tops. Her expression softened. "I loved making these," she said on a sigh. "Mrs. Cleary let me stay in class and miss recess to twist and bead to my heart's content."

She paused, counted the candy canes in her hand. "Seventeen," she said. "Originally there were twenty-four. A few got lost over the years."

"Candy canes are known to have legs," he joked.

"Socks run away in the dryer."

She walked to the tree and began hanging her childhood ornaments. Happy memories, Lander thought, as she stretched, but couldn't quite reach the upper branches. He'd like to help but he couldn't go high either. His side pained him with each pull of his muscles.

"I'll decorate the top if you have a step stool," he offered.

She placed the last of the ornaments on the tree, and then stepped back. She admired the evergreen from several angles. "It's perfect as it is," she finally said.

Dipping her head, she sounded sad when she added, "Last year I accidentally dropped our prized porcelain angel that topped the tree. My heart broke into more pieces than the angel. Gram was forgiving. Comforting me in that special way of hers. She convinced me not to worry, that she was hoping to shop and find a similar one, but she never found the time."

Lander rubbed the back of his neck, thoughtful. "I let my mother's favorite crystal star slip through my fingers a year ago," he said.

Abby's eyes rounded. "No, not you, too?"

"Yes, me too. I was on a ladder, holding the ornament by the metal hook. The hook loosened and the star fell, smashing to the floor in a hundred pieces." He grimaced. "The sound of breaking crystal stays with a man."

"Did you buy her a new one?" Abby asked, curious.

He shook his head. "The star was one of a kind and a gift from my father. It was irreplaceable. I knew my mom was crushed, seeing as how tightly she was holding on to every memory of him."

Tennyson took that moment to peek out from under the quilt beside Lander. The calico head-butted Lander's thigh, making him smile. The old boy wanted to be petted. Lander obliged.

"Your mother must have loved your father very much," Abby said with a catch in her voice. As if that sentiment tugged at her heart.

"My parents were deeply in love." He grew reminiscent. "My father was all business most days, but when it came close to Christmas, he became Santa Claus. He was a man who chose the perfect present for each family member. Making a list ole Saint Nick would envy, my dad bought the gifts early and hid them in the closet in the guest bedroom."

Abby grinned. "You knew about his hiding place?"

"Only by accident," Lander confessed. "I was sixteen and happened to be walking down the upper hallway when I saw my dad dart into the extra bedroom. He was carrying shopping bags. Big bags with red bows hanging out over the sides. He hadn't expected anyone to be home. My mother was at an organizational meeting and my sister had stayed after school for gymnastics. I had a football meeting but no practice, so I decided to come home afterward."

He released a slow breath. "I kept quiet, peeked around the door, and caught my father stashing wrapped Christmas gifts in the guest closet. Each one was decorated with a unique holiday flare. Striped foil paper, gold wrapping, and an antique red velvet box for my mom. My dad had a smile on his face. He looked so pleased with himself. I backed up, kept his secret."

He paused, then went on to say, "Because I knew he purchased early gifts, I prayed he had already bought something for my mother before he passed away. While my mother swept up the glass, I climbed down the ladder and headed for the guest room closet."

"Were there gifts?" Abby barely breathed the words.

He nodded, grinned, and said, "I found lots of presents inside the closet. Those meant for my mother were on the top shelf. I gathered them all."

He scrubbed his knuckles along his jaw. "Returning downstairs, I asked my mom to sit on the sofa in the living room. There, one by one, she opened my dad's gifts to her, each time her eyes tearing up. She celebrated their

Christmas several days early. In one of the gift bags was a small, clear crystal gift box topped by a red crystal bow dusted with gold. My father's card to her read: *I want you to have a gift every day of your life."*

He looked at Abby and saw the same emotion on her face that he felt in his heart. Her eyes were watery and she bit down on her bottom lip. She was equally touched by his father's gift to his mother as he had been. Abby understood the depth of his parents' love for each other.

"Our family Christmas turned out as good as it was going to get without my dad," Lander added, catching his breath. "At least my mother had a gift from him that would last a lifetime."

"Your dad knew your mom well," Abby slowly said.

"They did most everything together," he mused. "They had their own lives during the day, but come six o'clock, they were inseparable. Weekends, they were one person."

"Sounds very romantic," she said. Her voice was low; her expression thoughtful.

"They believed in commitment," he said, wondering why in the world he felt compelled to tell her that. She brought out emotions in him he'd never shared with anyone. "They didn't take each other for granted."

"That's how a marriage should be," she agreed.

He liked her way of thinking. Lightening the mood, he teased her, "Ever been in love, Abby?"

"Does ninth grade count?" she asked, returning to one of the boxes and removing the dark green flannel Christmas tree skirt. "If so, then his name was Jimmy Mayer. Smartest boy in my class."

She'd surprised him with her answer. "You like brainiacs?"

She spread the skirt around the base of the tree before answering, "Looks can fade, but smart never gets old."

So, she found intelligence sexy. "I graduated from high

school with honors," he said, trying to sound matter-of-fact, "then went on to college and graduate school."

His neck heated. What a stupid thing for a grown man to say. He sounded as if he were trying to compete with a ninth grader. Which, in truth, he had been. Pretty lame, he decided.

She glanced his way, and winked at him. "Handsome and brainy, you're quite a catch, Lander."

So he'd been told by many women long before Abby. But hearing her say the words had impact. She wouldn't compliment him simply to get his attention. Or initiate a date. Not this lady. Abby with the electric hair and sore toe was on her hands and knees smoothing out the flannel skirt and not trying to impress him. He liked that about her.

She'd just finished arranging the skirt when Tennyson got his second wind. Seeking attention, he crawled out from under the quilt and moved toward Abby as fast as his eighteen-year-old body would allow.

She saw him coming and stuck her hand under one corner of the skirt. She wiggled her fingers from beneath like a sock puppet. Tenn went cat crazy. He played like a kitten, attacking her hand and meowing with each pounce.

Abby laughed, and then looked at Lander. "Tennyson is playful today," she said. "He's got Christmas spirit."

He loved seeing her like this. She'd grown more relaxed over the course of the morning, Lander noted. The sleigh bells were hung and the tree was fully decorated, all but a few branches.

"Now what?" he asked from the sofa.

She made her decision. "You sit still and I'll hang the tinsel."

Tennyson had grown tired of chasing Abby's fingers, so he settled on the Christmas tree skirt and immediately went back to sleep. The cat could snore.

"Interesting tinsel," he said when she located a flat box. "It shimmers. I've never seen anything like it."

"Austrian tinsel," she told him. "The individual pieces are thin, made of metal, and eighteen inches long."

He noticed she'd started to hobble on her way back to the tree, favoring her right foot. She needed to get off her feet, as much as he needed to ice his side. They were recovering together.

Still, he couldn't deny her extra effort was worth it. The sparkling tinsel brought the tree to life. It became a bright, glittery magical thing. Once the electricity returned, the bubble lights would round out the decorations. Here stood one eclectic, vintage tree, he thought. Every ornament reflected Abby and her family. He hoped to add a few more memories to her life before he left for Philadelphia.

He chuckled when she drew back her arm and tossed the last pieces of tinsel toward the very top. They managed to catch on the branches, streaming down and covering the major gaps.

"Looks good," he said.

"I think so, too." She stood back then, appraising their efforts. "We did a good job, Lander."

We. He liked being included in her Christmas.

Yet, for all her enthusiasm, she looked a little sad. As if the enormity of the holiday rested on her shoulders. He didn't want her to slip back into her sorrow.

"What's left to do?" he asked, doing a visual sweep of the area. The living room was taking shape, appearing very festive.

She glanced at him, her gaze distant, as if she had been in her own world. "We need to unpack the musical snow globes, an assortment of candles, and the big Christmas stocking."

Big was an understatement.

Somehow, Lander wasn't surprised when Abby withdrew from one of the boxes a long, *long,* red knitted stocking decorated with a giraffe. She unfolded it slowly; he swore it stretched over six feet. He wondered about the giraffe design and why it wasn't Rudolph the red-nosed reindeer or a holiday moose.

"Where does it go?" he asked, setting aside his ice bag, then rising from the sofa to help her.

"Traditionally we hang it on the wall to the left of the fireplace," she said.

They crossed there together. She smiled as he reached up and attached the stocking to two large clip-hooks. "My grandmother knitted the stocking when I was ten," Abby said, running her hand across the top. "I had a fascination with giraffes that year. Gram asked me what animal I wanted on the stocking. She never blinked an eye when I told her. She purchased yellow and brown yarn and went with my choice."

Lander wrapped his arm about her shoulders and hugged her to him. "There's nothing wrong with a Christmas giraffe," he said, appreciating Abby's creative mind.

She leaned against him, all relaxed and warm, as if they'd spent a lifetime together. When in actuality it had only been one day. Time froze on the mountain during a blizzard, he thought. Closeness connected two people in a cabin buried in snow. Comfort came in liking the person he was with.

And he liked Abby a lot. He felt things for her that couldn't be explained. Sometimes the indefinable was the strongest emotion. Their connection seemed right to him.

He pressed a light kiss to her forehead, then asked, "Shall we do the snow globes next?"

She trembled a little, surprised by his quick kiss, he imagined, but was obviously pleased. She smiled at him and said, "The globes are much easier to handle than the stocking."

"Good to know."

They each unwrapped three large globes, then carried them to the mantle. "Any particular placement?" he asked, remembering how she'd teased him, requesting he move around the lead figurines. He wanted to get the globes right the first time.

"The white snow owl goes to the far right; the Christmas village next to it," she said, thinking. "The snowman and Santa Claus are always in the middle. We go to the left with the Disney characters glitter dome and the gingerbread man."

"Oh, yes, the gingerbread man . . ." His voice trailed off with the image of the peppermint-pecker-packing cookies. That wasn't his best memory. He happened to notice Abby's pained expression before she blew out a breath. Something seemed to be bothering her. But only for a moment.

She touched his arm once the globes were placed. Smiling now. So he didn't pursue the issue. "Close your eyes and listen," she requested. There was lightness to her voice, hinting of laughter.

Lander did as she asked. The room grew still, the silence soon broken by cranking and winding. He couldn't resist squinting when—

"No peeking," Abby said.

He shut his eyes tight. In a matter of seconds, an eclectic mix of holiday music brought merriment to the living room. He blinked, stared. Abby had wound all six globes, and a blend of "Frosty the Snowman," "Winter Wonderland," "Here Comes Santa Claus," "Jingle Bells," "Holly Jolly Christmas," and "Rockin' Around the Christmas Tree" combined for an interesting musical arrangement. Crazy and fun, the cacophony of sounds would fill his head for days to come.

They listened until the snow globes wound down. He watched as Abby skimmed her fingers over each one, like a mother patting each of her children's heads for a job well done. "A silly tradition to play them all at one time, but one I started years ago. Gram never complained about the music."

Lander rubbed his ears, which continued to ring. "Your grandmother had the patience of a saint."

Her eyes misted. "Yes, she did."

Once again he tucked her close. She slipped her arms about his waist as naturally as a wife would. She rested her head on his shoulder. He liked feeling the gentle rise and fall of her chest; the way she fit so nicely between his widened thighs. They stood together for a long time. So long, he swore he heard heavy breathing that wasn't all that musical.

Had she fallen asleep? "Are you snoring?" he finally asked, curious.

She tilted back her head, smiled. "Tennyson is snoring, not me," she said, releasing him. "The deeper he sleeps, the louder he snores. When his paws are moving, he's chasing mice."

Lander lifted his brows. At that moment the cat sounded like a lion.

"Let's unpack the candles now," she proposed. "I set them down on all the tables."

"Do you light them all at the same time, too?" he had to ask.

She scrunched her nose. "The scents would be over-powering and you couldn't enjoy their uniqueness. They're beautiful individually."

He inhaled a pale-blue pillar candle before he placed it on the coffee table. "White Ice," he said, noting the name. "Smells cold, like the outdoors."

She passed him a round candle, then said, "Burnt Vanilla Frost."

He liked that scent, too. Once the candles were situated

throughout the room, Lander returned to the couch and made a furniture adjustment. Not wanting to hurt his ribs further, he carefully pushed the overstuffed chair to the side, then angled the sofa directly toward the Christmas tree. He liked the view.

"The tree could use some presents." He spoke his thought out loud.

Abby caught her breath; put her hand over her heart. She looked like she'd just seen the Ghost of Christmas Past.

What had he said to cloud her eyes? To cause her to bite down on her lower lip? To make her shoulders slump?

"Abs?" he prodded, needing her to talk to him.

"I'm okay, Lander," she said on a sigh. "There are going to be moments like this when memories hit me hard. Your mention of gifts did just that."

"I'm sorry." And he meant it.

"It's not your fault. You can't predict how I'm going to feel or react, so don't try to soft coat the holiday," she said, breathing easier. "I'd ordered several boxes of my grandmother's favorite candy before she passed. When they were delivered, I didn't have the heart to give them away, so I stacked them at the back of the pantry. Out of sight, out of mind."

He wanted nothing more than to take her hand and squeeze it. To tell her everything would be all right. Instead he waited for her to catch her breath before he asked, "What kind of candy?" He had the occasional sweet tooth. Perhaps they could celebrate and share a box.

Her eyes brightened. "The best homemade candy from the Vermont General Store," she said. "There's cherry divinity, marzipan fruits, almond buttercrunch, and a tin of old-fashioned hard candy."

"I'm sure your grandmother would've been pleased with your selections," he said.

She looked at him thoughtfully. "I might wrap up a box and give it to you."

"That would hardly be a surprise, Abby, as you've already told me what I'd be getting."

For some reason that struck her as funny. She laughed until tears trailed from her eyes. He crossed to her and brushed them away with his thumb. "By the way, I do like almond buttercrunch."

She nodded. "Good to know."

He enjoyed their closeness. How she teased him and made him feel at ease. Her scent was warm and womanly. He breathed in a hint of spice and sentiment, knowing it wasn't just friendship he wanted from her. He wanted to kiss her and feel her tremble under his touch.

He appreciated the way she looked at him, wearing her heart on her sleeve, as if she knew him better than he knew himself. And she liked what she saw. "Come sit with me," he suggested, taking her hand and leading her back to the couch. He settled on one end and she on the other. All he could hear was the old Swiss clock ticking, reminding him their time together wouldn't last forever.

Lander swallowed hard. It wouldn't be easy to leave Pine Mountain. And Abby. She inspired him. Knowing her had brought back his own love for the holidays. No matter how crazy it was, he was convinced they had something together. He just needed more time. That time would melt away with the flicker of electricity and warming sunshine.

"We've accomplished a lot this morning," she mused, her smile soft, her eyes beaming. "The living room is very merry. Gram would definitely approve."

"How about you?" he asked, crossing one ankle over his knee. Getting comfortable. "Are you feeling the Christmas spirit?"

"More and more," she admitted, reaching out and touching his forearm. Her look was wistful and grateful. "Thank you for being patient with me, and for making this work. Had you not dragged in the tree, it would've died a slow death in the garage. The needles would've fallen off and I would have hauled the bare branches into the woods."

"The evergreen will live to see another day."

She looked at him then, her expression open. "You've given me a great memory, Lander. You're a good man."

Her words meant a lot to him. The women in his life politely thanked him for dinner and the theater. Or a long weekend getaway. Abby's appreciation came from her heart. She would now survive Christmas.

The corners of his mouth curved when he admitted, "There are a few things I like about you, too, Abs."

"Name one." She blushed, embarrassed at seeking his praise.

"I can name several," he said. "You're beautiful, generous, and kind. You love animals. You drag strangers from vehicles after a crash. You can cook over a fire. I'm fond of the way your hair spikes with static electricity. You're open and honest—"

She visibly flinched. "I'm honest?"

"Truth is important to me always."

She went suddenly still. The look on her face stunned him, as if she'd been caught doing something she shouldn't be doing. And regretted it deeply.

He had no idea what was behind her silence. "Abby?" he pressed.

She averted her gaze and stared into the fire. Her hands were clasped in her lap, so tightly her knuckles turned white. She'd crossed her ankles. She appeared to distance herself from him.

Concerned by her behavior, he moved down the couch toward her. "Talk to me," he requested.

"Confess to you is more like it." Her voice was tight, barely above a whisper.

"Confess what?" She confused him.

"I caused your car accident."

He ran one hand down his face. "That's impossible," he assured her. My God, the woman had saved his life. This was the last thing he expected to hear. "I got distracted by the box of gingerbread men with the peppermint-stick penises. I stared at them too long. It had nothing to do with you."

"It had everything to do with me, Lander," she said on a sigh. She looked so distraught, so unhappy, that he reached out to hold her. She slumped against his chest; buried her face against his shoulder. He felt her mouth move and he listened closely, never expecting her to say "I'm the erotic gingerbread baker."

Chapter 4

"**Y**ou bake X-rated cookies?" Lander sounded both surprised and amused. *And,* if Abby read him correctly, the man was also turned on. He curved his hands over her shoulders and set her gently away from him. "Wholesome Abby from Pine Mountain has a naughty side?" he asked with a chuckle in his voice.

She found it difficult to speak. "Naughty when it comes to my gingerbread men," she admitted.

He tilted his head and narrowed his eyes, studying her. "Naughty looks attractive on you," he said.

She breathed a little easier.

"Is your baking a hobby or a business?" He was curious. "Do you cook your erotic treats naked or wear a short holiday apron?"

He was teasing her now, and she didn't mind in the least. "It's a seasonal mail-order business," she told him without embarrassment. "I was testing the waters this Christmas. I have a website, but it's not public knowledge here in town."

He raised an eyebrow. "Pine Mountain is conservative?"

"Somewhat so," she confirmed. "You wouldn't find my G-men in the storefront window at the local bakery."

Lander grinned. "Your cookies are for those eighteen and older."

"You could say that." She sighed, then continued with, "I loved my grandmother's old-fashioned gingerbread cookies as a kid. They soothed my soul. After Gram passed away, I baked a batch and, in the process, decided to take them in another direction. Making them anatomically correct. I showed them to my friends Clara and Lily. They encouraged me to sell them. Discreetly, of course."

"Do you ever make gingerbread women?" he wanted to know.

"I could," she said, "but all my requests this year have been for men. I have a large order to bake for a bachelorette party in Las Vegas as soon as the electricity returns."

"Interesting . . ." was all he said.

She waited for his further reaction, for him to circle around and chastise her. To be mad at her. Or even disappointed. Instead his eyes darkened, and he looked at her in a way that warmed her belly. His smile came slow and lazy. And far too sexy. His lips were distracting.

"Let me ease your mind," he said, breaking the tension between them. "I was hungry when I left the community center, my stomach was growling. The road was icy and it was snowing heavily. I opened the box I'd bought at the cookie swap. I have to admit that seeing the X-rated gingerbread men all lined up in a row startled me. I stared too long. My car hit an icy patch and I couldn't correct the skid."

"I'm so sorry," she whispered, her voice barely audible.

He dropped a light kiss on her brow. "Who knows, I might've been as easily diverted by rocky-road fudge or marshmallow drops."

That brought a thankful smile to her lips. He was trying to make her feel better. She was grateful to him for not making fun of her or her attempt to make a business out of erotic cookies. It was no different in her mind from writing sexy books with sexy covers.

But her plain, brown cookie box had no warning cover, she reminded herself. No wonder the poor man had skidded down the side of a mountain when he'd opened it up. Nevertheless, she knew the truth and it wasn't pretty, no matter how hard he tried to dress it up. "Marshmallows aren't nearly as distracting as peppermint-stick penises."

"*Erect* peppermint penises," he emphasized.

Abby ran her hands down her thighs, mulling over what to do next. Lander was teasing her, not mad at her, maybe even liked her. A little. Should she encourage him? She might be letting herself in for a big disappointment, but she'd never know if she didn't try.

"How can I make it up to you?" she dared to ask him. "Ask for anything you wish, Lander."

He grew thoughtful; his gaze surveyed the scene, the holiday decorations, the tree. And her. Taking his sweet time. Slow to come to his decision. "You can kiss me," he said finally.

"A Christmas kiss?" she said, still cautious.

He nodded. "Why not? We can keep to holiday tradition. Do you have a sprig of mistletoe?"

She shook her head. "No mistletoe."

"Holly berries would do."

"No holly either."

"Work with me, Abby." He nudged her with his elbow. "What comes close?"

"I have wilted parsley in the refrigerator," she said. Now she was stalling, but just the thought of him kissing her sent goose bumps up and down her arms. The anticipation was enough to make her pulse quicken.

"At least it's green," he said.

She touched his hand. It would be amazing to kiss this

man. "Trust me, Lander, we don't need a vegetable hanging over our heads for us to kiss."

He twined his fingers with hers. "There's something I want to say first, and it needs to be said. I'm not feeding you a line, Abby," he added. "We've only just met, but I somehow feel like I know you."

She understood and wanted to tell him so. Surprisingly, her shyness left her, and for the first time in her life, she wasn't embarrassed to reveal what a man meant to her. "I feel the same way, Lander. It's not the length of time you know a person, but the depth of the connection."

"We have a strong bond between us," he added. "We're both survivors. I don't just mean the accident and you saving my life. We made the decision to carry on with our lives, whether it's our families' Christmas traditions or keeping alive the spirit of those we've lost."

He paused, appearing to give a great deal of thought to his next words. "This may sound crazy, but a part of me believes my father and your grandmother brought us together."

His thought didn't sound silly to her at all. Abby had the strangest feeling he was right. "It's a distinct possibility," she said softly. Gram would've liked Lander as much as Abby did.

He squeezed her hand. "Make a memory with me, Abby?"

Her heart quickened. "That we can do."

She initiated their first kiss. And she didn't hold back. She wanted to leave her imprint on his heart. From the first touch of their lips, he let her do what she would with him. He had a firm mouth that softened against hers. She stretched out each second, kissing him slowly and appreciatively. Loving the fact he responded with intimate ease.

Her heart sighed softly. Who knew closed-mouth kisses could be so romantic? she thought. They definitely were amazing. She cradled his chin in her palms, angled her head left, then right, then kissed him full-on. They bumped foreheads and noses, and he smiled against her mouth. His stubble rasped like sandpaper against the sensitive skin of her cheek. Stimulating and arousing. The scrape had her shifting on the sofa. Fidgety and stirring. Her breasts grew heavy and heat spread between her thighs.

Lander soon participated in their foreplay. He nipped one corner of her mouth. Bit down on her bottom lip. Then traced the crease between the two with his tongue. A craving rose within her, escaping her lips on a gentle moan. She longed for this man. To crush her breasts against his hard chest, to rub her hands over his shoulders. To feel his hot breath at the base of her throat.

Her body liquefied long before he encircled her in his arms. Their hips bumped, and their thighs grafted. He drew her knee over his leg, positioning her so he could stroke her lower spine, her butt, and the back of her thighs. She shivered, sensitive to his touch.

She responded in kind, curving her fingers over his biceps, and clutching his shirt in her fists. His front pocket bunched. She wished she could climb into his pocket and stay close to his heart long after he'd gone. Snuggle up and let him take her with him wherever he went. Where that was, she couldn't imagine. She refused to think about it, not now anyway. Especially when she had him all to herself. She lived in the heated joy of their moment.

Leisurely, masterfully, he ran his tongue inside her lower lip, then pushed deeper into her mouth, taking her breath away. She yielded and he explored. He glided his tongue over hers, time and time again. From sweet and tender to demanding surrender, his kisses stirred a sensual assault. He claimed her with experience and patience. And a growing intensity.

She wrapped her arms about his neck and leaned even

closer. He touched her then, a shifting glide of his hands over her shoulders, down her sides, then up and under her red waffle pullover. A delightful chill wiggled through her as the pads of his fingers played over her ribs. Unhooking her bra, he slid his hands underneath. Cupping her breasts, he thumbed her nipples. They crinkled in response. A sexual ache filled her.

She went full hands-on with Lander, too. Clothes were good, but naked was better. *Much* better. Her fingers had never moved as fast as they did now when she unbuttoned his white shirt, the wrinkled fabric cool to her touch. He helped her roll it off his shoulders, then drew her pullover over her head. The thin straps on her bra slid down her arms. Her breasts spilled from the lacy cups. She tossed her bra aside.

Returning to Lander, she rested unsteady hands over his well-toned chest. He was pure, potent masculinity. She smiled to herself when his pulse jumped a few beats against her palms. He was as turned on as she was.

She placed a kiss to his jaw.

He brushed her soft earlobe with his lips.

She bit his shoulder.

He flicked his tongue over the pale skin at her throat.

She nipped his shoulder. Then his left pec.

He licked between her breasts.

She laved his nipples.

Sensations fluttered her belly. Rocking her hips.

He shifted on the couch cushion, and she noticed his black slacks had tightened over his groin. His zipper now tented to accommodate his erection. That he was hard for her only heightened her pleasure. Dampening her panties.

A slight twist to the side, and he turned fully toward her. His dick pushed against her hip. She sensed his impatience, his eyes glazed with desire. She arched toward him, wanting to align herself with him.

Dipping his left shoulder, he lowered her to the sofa, only to pull back unexpectedly. He grimaced, grabbed his side, startling her. His breathing came hard and ragged, but no longer from arousal. That worried her. Sweat broke on his forehead and all color drained from his face. His expression was pained.

Abby crossed her arms over her bare breasts and blushed. "What's wrong?" she asked, concerned.

"My ribs," he murmured, his tone apologetic. "Bad positioning."

She felt awful. First, her G-men had sent him over a cliff, now their lovemaking had caused him pain. "We can stop—"

He shook his head, forced a grin. "Not on your life. I wanted you beneath me, Abby, but that's not going to work. There will be less stress on my ribs if you straddle me."

Straddle him. Her eyes widened. She rather liked the idea.

Lowering her arms, she boldly undid the button on his slacks and unzipped him, freeing his penis. She was awed by his size. The man was substantial. He lifted his hips off the cushion, and she slid down his pants before he could lend a hand.

Now sitting up straight, Lander had his own moves. He had her out of her black jeans in a heartbeat. Her cotton bikini panties were gone with a flick of his wrist.

She stared at him; he stared at her.

She swore the temperature in the room just got hotter.

They were both naked and breathing heavily once again.

"There are condoms in my wallet on the coffee table," he was quick to say before they went any further.

She nodded. The table was at arm's length. She passed his wallet to him.

He unfolded the leather, cracked and water-stained from

the accident. He located six foiled packets. He quickly stripped the seal on one and rolled on his protection.

He locked gazes with her. Lifted one brow. "Are you ready for us?" he asked.

"Very ready." *All her life ready.* She'd wanted him from the moment he'd walked into the community center, seeking directions. He was the handsomest man she'd ever laid eyes on. Knowing him as she did now, she also knew he was a person of compassion. They had many of the same values. Traditions. She more than liked him. Given time, she could fall in love with him.

Just looking at him naked turned her on. Every atom in her body sparked and responded to his nearness. Her hands shook when she slid her fingers through his hair, so crisp, thick, and dark. She traced his brow with her thumbs, then took a long moment to stare into his blue eyes, dilated from wanting her. That pleased her greatly.

She loved the arc of his cheekbones, the blade of his nose, and the strong line of his jaw. She admired his broad shoulders, the width of his bruised chest, and the symmetrical line of his ribs. He had a flat abdomen. And jutting cock. She circled him with her hand. The heated look in his eyes told her that her loving gesture pleased him. A lot.

Deliberately slow, she teased him with squeezing, releasing, strokes. His gaze narrowed, and he breathed in sharply. The tangible tightening of his entire body left her liquid.

Rising on her knees, she settled on his groin. The warm flesh of his thighs grazed her bottom. Tickling her. Her legs parted, and he ran his hands along the smooth inner skin. Back and forth, coming dangerously close to her most sensitive spot. Making her squirm.

"You have an amazing body," he said, appreciating her full breasts and rounded hips. He didn't seem to mind the slight softness of her stomach, which never seemed to flatten despite her fifty sit-ups each day.

Palming her bottom, he grazed the crease of her ass with his fingers. His grasp tightened, urging her on.

Anticipation touched them both.

Desire pooled in all the right places.

Their scents came together, a mating of his musk and pine and her cinnamon and vanilla.

Sex thickened the air.

She couldn't wait any longer. She splayed her hands on his shoulders, leaned forward, and took him inside her. Their contact drew a warm sexual heat from her. She grew restless.

Lander was restive, too. His mouth was hot and demanding when he again claimed her lips. She welcomed the intensity of his kiss, needing more of his mouth. More of his hands. More of him.

He gave her everything she wanted, and then some.

She became supersensitive. Her entire body sparked.

They went at it, hot and greedy. Desperate. Drawing breath from each other. Hers broke raspy and fast against his lips. His came hard and sharp.

She rolled her hips, and he slid his fingers between their bodies and rubbed her sex. He thrust more deeply, pulsing inside her like a heartbeat.

He drove her outside herself and into him.

The rhythm of their bodies in sexual sync.

Tension spiraled and they strained to reach completion. Her release came on a soul-shattering sigh.

His followed with a deep, guttural groan of satisfaction.

Timeless moments surrounded them. She kissed his chest right over his heart and felt it pound beneath her lips, steady and strong. He touched his lips to each of her cheeks and to the tip of her nose.

"That's a memory I'll never forget," he said, catching his breath.

"Me, neither," she sighed. *Never, ever.*

They remained together until their heartbeats slowed. Abby reveled in the afterglow, warm and protected in his arms. Her heart was happy; her body and soul content. In those moments the living room wrapped them in tradition and sentiment. Lander draped a quilt over her shoulders. The warmth of the fireplace kept them snug.

Forever crossed Abby's mind.

She wished with all her heart that time would stop and that Lander would linger long after the sun melted the snow on the mountain. But that was one Christmas wish no one could grant her.

She sighed shortly thereafter when Lander shifted beneath her. She slid off his lap and gave him some space so he could clean up and rid himself of his condom. Clutching the quilt to her breast, covering herself modestly, she said, "No running water, but you can grab a gallon of water and take a sponge bath."

"Bathe with me?" he asked casually, but there was an undertone in his voice that said his invitation promised more than just getting clean.

"I need to catch my breath," she said honestly. "But I will next time." The man had five condoms. She imagined what he could do with them.

"I'll hold you to that, Abby." He pushed off the couch and walked naked from the living room, a man who looked remarkably good in his skin. Wide shoulders. Tight ass. Muscular legs. Easy stride. If her lips weren't numb from kissing him, she would have whistled. Low and sexy. She heard him climb the stairs to the loft, and her heart warmed. She liked having a second person around the cabin. Lander filled it with his hearty laughter and eagerness to help her. Made her want to cook for him, watch sunsets from the top of the mountain, even pick up his dirty socks. It felt like a home again.

She glanced at the old Swiss clock on a side table near

the hearth. It was ten after twelve now. Over an hour had passed since they'd taken to the couch. She wished they could do it all over again. Every kiss, every pleasurable contraction, *everything*. It was the best seventy minutes of her life.

Lander had kissed, touched, and made love to her like no man before him. She hadn't had that many lovers, but those she'd had always raced to climax. She'd never felt a long-lasting emotional bond. Lander had seduced her with foreplay and feeling. As if he never wanted to let her go. He'd made her want him as much as he wanted her.

They'd both need stamina to make love a second time, she thought. Lunch would be nice, but she needed to wash up and change her clothes first. She rose, too, only to glance down on their discarded garments. What she saw tugged at her heartstrings. The arms of his white shirt were wrapped around her pullover, as if in a hug. Her jeans lay across the stretched out legs of his slacks. She smiled at how closely their clothes imitated their lovemaking.

She folded his clothes and placed them on the arm of the overstuffed chair. Collecting her bra, panties, and remaining items, she retreated to her bedroom. She set the clothes on her white hobnail bedspread, then turned and faced her closet. This called for something at-home casual, but sexy. But not *too* sexy. Foreplay with Lander was half the fun. She didn't want him so turned on that he went right to the main act. They'd be down to *no* condoms with snow still on the ground. Then what would they do?

Flipping through the hangers, she selected a pale-blue long-sleeved T-shirt with a Three Wise Women design on the front and a pair of navy leggings. She snagged a pair of socks from her dresser drawer, then wiggled her toe. Sex had taken her mind off its soreness, but it remained swollen.

After freshening up in the bathroom, she returned to the

kitchen a moment before Lander. Her smile broke when she set eyes on him in her old, faded plaid robe which she'd left hanging on a hook on the back of the bathroom door. The blue-and-white flannel strained across his shoulders, and the hem hit him at mid-thigh. Loosely tied at his waist, her housecoat gapped over his chest and at his groin. He revealed more than he covered. A shadow of his sex flashed with each footstep. Still, he looked amazing.

"I hope you don't mind that I borrowed your robe," he said, coming toward her. His hair was damp, yet he hadn't shaved. He smelled of almond soap and man. He pressed a light kiss to her lips; the scent of mint toothpaste was on his breath.

"I like you in plaid," she said. "The blue matches your eyes."

He grinned. "That's what I was going for."

"How about a light lunch?" she suggested.

"Don't go to a lot of trouble, Abs."

"Cooking from scratch isn't an option without electricity," she stated, "but the pantry is stocked with canned goods. I'll heat up some soup. Your choice: chicken noodle, tomato basil, minestrone, or black bean. I have a month's worth of oyster crackers."

"Chicken noodle works for me," he said.

It worked for her, too. "My grandmother made the best homemade soups," she reminisced, poking through her kitchen drawer, looking for an old-fashioned can opener. "Chicken noodle was a winter staple. Fat noodles and chunks of chicken in a tasty broth. I could eat it three times a day."

Lander looked toward the fireplace, then said, "The fire is low. Do you want me to add more wood?"

"Low flames are best when I'm cooking," she told

him, grabbing the opener from the back of the drawer. It hadn't been used in years. "Just place another log in the hearth once the soup is ready."

She went to the pantry, collected three cans of soup and a dozen packets of oyster crackers. Lander was a big man; she figured he'd enjoy two servings. Their meal came together quickly. Within a short time they again sat side by side on the couch, spooning chicken noodle soup piled high with round crackers from large ceramic bowls.

"I'll make s'mores for dessert," she offered.

His smile came slowly. "I haven't had a s'more since I was twelve."

"I had one last week," she confessed, not wanting to tell him she'd been sad and in need of comfort food. "It made me feel like a kid again."

"I'm in," he said. "You make the s'mores and I'll wash the soup bowls."

She liked that he shared in the chores, however simple they might be. He didn't stick up his nose at doing dishes and act like it was women's work. She soon returned to the kitchen. Opening a top cupboard door, she rummaged inside, pushing aside cans and pasta. What if she didn't have any chocolate left? Or the marshmallows were stale? She didn't have the heart to disappoint him.

The s'mores gods were on her side. She found a box of graham crackers, a bag of marshmallows, and two Hershey's candy bars on the shelf. She went on to layer the ingredients, then wrapped each one in aluminum foil. She cooked the s'mores on a flat cast-iron frying pan over the diminishing flames.

"Grab two paper plates," she called to Lander once the scent of chocolate permeated the foil. It smelled so good.

Sticky, gooey, delicious. They folded back the wrap and let their desserts cool. Finally, Lander couldn't wait any longer and dived in. "You have marshmallow lips." She laughed at him once he'd polished off his s'more.

"You have graham cracker crumbs on your chin," he tossed back at her.

Before she could swipe off the crumbs, he leaned in and licked them away, then kissed her with his marshmallow mouth. Decadent sweetness, Abby thought, as he penetrated her lips with his chocolaty tongue. She decided, right then and there, that s'mores were her new favorite dessert. She wished Lander would be around to enjoy them with her all winter long.

Taking a breather, they tossed their paper plates on the coffee table and, a second later, he drew her so close she felt at one with him. His robe gapped across his groin and his sex poked through the flannel panels. He was fully erect. A shift of each shoulder and he'd rid himself of the robe. She liked him in nothing but skin.

"You wear way too many clothes," he told her, drawing her long-sleeved T-shirt over her head. Her navy leggings disappeared next. "No underwear this time," he said. "I like your sense of freedom."

"I noticed you don't wear boxers or briefs either."

"Never have. They're too confining."

"We're both naked now."

He nipped the corner of her mouth. Her chin. The soft skin near her ear. "Let's take advantage of a second condom. Maybe even a third."

Abby found her way onto his lap, straddled him, and stayed there all afternoon. Until twilight stole the late afternoon haze from the day and darkness patterned the windowpanes. She rose only once, wrapping herself in the quilt, to light a candle; the air wafted with the cool, calming scent of White Ice.

Walking toward the window, she stared out into the

night. It was then she realized the wind had died. The snow had stopped falling. A chill that had nothing to do with winter invaded her. Her heart slowed, and a hint of sadness touched her. She was sated, tired, and wanted to sleep, yet she was afraid to close her eyes. Not wanting to wake to sunlight, electricity, and the deep rumble of snow plows.

She said nothing to Lander about what she saw outside. Instead she snuggled against his side and warmed herself with his body heat, wanting to keep him with her a little while longer.

Lander woke with a yawn and a stretch. He'd fallen asleep sitting on the couch. Cuddled by his side, Abby embraced him with her womanly warmth. They shared her grandmother's unfinished quilt. One end covered his groin, and the other concealed her breasts and belly.

She looked so peaceful, he thought. And so perfect for him. Her eyelashes were long and light brown. Her smooth skin pinkened with a morning blush. Her lips were slightly parted, and her breath puffed over his heart. He smiled over her static hair. So spiky, yet so silky.

All in all, this woman did it for him.

He wanted her in his life.

He would find a way to make her fit.

He sensed something was different in the light of day. He narrowed his gaze and looked around. Sunlight blinked through the deep snowdrifts outside the front window. The sky was a swirl of gray and blue. He listened intently, catching a noise that was barely a sound. Where was it coming from?

He finally located the soft gurgle. The string of bubble lights on the tree were now bubbling. He'd left the strand plugged in, so he would know when the electricity had been restored. The power must have come on during the night, sometime between their lovemaking and their need for sleep.

His stomach sank. Having the lights on moved up his departure date. Snow removal wouldn't be far behind, he assumed.

His time on the mountain was coming to a close.

He needed a private moment to put his life together again.

Cautiously, and not wanting to wake her, he slid off the sofa, then gently eased Abby down. He placed a pillow under her head and covered her with the quilt. She didn't move a muscle.

He reached for his pants on the arm of the overstuffed chair. He stepped into them, zipped and buttoned. His shirt came next. Pain splintered his side, and he knew he needed to see a doctor. That would come soon.

He picked up his cell phone off the coffee table and walked down the hallway, checking its reception. He finally got a signal at the back of the cabin. He found fifty texts from his mother and his sister. Their concern for his whereabouts and safety became more urgent with each message. Instead of texting, he gave his mother a call.

His mom's voice was faint, disjointed, sounding as if she were clear around the world and not ninety miles away.

She cried with relief upon hearing from him. He was brief and exact with his explanation; afraid he'd be cut off before he could finish telling her what had happened to him. He promised to come home as quickly as he could make arrangements to do so. He then disconnected.

It was decision time, he thought. He hated to leave Abby, but he had family commitments. Commitments made a year in advance. He couldn't immediately take Abby with him, but perhaps she could follow at a later date. He had a lot to figure out. He didn't want to leave her for long.

A head bump to his calf lowered his gaze to Tennyson. Lander would bet the old boy was hungry. Tenn had slept the afternoon and night away on the tree skirt. Lander figured the flannel was warm.

"Hungry?" he asked the cat.

The calico's purring indicated food would be good.

They walked back to the kitchen with Tenn weaving between his feet. For an elderly cat, he was pretty fast moving when it came to his meals.

Lander located a can of shredded tuna and chicken. It had a pop-top and came off easily. He smiled; the cat sounded like a buzz saw. He put the food on a paper plate and Tenn dug in. He ate as if he hadn't seen food in a week. Apparently a long night's sleep had given him quite an appetite.

Lander hunkered down beside the calico. In a low voice, he said, "Take care of Abby while I'm gone, big guy. I like her a lot and don't want her feeling left behind."

Tenn paused in his eating, and gave Lander as reassuring a look as an eighteen-year-old scruffy cat could give. His whiskers twitched, and he returned to his breakfast.

Lander stood back up. Glancing around the kitchen, he decided it was his turn to make Abby breakfast. She had a toaster, and he found a half a loaf of rye in the breadbox. He then scooped Santa's Helper into her coffee maker. He found a selection of homemade jams and jellies in the cupboard. He went with blackberry preserves.

Once their meal was prepared, he carried two paper plates and two steaming mugs to the coffee table. The scent of coffee swirled on the air, and Abby blinked herself awake. She gave him a soft smile and said, "Breakfast on the couch, lucky me."

She sat up, but didn't bother to get dressed. Instead she tucked the quilt over her breasts and between her thighs. Lander passed her a cup of coffee, and then settled down beside her. He sipped along with her, his lips pursed. He'd yet to develop a taste for the strong brew.

Abby eyed the bubble lights. "I see the electricity's returned," she said between bites of toast. He heard the slight catch in her voice. They both knew he'd be on his way very soon.

"I have cell service," he told her.

"Let me try my phone." She retrieved her own cell off the coffee table and checked for messages. "I have a text from Shane Griffin from Grady's Garage. He's the man I called from the site of your accident." She paused, read on. "Shane has towed your Mercedes to his garage. He's assessed the damage. Sadly, your car is totaled." Her voice sounded sympathetic. "Once you contact him, he'll pick you up and drive you into town whenever you're ready to arrange transportation."

"I'll get with him this morning, but I won't leave until tomorrow," Lander decided. "I want to spend another day with you, Abby."

"You do?" She looked surprised, but pleased.

"I'm not ready to leave."

"I'm not ready for you to go, either."

He was glad she felt the same way. "How close is your nearest grocery store?" he asked.

"Two miles down the mountain," she said. "Ridgeway's General carries the basics."

He finished off his coffee, then asked, "Will the store have the ingredients to make your gingerbread men?"

Abby nodded. "It should. I have an order to fill for that bachelorette party in Las Vegas. I'd planned to start baking the moment I had electricity."

"How soon before the snow plows reach us?" he wanted to know.

"Lights are on, so I'm guessing a few hours. Snow removal is down to a science in Pine Mountain."

"Let's plan our day," he suggested. He was a man of organization. "A shower is in order, and I hope you'll join me."

"The water will be cold," she warned him. "The cabin has a large hot water tank. It won't warm immediately."

"We'll raise goose bumps together." She shivered at his thought. Sexual chills were good. A fast shower with Abby was better than any prolonged hot shower alone.

"After we clean up, I was going to challenge you to a game of Naked Scrabble while we wait for the snow plows."

"Naked Scrabble?" She nearly spewed her coffee.

He grinned. "Naked adds challenge to the game."

"I'm sure it will," she agreed. "Once the plows clear a path, I'll drive down to the store and pick up what we need. You're welcome to come with me, if you like."

Lander debated. "What about mountain gossip?" he asked. "I imagine word would spread if you were seen with an unknown man."

"You're worried about my reputation?" She was touched by his concern.

He ran his hand down his face. "What we've shared is between us, not anyone else," he said with conviction. "I don't want whispers to take away from our time together."

"I understand," she said, "although Shane already knows you're at my cabin. He's a good man, and wouldn't start or spread rumors."

"Let's fly under the town's radar as long as we can," he said. "You'll get the needed ingredients for the cookies, and I'll help you bake and decorate them." He raised a brow. "Any chance we could make a few gingerbread women?"

"For your eating pleasure?" she kidded him.

"I would never object to you munching on a G-man."

"Licking, Lander," she corrected, giving him a sexy smile. "It's the best way to savor a peppermint stick."

He was hard in a heartbeat.

She set her mug and plate back on the coffee table, then crooked her finger and said, "It's shower time."

She rose off the sofa, and he was right on her heels. In his hurry, he accidentally stepped on one corner of the quilt that she'd wrapped around her. The patterned fabric loosened and shimmied down her body. The sight of her curves made his sex throb and his testicles tighten.

She walked into her downstairs bathroom, and he was out of his clothes before she'd turned on the water. She shrieked when he tucked her close and lifted her into the shower.

The spray pierced them both, as if they were being stabbed by icicles. Perhaps a cold shower wasn't his greatest idea, he mused, seconds later as he watched Abby hop up and down, favoring her sore toe, and shivering.

The water sluiced over her shoulders and her nipples hardened. He was surprised his sex hadn't shrunk. He apparently wanted Abby, even if they froze together like two halves of a popsicle.

She threw her arms about him, as if his cold body could warm hers. He was afraid he wasn't giving off much heat. She didn't seem to mind.

"Raspberry crème is both shampoo and shower gel," she said, removing a bottle from the bath caddy and pouring a small amount onto an organic sponge.

She scrubbed him head to toe. She worked quickly but thoroughly, touching, stroking, before taking a long moment to admire his groin. How he stayed hard was beyond Lander. Her gaze was so hot that he swore the water had begun to heat.

Then it was his turn to touch her. He added a bit more raspberry crème to the sponge, then washed her every curve. She went from hopping on one foot to becoming perfectly still as he appreciated the soft slope of her shoulders, the fullness of her breasts, and the soapy slickness of her sex. He inserted one finger between her folds, and he felt her clench. It would take so very little to bring her to orgasm. But not here beneath a spray that was as cold as rolling naked in the snow.

He switched off the valve and they stepped from the shower. She trembled as he toweled her dry. He threw back his head and closed his eyes when she next rubbed him down. She spent an inordinately long time drying his penis.

With his own sexual purpose, he eased her back until her bottom bumped the countertop by the sink. He didn't have a condom, but he had other ways to please her.

He went down on one knee, and gazed up at her.

Her eyes were wide and full of want.

The pulse at the base of her throat was visibly fast. Her breathing was uneven.

A heightened pink stained her cheeks, the flush moving to her upper chest.

He felt her up and kissed her down. Her nipples peaked beneath the flick of his tongue. He kissed along her rib cage, over her hip bone, then went on to tongue her navel.

He moved between her legs, nibbling the inside of her thighs. He traced the tender skin nearest her sex, then slowly slid a finger inside her.

She was wet for him.

The temperature of her body rose, and he felt her woman's heat. He wanted to taste her. She stilled, then opened to him. He sucked, teased, and controlled her pleasure. She sighed, closed her eyes, and let him claim her.

"Lander," her voice shook on a panting whisper.

She curved her hands on the edge of the countertop, clung tightly, climbing toward her climax.

He clutched her hips. Tongued her even deeper.

She gave way, and came with satisfying force. Her moan

rose from deep within her. Her knees started to buckle, and she was suddenly boneless. Lander pushed to his feet, drew her close, and let her lean on him. She seemed to sift inside him, all the way to his soul.

Kissing her lightly on the forehead, he eventually asked, "How about that game of Naked Scrabble now?"

"Or I could satisfy you."

He gazed into her warm brown eyes and was amazed by the depth of emotion he felt for this woman. The simplicity of holding her satisfied him as much as having sex. His feelings for her were strong and powerful, and what he believed to be long lasting, yet only time would tell.

"Scrabble can be arousing," he said, contemplating the rules. "We can have our own point system with each word. A kiss for placing letters on Premium Squares. A touch for double or triple letter values. Sex for the winner."

Abby laughed at him. "We both win if sex is the final prize."

"Let's go win that orgasm." He took her hand, led her toward the living room.

Naked Scrabble was Lander's undoing. Abby's nudity was a total distraction. How could he form words when he couldn't think straight? Abby played well, racking up points, and running away with the game.

The time soon came when she let him know what she thought of his skills. Crossing her arms over her full breasts, she accused, "You're a smart man, Lander, but I'm wise to your moves. You added a *y* to 'hand,' when you could've gone with 'handsome,' 'handful,' 'handicap'. . ."

Busted, he inwardly grinned. She saw through him. He was letting her win by playing short, going with easy words while she went with the more difficult. She'd either kissed or touched him with every move. He'd never enjoyed Scrabble more.

He glanced at their scores, tallied on a yellow legal pad.

"You're so far ahead of me, I'll never catch up," he said, more than willing to have her win.

"Do you concede?" she asked. The cloth bag that held the tiles was empty. Abby had only one letter left while he sat with six. He cheated, sneaking a peek at her final tile. An *s*, which could be used anywhere on the board, while he sat with *f, j, x, y,* and *z.* "Ox" appeared his only word.

He held up his hands, palms out. "You win, Abs."

"I can have my way with you?"

"Any way you want me." He boxed the tiles and board.

She climbed onto his lap, fitted him with the last condom, and took him so slowly his nostrils flared and his jaw locked. The corners of his mouth pinched in pleasure and pain. He was barely able to draw breath.

She closed her eyes when he worked his hand between them. Stroking her until she reached the edge. He held her there until the heat of the moment overtook them both.

They dissolved in sensual satisfaction.

Abby snuggled with Lander as they came down from their sexual high. She straddled him still. Her cheek rested on his shoulder. Her gaze was shuttered. He breathed in the raspberry crème scent of her hair, then nuzzled her neck. He placed a kiss at the soft spot beneath her ear.

He glanced toward the fireplace, and found the flames burned low. He debated adding another log, but decided that between the two of them, they generated enough heat to stay warm. Together they raised the temperature in the room by ten degrees.

Tennyson had eaten, and found his way back to the flannel skirt beneath the Christmas tree. He now stretched out, comfortable and content. Lander liked hearing him snore.

He also enjoyed holding Abby. Her breasts pressed

against his chest, and their bellies brushed. He was still semi-erect and sliding out of her slowly. He would be ready to take her again in a matter of minutes. She gave him a permanent erection. Despite his lack of condoms, they could still be creative.

A moment later, a rumble shook the mountain like an earthquake. Abby sat up and listened intently. Sadness shone in her eyes for several seconds before she grabbed the quilt and drew it to her breast.

"Snow plows," she said, recognizing the sound. "The crew is running ahead of schedule."

She pushed up on her knees, and eased from his lap. Sliding off the sofa, she scooted down the hallway. "I'm getting dressed," she shot over her shoulder.

He pulled on his wrinkled and worn white shirt and black slacks. He walked to the window and watched as the two plows shoved the snow aside, clearing the road. The drifts rose ten feet high. One of the removal vehicles turned into Abby's driveway, forging space for her to back her SUV from the garage.

Lander stepped away from the window, preferring no one saw him. He didn't want any embarrassment to come to Abby. Should someone see him at her cabin, it would be natural to assume they'd done more than play Scrabble. He'd let her be the one to spin her own holiday tale. If she even chose to mention him.

She returned to the living room, dressed warmly to face the elements. She wore both a cream-colored sweater and a shearling vest. Her brown corduroys were loose and lived-in. He found her knee-high boots sexy.

She grabbed her winter jacket off the hook, then turned to him. "I need to thank the crew," she said. "I'll follow them down the mountain to the store."

She bit her bottom lip. "This might be a good time for you to call Shane Griffin at the garage." She gave him the mechanic's number from memory. Her voice caught on the last digit, as if saying it brought their time to an end. He felt much the same.

She came to him before she left. Rising on tiptoe, she kissed him full on the mouth. "Miss me while I'm gone?" she asked.

"I missed you the moment you left my lap," he said honestly.

She smiled, kissed him again, and was gone.

He heard the door open then close, and was relieved when her engine turned over. The garage door lifted, and he moved to the window and watched her drive away. The snow plows roared ahead of her. Her windshield wipers swished. He saw her wave, and he waved back. Her smile was small, forced.

His heart felt heavy. She would return with her baking supplies. They'd make erotic gingerbread men and women, then—what? Have a final night together before he headed out the next morning.

He hung his head. Time sifted through his fingers, faster now as his departure neared. He would be gone in twenty-four hours. The pain in his side seemed minimal compared to the ache about his heart. Abby had gotten to him.

He returned to the couch, waited out her return. Tennyson woke in the middle of a snore, startling himself. The calico padded across the floor, and attempted to jump onto the couch. Lander saw he wasn't going to make it, and gave Tenn a boost. The calico made himself at home, settling beside Lander, resting his head on Lander's knee.

For the first time, Lander noticed a small basket of magazines situated beneath the coffee table. He reached for a *People* magazine, fanned the pages, and got the Hollywood scoop. Abby Denton, he read her name off the address label. He peeled off the label and put it in his pocket, in case he needed her location at a later date.

He had one phone call he wanted to make before Abby returned. He took a deep breath and called Shane Griffin. The mechanic seemed to be a nice guy; accommodating, too. He offered to pick up Lander the following morning, so Abby wouldn't have to drive him into town. Lander agreed. He preferred to keep his relationship with Abby low-key. Until they became an official couple.

She showed up a short time later, and he met her at the side door to the garage. She was loaded down with groceries. He took three of the four paper bags from her.

"Did you buy out the store?" he asked, eyeing the contents.

"Ridgeway's was crowded," she told him. "People are digging out after the blizzard. I got roped into more than one conversation."

She paused, glanced at him, and grinned. "The owner of the store told me I had a 'holiday glow.' " She used air quotes.

"Blizzard sex will put color in your cheeks."

Abby blushed, but agreed. "I bought everything I needed for the gingerbread cookies," she said, as she unpacked the paper sacks. Once the first sack was empty, she dropped it on the floor.

Lander raised an eyebrow, and she explained, "A toy for Tennyson when he wakes up."

She moved about the kitchen now, locating a mixing bowl, measuring cups and spoons. "I'll put the recipe together, then set the dough in the refrigerator for two hours. Sometimes I leave it overnight, but since I have limited time, I'll need to bake and decorate today, then pack and mail the cookies in the morning."

"How can I help you, Abby?" he asked.

"I'll blend the ingredients, and you can search the pantry for anatomical enticements."

He rubbed the back of his neck. "Like peppermint sticks?"

"Those work, as would red licorice." She winked at him. "Be creative, Lander."

He found the pantry to be a minimart. He went item by item, imagining the perfect combinations. His arms were weighted down with jars and cans by the time he returned. He laid out everything he'd chosen on the round dining room table. He pulled out a chair, sat, and watched Abby translate her grandmother's old-fashioned recipe into erotic gingerbread men.

He rested his elbows on the table top, and asked, "Have you always wanted to bake?" He was curious.

She took time with her answer. "Baking soothes me, and each recipe has a memory attached to it," she said with feeling. "Gram's gingerbread was always my favorite. Her double-chocolate-chip cookies were like a crooked finger, beckoning me home as soon as I'd step off the school bus. Her angel food cake was pure heaven."

Lander wished he'd had the opportunity to meet Ada, though he felt he knew her through Abby. Memories kept one's spirit alive. Ada would always be a part of the cabin.

The sound of the electric hand mixer woke Tennyson. He padded across the living room to the kitchen. The paper sack caught his eye, and he slunk low. He poked his head inside the opening, then retreated. His meow was fierce as he extended his claws and attacked the sack, ripping it to shreds.

Once Tenn had destroyed the sack beyond recognition, Abby grabbed a broom and dust pan from a narrow closet and swept up the mess. "He had fun," she said, humor in her voice. "He used up most of his energy, too. Chances are good he'll sleep again."

Her prediction was correct. The calico lay down by

Lander's feet and twitched his nose. Vanilla, brown sugar, and molasses sweetened the air. A few more ingredients were added, and the dough was soon ready to refrigerate. She then whipped up three flavors of royal frosting. By that time, Tennyson again snored.

She turned to Lander and smiled. An easy smile of accomplishment. She blew her bangs out of her eyes. Wiped her forehead with the back of her hand. A hint of flour powdered the sleeve on her sweater, and a bit of brown sugar speckled her wrist.

This was her domain, he realized. She was relaxed and happy as she loaded the dishwasher. He liked the sway of her hips when she wiped down the countertop. Should her business take off as she hoped, she would need a much bigger kitchen. He wished her every success.

"What's on your Christmas list?" he asked her.

She crossed to where he sat, pulled out a chair, and joined him at the table. "I had only one wish," she said on a sigh. "The Historical Society of Philadelphia offers a Christmas Eve tour through the mansions on Chestnut Hill each year. Before Gram passed away, we'd written to the sponsors and requested an invitation. We weren't selected."

Lander was familiar with the holiday tour. He'd seen it advertised. Those on Chestnut Hill decorated lavishly. They spared no expense. The prominent families opened their doors to forty visitors, many of them historians or librarians.

"Perhaps next year," he offered hopefully.

"I'll keep trying," she said. "The only other thing I'd like to see happen someday would be the expansion of my Internet business to include additional holidays."

"Valentine's Day would draw customers," he said. "You could decorate with candy hearts, chocolate nut clusters, and red-and-white unicorn suckers."

"Unicorn suckers, huh?"

"They're pointy."

"How about you, Lander," she asked, "are you on Santa's naughty or nice list?"

"His naughty list, once I decorate the gingerbread women."

"We'll both get coal in our stockings this year," she teased him.

Two hours passed in the blink of an eye. They'd touched on so many topics. Abby had a depth he appreciated. They were similar in many ways. She liked to read and was a woman interested in art. She lived in ski country, but hadn't advanced beyond the bunny slopes. She could laugh at herself. He liked the way she teased him, too. She did the daily crossword puzzles in pen and kept up on current affairs. She loved winter, the heavier the snowfall the better.

Beside him now, Abby stretched out her legs, then rose from her chair. "It's time to roll out the dough, cut the cookies, and bake them. Once they cool, we'll decorate."

She preheated the oven and got to work. Using her grandmother's old-fashioned cookie cutters, she made three dozen Las Vegas gingerbread men for her order, along with four extra for Lander to test his skills.

Thirty minutes later, she was sliding them off the cookie sheets and onto the dining room table, now covered with wax paper. Three piping bags were filled with white, green, and red frosting. They would use small spatulas to spread the icing.

"I'll decorate the men and you can have fun with the women," she said. "The lady who placed the order requested all the G-men look alike, so there'd be no squabbles over who ate which one."

Lander couldn't believe how meticulously Abby worked. Her hands were steady; her gaze was intent. All the cookies had mini-chocolate-chip eyes and thin candied orange slices for their mouths. They wore red frosted vests with white piping, short red pants and matching boots. Between their chunky gingerbread thighs she designed green wreaths with peppermint-stick penises—sticking straight out.

After watching her for a short time, Lander got busy, too. He spread a thin layer of white frosting over one of his gingerbread women, then sprinkled her with sparkling green and gold sugar. She glimmered.

Abby cut him a glance and said, "Very Tinkerbell."

He had to agree. The G-woman looked more Disney cartoon than erotic cookie. So much for his first attempt. He decided she'd make a nice snack. "The gingerbread is delicious, Abby," he said, after taking his first bite. It was the best he'd ever tasted.

"I have milk leftover from the recipe," she offered. "It's in the refrigerator."

Milk and cookies. It had been a long time since he'd enjoyed such a treat. He poured them both a glass.

His second effort at decorating fared better. He used frosting for the eyes and mouth. What he hoped would be a sexy smile turned into a sneer. He removed the icing with the spatula and tried again. And again.

Abby nodded her approval after his fourth attempt. "That smile says come and eat me," she said.

He used small yellow gumdrops for the gingerbread woman's breasts. Debated on how to decorate her crotch. He went with shredded coconut. Which drew Abby's laugh.

"Good choice," she praised once she'd stopped laughing. "You're getting the hang of it, Lander."

He had two cookies left, and an idea he thought might please her. He didn't tell Abby what he planned; he wanted to achieve the desired result first. Placing the cookies side by side, he imagined them as a bride and groom.

He then began to decorate.

He reached for the piping bag of white frosting and started with the bride. He made a border around her head, then flared the white at her shoulders like a wedding veil. So far so good, he thought. He gave her mini-marshmallow breasts, dabbed the nipples with pink sparkle sugar.

Returning to the white frosting, he drew a wavy, crinkly skirt. He left enough room for a miniature chocolate-covered cherry at her crotch. He added white shoes, with girly straps at the ankle. His final touch came with green M&M eyes and his signature sexy red icing lips.

Abby had stopped her own decorating and was watching him now. She drew in a breath and said, "Lander, that's amazing. You have erotic cookie talent."

He grinned at her. "Now for the groom."

He dabbed the edges of the G-man's head with white frosting, then curved a short whip of black licorice over the icing and attached it. The hair stuck. Raisin eyes worked nicely. He upped the ante by giving the groom an even sexier grin than his bride.

He spread vanilla frosting for the formal shirt, and added mini chocolate chips for the buttons. The black licorice came in handy a second time, as Lander used it to make suspenders to hold up the white pants. At the groin, Lander went with two peanuts and a cinnamon stick.

"I'm impressed," Abby said. "I'll add your specialty cookies to the order. The bride will love them."

He rubbed his hands together and stepped back from the table. "My work here is done."

She finished up her own cookies, and the table flared with penises. Lander moved to the couch, prepared to relax. Abby cleaned up and joined him shortly thereafter. "The gingerbread cookies need to set, then I'll pack them in a corrugated box with bubble wrap and popcorn," she told him.

He'd hoped their day together would pass slowly; instead it quickly got away from them. They fooled around, then simply held each other. They laughed, and then grew still. Tennyson woke and, with Abby's assistance, settled between them on the sofa. In the afternoon silence, their closeness deepened. Neither of them found small talk important. They took the time to embrace the moment and appreciate each other.

Abby fixed them fried-egg sandwiches for a midnight supper. After that, they snuggled under the quilt, so comfortable and cozy they drifted off.

To Lander's disappointment, he woke to sunshine filtering through the living room window. Bright and warming. The old Swiss clock read eight-thirty. Today would be a difficult one, he knew. Shane Griffin was to pick him up at nine o'clock. He had very little time to say good-bye to Abby. He gently nudged her awake.

She stirred, and gazed up at him. Her expression was sad and guarded, as if she were afraid to face the day. "You're ready to go?" she asked him, a catch in her voice.

"Close to it," he returned.

"You don't have anything to pack."

"I leave as I arrived," he said, "with my muddy coat, torn shirt, and wrinkled pants. My socks have holes, and my shoes have cracked. Part of one sole is missing."

She leaned her head on his shoulder and said, "I think you look handsome."

"Love can be blind," he surprised himself by saying.

She managed a small smile. "I see you just fine."

"Today isn't good-bye," he assured her. "We'll connect again soon. I promise."

She nodded, but didn't seem convinced.

The sound of a horn in the driveway brought their conversation to an end. Shane Griffin had arrived. Fifteen minutes early. He sat in his tow truck and let it idle as he waited for Lander.

Abby panicked. "You haven't had your coffee."

He kissed her lightly. "I'll grab a cup in town, although it won't compare to Santa's Helper," he teased her as he rose from the couch.

He drew her up beside him. She'd slept in her sweats. He held her so close she felt a part of him. She hugged him back. He rested his chin on the top of her head, letting the static strands tickle his cheeks. "Soon, Abby," he repeated. "we'll continue where we've left off." He then released her. Hating to do so.

She lowered her arms and he saw her hands shake. He heard her swallow, catching the mist in her eyes before she rapidly blinked.

"Bye, Lander, have a safe trip," she said so softly he wasn't sure she'd even spoken.

"Later, Abby." He gave her one final kiss.

His ruined cashmere coat hung on a hanger by the door. He put it on. His own hands trembled. He had a lump in his throat and his heart felt heavy as he walked toward the door.

"Meow."

Lander glanced down and noticed that Tennyson was trailing him. He bent and gave the cat a final scratch behind his ear. "Remember our agreement," he whispered to Tenn. "Take care of our Abby."

The calico head butted his palm, giving his word.

He had his hand on the door handle, when Abby called, "Wait, just a second."

She hurried down the hallway to the pantry, returned in a matter of seconds. She carried several boxes, which she quickly packed in a paper sack.

Approaching him, she said, "Merry Christmas. I wanted

you to have the holiday goodies I'd ordered for my grand-mother. Enjoy them, Lander."

"Oh . . . Abby." He sighed. Her gifts were telling. She'd come a long way, and was now able to part with the presents once intended for Gram. She'd given them to him.

She pushed him lightly. "Don't make Shane wait any longer. I'm sure Grady's Garage is busy after all the snow."

The blizzard had brought them together.

The sunshine now drove them apart.

Lander decided the moment he cleared the door that he wanted to not only spend this winter but each season in the year ahead with Abby Denton.

Chapter 5

Ten days had passed, and Abby hadn't heard from Lander. It was as if their time on the mountain had been no more than a dream. Sadly, she'd wakened.

Tonight was her night, and she was about to celebrate her good fortune. She would be touring Chestnut Hill. She clutched the engraved invitation in her hand. Gold ink, heavy brocade white paper. First class all the way. She couldn't believe a last-minute cancellation had landed her on the excursion. She'd never felt so lucky. She only wished her grandmother was here with her. She believed Ada was with her in spirit.

Abby had driven to Philadelphia, and left her SUV in the parking lot at the historical society. That's where she'd boarded the luxury tour bus. The bus now dropped its passengers off in front of the first home.

She stood beneath a Victorian-style cast-iron street lamp. Pushing up the sleeve of her jacket, she glanced at her watch. It was seven o'clock. The pale-blue twilight now darkened to a deep navy sky. The night was cold but clear, with just enough stars to support the soft glow of the corner light.

Twelve of the city's oldest mansions were included on the tour and she couldn't wait to get started. Six homes bordered each side of the street. A park curved at the cul-de-sac, land recently purchased by the historical society.

The tour guide and historian, Winston Moore, collected his group and proceeded to the first Victorian mansion. The brick sidewalks were safely cleared, and the magnificent Christmas lights on each estate shone across the freshly powdered snow, lighting her way.

Winston appeared elderly with his white hair and rounded shoulders, but his step was spry and his manners spoke of an era gone by. He wore a herringbone wool coat with a red velvet vest and a white pocket square tucked into his lapel, perfectly pinched and standing up in a puff, Abby thought, smiling to herself.

His knowledge of Chestnut Hill was unmatched. He shared stories of old family money and the skeletons in turn-of-the-century closets. Passion and prejudice. Scandal and deception. Abby absorbed every word, her eyes widening. It was better than any family friction on TV reality shows, she decided. The details of fortunes lost and lovers taken seemed juicier somehow when the characters had *that* much money.

The 1870 Ebenezer Grange Mansion bore a striking resemblance to the home from the Addams Family, she thought, as she climbed the gray stone steps and entered the main hallway. An entry fire had been set. The hall was toasty. She unbuttoned her jacket and listened as Winston introduced three of Ebenezer Grange's descendants presently gathered to greet the tour. A husband, wife, and their daughter. They were dressed formally.

Black tie and slicked-back hair gave the gentleman a GQ look, while the lady and young girl complemented each other in matching deep burgundy silk dresses trimmed with elegant black braid. The mother was stylish in black suede pumps and her daughter wore patent leather Mary Jane shoes.

The guide then gave an accounting of the cloth merchant's fortune and family tree. "Ebenezer Grange primarily dealt in coarse twill and worsted weft, but he preferred silk and fine linen for his own shirts and undergarments," he said with a smile. "Grange was known to be tight with his money, although he doted on his only son. A bit of a chauvinist as well, he was convinced his wife's place was at home. He went on to travel the world with his heir."

He next steered the group toward the drawing room to enjoy the Victorian Christmas tree. "The Blue Spruce has been traditionally decorated with apples, tangerines, walnuts dipped in egg white, and strings of cranberries and popcorn," he told them. He added that sampling was not permitted.

Abby took it all in. The lighting came from wall sconces and clusters of pale tapers in crystal candle holders. Vintage holiday cards from days long past were displayed on the top of a baby grand piano. A pianist and trio of singers dressed in green velvet robes sang carols. "O Christmas Tree" followed "I Heard the Bells."

The familiar melodies took on a rich, ebullient tone in this grand house, adding to the special holiday moment. Abby loved it, yet she couldn't help but feel a twinge of loneliness. This beautiful family and their traditions reminded her that she would never again know the warm touch of her grandmother's hand on her arm urging her to hurry and heat up the cocoa so they could enjoy the bubbling lights on the Christmas tree. But with sadness also came a different emotion.

Joy.

The memory of Lander's arms around her. His lips on hers. Her body melting into his. She was grateful for the time they'd had together. He'd been caring, affectionate, and great in bed. He was a present under her tree that she'd never expected. She'd hold his memory in her heart forever.

Layne Marshall, the woman who'd sat next to Abby on the luxury bus, nudged Abby with her elbow. "It says in the brochure that Earl Grey tea, cinnamon scones, and shortbread cookies will be served in the formal dining room."

"Sounds delicious," Abby said, her voice catching in her throat. She breathed deeply, trying to keep her emotions at bay.

The two women walked down the hall, in search of the holiday fare. They were not the first to arrive. Others from the tour were already gathered around a circular table, sipping tea and enjoying the elegant service.

Their tour guide allowed them fifteen minutes to further explore the lower level of the mansion. The upper two stories were reserved strictly for family.

Winston Moore soon tapped his watch, moving them along. The Granges' staff were gracious hosts. They gave everyone a gift bag of goodies on their way out. Creamy milk chocolate stars and imported marzipan along with beautiful ornaments ready to hang on the tree.

Once outside, Abby saw that it had started to snow. The sidewalk between the mansions was now patterned with fat snowflakes. Layne preceded Abby through the front door of the Eugene Freemont Home. The 1848 Greek Revival was majestic, Abby thought, with its front façade of soft-toned brick, five bay-width and six fluted Ionic columns.

Wreaths and swags of garland greenery decorated the main entrance with its high ceilings and tiered chandelier. Enormous pink and red poinsettia plants added color to the entry hall. A father and his son welcomed them with smiles and handshakes.

"Eugene Freemont founded Freemont Inns, the opulent hotel chain throughout the northeast," Winston told the group. "However he never stayed overnight in one of his own holdings. He preferred his own bed."

Abby understood how Freemont felt. She wondered if she'd made a mistake, reserving a room for tonight in Philadelphia. She didn't like to leave Tennyson for too long a time, even with a pet sitter. She also liked sleeping in her own bed. She still couldn't forget Lander. His presence lingered at the cabin. She missed him. A lot.

Winston pointed everyone toward the double parlor. "This home was decorated in a Napoleon Bonaparte motif. Don't miss the spectacular circular staircase rising, seemingly without support, in a domed cylindrical chamber at the rear of the house. It will amaze you."

He paused, then added, "Enjoy hot apple cider and an assortment of Christmas cookies in the library. The Freemont chef makes the best sugar cookies in Philadelphia."

Abby wandered through the mansion. Time seemed to stop in the Greek Revival. The furniture, gilt-wood mirrors, and the wool Brussels carpet in a geometric-floral pattern were resplendent, evoking memories of another era. She caught up with Layne at an elliptical table in the library.

"This is my third snowman," her friend said, holding up the cookie and licking the sugar off her lips. "They are so delicious. They don't even need frosting."

The sugar cookies on the sterling silver tray were disappearing rapidly. Abby took one, then accepted a crystal cup of hot cider from one of the servers circling the room.

She hated to leave the mansion, but the tour guide needed to keep them on schedule. The next two Victorian homes passed in a blur. She wished she could spend more time at each one. History lived and breathed within the walls.

The stars seemed to brighten and there was something

in the air that she couldn't quite place when she strolled up the walkway to the fifth home, an 1885 Italianate Victorian.

The Reynolds House called to her in a way she'd never experienced. She had an immediate affinity for the mansion. As if she was coming home. She shivered, suddenly as nervous as she was curious.

She stared for a long moment at the bracketed cornices, parapets, and square towers above the three-story roofline. She'd read in the brochure that the balconies were made of both stone and wrought iron. She swore she saw the shadow of a man standing at the window on the upper balcony. She had the strangest sensation she knew him. She shook off the feeling. Could anything be more ridiculous?

"Miss," Winston called to her from the double portico. "Please come and join the others."

Abby took the steps to the wide porch. The tour guide held the door for her. She walked in and stopped dead. She couldn't have moved if someone had paid her.

Positioned in the center of the wide foyer, a six-foot-long, two-story gingerbread house welcomed visitors. It was intricately and beautifully decorated. Abby had never seen anything like it. She breathed in the sugary scents of gumdrops, peppermint sticks, marshmallows, wafer cookies, royal icing, and a dozen other candies.

She felt suddenly lightheaded. Knocked off balance by her uncanny feeling that something strange was going on here. She swayed, bumping shoulders with Layne. She was quick to apologize. She locked her knees, stood up straight, then fisted her hands to calm herself.

"The Reynolds family will join us in the formal living room," Winston said, motioning everyone to the right.

"Note the two marble fireplaces and the extravagant woodwork throughout," he commented. "Reynolds House has sixteen rooms and the original hardwood floors. There is a Christmas tree in every room of the house."

The group murmured over the enormity of decorating so many trees. Abby's heart warmed with the memory of Lander dragging her evergreen in from the garage. She could still hear the *thump-thump* of the trunk along the hallway as well as see the resolute expression on his face. He'd been determined that she have a good holiday.

Winston cleared his throat, drawing everyone's attention back to him. "The mansion is affectionately called The Vault. Lawrence Reynolds was in banking. Yet, oddly enough, he never trusted his own money to the business safe. Instead, he had his own bank vault built in the basement of his home. It remains there today."

"That vault is now used as a wine cellar," a man's deep voice added from the doorway. "My family trusts the Reynolds Bank."

Those gathered were all smiles and soft chuckles. All but Abby. She stood frozen to the spot. Her back was to the entrance, yet she recognized his voice. How could she not? Deep, resonating, and with so much sex appeal, her entire body tingled.

As discreetly as was humanly possible, she turned and peeked around the broad shoulders of the man blocking her view. She inhaled slowly and kept her focus. Yes, it was definitely Lander, well dressed and handsome in a black suit, crisp white shirt, and red-and-green striped holiday tie.

Fortunately for her, she stood in the middle of the crowd and he had yet to see her. *Reynolds.* She now knew his last name. And that he came from old money and lived in a historic mansion.

Realization settled heavily within her. No matter how many ways she spun the facts in her head, they didn't change: the two of them were at opposite ends of the social and financial spectrum. Her heart squeezed. She wished at that moment she was back on Pine Mountain. Safe, snug, and cozy in her cabin. There she could still hold on to her dream of Lander coming back to her. Here in this opulent setting, the dream crashed like a snow globe falling to the floor. She wasn't ready to face him. She didn't want him thinking that she'd chased after him to the city. She'd wanted him to make the first move in seeing her again.

She shifted behind the big man in front of her. Each time he moved, she moved. She became his shadow.

Beside her, Layne whispered, "That's one good-looking man. I'd love to find him in my stocking on Christmas morning. Him and his millions."

What would the woman say if Abby told her that she'd found him in his car in a ditch twelve days ago? Her erotic gingerbread cookies had caused his accident, but she had saved his life. They'd bonded during the blizzard. Yet when the sun broke through the clouds and the electricity flickered on, Lander had returned to Philadelphia.

She hadn't expected him to stay at her cabin. But she had thought he might call. Although cell phone service on the mountain was minimal at best. There had been no Christmas card, as he'd promised. Seeing him now made her shudder. She felt like an intruder in his home, even if she'd received a coveted invitation for the tour in the mail.

Abby caught glimpses of the two lovely women who soon joined Lander. Both stood by his side and slipped their arms through his. The ladies were striking, Abby thought. Impeccably dressed and with an air of sophistication.

"I'm Lander and this is my mother Catherine and my sister Angela," Abby heard him say. "We welcome you to Reynolds House."

She immediately felt drawn to the older woman, knowing as she did about that special final Christmas gift from her husband and how much he'd loved her. How strong a connection they'd had, even after he was gone. She envied her that love, and hoped to find it for herself someday. She didn't want to admit it, but she'd hoped to have it with Lander. Some things weren't meant to be, no matter how much you wished them so.

She watched as several members of the tour moved forward to shake hands with the family. The man in front of Abby did so as well. She was suddenly in the open and vulnerable. Her heart was fragile. She darted behind the Christmas tree. A gorgeous tree, she noted, decorated with clear glass balls, white snowflakes and doves and—her eyes rounded—*gingerbread men.*

She stared overly long into the face of the M&M-eyed cookie. He stared right back at her. His round O of a cinnamon-candy mouth showed he was as surprised to see her as she was to see him. He wore white powdered sugar mittens and black licorice boots.

The only thing missing was a peppermint-stick penis.

"The Reynolds family will be serving an orange-custard tart and a sticky toffee bundt cake in the parlor," Winston announced in his scholarly voice, though Abby detected a gleam in his eye when he mentioned the tart. "There will also be a Yule punch, a traditional family recipe."

Abby peered through the branches of the tree, straight toward the hallway. The entrance had cleared. The Reynolds family now circulated among the tour guests, laughing and chatting, their gestures elegant and worldly. Reminding her that she didn't belong here.

Lander moved around the perimeter of the room, getting closer and closer to where she stood. Abby was certain he had spotted her. She felt his eyes on her, from the top of her head down to her still-sore big toe. And everywhere in between. *That* set her pulse racing. She prayed she wasn't blushing as red as the poinsettias decorating several side tables. Perhaps this wasn't the best hiding place after all, she thought.

She mentally calculated her escape. She figured it would take her thirty steps to reach the entry hall, if she walked fast. Once there, she hoped to clear the door without him stopping her. She had no problem waiting outside for the group. It was cold, but not freezing. She had to take the chance. Besides, she'd welcome the numbness so she wouldn't have to feel the ache in her heart. She'd missed him; seeing him like this only made it worse. Because now she knew she could never have him.

She closed her eyes, counted to ten, worked up her courage—

"Hello, Abby," Lander whispered near her ear. His hot breath chilled her to the bone.

The man had approached on cat's feet. His low voice startled her; so much so, her eyes went wide, and she backed deeper into the tree, nearly losing her balance. Several ornaments shifted and shook, but she didn't look at him.

With a shaky hand, she steadied a dove before it slipped off its hook. Pine needles poked her bare knee between the hem on her gray wool skirt and the top of her black winter boots, making her skin itch. She gave a quick scratch.

A flash of Lander dragging in her evergreen shot before her eyes, making her feel even more miserable. How she wished they were back at her cabin, just the two of them. No mansion, no tour, and no visible differences between them.

She finally made eye contact with him. Her breath caught in her lungs, nearly strangling her. "Lander" came out hoarse.

He stood before her, tall and magnificently male. A

hush came over her. The soft blue glow of the Christmas tree lights was the same color as his eyes. He'd gotten a haircut since she'd last seen him. He was smooth shaven. His cologne was subtle, hinting of amber, musk, and man. Gently, confidently, he cupped her chin with his hand, then ran his thumb across her lower lip. "I see you received my invitation," he said, looking pleased. "I'm glad you could make it."

His invitation. "So it was you who granted my holiday wish to tour the historic mansions," she said. The Reynolds name could pull the proper strings. "Thank you, Lander." She'd always be grateful to him. "Why did you invite me?" She needed to know.

"I wanted you with me on Christmas Eve."

Had he said what she thought he'd said? Her stunned expression elicited his explanation. "The formal invite was mailed late, but I still hoped you'd accept. Tonight I stood at the upstairs balcony window and watched for you. I hoped Santa would grant me my wish. I was one happy man when you walked up the sidewalk."

She'd seen his shadow. And sensed his presence. "I fell in love with your home the moment I saw it," she confessed, not moving an inch, as if she could. "But I had no idea it belonged to your family."

"I'm pleased you like it, but how do you feel about the man who lives here?" he asked, genuinely interested in her answer. He appeared rather nervous, and nothing like the self-assured man she'd known in Pine Mountain.

She gave him a small, reassuring smile. "I rather like him, too."

His expression relaxed as he exhaled his relief. He looked at her now as he had at the cabin, with both compassion and desire. Leaning close, he gently kissed her lips. A promising kiss that would have to suffice until they had more privacy.

He glanced at the tree, then asked, "How do you like my gingerbread men?"

She scanned the ones she could see, and couldn't help but grin. "I like the one decorated in a Santa suit. The G-man with the green frosted bow tie, vest, and shorts is cute, too." She paused, then continued tongue-in-cheek, "It's what's beneath those outfits that counts the most."

"No peppermint sticks or peanut testicles," he said, lowering his voice for her ears only. "The cookies are soft gingerbread, not hard."

Abby couldn't help but laugh. She loved his humor. He shared in her secret of creating erotic cookies. She trusted him not to tell anyone else.

From the corner of her eye, Abby saw his mother and sister approach them. They were both smiling. "Is this your Abby?" the older of the two asked Lander.

"My Abby," he confirmed easily, tucking her to his side. "Catherine and Angela, meet Abby Denton," he said.

His Abby. She needed a moment to take in his words. Yes, it was true. He'd claimed her as his. Tears filled the corners of her eyes. Happiness pushed the last of the holiday sadness from her heart. It was the most romantic moment of her life.

"I'm pleased to meet you both," she managed to say.

Catherine welcomed Abby to their home with a hug, as did Angela. His mother's hug was fragile, yet warm. Angela embraced Abby as if Abby were her sister. Their acceptance of her was overwhelming, as if they were welcoming home a long-lost daughter. Once Angela released her, Lander took her hand in his. Their fingers laced, and she felt secure and safe by his side.

"It's time we met, Abby," Catherine stated with an affirmative nod. "My son is quite fond of you. He told us about the blizzard, the accident, and how you saved his life."

Abby's heart swelled at hearing the woman's words.

"My mother and I will always be grateful to you," Angela added with a sincerity that touched Abby. "We were worried sick when he didn't contact us for several days. We thought the worst." Her hands shook and Abby could see both mother and daughter still hadn't totally recovered from living through the nightmare of not knowing what had happened to Lander.

She wanted to tell them she'd almost died when she found him, his lips blue, his heart barely a murmur in his chest. But she didn't. Why make them relive the accident again? He was home safe now, and that's all that mattered.

"Cell phone service on the mountain isn't always reliable," Abby said truthfully.

"From what I understand, you were both injured following his car crash," Catherine continued. "Lander hurt his ribs and you injured your foot. I insisted he see our family physician upon his return."

"X-rays indicated two of my ribs are fractured," Lander told Abby, holding his side. "How's your toe?"

"I saw my doctor, too," she admitted. "My big toe is broken. It still hurts when I stand too long."

"Do you need to sit down now?" Lander immediately asked, concerned for her.

She shook her head. "I've waited years to take this holiday walking tour," she reflected. "I'll tough it out."

"You are both strong and brave in so many ways," Catherine said. Her voice held respect and admiration.

"Abby is an amazing woman," Lander agreed. His gaze warmed as he squeezed her hand. Abby squeezed back. She'd always have this special moment to remember, no matter what happened between them.

Several minutes passed in which he and Abby did no more than stare at one another. She got lost in his eyes. Memories of their time together silently passed between them. Each knew what the other was thinking. When his lips twitched and his smile spread, sexual chills raised goose bumps all over her body. Her stomach quivered, and she felt far too hot to be wearing her winter clothes. A lacy holiday red nightgown came to mind. To Lander's too, by the look in his eyes.

Beside her, Angela cleared her throat, drawing their attention back to the moment at hand. "My brother mentioned you have a cat named Tennyson," she said. "I'm a cat lover, too."

"Tenn didn't make the trip," Abby said. "I have my nearest neighbor on the mountain pet sitting at my cabin. Bernice has recently adopted a female kitten named Pippa, who, according to Bernie's last text, is madly in love with my old boy. Tennyson has yet to commit to liking Pip. They're only together for a short time. I was planning to return to Pine Mountain after the tour."

She saw Lander frown, but decided his look of disappointment about her leaving was wishful thinking on her part.

"Next time you visit, you'll have to bring Tennyson with you," Angela encouraged her. "The house is huge, and there are lots of rooms to explore."

Next time she visited.

She meant to be kind, but Angela's words were a dose of reality, and they left Abby uneasy. Visiting meant she would come, and then go. There was no permanence in a visit. She realized in that moment how much she wanted to stay. Stay and feel Lander's arms around her again, his kiss upon her lips. All the wishful thinking in the world wasn't going to change that. She longed more than ever for the safety of her cabin.

She inwardly sighed. What had she expected? That she'd take up residence here like she was family? She hadn't known Lander that long and she'd only just met his mother and sister. She'd be leaving when the tour guide ushered everyone toward the front door.

Abby took notice that the crowd had thinned out around them. Only one person continued to admire the tree. The enticement of two special desserts and a Yule punch had drawn everyone to the parlor. She wondered if she should excuse herself and join the others? When all she wanted was to remain by Lander's side. To feel his heat and strength. To know he still desired her.

"I have a gift for you," he said, interrupting her thoughts with a pleasant surprise. Releasing her hand, he bent down, shifting several presents around the base of the Christmas tree, until he located a small rectangular box wrapped in silver foil with a red satin bow. Straightening, he handed it to her. "Merry Christmas, Abby," he said.

She took the gift, and her hands shook slightly. She wanted to cherish the moment. The box was almost too pretty to unwrap.

"We'll leave you two alone," Catherine said, stepping back and allowing them their privacy. "Angela and I should be good hostesses and circulate with our guests."

Angela nodded, agreeing with her mother. "We'll chat again soon," she said to Abby, laying a hand on her arm in friendship. The two women then walked toward the parlor.

Lander gently nudged her with his elbow. There was a sparkle in his eye when he said, "Open your gift, Abby."

She was all thumbs as she removed the bow and decorative foil. She knew in her heart his gift would be something special. Her eyes watered and her vision blurred as she lifted the lid on the white lacquered box. She could barely see the delicate angel through her tears.

"She's exquisite," she said, her voice shaky, as she carefully unwrapped the new top ornament meant for her tree.

"It's an antique angel," Lander said, wiping her tears

from her cheeks with the pad of his thumb. He then gave her the history behind his gift. "From the eighteenth century, and formed of plaster, the angel was made in France. The paper robes are covered in brass foil. The head is painted porcelain and her wings are pleated gauze. The halo is made of hair-thin curved glass rods."

Abby couldn't take her eyes off her present. "I love your gift, your sentiment, and tradition." She grew quiet and felt a moment of awkwardness. This was the last thing she'd expected. "I don't have anything for you, Lander."

He wrapped his arm about her shoulders and drew her close to him. She shifted the gift box so as not to squash the angel between them. "You're here, Abby. You're all I want for Christmas."

Her throat grew so tight she couldn't speak. She could only rest her head against his shoulder and breathe him in. Lander seemed to understand. He drew her so close, they nearly became one person. She swore she could feel his heart beating within her.

The sound of departing footsteps echoed on the hardwood floors of the entrance hall. "This way, please." She heard Winston Moore direct his tour down the hallway and toward the front door. "The next mansion on our tour is known as Lavender House. You will find the home decorated in shades of purple. In the summer months, the owners take the color scheme to the garden and grounds with hybrid chrysanthemums, hydrangeas, and deep purple lilac trees."

The guide stood back until all the guests had scooted out the door. Everyone but Abby. "Miss?" Winston prodded her along. "The Reynolds family is ready to lock up now."

There was a moment when her heart squeezed with the fear she'd have to leave, but the pressure eased when Lander said, "Abby is family. Her tour stops here."

Winston raised a brow. "Sir, this is highly unusual. Are you certain?"

"I've never been more sure of anything in my life," Lander told him.

"Very well, then." The guide cast them both a second look, giving Lander a moment to change his mind, before he slipped out the door.

"I'm family?" Abby liked saying the words out loud.

"I think you'll fit in perfectly," he said. "We need to spend more time together. I want our relationship to work."

So did she. With all her heart. She was going to do her best to show him that they were meant for each other. She truly believed that something other than fate had brought them together.

She listened as he suggestively whispered near her ear. "Stay here tonight, Abby."

"I'd need to cancel my hotel room." Which she'd be happy to do. "I'll also call Bernice and have her extend her stay with Tennyson."

"We have a guest wing upstairs on the second floor, or you can stay in my master suite on the third," he said. "Tomorrow we'll return to Pine Mountain and Tennyson and spend Christmas Day at the cabin."

She'd seen the wide staircase at the back of the mansion when she'd entered his home earlier. Garlands wrapped the polished wooden railings. An inside balcony overlooked the entrance hall. She wanted to climb those stairs. To spend the night with this man. *Her* man.

"I'll join you in your suite," she said without hesitation. "My second Christmas wish just came true."

His arm was still around her, and they bumped shoulders and hips as they headed toward the staircase. She clutched the antique angel and lacquer box to her chest. With each step, the air warmed, shimmered, and she sensed her grandmother's presence.

"Thank you, Gram, for bringing us together," she said softly beneath her breath.

"Thank you, Dad, for Abby," she heard Lander murmur beside her.

Abby knew then that she and Lander Reynolds would climb these stairs for years to come. They would spend a lifetime of Christmases together.

Happy tears filled her eyes.

Her heart felt great joy.

Today's special moments would be tomorrow's loving memories.

Kate Angell says these Gingerbread Men are orgasmic: decorate to taste, and try them for yourself!

OLD-FASHIONED GINGERBREAD MAN COOKIES

5 to 5½ cups all-purpose flour
1 teaspoon baking soda
¾ teaspoon salt
2 teaspoons ground ginger
1 tablespoon ground cinnamon
½ teaspoon ground nutmeg
½ teaspoon ground cloves
1 cup (2 sticks) unsalted butter, at room temperature
1 cup packed light brown sugar
1 large egg, at room temperature
1 cup unsulfured molasses
1 teaspoon vanilla extract

Combine the flour, baking soda, salt, and spices in a large bowl; set aside. In the bowl of an electric mixer, beat the butter, brown sugar, and egg on medium until smooth. Add the molasses and beat until fluffy, about 2 minutes. Add the vanilla. Stir in the flour mixture 1 cup at a time, blending until smooth. The dough should gather into a semi-firm mass. (If it's not firm, add another ¼ to ½ cup flour, but not enough to make it crumbly.)

Turn the dough onto a lightly floured surface. Divide in half. Flatten into disks and wrap in plastic. Refrigerate at least 2 hours or up to 1 week.

After dough has set, preheat oven to 350°F.

On a floured surface, roll each disk to ⅛ inch thick. Use gingerbread-man cutters to make shapes. Transfer them to a large, parchment-lined baking sheet, spacing them about 1 inch apart. Bake until firm to the touch, about 12 minutes. Cool slightly before transferring to a rack.

Decorate in as sweet or as erotic a style as desired!

Makes approximately 2 dozen cookies.

Sugar and Spice

KIMBERLY KINCAID

Chapter 1

November 9

"**D**idn't anyone ever tell you making frosting on a Friday night will make you go blind?"

Lily Callahan pushed her glasses up the bridge of her nose, marking her spot in the tattered recipe book with an index card even though she could make the cake on the page while in a coma. Her gaze traveled from the care-worn notebook to the doorframe of her kitchen, where her friend Clara stood grinning.

"First of all, it's fondant, not frosting. And secondly, I'm pretty sure that's an urban legend." Lily lifted a brow and smiled before bending down to grab her mixer's hook attachment from one of the kitchen's three overstuffed cabinets. If she stood in the dead center of the room and extended her arms, both sets of fingertips would easily kiss the lemon-yellow walls on either side. A galley kitchen was right up there with fickle oven temperatures and overmixed cookie dough in Lily's nightmare department, but affordable space was at a premium on a baker's budget, even in tiny Pine Mountain. She'd long since learned to make do.

Clara ditched her easygoing expression in favor of something more serious and pushed off from the doorframe that barely encompassed her thin shoulders. "If it wasn't, you'd have been completely sightless five years ago. It's okay to leave work behind every once in a while, you know," she said, sidestepping the stack of Tupperware bins housing Lily's vintage cookie cutters and cake molds.

"Not when I've got thirty-six hours and counting to make a three-tiered princess birthday cake, complete with edible glitter and handmade fondant tiaras." Lily deposited the dough hook and the spotless seven-quart bowl belonging to her trusty Viking mixer into her friend's outstretched hands.

"You know I have no idea how to use this, right?" Clara examined the dough hook with an equal mix of curiosity and doubt. "I mean, other than as a back scratcher."

"Don't even think about it, or I won't make your offering for the Christmas cookie swap next month."

"That's not funny, Lily! You know I can't even boil water. And if Abby makes my cookies, she's liable to spike them with some kind of aphrodisiac or something!"

Lily couldn't suppress the tiny chuckle brewing on her lips, both at Clara's reaction and the mention of their other best friend's mail-order erotic sweets business. "Not if she wants to keep her business a secret, she won't. Anyway, you know I would never really leave you high and dry. Just keep me company while I make this cake, okay?"

Lily maneuvered around the case of confectioner's sugar sitting in front of her pantry. Good thing she used so much of the stuff—it made trying to cram the boxes into the already overflowing space a nonissue. God, she hated working out of her apartment. But making the rent on this place was hard enough. Affording an actual storefront was about as feasible as climbing Mount McKinley. In hot pants. During a blizzard.

"It's five o'clock on a Friday evening and you're about to be up to your elbows in powdered sugar and corn syrup," Clara pointed out, her tone carrying more mischief than heat. "Admit it. You're having a love affair with your job."

Lily shrugged. "It could be worse. At least my job doesn't use movie quotes as its primary means of communication, conveniently 'forget' its wallet four dates in a row, or think dinosaurs are just one big conspiracy theory." That last one had been her personal favorite. If she didn't know better than to believe in hokey superstitions, she'd swear she was cursed in the dating department.

Clara bit her lip, but her giggle filled the cozy kitchen work space regardless. "I forgot about the T-Rex guy. What did that last, three dates?"

"Two and a half," Lily corrected, balancing a giant bottle of corn syrup in the crook of her elbow while she looked for the shortening. "I politely feigned a raging headache after he tried to convince me to pitch my iPhone into the nearest garbage can to avoid falling prey to The Man."

"Okay, so that guy was a little whack-a-doo." Clara put the bowl and dough hook on Lily's only available counter space and turned to give her a thoughtful look. "Still, a relationship with powdered sugar and pastry dough can't be good for you, either."

"It's better than the alternative." At least Lily knew where she stood with the pastry dough. "And anyway, I don't see you out on some hot date tonight."

"Please. We're swimming in the same dating pool, remember?" Clara rolled her eyes. "Anyway, I have something important for you. Even though it'll only make you work harder," she said, moving back to the spot by the entryway where she'd left her bag.

Lily's curiosity slowed her hands over the perfect O of the mixing bowl beneath them. "According to you, that's impossible, remember?"

"If anything will make you push the boundaries of impossible, it's this." Clara whipped a sheet of printer paper from her bag. "We're running this in tomorrow's paper. Apparently, the resort just made the announcement."

Lily's gaze snagged on the elegant logo emblazoned across the top of the page, her heart kicking against her ribcage. As a columnist at the *Pine Mountain Gazette*, Clara was privy to all sorts of juicy news. "Is that from Pine Mountain Ski Resort?"

"I thought that might get your attention."

Hoo-boy, Clara wasn't messing around. The resort was Pine Mountain's lifeblood, not to mention one of the most gorgeous places on earth. The fact that the lush, wintry setting was only ninety minutes from Philadelphia made it one of the most popular ski spots in the entire Blue Ridge.

Lily's curiosity lifted to a full simmer. "More buzz about their plans to revitalize?" Although Pine Mountain Resort had a reputation for being upscale yet not overly formal, their culinary services—including the restaurant on site—garnered lackluster reviews at best. It was no secret in the cozy town that a complete revitalization was in the works.

"Not quite." Clara placed the single sheet in Lily's sticky hands. At about the third paragraph, it started to flutter beneath her grip.

"Oh my God. They're running a Christmas cookie contest."

"That they are," Clara agreed. "I heard they're looking to bump up their reputation to attract a top-notch chef to run the new restaurant. Showing that they can bring in the crowds won't hurt, and a contest is a great tie-in to the food itself. Gotta admit, it's pretty brilliant marketing."

No way. No *way.* "Top prize is ten thousand dollars, Clara. As in, ten thousand tickets out of this kitchen and into my very own storefront!"

While Lily's cake catering business had been steadily

growing, she was limited in what she could do from her own kitchen, both in scope and home-business catering regulations. With the right placement and a great business plan, owning her own bakery could vault her from small-time to the big leagues in about two seconds flat.

And if she won this contest, it wouldn't be just a pipe dream, because she'd have enough money to put down as collateral on a loan.

Lily's brain spun like egg whites just shy of meringue status, and she swung her gaze back to the printout in her hand. "The first round is in thirty-four days. Oh, God, I need to go through my recipes and brainstorm so I can make an outline. I have so much work to do!"

"I knew you were going to dive into this headfirst." A smile poked at the corners of Clara's mouth, dissolving any sternness her voice might have carried. "Just remember, if you work yourself to death, you won't be around to cut the ribbon at your own grand opening."

But Lily wasn't having it. "If there's anything I know, it's that hard work and careful planning equal big strides." It had been her creed the minute the first cake came out of her Easy-Bake Oven twenty years ago. "I've got to be in it to win it. One hundred percent."

Clara rolled up her sleeves. "All righty then. Where do you want to start?"

The grin on Lily's face felt delicious. "With the rules, of course." She'd be damned if she'd risk her shot by not knowing every last one of the stipulations by heart. "By the time I'm done tonight, I'm going to have a surefire plan to walk away with that prize."

"I know you've got balls of solid rock, man, but breaking into La Luna's wine cellar at one in the morning is pushing it, even for you."

Pete Mancuso ignored the doubt in his buddy's voice

and cursed as he tried—and failed—to jimmy the lock on the restaurant's wine-cellar door with his grocery-store bonus card.

Maybe it was the grueling eleven-hour shift he'd just put behind him, or the thought of the impending ninety-minute drive back home to Pine Mountain, but picking a lock wasn't as easy as it used to be. Realizing he'd be captain of a sinking ship if he kept it up, not to mention having some explaining to do at Joe's Grocery for his shredded bonus card, he took a step back to assess the situation.

"It's not breaking and entering. We work here, and we're already in the kitchen," he pointed out to his fellow chef, Jake Donovan. "We're just bending the rules to get a special ingredient after hours, that's all."

Jake laughed, the sound echoing off the pristinely scrubbed blue-tiled walls of the kitchen behind them. "Maneuvering around the lock with a credit card is more like fracturing the rules, don't you think?"

"Potato, potahto. Amazing how much gray area there is in bucking authority, isn't it?" Pete reset his card, holding it perpendicular to the door before sliding it into the hairbreadth of space between the locking mechanism and the wooden jamb.

He leaned against the door, applying just enough pressure before continuing. "Anyway, the dessert that's prompting this little recon mission will be worth every bite." Provided he could actually pop the lock and get on with it, anyway. Damn, he was losing his touch.

"Uh-huh. So why did you wait until Martine left for the night to sneak in, rather than just asking for the key at a normal hour?" Jake tossed a nervous look over one huge, white-jacketed shoulder, as if speaking their boss's name out loud would conjure the old battle-axe from nothing more than two syllables and bad karma.

Pete maneuvered his way around the question, but wasn't as lucky with the finicky lock. "One in the morning *is* a normal hour. And don't worry about Martine. She won't be complaining when she can plate this dessert for fifteen bucks a pop."

"Get serious. There's not a scenario on the planet in which Martine doesn't dog somebody about something. And you, my friend, are her favorite chew toy."

He had a point. "Still. I can't make a chocolate brandy genoise happen without liquor. And this dessert is going to be too good to let go. Ah!" The locking mechanism caught on Pete's bonus card—finally—and slid out of the way with a telltale click. "See? Piece of cake."

Jake's expression translated to a wordless version of *really*? "Does pastry chef humor have to be so cheesy?"

"Only for you, dude," Pete said, kicking up a brow as he stepped into the hushed, temperature-controlled space of the wine cellar.

Under normal circumstances, he might be tempted to take in the dazzling collection of higher-end ports and Bordeaux that Martine kept on hand in case they snared some equally dazzling clientele. But Jake wasn't wrong when he implied she'd have a kitten if she caught them raiding the liquor supply, especially if she knew where Pete had set his sights. He skimmed his fingers over the narrow wooden shelves, taking in the array of gently reclined wine bottles before he reached a deeper ledge in the back corner of the tiny space.

"Bingo." Pete grinned, sliding a distinct, multifaceted bottle from its spot in the shadows.

"Jesus, Mancuso. I know I don't have to tell you that's a two-hundred-dollar bottle of liquor." Jake's gaze flashed over the bottle of Rémy Martin XO before landing on Pete with an equal mixture of dread and doubt. "Martine is going to kill you. And then she's going to fire your ass."

"Don't be such a pessimist. It's not like I'm going to drink it myself. It's for a dessert," Pete said, even though he knew his buddy was closer to the mark than he'd admit out loud. Okay, fine. So technically Pete was pushing it with this little endeavor, but come on. No one had ever accused him of being conventional, and he certainly hadn't made it up the ranks in the Philadelphia restaurant scene by doing something as boring as following the rules.

Too bad talent and vision didn't always make up for that. Case in point: while he might be able to create desserts sumptuous enough to make nuns swoon, Pete's reputation as a by-the-book employee was patchier than overworked pie crust.

He stuffed down the thought and fixed his friend with a reassuring half-smile. "I just need enough brandy to soak into the genoise sitting on the cooling racks. With the praline buttercream and dark chocolate ganache that's going with it, the extra layer of complexity from the liquor will make Martine—and everyone in the dining room tomorrow night—forget their names, let alone wonder where the brandy came from."

Jake let out a low whistle. "Okay, that's good, even for you. But why the sudden urge to create something over the top? You trying to impress someone I don't know about?" He led the way out of the wine cellar and back through the belly of the main kitchen.

"I live over the top. But since you asked . . ." Pete's half-smile unfolded into the real deal as they rounded the corner to the dessert station at the end of the line. "Rumor has it that Conrad Le Clerc is leaving L'Orangerie."

"Get the hell out of here." Jake froze in front of the cooling rack, a sheet pan of double chocolate cake mid-slide on his palm. "The guy has worked there since we were like in the third grade. He's leaving *now*?"

Pete nodded, liberating the pan from Jake's hands to

place it on the stainless steel table that took up the bulk of his station's work space. "He's opening a patisserie in the French countryside with his wife, just as soon as they can replace him. Which means L'Orangerie is going to be in the market for a pastry chef."

The unspoken implication hung in the air just long enough for Jake's eyes to go as round as pie plates. "Don't take this the wrong way, but you might need more than a two-hundred-dollar bottle of brandy for this. L'Orangerie is the most upscale restaurant in the city, bar-freaking-none. Do you have any idea how many people are going to throw down for that job?"

Pete knew, all right. Good thing he was a sucker for bad odds. "Oh, this genoise is just the tip of the iceberg. From now on, I'm going to do everything I can to get people talking about my dishes. Landing that job would be huge, and I'm going after it with all I've got."

His desserts always had been better than his rebellious reputation, and if anything could distract L'Orangerie's owner from the latter, it would be what Pete put on the plate. So what if he fractured a few rules to get there? He was still a damned good chef, and landing this job would prove it.

"You know, if you really want to get your desserts no-ticed, maybe you should do that cookie thing," Jake said, snagging Pete's full attention.

"What cookie thing?"

"You know, the thing Pine Mountain Resort is doing to drum up PR. That contest for the best Christmas cookie recipe." Jake pulled his iPhone from his back pocket and flicked the screen to life. "Didn't you see the call for contestants on their blog today?"

"No." He'd been too busy baking pumpkin tartlets and dodging Martine's serrated glances. Pete took the phone from Jake's hands with a weird thread of anticipation jangling in his veins, and it only grew stronger as he read. "Holy shit. This contest definitely isn't small potatoes."

"More like filet mignon, man. Rumor has it they're looking to go all out on this thing to grab as much good press as possible."

"Mmm." Pete had heard from more than one person that the resort restaurant had been tanking big-time lately. Looked like they could both use a pick-me-up in the reputation department. "The qualifying round is only a month away."

Jake leaned against the stainless steel table with a nod. "Yeah, I guess that's part of the deal. They're doing exclusive coverage on their website so it can be up to the minute. None of that Christmas in July crap for them. Guess they want their shining stars this season, no waiting."

Pete stood tall, exercising every inch of his six-foot frame as his resolve settled into place with unyielding certainty.

"If a shining star is what they want, they'd better gear up. This contest is a one-way ticket to the best job in Philly, and I'm going to win it. Hands down."

Chapter 2

December 13

Pete made his way to the main entrance of Pine Mountain Ski Resort, wishing like hell the powers that be had gone for that Christmas in July thing after all. They might only be a few weeks removed from Thanksgiving, but man, he wished he'd had the foresight to at least grab a heavier coat before diving headfirst into this winter wonderland.

Not that the scenery wasn't postcard-perfect up here in the Blue Ridge, with the weathered stone main lodge flanked on either side by powdery trails and pine trees thick with snow from last night's storm. Hell, even Scrooge himself might be tempted into a Norman Rockwell–flash of good cheer at the lush Christmas greenery and softly lit luminaires glowing in the late-afternoon light.

But Pete was too busy freezing his ass off to enjoy it.

The bitter wind at his back made him grimace. Truly, it was enough to make even the most hopeful competitor want to ditch it all for the warm comforts of home, and the first event wasn't even until tomorrow morning.

Not that any of the other contestants had much of a chance even if they made it through the still-snowy roads for this evening's check-in. While he respected anyone who had the courage and talent to throw down in a contest of this caliber, there was a zero percent chance Pete wasn't walking away with the whole shebang. Especially since Martine had been *thiiiis* close to making his leave of absence permanent when he told her how much time he needed off for the competition.

He was so busy knocking his resolve into place that he didn't see the blonde in his path until collision was a foregone conclusion.

"Oof!" Out of sheer instinct, Pete's hands flew around her in an effort to keep them both from tumbling ass over teakettle. The woman returned the favor in a rush of wooly gloves and scattered papers, and damn if her hands weren't a whole lot steadier than her feet.

Double damn if her body didn't feel sexy as hell pressed against his.

"I'm so sorry!" the woman said, at the exact moment he uttered the same words.

And then he realized who she was.

"Lily?" His thoughts jammed to a halt at the hard shot of heat zinging through him at warp speed. In spite of his crazy work schedule, he'd seen her around town dozens of times since he moved here five years ago—after all, Pine Mountain was your basic cozy map dot. But with her prim and proper demeanor, she'd never once made his nerve endings sizzle like this.

Of course it didn't hurt that they were currently tangled together from neck to knees.

"Oh my God. *Pete*?"

The pretty flush creeping over her cheeks kept his hands firmly in place as her realization caught up to his. Propriety dictated he should let go and step back, but man, her arms felt hot wrapped around his shoulders.

"Are you okay?" he asked, the undeniable and totally unexpected heat in his blood not budging an inch.

Lily's eyes rounded behind a set of stylish, burgundy-framed glasses, her grasp going tighter on the back of his jacket for just a breath before she frowned. "Yes, I'm . . . oh, my papers!"

Just like that, his arms were empty.

"That's what I get for trying to walk and read at the same time. Damn it, I had it all in order, too," she muttered under her breath, bending low to pluck the pages from the salt-crusted walkway.

"That's a lot of literature. Are you writing a book?" His gentle teasing fell victim to her deliberate movements as she gathered her work, prompting him to kneel down to help her despite the clear indication she didn't need it.

"Don't get cute with me, Pete Mancuso. You broke up with my best friend in front of the whole grocery store."

"Huh?" Under the circumstances, it was sadly all he had. "Are you talking about the phone call I had with Clara a couple days ago?" They hadn't even been going out, for God's sake.

At least *he* hadn't thought so. They'd had a business meeting, but as soon as he realized Clara had mistakenly hopped on the dating train, he'd called her to gently set the record straight.

Who broke up with someone in the grocery store?

"You embarrassed her in front of half the town." Lily's dusky blond lashes fanned over a set of startling baby blues. She shifted her weight and sprang back to standing with efficient fluidity, as if she had energy banked under her skin and was saving it for later.

The move would be pretty hot, if she wasn't so serious about it.

"Listen, Lily, I'm not sure what you're talking about. I thought Clara and I could hook up for a business thing. But I didn't think she'd take it as, uh, us just hooking up."

"So you admit that you only asked her out to get your name in the paper?" Lily looked at him the way someone might inspect a loaf of bread for hidden spots of mold.

"No. I mean, I didn't ask her out." Okay, fine, so he'd been looking to drum up a little positive buzz by getting a mention in the paper, but how was he supposed to know the woman had harbored a crush on him? "I meant it as a business thing, period, but she got the wrong idea."

"Oh." Lily's tone dipped, but just by a notch. "What about the phone call then?" She pushed her glasses up the bridge of her pert nose, and wow. Her expression might be all work and no play, but those dark blue eyes sent another shot of unexpected warmth right through him.

"I was just trying to let her down gently. I'm not sure how half the town got involved, though. Or Joe's Grocery."

Her eyes rounded for a split second before she jammed them shut in a classic oh-crap expression. "Well, ummm . . ." She still looked skeptical as hell, but not nearly as unbreakable as a minute ago. "It's a small town, word travels fast. I guess it doesn't really matter. Anyway, I've got a ton of prep left to do."

He skimmed a covert gaze from the neat bundle of blond hair at her nape to the sensible black kitchen clogs on her feet, his gut tightening.

Of course. She had a custom-cake business, for Chrissake. He should've known she'd be all over this contest.

Time to recalibrate.

"I guess I'll see you tomorrow, then." Pete watched the fresh layer of understanding wash over her features, followed by twin spots of pink on the apples of her cheeks. Damn. At least her blush would keep him from freezing.

"You're competing too?"

"'Fraid so," he said. "Winning this thing will be a pretty

big boost for my career. It'll put me on the fast track in the city, that's for sure."

The austere expression Lily served up made him tack on a cocky smile just to see if he could temper it. God, he loved a challenge.

"You're awfully sure of yourself, aren't you?"

Something unfolded deep in his belly, prompting him close enough that their breath commingled in puffy wisps of dissipating heat. "I wouldn't last a day in this business if I wasn't."

Okay, yeah, maybe he was trying to knock Lily off her game a little. But being that straitlaced couldn't be healthy, and part of him wanted to see what it would take to rattle her.

The other part just liked her blush.

"Oh." Her bow-shaped mouth parted just enough to allow the word out, and for the barest moment, all that austerity fell away. The wind that Pete had cursed just minutes before made another appearance, only this time it stirred a few honey-colored strands from the knot at the back of her head.

Suddenly, his distaste for Mother Nature dropped a couple of pegs.

Lily blinked, but then gave a firm head shake as if resetting herself. "Well, then. I guess I'll see you in the morning."

"I hope so." The well-hello-there stirring behind the fly of Pete's Levi's seconded the sentiment. "Good luck tomorrow."

A faint yet unmistakable smile ghosted over her lips. "I appreciate the good wishes, but I believe in hard work, not luck."

Oh, no way. No *way* was he going to let Little Miss By-the-Book have the last word. She might be cute and all with that sudden, sassy smile on her face, but a guy had his pride.

Pete turned his reply over in his mouth, savoring it like a bite of decadent cheesecake before letting it roll off his tongue with a smile.

"You might not want to make that an either-or, Blondie. See, I came here to win this thing. Which means you're going to need all the luck you can get."

Sixteen hours, one cold shower, and four cups of coffee later, Lily still couldn't get the feel of Pete Mancuso's leanly muscled arms out of her head. Which was crazy, really, considering he was the most arrogant smooth talker she'd ever laid eyes on.

With a smile like that, laying some other parts on him wouldn't be bad, either.

Lily's spine went ramrod straight and she snuck a covert glance from side to side, as if the naughty thought had been broadcast in Dolby stereo. Okay, fine, so those emerald-green eyes fringed by eyelashes thick enough to be unfair on a man were one hell of a one-two punch. But it didn't make up for the fact that the guy was ego on a stick, even if his side of what had happened with Clara did make sense.

Not that it mattered. Lily might not have gone to a fancy culinary school in Philadelphia, but she'd still been around enough chefs to know Pete's suave, I-know-best type. She hadn't spent the last month refining her skills and perfecting countless cookie recipes just to be upended by an overly confident pretty face.

Even if Pete's smile *had* threatened to knock her knees out from under her.

"Ladies and gentlemen!" The voice coming through the microphone set up at the front of the room belonged to Chase Bishop, the resort's event planner, who flashed the contestants a dazzling smile. "If we could please have your attention, we'd like to get started. Welcome to Pine Mountain Resort's Christmas Cookie Competition."

He continued through some obligatory thank-yous to the contest sponsors, who were no slouches in the culinary world. Looked like the resort was as serious about their public relations as they were their food.

And their prize money. Lily scooped in a deep breath, doing her best to let it calm her as she waited impatiently for Chase to get to the meat of things. They'd been given disappointingly little by way of specific details for each round, and although Lily had scoured the rules and regulations until her eyes had gone numb, all she'd unearthed besides the dates for each event were a full list of what would be available on site and the declaration that she should be ready for anything.

After four weeks of meticulous prep, Lily could eat *ready* for breakfast.

"As you know, there will be four rounds of competition spanning the next ten days. In between rounds, competitors will have the chance to practice in our test kitchens as well as participate in interviews for our online publications, including our blog."

Chase gestured to the pair of cameramen hard at work by the podium, and the notion caught her off guard. As a one-woman business, Lily had never even had a coworker, much less been filmed on the job.

Not that it made much difference, really. She had a plan, and that plan was to win. Film or not, she was going to sail through today's elimination, no matter how many swagger-soaked pastry chefs stood in her way.

Chase continued. "For today's event, our goal is to narrow the field while showcasing your talent. In order to do that, we're going to put a twist on things."

Lily's gut did a free-fall toward her toes. Why did they

have to mess with a perfectly good set of guidelines? Her fingers itched to get to the stations set up just over Chase's shoulder, to measure out precise amounts of flour and sugar and butter so she could watch them form more than just the sum of their parts.

Instead, there was a *twist*.

"Each of you will have thirty minutes of planning and one hour of baking time, including plating, to come up with a holiday-themed cookie incorporating the red or green ingredient in the gift basket at your station. Each basket has a matching counterpart. You will be judged in a single elimination round against whoever has your matching ingredient."

Chase lifted a red basket decorated with tiny pine trees, and Lily's nerves evened out. She was pretty good on her feet. As long as there wasn't anything too weird in there, this would be no sweat.

"However," he proceeded, reclaiming her attention, "to go along with our Christmas theme, we're adding some goodwill to the mix. Like your baskets, each of you will have a counterpart."

Lily's calm curdled in her veins as Chase went on. "Contestants will be paired up with another competitor to make this round a collaborative effort, with both members of each winning team advancing to the next round. Workstations are labeled with both partners' names. You have ten minutes to find yours, and your partner, starting . . . now!"

With her heart thumping in her ears, Lily methodically moved up the aisles of temporary workstations, coaching herself through every step. Okay, so collaboration was a bit outside of her comfort zone, but if those were the rules, she could make it work. She *had* to. She'd come here to win, and she'd be damned if she'd let a surprise like this knock her out of the game.

But as Lily's eyes landed on her workstation, and more important, her partner's slow and sexy half-grin, she realized teaming up wasn't going to be a twist so much as the mother of all freaking corkscrews.

Chapter 3

"**L**ooks like fate has plans for us, huh Blondie?"

No way. *No way no way no way.*

Lily cracked open one of the eyes she'd involuntarily squeezed shut, hoping her brain had just gone a little haywire from the stress of the competition.

Pete Mancuso leveled her with a smile so hot, she felt it under her skin.

"I'm not sure fate has anything to do with the random pairing process." She shifted to hide her wince. This was no time for her inner philosopher to go on parade. Why couldn't she bite her nails like a normal person instead of spouting technicalities when she got nervous?

But rather than point out her geek streak, Pete just rumbled out a laugh, and God, it was even more unnerving than his smile. "If you say so."

The large digital screen above their workstation flashed its bright red display, and Lily sprang into action despite the warmth prickling through her treasonous lady bits. "We can argue semantics later if you want. But that timer is going to hack into our planning time any second now. We need to focus on the kitchen."

A resort staffer wearing a Santa hat passed them their festive little basket along with express instructions not to open it until Chase gave the word, which came a few minutes later. Lily flipped the red and green lid, wasting no time as she dug in with both hands to unearth . . .

A pomegranate.

"Okay." She cradled the jewel-colored fruit in one palm while reaching for her notebook with her other hand. "We should probably start with a flavor profile, then we can outline—"

"We need a recipe, not an outline." A frown unfolded beneath Pete's five o'clock shadow as he scooped three more pomegranates from the bottom of the basket.

"How else are we going to organize our thoughts?" Exasperated, Lily knotted her arms over the double rows of buttons on her chef's jacket. Come on, this was baking 101, for God's sake.

"By taste, that's how." Pete reached up to the magnetic strip splitting the difference between the two sections of their workstation and pulled a kitchen knife down with a metallic flash. Before she could protest, he sliced into the pomegranate in front of him and plucked a handful of tiny seeds from the parchment-colored flesh.

"You can't do that!" she protested, but it only prompted him to pop them into his mouth with a flourish.

"Why, am I going to get busted by the pomegranate police? No flavor profile on the planet can compare to good old-fashioned tasting. Here." He popped a few more seeds from the pith and deposited them in her hand. "See for yourself."

Wishing she had time to argue—because *damn,* he was infuriating—Lily reluctantly played along.

It had been a while since she'd actually tasted the ingredient, and the little burst of velvety juice paired with the unexpected crunch of the seeds reminded her to do it more often. Still, while the snack was nice and all, they had work to do.

"I could make a reduction, some kind of syrup we

could use as a substitute for molasses." She started scratching out ideas on the page, but Pete shook his head.

"There won't be enough time to cool it to a workable
temperature. And if we try to use hot syrup, it's only going to end up a hot mess. Same as if we tried to make jam
for a thumbprint."

Damn it, he was right. "All right, what about using the
juice then?" Lily started rooting through the decked-out
workstation in search of a blender.

"Think outside the box, Blondie. These little babies are
great just as they are. Let's use 'em that way."

Lily's pen stopped short over her page of meticulous
notes. "I'm not sure I follow."

"We could bake the seeds into shortbread, maybe throw
in some pistachios for another layer of flavor." Pete slung
his lean frame against the edge of his work table, looking
more like he was having a casual beer with friends than
competing in a contest that could make or break someone's career. "Or instead, we could concentrate on citrus
and use lemon zest for added punch. We can decide on
that once we get started. What do you think?"

He had to be kidding. "You want to just make it up as
you go?"

"For the smaller stuff, sure. Why not? An outline's just
constricting."

This was exactly why Lily hated the whole "twist" thing
in the first place. Too much likelihood of getting paired up
with *insane* people.

"Look," she said, dragging in a deep breath. Staying rational was her only shot at avoiding meltdown status. With
eighteen minutes to go on the planning clock, she had to
buckle down if she had a prayer of salvaging this, no matter how tempting it was to lose her cool. "You might feel
comfortable winging it, but this is a big deal to me."

She pitched her voice lower, and although she meant

for it to convey her seriousness, a thread of despair rode out on her words. "I'm not going home today."

In a blink, Pete's smile vanished, his dark eyes sparking with something Lily couldn't quite name.

"If it'll make you feel better to write it all down, then you should." But rather than being condescending, or even teasing, his words carried simple honesty. "I'm not going home today, either. So let's do what it takes to get this done, me and you."

"O-okay." She would've stayed mired in shock, but the sight of the camera crew buzzing around the periphery of their workstation served as a stark reminder of why Lily was there.

And more important, what was at stake.

She nodded, just one quick drop of her chin before her mental Rolodex kicked into high gear. "Using the seeds in shortbread seems like a good idea, but I'm not wild about the citrus. What about white chocolate, to really knock home the Christmas theme? The colors would present well, and the flavors play nicely together."

They went back and forth, with Lily furiously scribbling notes and dividing tasks between them as they discussed the merits of different ingredients and methods to come up with a workable plan.

"Right. So that'll do it, don't you think?" she asked, handing Pete his half of the outline while trying to shake the cramp from her hand.

Pete's cocky smile went on one hell of a comeback tour, and it caught Lily right in the chest.

"It's going to have to. Our time is officially up."

Despite living in a world where being off by a couple of grams spelled total disaster for a recipe, written directions gave Pete the shakes. But he had to give credence to the skilled ideas behind Lily's brainstorming.

Even if she had highlighted them in two different colors.

He rocked back on his heels and tuned out the suit from the resort as the guy reiterated the rules for the camera with a toothpaste-commercial smile. It hadn't been lost on Pete that one of the film crews had taken a liking to Lily, although as best he could tell, she was oblivious to their presence. Her focus was so sharply honed, it made a samurai sword look like a butter knife, and something about the way she'd vowed not to go home had traveled right to the depths of his gut.

Of course, the flush of fiery determination on her cheeks didn't hurt either. *That* had traveled to a decidedly different part of his anatomy.

Pete tightened his mental vise over the thought and cracked it like a walnut. He hadn't come here to be derailed by thoughts of a prickly caterer, no matter how sexy her blush was. His career was his main focus—his only focus—and he was going to earn a top-notch headline for his résumé. No matter who he had to work with.

"All right, competitors!" the host said with one last smile. "Get ready to get baking, because your time starts . . . right now."

Lily sprang into action, her graceful movements in complete discord with her linebacker-tough expression. She was going to best him right out of the gate if he didn't get his ass in gear, and no way was he having that.

They'd divided their tasks evenly, starting with prep, and Pete didn't waste any time removing the crowns from the fruit in front of him. He sectioned each one with practiced strokes, digging into the soft, pale membrane to free the dark red seeds.

"Don't you want a bowl of water for that?" Lily's pretty blue eyes flicked over his hands from her spot on the other side of the workstation, where she was shelling pistachios with nimble movements.

"With only an hour on the clock? No way." The textbook method of submerging pomegranates in cold water so the seeds could gently separate from the pith was time-consuming as hell. Pete could do it faster *and* better on his own. "You don't have to worry about me crushing the seeds, Blondie. I have a light touch."

She flattened her palms over the stainless steel countertop, and God, her poker face was exquisite. "Well, don't be afraid to use it. I'm going to have this shortbread dough mixed up in ten, so I'll need them by then."

Ouch. She really was made of sterner stuff than her angelic face and slim frame suggested. Although come to think of it, he never did like a pushover, especially in the kitchen.

Lily hustled to the pantry for the dry ingredients, but Pete focused on his task. The seeds were the central ingredient in the shortbread, and just because he didn't use conventional methods to get them out didn't mean he'd scrimp on work ethic. He seeded each fruit gently, then treated the pistachios to a fastidious chop.

He orbited around Lily with ease as they worked, folding the pomegranate seeds and pistachios into his half of the dough. An idea swirled in his head, coaxed by the butter-rich scent of the unbaked shortbread, and it was too delicious to ignore.

"Hey, Lily, I think we should change up the chocolate thing." The idea multiplied, becoming more insistent as Pete looked at the kaleidoscope of colors on the parchment-lined baking sheet, and yeah. It was *perfect* for this recipe.

Her blue eyes flashed up from the fluffy, pale yellow dough in her mixing bowl. "But we have a plan."

"Forget the plan for a second. What if we—"

"No." Lily didn't waver, not even breaking stride with the shortbread dough. "It's too risky to change things with . . ." She paused, but only long enough to spare a glance at the countdown clock above their station. "Thirty-two minutes to go. We're still not quite sure how much the altitude will affect baking time. We don't have time to change the plan."

A ribbon of anger uncurled in Pete's belly, low and hot. Okay, so she was talented—her knowledge told him plenty, and her movements and technique filled in the rest of the blanks. But that didn't mean he was going to let her go all Frosty the Snow Chef on his ass.

He handed her some pomegranate seeds, but when her fingers cupped the bowl to take it, he didn't let go. "This is better than the outline. Take a risk, for Chrissake."

"We're wasting time," she said, her voice catching on the last word.

"I want to win, too, Lily. Just trust me."

Her lips parted, and in that fraction of a second, he knew he had her.

"Competitors! We are at the halfway point. You have thirty minutes to go," chimed a voice from the host's podium, and Lily stepped back toward the mixer as if breaking from a trance.

"No. The chocolate makes a huge difference in this recipe. I'm not risking my chances on a spur-of-the-moment change to a key ingredient. I'm sorry," she said, and walked away.

"I'm sorry, too, Blondie," Pete whispered under his breath. "But I need this win."

As soon as she returned her attention to her half of the shortbread dough, he headed straight for the pantry.

Time flew from the clock in a blur of blending, baking, and slicing. In the time it took him to blink, both batches of shortbread were cut and on the cooling rack, awaiting the final layer of melted chocolate he was tempering over the double boiler.

Pete had to admit Lily's idea of cutting the cookies into long triangles rather than traditional circles had been brilliant. The pistachio and pomegranate–studded wedges bore resemblance to holly trees, and with the chocolate mixture he'd carefully constructed, they'd be over the top in both presentation and flavor.

"What the hell is that?" Lily's eyes widened, liquid blue and pissed off, but he met them with equal measure.

"It's dark chocolate."

She eyed him as if he'd lost his marbles. "But we agreed to dip the cookies in *white* chocolate."

"I *agreed* to do whatever it took to win." It wasn't his fault she was too inflexible to see that this would work.

"But this changes the entire dish, from flavor to presentation. Messing with it without thinking things through is crazy."

Holy stickler, this girl was tough! "It's not crazy. The shortbread is sweet enough on its own. If we go with this, it'll add just enough complexity to play off the other ingredients while still showcasing the pomegranate. If we'd stuck with the white chocolate, we'd have lost the other components."

Lily jammed her hands against her hips, insistent. "This wasn't the plan!"

"No, it wasn't."

With a thick kitchen towel wrapped around his hand, Pete removed the insert from the double boiler and walked the perfectly tempered glossy mixture over to the cooling rack. The clock showed six minutes left for plating, which was just enough time to get them drizzled so the chocolate could set up.

As long as he did it right now.

"What if this backfires?" Lily asked, her voice no higher than a whisper. "Did you even stop to think about that?"

"No." But before she could protest, Pete continued, matching her tone with every inflection. "Look, my fate rides on this, too, Lily. It's not going to backfire. I promise."

Chapter 4

Lily looked down at the three plates of shortbread trian-gles, complete with satiny crisscrosses of dark chocolate, and tried with all her might not to throw up. Their competition had presented first, and although the rules dictated one team couldn't watch the others' presentation, their ear-to-ear smiles as they passed through the green room said enough.

She and Pete were going to have to knock this thing out of the park if they wanted to win. And like idiots, they'd bucked a perfectly good plan.

"You want to present?" The low rumble of Pete's voice pulled her back to the competition floor. "After all, you're better spoken than I am. Not to mention prettier."

"All the sweet talk in the world won't keep me from being furious with you," she whispered, although the involuntary smile tugging at her lips made her the world's biggest liar. Was it really too much to ask for that cocky little half-smile of his to be more aggravating than hot?

"It's not sweet talk if it's true. And you won't be mad when we win." His murmur curved around her ear, and he passed the tray of shortbread to an event staffer as the judges settled at the podium.

Lily's jangled nerves took a backseat to her quiet snort. "I'm immune to your charm."

Pete reached out, brushing her forearm with a light touch Lily felt on every inch of her skin.

"Just make sure the judges aren't immune to yours, okay?"

Before she could respond, or hell, even start breathing again, Chase stepped up to the podium. "Welcome, team two. Before we begin, I'd like to introduce our judges. On the left, we have Martin Alexander, local developer and owner of several bakeries in the Blue Ridge. Next is Olivia Reece, one of our executives here at Pine Mountain Resort. And lastly," Chase paused for emphasis, effectively drawing all of Lily's focus to the judge at the end of the table as he said, "We are thrilled to have Chef Carly di Matisse all the way from New York City."

Right. Because what Lily *needed* was more pressure. The chef had her own cable TV show, for God's sake!

"All right, contestants." Chase gestured to the spot where she stood, side by side with Pete. "Whenever you're ready."

Lily did her best to stamp anything but certainty from her expression, cranking up her smile as she took a step forward. "Good afternoon. My name is Lily Callahan, and I'm one half of Team Pomegranate."

The judges chuckled politely, bolstering her just enough to continue. "Our offering today is a pomegranate pistachio shortbread with a dark chocolate glaze. Chef Mancuso and I wanted to spotlight the secret ingredient by pairing it with flavors that complement its natural vitality without being overwhelming. Please enjoy."

Lily clasped her hands over the front hem of her chef's jacket in an effort to keep them steady. She swung her attention from the podium, desperate for something—anything—to keep her grounded while the judges took that first fateful bite.

Her gaze landed with a direct hit on Pete's shadow-stubbled smile.

"Interesting." Martin Alexander's voice cut through Lily's surprise, drawing her back to reality with a resounding thud. "Can you tell us a bit more about why you chose shortbread rather than, say, a traditional sugar cookie base?"

The straightforward question narrowed her focus, and Lily answered it along with a follow-up question from Olivia Reece. The tension in her shoulders kicked down a notch as they tasted and took notes, and for the first time since they'd deviated from the plan, Lily took a full breath.

"Hmm. I'm not sure about this dark chocolate." Chef di Matisse tipped her head, her expression completely blank. "What was the thought process there?"

The breath Lily had just taken jammed in her lungs like a scoop of cold marmalade left in the bottom of the jar.

Pete stepped up beside her, easygoing confidence infusing each of his words. "The dark chocolate was meant for just a touch of emphasis without trying to outshine the other ingredients. A teaser, if you will, to let the pomegranate's flavor shine through."

Chef di Matisse frowned. "I see. Still, it's a bit risky to go sparse on flavors in a dessert. Perhaps something sweeter might have worked a bit better here."

With that, Lily's gut—and all her hopes with it—sank like a stone.

After a few more notes and a hushed conference between the judges, the decision was made. Lily's feet felt sloppy beneath her as she and Pete made room for their fellow contestants, every move amplified by the fact that two of them were about to be sent home.

"Lily." Pete's whisper found her ears in a cross between encouragement and an apology, but she kept her eyes fixed on the judges' podium.

Mostly so he wouldn't see they were rimmed with hot tears.

"Well, this was a very close call," Chase began, the results slip in his hand. "You're all clearly talented and innovative, and the judges felt both desserts had merit. In the end, though, flavor tipped the scales by just one point." His gaze landed on her and Pete, and oh, God, couldn't they just get this over with?

"Congratulations to Lily Callahan and Pete Mancuso, who will be moving on to our next round!"

Lily gasped, unable to form a decent thought, much less get something down the chain of command to her mouth.

They'd done it. They'd won the first round.

She wasn't going home.

"Yes! Lily, we made it!" Pete threw his arms around her in a gleeful embrace, surprising her right off her feet. Since her only choices were to clutch him back or tumble to the floor, she held onto his sturdy shoulders while he swung her around. Words floated by, scraps of sound and movement she was sure were important, but the only thing Lily could focus on was Pete's mouth as he lowered it to hers.

Lily tasted like peppermint and total surprise, and the feel of her lips under his, all soft and pliant and warm, sent a bolt of *hell yes* right down his spine.

"Oh!" They parted on a soft exhale, and Lily blinked up at him from behind her glasses. It had been a perfectly PG kiss, just a spur-of-the-moment thing born of the excitement of winning, really.

Damn, he wanted to kiss her again. And slower.

"I told you that you could trust me," he said, lowering her to her feet while trying to recover the grin he wore like a shield. She took a step back, ghosting a hand over her lips with a nod.

Whatever she'd planned to say in response got lost in the rush of shaking hands with the opposing team, thanking the judges, and the obligatory post-round interviews with the camera crew who'd been milling close by. Time moved at a startling clip as an event planner whisked him away to go over the itinerary for the next few days, complete with sign-up schedules for the test kitchen, more interview slots, and information on some group charity-event thing the night before the next round.

Pete stuffed all the pages into a folder, making a mental note to breeze over them later. The only page he cared about right now was today's score sheet, and since it wasn't in his packet and they'd all been delivered, there was only one person who could have it.

And only one place that person would probably be.

He sauntered back to the competition floor, which had long since quieted from the earlier excitement. Sure enough, Lily sat perched on a stool at the counter in their work space, her standard-issue serious demeanor locked into place as she looked up from the slip of paper between her elbows.

"It looks like the judges all felt the shortbread itself was good, although none of the scores for that component were perfect."

Pete bit down on the urge to laugh, although not with malice. He should've known she'd get right to it. "That seems a bit conservative, but okay. What else did they have to say?"

The furrow in her brow paved the way for a frown. "The chocolate caused quite the controversy. Chef di Matisse gave us a two out of five for overall flavor, citing the chocolate as most of her reason."

"What about the other two judges?"

She paused. "Martin and Olivia both gave it perfect marks in that category."

Pete shrugged, leaning against the stainless steel counter

beside her. "You can't please everybody, I guess." Still, two perfect marks out of three plus the win? He'd take it.

"It was a huge risk." Lily fastened him with a hard stare. "And an unnecessary one. We only won by a point."

He stiffened, but didn't change his tone. "Okay, but we did win. Who cares about the margin?"

"I do. It was both our futures hanging in limbo. You should've known better than to put stock in a whim that nearly cost us everything."

"Hey." The word was out before he could stop it, a clear prickle of irritation riding on the assertion. "That whim got two perfect scores. I don't hear you complaining about that." Not to mention taking the shortbread from great to fucking stellar. Like any decent chef, Pete had tasted the final product before it hit the plate. No two ways about it; they'd earned their win.

"You're missing the point. It was a complete gamble, and it could've easily gone the other way." Lily's voice gave a slight tremble, betraying the vulnerability beneath her tough exterior. "We really could've lost, and it wouldn't have been just you going home."

The tender thread of emotion weaving over her face pushed him toward her, close enough to see the tiny flecks of gray in her dark blue irises.

"Any time we compete, we could lose and go home. It's a high-risk, high-reward game."

"See, that's where we differ. To me, this isn't a game at all."

Lily's eyes flashed over his, as wide open as the rest of her, and the expression on her face stirred up an emotion he couldn't quite identify, until it smashed into him all at once.

It was remorse.

The vulnerability flickered for just a second longer before Lily snuffed it out with a curt nod. "Either way, I suppose you're right. It doesn't matter. Looks like we're back to being competitors, so best of luck in the next round."

She extended a hand, and Pete found himself caught squarely between wanting to argue with her until they both dropped and kissing her until her fierceness turned into something entirely different.

But the sound of a masculine voice being cleared stopped him from doing either.

"Excuse me, I don't mean to interrupt." Chase Bishop stood a few feet away, with his hands casually stuffed in his impeccably tailored pockets. "I was hoping to have a word with you."

All the better. As turned on as Pete was by the challenge of figuring her out, Lily was right. They were competitors, and if anything, getting through today's round only solidified his determination to win the whole thing and skyrocket his career to the big leagues. His best move right now was to walk away so he could focus on exactly that.

"Right. I'll leave you two to your privacy." Pete turned toward the rear exit, but Chase stopped him in his tracks.

"Actually, I need to speak to both of you."

Lily's face went the color of chilled cream. "Is there a problem with the competition results?"

"No, no, nothing like that," Chase assured her, and the relief clattering through Pete's veins looked like a perfect match for the expression breaking over Lily's face. Chase smiled. "In fact, it's rather the opposite."

"I'm not sure I understand," Lily said, and Chase pulled a BlackBerry from his pocket like it was the obvious answer to her confusion.

"As you know, we're updating our blog rather frequently as the contest unfolds. We're also cross-promoting with a few culinary sites, as well as our sponsor's Web pages. That way both the contestants and the resort have the opportunity for some great media exposure."

Pete nodded. He'd come here to pad his reputation through his résumé, so none of this was news. "Okay, so what does that have to do with our results?"

"As it turns out, footage of you and Ms. Callahan was selected for one of today's spotlights. It went live two hours ago, and you've already received . . ." He paused to check his phone. "Just over three times more hits than the next-place clip, and more than the rest of them combined."

Whoa. Even Pete, who usually preferred experience over engineering, knew that was a lot. "But dozens of teams competed today. What's so special about us?"

Chase lifted a brow. "People seem to feel you two have great on-screen chemistry."

Oh *hell*.

"All those hits were for us kissing rather than baking?" Lily asked, her voice so soft he couldn't get a read on it.

"Most of the segment showed the two of you working together. First and foremost, this is a cookie competition. But you two are a dynamic team. And if I'm being honest, the kiss probably didn't hurt."

"So what does this have to do with anything? The team event is over." Pete felt the words low in his throat, but it still didn't stop him from putting some gravel to them. He might've wanted the win for his career, but he hadn't kissed Lily as a PR scam.

He'd kissed her because it felt right.

"Technically, yes. The team task is over. But we'll be filming everyone at the group holiday event tomorrow and throughout the week in the test kitchens anyway, to prepare new teasers and generate interest in the competition. During the course of those sessions, we'd like to do another segment on you . . . together."

"You want us to be all buddy-buddy just to boost exposure?" Lily knotted her arms over the front of her chef's whites, but Chase was quick to assure her.

"It's not just to enhance the resort's PR, Ms. Callahan, although yes, there is that. And we're not asking you to do anything you're not comfortable doing." The unspoken reference to their impromptu kiss hung heavy in the air. "But one of our goals is to showcase our competitors' culinary talent to boost their personal reputations. Not everyone can win the prize money, but it's our hope that more than one of you can walk away with something beneficial from the competition."

Lily didn't argue, but still didn't look convinced, so Chase continued. "We received thousands of hits today, and it was only the opening round. The people who watched those clips aren't likely to forget your name too soon." He flicked his glance from Lily to Pete, tacking on, "Or yours."

No two ways about it—it was a veritable treasure trove of kickass marketing, not to mention the very thing Pete had come here to do. Plus, surprising as it had been, he and Lily had worked well as a team. This really was a win-win for both of them.

Provided he could keep his libido in check, and that Lily would actually agree.

Chapter 5

Lily cradled the phone in her hotel suite to one clammy ear and dialed Clara's cell phone number. She might not believe in crazy superstitions like luck, but the mystical power of best girlfriends? Now that she'd follow to her very last breath.

"Hello?"

"Oh, thank God!" Relief spilled through Lily's veins at the sound of Clara's voice on the other end. Trying to explain an Internet lip-lock with the guy who had inadvertently embarrassed your best friend in the middle of the town grocery store was *so* not something one could do in a voice mail.

"Lily? Is everything okay?" Clara's concern made it over the line loud and clear, and Lily winced. Better to just come out with it. After all, the kiss hadn't meant anything.

Never mind that she couldn't stop revisiting it in her brain on a continuous loop. In brightly vivid 3-D. With the sexy rumble of Pete's voice echoing through her mind in surround sound.

"Yes . . . no. Did you, um, see any of the competition online today?" She fidgeted with the phone cord. For someone who didn't trust anything other than what she could see in front of her, Lily sure was saying a lot of prayers today.

Clara gasped. "Your competition! Lily, I'm so sorry. I've . . . been kind of tied up with something here, and I must have missed it. How did it go?"

"Well, the good news is that I made it through the first round." Lily paused while Clara squealed her congratulations, then delivered the rest in a rush. "But the, um, bad news is that I was partnered with Pete, and when we won the round, he got kind of excited and, well, he kissed me. In front of a camera. And footage of it might be floating around the Internet. A lot. God, Clara, I'm so sorry!"

Silence hummed over the line for a long second before Clara sighed. "I should've figured he'd enter the cookie competition. He did say he wanted to focus on his career."

"So you're not mad about the kiss thing? I swear I had no idea he was going to do it." Lily swallowed hard and closed her eyes. Although that was the God's-honest truth, she couldn't deny the bolt of raw electricity that had sizzled through her when Pete kissed her.

Or that she wanted him to do it again. Without the cameras rolling.

Clara's small chuckle was the last thing Lily expected, but exactly what she got. "Of course I'm not mad. In fact, good luck with him."

"I'm *so* not interested in Chef Smiles-a-Lot! It was just a heat-of-the-moment thing that took me by surprise, and I didn't want you to hear about it in town." Pine Mountain's grapevine might as well have been constructed from steel-reinforced cables with Kevlar coating. No way was this not going to make the rounds.

"I don't think you have anything to worry about there," Clara said, her voice tinny on the other end of the line.

Lily pulled the receiver away from her ear for inspection. Cell phone connections were precarious at best in the mountains. "Are you sure you're okay?"

"Yeah, I've just got a lot on my plate right now. You probably wouldn't believe me if I told you. Which I can't because I've got to go. But don't worry about Pete, it's ancient history. Good luck in the next round of competition. I'm rooting for you!"

They said their good-byes, and Lily replaced the receiver with a shake of her head. She should be relieved that Clara seemed to have put Pete firmly in her rearview mirror. But rather than feeling comforted by their conversation, a fine layer of unease dusted over Lily like freshly sifted powdered sugar.

Because she was fresh out of reasons to not work with the cocky-as-hell pastry chef.

Twelve hours after she'd uttered the fateful, ridiculous *yes* that landed her in the test kitchen with her smirk-happy nemesis and a two-man camera crew, Lily cursed the very nature of the word. Someone had failed to mention to her nether region that this culinary bender with Pete was for the benefit of the blogosphere, and not the boudoir. If it hadn't been so long since she'd actually *seen* the boudoir, it wouldn't be so bad.

But as it stood, her concentration had more holes than a dozen boxes of donuts.

"Morning." Pete strolled into the test kitchen that had been set up adjacent to the resort's main restaurant kitchen. Having worked her entire career in a kitchen the size of a walnut, the sheer dimensions of Pine Mountain's amenities blew Lily's mind.

Along with reminding her what would be well within reach if she won.

"Morning." Lily tucked her pencil into the tidy knot of hair at the nape of her neck and flipped her notebook closed. Just for one day, she could play this little game. All she had to do was keep her cards glued to her vest as they practiced their recipes for the cameras. No problem.

"What's that?" she asked, eyeing the pair of cheery red and green to-go cups in his hands. The coffee at the resort's breakfast buffet had been bitter at best, with the rest of the offerings equally unappealing. It was little wonder that management was looking to replace their head chef and culinary staff.

Pete's mouth fell into that overconfident grin she wanted so badly to hate, sending a trail of good-morning-to-*you* right to her center. "It's my way of saying thank you for being willing to work with me again after my chocolate stunt. While I can't apologize for taking the risk, I should've realized it would upset you. I'm sorry."

"Oh." Shock rippled through Lily at the unexpected sentiment. "Well, we did get some great marks for flavor, so I guess it wasn't all bad."

He held up the coffee. "Call it even?"

"Sure." She peeked at the kitchen's periphery, where the camera crew was gearing up. "Is it from the buffet?"

"Hell no," Pete said, then snuck a covert glance around to make sure no one heard him. "That stuff was thicker than the motor oil in my Jeep. This is the real deal."

He slid one of the cups across the counter until it rested about an inch from her fingertips. A thin ribbon of steam curled up from the notch in the lid, filling her nostrils with rich, earthy goodness.

"Thank you." She cradled the cup in her palm and took a polite sip.

The instant the flavors met her taste buds, all hope for decorum hit the fan. The deep richness of the coffee and the velvety glide of cream loosened a groan from her chest, and she wrapped her other hand around the cup in a possessive *gimme!* gesture. Her next three sips grew progressively enthusiastic as her senses and stomach joined forces in a greedy demand for more.

"Oh my God," she murmured, pausing to lick an errant dribble from the plastic lid. The delicate layer of whipped foam was a perfect partner for the warm comfort of the coffee itself, and Lily took another deep draw with a satisfied moan. "This is amazing."

"Glad you like it." The unexpected huskiness in Pete's voice strummed its way through her belly, and she blinked up at him in surprise.

"Sorry." Cheeks burning, she lowered the half-empty cup and reached for a napkin. Had she really been *licking* the cup? No wonder he was staring. "I guess I need caffeine a little more than I thought." Lily made a move toward the kitchen so they could get started, but Pete stilled her movements with a surprisingly gentle brush of his hand.

"Then by all means, you should finish." His eyes sparked with something dark and forbidden, and Lily felt it all the way to her traitorous toes.

Whoa.

And then, just as fast as it had appeared, the look on his face was replaced by that familiar, confident smile. "Told you it was the real deal."

She took another sip, albeit a smaller one than her last few, and shook off the image of Pete's fleeting expression. Clearly, her happy-happy java endorphins were getting the best of her. "Did you make it?"

"Yeah. The guys in the main kitchen were pretty accommodating about letting me in, but only after I promised to make them each a cup of the best coffee they'd ever had."

Her jaw dropped, and she placed her cup on the counter with a stare. "You just waltzed right into the resort's kitchen and used their equipment?"

"I asked first, and then I bribed them with the coffee. Even bad kitchen staff is territorial about their stuff."

"Are there any rules you find sacred, or are you equal opportunity about breaking them all?" Although she meant the question seriously, Lily couldn't deny the curl of forbidden curiosity winding through her in anticipation of his answer.

Pete stepped closer, turning her curiosity on its ear. "Are there any rules you're willing to break, or are you equal opportunity about following them all?"

For a second, they stood there, inches apart, and Lily wanted nothing more than to press up on her toes and kiss him, *really* kiss him, until they both were breathless.

But the sound of tinny jingling yanked her squarely back to earth.

"Oh, ah, excuse me," said the cameraman as he reached up to steady the decorative wreath he'd brushed against. "We're ready whenever you two are."

Saved by the jingle bells.

"Great." Pete stepped away, turning toward the cavernous test kitchen with his hallmark confident smile. The cameraman gave them a spiel about acting natural, just doing what they'd normally do, and a whole bunch of other things that were statistically impossible to manage while being captured on film. But this was their only baking session of the day, and Lily would be damned if she'd lose out on practice time by worrying about the cameras. Even if they were currently capturing her every move.

"I was going to play around with some classics today," Pete said, snaring her attention as he pulled some butter out of the lowboy. "What do you think?"

Lily proceeded with caution, sticking to her completely generic guns on strategy. "Classics are good." She pulled out some butter of her own. It wouldn't hurt her to work on some basics. If the first round had shown them anything, it was the importance of having a solid base.

"I know everyone thinks of chocolate chip, or oatmeal raisin, or even good old-fashioned sugar cookies as classics. But me? I'm all about the gingersnaps."

Surprise popped through her veins, and her words flew out before she could hold them back. "Get out of here! They're my favorites too."

"Great minds." Pete jerked his head toward the pantry, and Lily fell into step beside him. "I kind of go all in with gingersnaps. The bolder, the better."

She bit back a wry smile. "That seems to suit you."

Please. He might as well have "go big or go home" tattooed on his forehead. Lily shrugged as she stood on her tiptoes to grab the turbinado sugar, but Pete beat her to the punch.

"I take it you're more of a traditional girl," he said, placing the container in her hands with a look as warm and decadent as fresh-baked brownies.

"Oh." The word escaped as more sigh than declaration, prompting a flush of warmth to parade over her cheeks. "Thank you."

Her answer amped his expression into a full-on laugh. "You've never worked in a professional kitchen, have you?"

The chill that gripped her body spilled over into her words, canceling out all the warm fuzzies she'd just felt. "What's that supposed to mean?"

"Not what you think it does. You're just awfully polite." He grabbed a container full of candied ginger before making his way back to the test kitchen, the cameraman a subtle yet definite presence in the background.

Lily chose her words with care, but didn't censor herself, either. "How are good manners a bad thing?"

"They're not. It's just that professional kitchens tend to be a lot more . . . volatile than that."

She lifted a brow at the euphemism. Professional kitchens could be downright cutthroat. She didn't need a fancy culinary degree or experience in the city to know that. It had been the first thing she'd learned in her community college baking courses.

"I've always preferred to work in my own environment. It's why I'm here, actually."

Pete paused, turning his attention from the crystallized ginger on his cutting board to her face with obvious curiosity. "Really?"

Lily caged her groan, but barely. The seamless way she and Pete moved around each other in the kitchen had put her so at ease, the words just popped out.

So much for keeping things close to the vest.

"I run The Sweet Life out of my own kitchen, but it's getting more and more difficult as my client list grows. Between the home business permits and the lack of space, it just makes sense to go the next step and move to a storefront."

Lily might have to share a little more factual information than she'd intended, but her personal life wasn't up for grabs. No way was she going to let Pete—not to mention everyone in the blogosphere—in on the fact that starting her own bakery didn't just make business sense. It would also fulfill a lifelong dream.

One that no one in her family had ever been able to accomplish.

"That's quite the expensive endeavor." Pete's expression was startlingly grin-free as he coaxed a small mountain of flour onto his food scale.

"Yup." She focused on the tasks in front of her, letting the movements soothe the ragged edges of her nerves. As far as Lily was concerned, anyone who claimed baking was more stress than therapy was full of crap, even if said baking was being done under Big Brother's watchful camera lens. "What about you? What would you use the money for if you won?"

"I haven't given it much thought, to be honest."

The answer, along with the sincerity of Pete's delivery, nearly knocked the sheet pan out of Lily's hands. "I'm sorry?"

"I'm not really in it for the money," he said, reaching for the molasses. "For me, it's more of a prestige thing so I can land a better job."

"Better than La Luna?"

A wicked gleam flashed over his eyes. "Ever heard of Conrad Le Clerc?"

Whoa. "Of course. I used to daydream about going to L'Orangerie's Sunday afternoon tea service as a kid." Okay, and maybe as an adult, too. Not that she'd admit to Pete why she'd never actually gone. "The place is incredible."

"Le Clerc is retiring to France," he said, the implication taking a minute to elbow its way into her brain.

"And you want to take his place." No wonder Pete wanted this win so badly. With bragging rights like that, he'd vault right to the top of the short list for any job in the city.

"Mmm hmm. Like I said, it's all about the prestige."

They continued to work side by side, punctuating the companionable silence by sharing basic techniques and ideas for their very different takes on the spicy-sweet cookies. Pete's version yielded a soft, oversized cookie, as bold in flavor as it was in size. But when he pulled them from the oven during the last two minutes of baking to sprinkle them with just a bit of crushed peppermint candy, she couldn't contain her surprise.

"You can't pair those flavors. They're too strong."

Pete sent a devastating grin over his white-jacketed shoulder from his spot by the oven. "Says who? People put peppermint candies on gingerbread all the time. It's really just a twist on that."

Lily's mind went without pause to the X-rated gingerbread men her friend Abby had gifted her "for luck," complete with peppermint-stick penises, and it was all she could do not to choke on her tongue.

"Wow, are you okay?" Even the cameraman looked a little concerned as Pete slid his cookie sheet back into the oven and rounded the corner to pat her firmly on the back.

"Never better," she croaked, finally gaining enough composure to finish her cookies.

When both batches came out of the oven and had been transferred to cooling racks, the cameramen wrapped things up and headed out. Lily tidied her station even though event planners had told her it wasn't necessary. Washing out mixing bowls wasn't exactly a party, but it was part of the process, and she loved it all.

"So now that the cameramen are gone, you want to tell me the real reason you want to open your own bakery?" Pete asked, pushing up the sleeves on his chef's jacket as he grabbed a clean dish towel from the stack over the sink.

Warning bells clanged in her head, but she stood firm. "I did tell you. I'm outgrowing my space, and moving to a storefront is the next logical step."

"That's a great story. Except you don't believe a word of it, do you, Blondie?"

Shock froze Lily to her spot on the kitchen tiles. "How do you know what I believe?"

But rather than match her unease, Pete just nonchalantly took the clean bowl from her hands and started to dry it.

"You get a look on your face when you're baking, and it definitely isn't prepackaged like that answer. If you don't want to talk about it, that's cool by me, but you're going to have to sell that next-logical-step thing to someone else."

Pete was right. She *didn't* have to talk about it. In fact, it was perfectly acceptable to just clam right up and stick to her story like she'd planned.

But instead, Lily told him the truth.

Chapter 6

"You don't know this because you grew up in the city, but I'm the only Callahan who's ever gone to college. Or even come close, really."

The words were barely a whisper, yet the emotion attached to them hit Pete with startling gravity. "Wow."

Rather than carry any trace of bitterness, her words remained soft. "I know it might not seem like a big deal to you, being a classically trained pastry chef from Philadelphia and all, but it's a huge deal for my family."

Pete's gut double-knotted at her assumption, but he said nothing. His past wasn't a boat that needed rocking, and anyway, he didn't want Lily to stop talking.

"My parents are great, but they were raised on hard work, both in mining families." She moved her hands through the suds in the sink as if the movements soothed her, talking as she went. "They got married at eighteen, and I'm the youngest of five kids. There was never a shortage on love, even when we didn't have a whole lot else."

"Still sounds like a nice childhood," he said, and the scrape in his voice wasn't lost on him.

Thankfully, Lily didn't catch it. "It was. But as much as I respect my parents, I always yearned for something different than a blue collar life. Not because I didn't want to be like them or my brothers and sisters, but because I wanted to give something back. So after graduation, I worked nights and weekends waiting tables at the diner in town and paid my way through Riverside Community College one semester at a time."

Pete pulled back to look at her, surprised. "You worked your way through college by yourself?"

Lily stood a little taller, but didn't break stride with the dishes. "It was worth it. I got my degree in business and took some baking classes while I was there too, although I taught myself most of what I know in the kitchen."

Jeez, she was made of some really stern stuff. And now the why of both her work ethic and her serious demeanor made a hell of a lot more sense. "So why do all that just to stay here? With your skills, you could snag a job in the city, no problem." It seemed like a no-brainer, really. There were worse things than drowning in work, and she'd make more money in Philly, for sure.

But she shook her head, resolute. "Because I love Pine Mountain, and it'll always be my home. Just because I want a different kind of happiness than the rest of my family doesn't mean I have to leave here to get it. I mean, it's not where you are that makes you successful, it's *what* you are."

Pete buckled down over the urge to flinch, forcing away thoughts of both his past and his own career. This wasn't about him, anyway. "So that's why you really want to win this contest."

Lily nodded, a wisp of blond hair falling over her cheek as she dropped her chin toward the bubbles in the sink. "Between here and Riverside, I do pretty good business with custom cakes, but it's only enough to stay steady. Ten thousand dollars is just enough collateral to qualify for the loan I need to open up a storefront on Main Street. I could expand to more than just cakes and the occasional

dessert tray for church socials. It would mean daily customers."

She opened her mouth to continue, but the pink stain
on her cheeks beat her to it. "Sorry. This all probably
seems silly to you. I mean, you've trained in some of the
fanciest restaurants in Philadelphia, and La Luna is just . . .
well, a far cry from my tiny kitchen."

Damn, her blush made him crazy, and his words tumbled out without his brain's permission.

"You're a really good baker, Lily. Better than a lot of the
yahoos I've seen in the city. And your dream doesn't seem
silly to me at all."

"It doesn't?"

"No." He dipped his chin to meet her lowered eyes. For
just a second, Pete saw that same heat he'd caught when
he first bumped into her outside the resort, and it reached
in and grabbed him with palpable force, guiding him forward until they were as close as they could get without actually touching.

Lily was an enigma, all right, with all that austerity
banking the fire inside her. And right now, he wanted to
unravel her piece by piece.

Her gaze flared, dark and translucent blue, but she didn't
step back. His brain screamed that touching her was a
tremendously stupid idea, but his mutinous body sent a
hand to tuck that loose strand of hair behind her ear anyway. "It seems honest. Like you."

"Oh." The word was nothing more than a honeyed
murmur, and all the competition titles on planet earth
couldn't have bribed his hand from its resting place on her
shoulder. Her lips parted, and the lush sigh that spilled
from them belied her next words.

"We should . . . we should finish these dishes and pack
up our cookies," she said, arching up under his palm. Christ,
even the chaste column of her neck burned him with the

intensity of a live wire, innocuous to look at but scorching to the touch.

"I know." His voice paired gravel with a whisper, and the bowl between her fingers slid into the soapy water beneath them in response.

Lily lifted up on her toes and canted her head back gently, fitting her body to his touch. "We should . . . could you . . ."

Pete sifted his hands upward, loosening the silky knot of hair at her nape. "Finish drying the dishes?"

"Kiss me," she said, closing what little space remained between them in a single rush.

The electric heat he'd found a moment ago with his hands was nothing compared to what met his mouth, and he dived into it on pure instinct. A sudden burst of wicked surprise hit him full-force as she opened her lips without coaxing, but he didn't try to temper the move by slowing down.

He tunneled his hands through the blond waves now spilling over her shoulders, holding her fast as he explored her mouth with his lips, tongue, and the edge of his teeth. The velvety groan it lifted from her chest only spurred him on, and when she bowed against him in a tight arch, he returned the favor without thinking. Bracing his hands around her back to absorb any potential discomfort from the hard edge of the countertop, Pete notched his body against Lily's in a thrust that left nothing to the imagination.

And he had a really good imagination.

"Still worried about the dishes?" he asked, dropping a trail of kisses around her ear. She tasted heady and sweet, like every rule he'd ever broken, and he teased her earlobe with the edge of his bottom lip before moving on to the soft hollow where her shoulder met the edge of her chef's jacket.

"Yes. No. Oh, God that feels good," Lily whispered, her voice soaked with want. She pushed back against him, the soft heat of her hips making him impossibly hard as she wrapped her hands around his shoulders. "Forget the kitchen. Just don't stop doing that."

Her words echoed in his head, pulling a thread he couldn't ignore. Kitchen. Cookies. Cameras.

Competition.

"Lily." Pete took a step back, even though every part of him from the neck down gave him some serious what-for. "We can't . . . I mean, we shouldn't . . . someone could see us," he finished lamely, but the damage was done. The warmth in Lily's expression morphed from passion to chagrin right before his eyes, and she nodded crisply as she put even more distance between them.

"Right. I apologize for getting carried away." She drew in a deep breath, and hell if the resulting swell didn't make her standard-issue chef's jacket look as sexy as racy lingerie. But by the time her words made it around the image jamming his brain, she'd cleared the entire stretch of space to the exit.

"Wait, Lily, I—"

"No, I think you got it exactly right." While her words carried more honesty than heat, they punched through the quiet all the same. "We really *can't*. I can't get distracted. There's too much at stake."

For a split second, Pete wanted to argue with her, to tell her no win, no prestige, no money was worth how good she'd just felt coming undone in his arms.

But she was right. They were competitors, both with their eye on the same prize and neither one willing to give an inch. Any time they spent together other than for the cameras was just going to destroy their concentration, no matter how compatible their work habits were.

Or how hot their chemistry.

Pete blanked his expression and his voice to match. "I suppose you're right."

This was the smart play, no matter how bitter the rest tasted. "I guess we're done here, then," he said, taking one last glance at her before letting her walk away.

Pete stood by the curved staircase in the resort lobby, taking in the tastefully decorated fifteen-foot Douglas fir and blazing stone fireplaces with tired eyes. The last thirty hours, complete with intensive kitchen sessions, personal interview spots, and last-minute recipe prep for tomorrow's elimination round, had demanded every ounce of energy he could muster. The remaining fumes went toward necessities, like brewing enough coffee to jump-start a town full of zombies and making sure he had pants on when he left his suite.

And thinking about Lily, which—much to his chagrin—outranked both of the above.

Although they had one more scheduled camera session at tonight's charity event, Pete was certain Lily would politely bow out, not that he could really blame her. He hadn't caught even a glimpse of her since she'd left their joint session yesterday morning, which should be a good thing. After all, the crown jewel of pastry chef positions was within his reach. All he had to do was stay focused on winning, and he could kiss his rigid boss and her even more rigid rules good-bye.

Now if he could just convince his body to stop double-crossing his brain with an endless supply of reminders from the hottest kiss of his life, he'd be all freaking set.

"Ready for tonight's fundraiser, Chef?" Chase Bishop's voice knocked Pete firmly from la-la land as the host approached him with a genuine smile, and he reset his focus for the umpteenth time today.

"Sure." Pete returned Chase's gesture with his standard

half-grin. "And you can call me Pete. You know, since there are no cameras rolling yet."

Chase held up his palms with a chuckle. "Hard habit to break, I guess. Hey, speaking of cameras, I meant to thank you and Ms. Callahan for agreeing to do another spotlight together. The first one is still pulling in steady numbers." He pitched his voice lower, shifting casually to close off their conversation. "Just between me and you, *Delectable* magazine has expressed interest in doing online coverage leading up to the final round."

Surprise ricocheted through Pete's veins. "Are you serious?"

Delectable was a hip, up-and-coming publication popular with both foodies and culinary professionals alike. Getting a mention was a big deal, but an entire spread on their website? It was a pastry chef's wildest dream.

"We're still finalizing the details, so it's pretty hush-hush. But since the first spot with you and Ms. Callahan was so popular, you two might want to brush up on your smiles."

Pete froze, despite the warmth and merry bustle in the lobby. "You think they'd keep us together even after tonight?"

"I think they'll give everyone equal consideration," Chase said, honesty blanketing his words. "But I also think they've seen the same numbers I have. I know what I'd do."

Unease trickled through him like cold dishwater in a sponge. Okay, yes, an online magazine spread like this was a crazy-good opportunity, one Pete would be insane to pass up. But . . . "To be honest, I'm not sure that would be the best idea."

"No?" The surprise covering Chase's face was complete, and Pete plowed on before he lost his nerve and recanted.

"It's not that I wouldn't want to." So far, so good there. Christ, he couldn't believe he was about to opt out of this. At least he'd make up for it when he won. "I'm just not sure Lily would feel the same way, and I wouldn't want her to feel uncomfortable about it."

"Wouldn't want me to feel uncomfortable about what?"

Pete swung his gaze toward the grand curve of the staircase at his back just in time to see Lily descend the last two steps, brows upturned. Her blond hair shone gold against the firelight in the soft glow of the lobby, dusting the shoulders of her red sweater as she fixed him with a wide-open expression that hit him right in the solar plexus.

God, she was beautiful.

Thankfully, Chase saved Pete's bacon by actually forming intelligible words. "We were just talking about the spotlight," he said, shuffling the subject ever so slightly. "The event committee is really grateful you both agreed to be filmed together at tonight's coffee and dessert to benefit School Days."

Lily gave Chase a polite smile. "Well, it's a great program. Having lived here my whole life, I know there are lots of working parents who need a safe place for their kids to go after school. And asking the remaining contestants to serve the cookies from today's baking session is brilliant."

Apparently, Pete hadn't filled his surprise quota for the day. "Tonight's fundraiser is for School Days?"

"Yes." Chase's brow dipped in concern even though his smile didn't budge. "Didn't one of the event planners review it with you? It should've been in your packet."

Damn it, he knew he'd forgotten something. Who knew there'd be something of actual importance in there? "Oh, right. It must've slipped my mind. But Lily's right. It's a great idea."

Chase nodded, his expression back in happy-host territory. "We're glad we could help raise money by sponsoring the event. Speaking of which, I'd better get out to the community center for some last-minute preparations. See you two there."

Chase made his way through the throng of guests sipping hot toddies and enjoying the Christmas carols being played by the pianist. The ski trails, visible through the huge expanse of windows across the back of the room, popped bright white against the velvety darkness of the mountains beyond. The scene was cozy despite all the people milling about, and it chipped away at the tension knotted in Pete's shoulders.

As soon as Chase was well out of earshot, Lily said, "I owe you an apology for storming off yesterday. It wasn't very professional of me."

The taut pull that had just left Pete's body threatened a comeback at the look on her face, but he refused to give it its due.

She'd been straight up about her past, and while he knew he couldn't return the favor, he owed it to her to at least tell the truth about the here and now.

"You don't owe me an apology, Lily. I was there, too. If anything, I should apologize to you for being out of line. I know you have a lot riding on the competition, and I'm sorry if I distracted you."

She blinked, and the soft firelight reflecting against her deep blue eyes made them sparkle. "What do you think? Truce? Until tomorrow, anyway."

"Truce," he agreed, tipping his head toward the main entrance. "Come on, I'll even give you a ride to the community center. You've never really lived until you've hit slushy side roads in a Jeep."

"Wow. You sure know how to impress a girl." Her tone might've carried all the by-the-book seriousness as usual, but there was no denying the hint of a sexy smile on her bow-shaped mouth.

Oh, this was going to be a long night.

"That's nothing," he said, opting for humor over heat. They'd *just* called a truce, for God's sake. "If you're really lucky, we might find a slippery parking lot on the way. I don't mean to brag, but I was the donut king at Parkview High School."

"No thank you. The only donuts I do are in the kitchen." She slid into a navy-blue coat that nearly matched the color of her stare, buttoning the thing all the way up to her chin, and he pulled back, surprised at her overly stern demeanor. But then that tiny whisper of a smile blossomed fully over her lips, bubbling up into a hot-as-hell laugh as she turned toward the door.

"Oh, relax Mancuso, I'm only kidding. Stop by the parking lot behind the hardware store on your way to the community center, and I'll show you the best stretch of unplowed asphalt in Pine Mountain."

Chapter 7

It was a good thing Pine Mountain Community Center had a public bathroom, because by the time Lily and Pete rushed through the main entrance, she was fairly certain she'd reached her holding-it limit from all the laughter.

"I told you it would work just as well in four-wheel drive once you turned off the stability control," she said, feeling the resulting ache in her side as she nudged him. It had been ages since she'd done donuts in a snowy parking lot, even though they racked up tons of powder every winter.

Come to think of it, it had been ages since she'd laughed like that, too.

"Okay, okay. You were right." Pete helped her out of her coat, hanging it carefully in the entryway closet before following suit with his own. "Do I even want to know where you learned to drive like that?"

"I went to high school too, you know. Only we have a lot more snow and open space out here in the hinterlands." The smell of brewing coffee mingled with the muted chatter from down the corridor, warming Lily's spirit even further. While she loved all the holiday celebrations in Pine Mountain, there was something extra comforting about Christmastime in the small community. Her mood was so pleasantly joyful that when Pete extended his elbow in offering, she twined her arm around his without a second thought as they headed to the main hall.

"Yeah, I have to be honest, being at the resort for the last couple of days has opened my eyes a little. I don't think I ever noticed how nice it is up here this time of year," Pete admitted.

Lily drew back to look at him, confused. "But you've lived here for five years now, haven't you?"

He paused, but then ironed out the hitch with a shrug. "Sure, but I'm not really around much. Between the commute and the hours, the only thing I really have time for when I'm here is sleep."

"So why live all the way out in the Blue Ridge? I mean, you grew up in Philly, right? And the back and forth has to be hellish." Of course, Lily was biased when it came to her hometown. She loved everything about Pine Mountain, from the quaint row of shops on Main Street to the larger-scale grandeur of the ski resort. She'd heard whisperings when Pete first moved here that he had a sister who lived in Riverside. But even so, Lily couldn't make sense of Pete living here if he had a great job in the city.

"It's a long story, and not nearly as good as the cookies we're about to serve up. After you."

Lily blinked, startled to already be at the entrance to the community center's main meeting room. "Oh, thanks."

"Lily! Pete! I'm so glad you're both here." The director of the community center made her way over with a grin.

"Hi Marianna." Lily greeted the woman with a smile and a hug. "It looks like some of the roads are finally clearing from last week's storm. This place is packed." She gestured to the busy room, dotted with tables draped in red and green and jam-packed with townspeople and resort staff.

"It doesn't hurt that Shane Griffin and Jackson Carter

offered to personally clear anyone's driveway in exchange for a donation," Marianna said, tipping her head at Pine Mountain's local mechanic and his super-sized contractor buddy.

"Nice," Lily agreed. "What do you need us to do?"

"Chase and I thought it would be fun to have the contestants team up with some of the local kids to serve our guests. As you can see, we've sold every seat in the house, so you guys will be on your toes."

"We're kind of used to that," Pete said, and heck if his provocative little half-smile didn't have a perfectly charming counterpart.

Was he *trying* to kill her? It was bad enough she'd lost control and initiated that kiss the other day. And now, despite the fact that Pete had been the one to put an end to their steamy lip-lock, all Lily could think about was doing it again. And again. And . . .

Marianna's grin snapped Lily's focus back to the matter at hand. "It's good news for us, since all the proceeds from tickets go directly to getting School Days up and running. Still, feel free to talk up additional donations. We need all the help we can get."

Concern pinched at Lily. "Are you still having trouble raising enough money to kick off in the New Year?" she asked, taking the red-and-white striped apron their hostess offered and passing the more masculine dark green one to Pete.

"We're doing our best," she said, but the tight lines beneath her smile were evident. "Anyway, tonight is about fun. And fame, apparently." Marianna pointed to the camera crew making their way across the room, her expression becoming more relaxed. "I've got to get back to the guests, but thanks again for helping out."

The camera crew descended upon Lily and Pete in a flurry of quick moves and expensive equipment, testing the lighting and reminding them to act natural just like they had the other day. Lily tamped down a snort at the possibility, surveying the room as a tech fiddled with a camera that probably cost as much as Lily's car.

"Is that . . . mistletoe?" she asked, adjusting her glasses to make sure she was seeing properly. No less than fifty bunches of dark green leaves hung around the spacious room, suspended by fat, red ribbons

"Oh, yeah. The stuff is everywhere. Apparently some of the locals thought it would be fun." The tech shrugged.

"I'll just bet they did," Lily muttered. God, this was the only thing she hated about living in a small town. But what could she expect? Pine Mountain thrived on juicy news, and everyone there had to have seen that video clip of her and Pete winning. And kissing.

Wait a second . . .

Ducking the attention of the crew as they finalized their setup, Lily turned toward Pete, whose brow lifted in direct proportion with her growing smile.

"That's a hell of a look you've got on your face, Blondie. I'm not sure if I should be intrigued or run for cover." He shifted toward her, green eyes warm and sparkling with mischief, and yeah, this would be *perfect*.

"Tell me something, Chef. Exactly how far are you willing to go in the name of charity?"

Pete had never been a fan of traditional kitchen wear, but he was suddenly grateful as hell for the swath of thick green fabric knotted around his hips. Who knew something as simple as a Christmas apron would save him from announcing to a roomful of people that the woman next to him was driving him mad?

"You sure about this?" he asked, although he had to admit, her plan was nothing short of brilliant. The fact that it would put them right back in the spotlight didn't seem to bother her.

Nor did the prospect of how they'd get there.

"I wouldn't have suggested it otherwise." Lily squared her slim shoulders. "If Shane and Jackson can clear driveways all in the name of charity, a couple of very public run-ins beneath the mistletoe is the least we can do."

Unsure whether he should be offended by her clinical approach or aroused at the prospect of kissing her again, Pete decided to split the difference with some cool nonchalance. "Nice to see there are some rules you're willing to bend for a good cause."

"It's perfectly within the boundaries of the rules." Lily scooped up a tray full of iced sugar cookies, but not before he caught the pink tinge climbing up her cheeks. "We're simply doing the assigned video segment. This just gives School Days some good press on top of it. And if even half the people scoping out our Internet clips make a small donation as a result, it'll be worth it." She dropped her voice to a whisper. "We should probably come up with a schedule. You know, so we meet up often enough under the mistletoe."

Pete laughed. Even her spontaneity had a plan. "Lily, the stuff is everywhere. Why don't we just wing it?" He cut off the protest brewing on her lips. "Just for the sake of keeping it natural?"

Her brow curved in thought. "Oh. I guess that makes sense."

Pete subtly checked his apron, half-certain that all the fabric on the planet wasn't going to hide how badly he wanted to do a test run on one of those kisses, sans audience. "See you under the mistletoe, Blondie."

They separated, weaving their way through the crowd. The setting was festive and comfortable, just like at the resort, and it smoothed out the unspoken tension of tomorrow's impending elimination round.

The sight of Lily putting her arm around a young blond girl with a snowman-print apron as they passed out cookies together didn't hurt. She looked so in her element, handing out sweets and laughing with the recipients, that it made joining in easy and inviting.

Pete moved from table to table, talking up the locals he knew and introducing himself to those he didn't. He knew he should play it cool and hang back a few more minutes so their little publicity stunt didn't seem contrived, but the prospect of kissing Lily again had him gravitating toward her before he could stop himself.

Then, out of the corner of his eye, Pete caught a glimpse of someone leaning against the wall, sticking to the shadows. The kid looked smack in the middle of puberty, definitely no longer a boy, but not quite a full-on teen. His brown hair was just a shade too long, his threadbare sweatshirt just a bit too small, and everything about him hollered at Pete like a drill sergeant, forcing his feet temporarily off course.

"Hi," Pete said, blending into the background next to the kid like a pro. The boy sent a look of both disdain and curiosity in Pete's direction before he finally shrugged.

"Hey."

"You hungry?" Pete nodded down at the tray of gingersnaps in his hand.

The kid's eyes went wide for just a breath before he returned his glance to his beat-up sneakers. "Those are for the real people, aren't they? I mean, the people who paid for tickets, and stuff."

Pete forced his words past the ache lodged firmly in his sternum. "Don't worry, there are plenty. Plus, every good chef tastes his finished product, and it just so happens I made these myself." He held up the tray in offering.

"Guys can be chefs?" The kid looked at him, dubious.

"Yup. In fact, most chefs are." Pete took a cookie off the tray and popped it into his mouth like it was nothing.

"I didn't know that." He hesitated, but then slipped a cookie from the tray.

"I didn't either, when I first started." Pete shifted the tray to one hand so he could extend the other. "Pete Mancuso."

The kid looked genuinely surprised at the equality of a simple handshake. "Uh, Lucas. Lucas Ford."

"Well, Lucas, I heard the contestants are supposed to team up with someone to serve these cookies. I could use a right-hand man. You up for the job?"

"I don't know." Lucas's eyes took an up and down trip over Pete. "Do I have to wear an apron?"

Pete didn't even bother containing his laugh. Christ, this was a kid after his own heart. "I usually stick with a chef's coat, but today I made an exception. I'm sure Marianna would let you slide, though."

Lucas took a bite of his cookie, as if to buy time before he answered. "Okay. I guess that's cool then."

"Great." Pete pointed to the prep area at the back of the main room. "While the apron's optional, hand washing isn't. Why don't you go scrub up and find me when you're done? Then we can tackle this crowd together."

Lucas grunted an agreement before heading off, but Pete needed a minute before rejoining the fray. He let his eyes wander around the room until they automatically landed on Lily. The serious knit that usually graced her brow had softened to pale gold, and as she smiled, she looked as honest and pretty as a room full of daylight. She was clearly caught up in the moment, lost in what she was doing, yet sure with the sheer thrill of it.

As Pete watched her, with time both stretching out and stopping all at once, he knew exactly how she felt.

★   ★   ★

It took exactly twelve more minutes before Pine Mountain's decorating committee got what they'd been hoping for with all that strategically placed Christmas greenery.

Not that Pete had been counting.

"Why, Lily Callahan! It looks like you and Pete are under a sprig of mistletoe." A sweet-looking elderly lady pointed knowingly to a spot over their heads, and damn, Lily's flush made the whole thing look completely genuine.

"Oh! I guess we are, Mrs. Teasdale. Did you know that mistletoe is most commonly found on apple trees? It dates back as far as ancient times."

Mrs. Teasdale laughed. "Lord, child. You always did blurt the strangest things. Now go on and kiss that young man. You don't want to bring bad luck to School Days, now do you?"

"No. I . . . I guess not." Lily turned then, and Pete scanned her face with care. As badly as he wanted to kiss her, he wasn't going to do it if he saw even the slightest hint of doubt in her eyes.

But she met his gaze with a very tiny, very certain nod.

He leaned down, purposely leaving a decent sliver of space between everything but their mouths for propriety's sake even though his body screamed in protest. Lily's lips were just as soft as he remembered, and even though he barely brushed them with his own, the taste of her sent a streak of heat to his very core.

Holy hell. If he were on Death Row, he'd choose this woman as his last frigging meal.

But then a smattering of applause filtered past his subconscious, reminding him not just where he was, but what he was doing.

And more important, what he *shouldn't* be doing.

"Well, no bad luck there," Mrs. Teasdale said with a twinkle in her eye as he and Lily parted.

"No ma'am." Pete armed himself with a smile, realizing belatedly there was a zero percent chance the camera crew had missed the opportunity to capture the whole thing. Sure enough, a guy in a backward baseball cap stood less than five feet away, camera going full speed, bringing him even further back to reality. It was a publicity stunt, nothing more. The fact that he'd get a boost out of it while promoting a good cause didn't hurt, either.

Pete spent the next two hours alternating between talking up School Days, trying to coax casual conversation out of Lucas, and kissing Lily at fairly regular intervals. The more they bumped into each other accidentally on purpose under the mistletoe, the happier the guests became. They gushed about the magic of the season, diving into their purses and wallets to make one last donation, and the camera crew ate it up like candy. By the time the last cookie had been served and the crowd dwindled to stragglers, Pete's mood was damn near unbreakable.

"Correct me if I'm wrong, but I believe we hit every bunch of mistletoe in this place." He gestured upward to a particularly large collection of greenery before tossing his apron into the bin Marianna had brought out for dirty linens.

"That may be an exaggeration." Lily's prim words were no match for the ear-to-ear stunner on her face. "But suffice it to say, our next spotlight will probably be as popular as our first."

"Does it bother you?" Pete fell into step with her as they headed toward the exit. The camera crew had long since packed up for the night, allowing them to speak freely about Operation Mistletoe.

Lily's brow puckered over her frown. "It was my idea, remember?"

He remembered, all right. "I just want to make sure you don't have any regrets, I guess."

"Regrets are a waste of time. It makes more sense to change things if you don't like them rather than worry about what's done."

The matter-of-fact explanation made so much sense, was so undeniably *Lily* that he had no choice but to laugh. "Fair enough."

Pete slid her coat over her shoulders before pulling on his own, ushering Lily through the double doors of the red-bricked community center. A now-familiar figure captured his attention from beyond the reach of the street-light, and although the kid's back was to them, Pete recognized him in an instant.

"Lucas!"

He stopped, but didn't turn around for a long second. It gave Pete and Lily time to cross the parking lot, their breath scattering in smoky wisps from the bone-rattling cold.

"Lily, you met Lucas earlier, right?" Pete tipped his head toward the kid, who wore nothing more than a jean jacket that had seen better days. He had to be freezing.

"I sure did. He handed out every last one of my ginger-snaps." She gave Lucas a warm smile, and he returned it with a tentative one before stuffing his hands in his pockets.

"Everyone said they were good." Lucas directed the comment more to the pavement than Lily, and it struck Pete how painfully shy the kid really was.

"Smart crowd." He skimmed a glance over the scattering of cars left in the parking lot. "Are you waiting for a ride?"

"Oh, uh, no." Lucas slumped further into his jacket, but didn't elaborate. Man, the poor kid would never make it home without frostbite, even if he lived close by.

"Well you're in luck. I'm already giving Lily a ride. Why don't we take you wherever you're headed, too?"

That got Lucas's head to pop up. "That's okay. I mean, it's cool for me to walk."

Lily's expression turned to pure determination, but Pete gave her a tiny, silent head shake before turning to Lucas with the most laid-back glance he could work up. "That's too bad. I was kind of hoping for some help."

Both Lucas and Lily shot him quizzical looks, although hers wore a healthy smattering of *what the hell are you up to?* But this kid would only retreat further if they strong-armed him, even with the best intentions.

It was something Pete knew by heart, and in that split second of realization, he knew exactly what he'd do with the contest money if he won.

"Yeah. Lily and I have a friendly debate going about which is better for a chocolate chip cookie. I'm a big fan of chewy, but she thinks thin and crisp is the way to go. I was hoping for a little input in case I decide to make them in the next round tomorrow, but . . ."

"Oh." The word thudded between them, both hesitant and hopeful. "I kind of like both."

"Maybe you could tell us why? There's nothing better than an unbiased opinion," Pete said, tipping his head toward the Jeep. "And I could give you a ride home, as my way of saying thanks."

"Just for telling you what I think?"

But it was Lily who tipped the scales with her quiet, sincere nod.

"Absolutely, Lucas. After all, we could use the help."

Chapter 8

Lily snuck a glance at her bedside clock for the sixth time in ten minutes and grunted her disgust. It wasn't terribly late, but between her nerves over tomorrow's elimination and the thoughts crowding her head from earlier tonight, the chances she'd actually drift off any time soon were slim to none.

And slim was looking pretty anorexic.

She forced herself to sink further down into the luxurious bedding, willing relaxation into her overwound muscles. She was in one of the most gorgeously appointed suites in the entire Blue Ridge, for God's sake. Letting go of her tension should be a walk in the park in a place like this.

If only she could dislodge the image of her cocky counterpart from the front-and-center spot in her brain, maybe she'd get a little shuteye.

Okay, so their little performance tonight had garnered the results they'd hoped for, enhancing donations by creating good cheer and getting School Days' name in the media. But it also had some results she hadn't counted on, namely the heat brewing in some very delicate places, and the one thought Lily could no longer ignore.

She wanted Pete Mancuso. Badly.

Which was demented, not to mention totally irrational.

He was a risk-taker—borderline arrogant, really—and he wanted to win this competition as much as she did.

But he's also kind and smart and decent, came a whisper from within, and even though she wanted to ignore it, she couldn't.

Pete had known exactly what to say to Lucas to put him at ease, from the minute they'd all climbed into the Jeep to the easygoing "See ya later" he'd given up when they dropped the boy off. Lily knew Pine Mountain well enough to recognize that Lucas lived in one of the most rural sections of town, and one of the poorest. Coming from a family of little means, it was easy for Lily to see the subtle signs in hindsight.

What she *didn't* see was how Pete had picked up on them, and well before she had, to boot.

You could ask him, whispered the voice again, and okay, now she was really going crazy. She couldn't just show up at Pete's hotel suite at ten o'clock at night in her pajamas, asking him all sorts of personal questions. It was insane. It was impolite. It was . . .

Totally, unequivocally forbidden, and she wanted nothing more than to do it.

Before reason could glue her to the bed, Lily flung back the coverlet and stood up. So what if this was the most impulsive thing she had done since . . . well, birth. Pete broke the rules all the time. He probably wouldn't think it was all that crazy to find her knocking at his door. In fact, he probably did this kind of thing before he even finished his morning coffee.

Lily jammed her feet into her shoes and scooped her hair into a ponytail. If worse came to worst, she could always excuse her visit with a baking question and be back in bed in five minutes flat. The presence of a backup plan bolstered her, guiding her feet right out the door and down the thickly carpeted hallway.

Lily had heard Pete ask the hotel staff for some extra coffee filters the other day, and at the time, she'd thought it a product of her meticulous brain that his room number had stuck in her head like molasses clinging to a measuring cup.

Only now she knew her brain had nothing to do with it.

Losing her nerve wasn't an option, though, and now that she had a plan, complete with a solid backup, she'd damn well stick to it. Lily placed a businesslike knock on the door in front of her, straightening her shoulders with a nod. This was no big deal.

But then the door swung open, revealing a slightly rumpled pastry chef wearing nothing but a pair of low-slung basketball shorts and a smile, and Lily's plan spontaneously combusted.

"Something tells me you're not here to borrow a cup of sugar," Pete said, and holy *shit,* how had she not factored possible shirtlessness into the equation? After all, plenty of guys slept without a shirt on.

Not to mention plenty more who slept in the nude.

"Oh!" Lily squeaked. She should've known better than to think she could pull off something this risky. "Ah, no. I just . . . I had a question." Why, oh why hadn't she come up with a getaway question *before* she'd knocked? The impossible silence hurtling over the threshold made her blurt the first thing that flew into her head.

"Did you know that there are six different kinds of peepholes you can have installed on a door for security?"

Pete's brow popped, and he turned to look over one shoulder at the peephole in his door, muscles flexing just enough to make Lily lightheaded.

"You got out of bed to tell me that?" The smile tugging at his lips was undeniable, and the sight of it guided even more embarrassing honesty out of her, despite the risk.

"No. I got out of bed because I want to know why you were so nice to Lucas."

Pete's smile vanished, but he stepped back into his room. "Come on in."

Lily tiptoed into his suite, which was a mirror image of hers, if a bit messier. Pete took a T-shirt from a duffel bag on the floor, pulling it over his head as he sat down on the half-made bed. Having no idea what the protocol was for barging in on someone like this, she perched on the edge of the desk chair across from him and just came out with it.

"I'm sorry for being so forward. It's just that not a lot of people would've even noticed Lucas tonight, much less known exactly how to make him feel comfortable, but you did."

He shrugged, a singular tight jerk of his shoulders to match his clipped response. "I was just nice to a kid who looked like he needed it."

But Lily hadn't gotten out of bed for canned generalizations, and she wasn't going back to her room without answers. "I think there's more to it than that."

"What else could there be?"

Lily drew in a breath. Screw it. If she was going to hold back, she wouldn't have knocked on his door in the first place.

"I don't know, Pete. But the more time I spend around you, the more I see someone different from the hotshot pastry chef who smacked into me last week. And it wouldn't be such a big deal, except . . ." She paused, her heart now kicking full-throttle against her ribcage. "Except I really like the guy I see."

Pete jerked back to look at her. "I'm not as nice a guy as you think."

"I don't believe you."

"No?" His eyes went dark green and wide with sur-

prise. He pushed off from the bed to cut the space between them to mere inches, kneeling in front of her to
look her right in the eye. "If I was a nice guy, I wouldn't
be thinking about how much I want to kiss you right
now."

Lily's breath sped up, her nipples tightening beneath the
thin cotton of her pajama top as Pete edged between her
knees, stroking his thumb over her bottom lip with excru-
ciating care.

"You wouldn't?" she whispered, and oh God, she'd
never felt anything so right in her life.

He shook his head before dipping his mouth within an
inch of hers. "If I were in any way decent, I wouldn't be
remembering how you taste like fresh peppermint, right
here."

Lily was helpless against the sigh pushing up from her
chest, and Pete's lips curled into a wicked smile before he
turned toward the shell of her ear.

"And if I were the guy you think I am, I damn sure
wouldn't be wondering if the rest of you tastes the same
way."

The words snapped Lily's last tenuous thread of control,
and she turned her mouth so close to his, she could feel
the heat of his exhale.

"Then maybe I'm not the woman you think *I* am, because I want you to find out."

They came together in a hot rush of breath and limbs
and total desire, and she dug her hands into the soft material covering his shoulders, welcoming the feel of his body
beneath. Pete let out a pleasured groan, rocking against
her for momentum as he scooped her from the chair to his
lap in one swift motion. Under any other circumstances,
tumbling to the floor might be troublesome, but with
Pete's hard-in-all-the-right-places body beneath hers, Lily

not only didn't care, she never wanted to move from her spot.

"Oh, God, that feels so good." Lily notched her body over his, covering his chest with her own as she pressed against him from shoulder to hip.

Another groan broke from his mouth, and he shuddered beneath her as her knees widened over the lean expanse of his hips. "Jesus. Lily, please be sure."

She pressed her palms against the lush carpet, pushing up to look him in the eye. "No regrets, remember? I'm sure."

His chuckle was a dark, seductive counterpart to the delicious tension pulling her taut. "Okay. But if we're going to do this, let's do it right."

He levered to sitting, his hands covering the swell of her ass as he reached around to sweep her fully into his arms. In one fluid move, Lily was weightless as Pete stood and carried her across the carpet. He lowered them carefully to the bed, placing her in the center of his lap before sliding his hand over her heart to release the buttons on her pajama top one by one. The rasp of the fabric on her nipples was such a contrast to the cool air that Lily bit down on her lip in an effort to not cry out as Pete slipped it from the frame of her shoulders.

To her surprise, he didn't move quickly or touch her with any of the hard passion of a few moments ago. Instead, he was reverent, touching her body in slow, sweet caresses as if she was a lazy Sunday morning and he had all the time in the world to savor her.

"Pete." Lily squirmed against him, the ache building between her thighs making her impatient. But he refused to give in, simply pinning her with a look so utterly sexy, it stayed her movements.

"I told you. I'm not a nice guy."

His hands shaped the back of her ribcage as he drew her close, trailing kisses down her neck as his fingers climbed gently up her spine. She arched to give him unbroken access, feeling his smile against her skin. The sighs that left her with every touch would've been embarrassing, except even those felt deliciously good as they spilled past her lips.

"God, you are beautiful." Pete's hands moved in a lazy trail from her back to her shoulders, tracing the heated path of his kisses, and Lily was certain she'd drown in the sheer want coursing through her. When he finally set his attention on her breasts, she gasped at the feel of his callused fingers on her sensitive skin.

Another smile curved into her flesh as he dipped his head lower, and oh *God,* Pete's stubble felt even better than his fingers on her needy skin. Cupping his hands to test the weight of first one breast, then the other, he drew in one nipple, tight against his tongue. The ache between her thighs became an absolute demand, and Lily rolled her hips into his, driven by need.

Pete curled his hand upward in response, holding her tighter. When his fingers joined in with the wicked movement of his mouth as he teased her, Lily knotted her legs around his waist, thrusting against his erection in a greedy push.

"You're not playing by the rules," he ground out, stopping his ministrations only long enough to let the words escape. But for the first time in her life, Lily didn't care about playing fair. Hell, she didn't care about anything unless it involved having this man inside her body.

"You're not really going to turn into a stickler on me now, are you?" Lily moved back to slide her hand between their bodies. Her palm met soft fabric over rock-hard intentions, and a muscle ticked beneath Pete's stubble as she stroked his cock.

"Only if turnabout is fair play." He eased her back to the

pillows, filling her belly with butterflies as he shifted forward for another searing kiss. She gripped the hem of his T-shirt as she pressed up to return it, and within seconds, both the shirt and her pajama bottoms lay in a heap on the floor.

She knew she should be self-conscious in the low light of Pete's room, wearing nothing but a pair of light blue panties and a tremble on her lips, but the feeling that had steered Lily down the hallway in the first place remained.

This didn't feel crazy or brash or impulsive. It felt right, like it was made exactly for her.

"Still sure?" Pete asked, as if her thoughts were broadcast on her face, but she only nodded.

"You?"

"Are you kidding?" He slid under the covers, pulling her close against him in answer. "I've wanted you since the minute I saw you."

His hands were on her like wildfire, hot and out of control as he coaxed sensations from her body she'd only fantasized about. Lily returned the favor, running her hands over the leanly muscled expanse of Pete's chest, letting her fingers follow the scattering of dark hair leading from his navel to his waistband.

"Not yet," he murmured, capturing her wrist in one palm. But when she whimpered her displeasure, he parted her knees with a gentle press, green eyes glittering as he slid down her body.

"First, I want to find out the answer to my question."

Sparks shot through Lily's belly as he slipped her underwear from her hips, trailing kisses from her breasts to her belly button. He paused for just a minute to rim her navel with a lazy sweep of his tongue, causing her whimper to make a repeat performance.

But then he settled on the heat between her thighs, and she promptly forgot her name.

"*Oh,* God." Lily's fists knotted over hot handfuls of cotton as she gripped the coverlet beneath her. But Pete refused to rush, pleasuring her in long, languid strokes with both his hands and mouth. All of Lily's tension and unanswered need stretched together into one fine point as he touched her so flawlessly, until the mounting pressure hovered on the bright edge between reason and release.

She tumbled over without a second thought.

Waves of pleasure splashed through her, covering even the smallest places as she came with a keening cry. Pete lightened his touch by slow degrees, slipping from the cradle of her hips only after he'd wrought every last shudder from her body.

"You are stunning like this." He placed the whisper in the space between her neck and her shoulder, although Lily felt it all the way down to her toes. She reached for him, guiding her hands around his face as she fixed her eyes on his, unwavering.

"I don't want to wait anymore. I want you, Pete."

Pete's quick fumble through the bedside table blessedly produced a condom, and Lily wrapped her hands around his waistband as he returned to the threshold of her hips. She lowered the last garment between them, shocked to find even more need swirling within her as he rolled the condom on and slid his length along her aching folds.

"Now. *Please.*"

Slowly, he pressed his cock into the heat of her body, stealing every ounce of her breath as he stretched her completely.

"Lily." Her name passed through his lips on a ragged groan. "You feel so good," he said, sliding back just to surge forward and fill her again.

"Please . . . don't stop." Lily matched his rhythm, sensual pressure rebuilding in her core with every thrust.

Pete braced himself on his forearms, grazing her skin

with each movement, and the brush of his chest on her nipples made her gasp. Wrapping her fingers around the tight muscles in his hips, she held him in place, lifting her body to meet his again and again until she began to quake with familiar, brilliant release.

"Ah, God, Lily." Pete ground out her name, and she chanted his in return, arching up to take him until he leaned down to cover her. He gripped the curve of her shoulders with rough palms, answering her thrusts with more of his own until he began to shudder on one final groan, holding her tight to his body as he came.

They lay together beneath the sheets, panting and spent in a tangle of limbs as Lily regained her body. Minutes dropped off the clock, but whether it was two or two hundred, she couldn't tell.

And in that moment, Lily realized that for all the meticulous planning that had led her down the hall, she had absolutely no clue what to do next.

Chapter 9

Of all the things Pete could imagine doing the night before an elimination challenge, having the most intense sex of his life was nowhere near the top of the list. In fact, the only thing that seemed less likely was doing it twice, then falling asleep wrapped around the woman in question.

Which made Pete two for two in the *no fucking way* category.

In his defense, he hadn't *planned* on having sex with Lily, not even when she'd appeared on his doorstep wearing soft pink pajamas that matched her hot-as-hell blush. He'd even tried to warn her by telling her outright that he wasn't a nice guy, but then she'd done something that kicked his resolve right out from under him.

She'd played it straight, and the simple honesty made him realize exactly how much he wanted her, too.

A little problematic, since not only were they vying for the same prize, but Lily had also managed to glimpse past the cocky façade he'd worn like a suit of armor for half his life. Something about her no-nonsense disposition tempted Pete to trust her with the rest of it, to lay it all on the line and let her see everything. After all, she'd grown up in difficult circumstances too.

The only difference was, she had a family who loved her, whereas Pete had parents who only stopped drinking long enough to tell him and his sister how worthless they were.

"Hey." Lily's soft voice broke through his trip down bad-memory lane as she sat down next to him, and the bright morning sunlight pouring in through lobby windows had nothing on her glow. "I'm glad I caught you. I grabbed some bagels and juice from Joe's. We only have a few minutes to get to the competition floor, but you should probably eat."

His smile was involuntary, in spite of the thoughts she'd interrupted. "You always eat a balanced breakfast, don't you?"

She paired her return smile with an eye roll. "It doesn't hurt to start out healthy. Breakfast *is* the most important meal of the day."

Pete laughed. "I'm going to make you a banana split one morning. Bet it'll change your tune."

The implication hit him only after the words were out, and he cleared his throat in an effort to smooth over it.

Christ, he wanted to spend more than one night with her.

Lily's movements screeched to a halt, her blue eyes flying wide before she dropped them to her hands. "Well, at least there's fruit in a banana split," she said, dodging the subject as she finished passing him a white paper bag printed with Joe's logo.

But being with her had been the best thing he'd felt in who knew how long, and suddenly, he didn't want to skirt the issue. "Lily, look at me."

Surprisingly, she did, and it made telling her how he really felt a foregone conclusion. "I know we didn't plan for this to happen, and that it has the potential to get . . . complicated."

She exhaled audibly over a wry smile, but still held his gaze. "That's one way of putting it."

"But I don't care."

"You don't?" The shock on her face was plain.

"Look, I'm not saying I don't want to win, because I do. But when I look at you, I like who I see, too. And that doesn't happen a lot." Okay, so it didn't even happen intermittently, but the last thing he wanted to do was freak her out fifteen minutes before they went into the kitchen.

"So where does that leave us?" Lily asked, so straightforward that he had no choice but to answer her with the same honesty.

"Right here together, I guess."

She sat with him as he ate, and although they didn't speak, the quiet settled over them like a blanket, drawing them together. Finally, Lily glanced at the hallway leading to the competition floor, and Pete's chest tightened as he squeezed her hand.

"Go. I know you're dying to get ready for them to let us in."

Her sheepish expression told him he'd been spot-on in reading her, but she didn't let go of his fingers. "Are you sure?"

In that moment, Pete knew his life was about to get a hell of a lot more complicated, because as much as he didn't want to go home today, he didn't want Lily to go home, either.

As crazy as it was, he wanted to be with her, and not just for a night or two.

"Yeah, Blondie. I'm sure."

Pete pressed his palms against the countertop in his assigned station, trying to absorb enough of the steely coolness to soften the edges of adrenaline in his veins as Chase Bishop took the podium.

"Good morning, contestants." Chase dialed his smile to

the on-air setting as he nodded to the group. "Welcome to our next elimination round. We'll be narrowing the field to ten finalists today, which means each of you will need to bring your A-game if you want to advance. In keeping with our Christmas theme, today's challenge is to create a cookie based on your best holiday memory."

Pete's gut sank as Chase continued. "You'll each have fifteen minutes to plan and an hour to bake and plate your offering. While flavor and technique will be deciding factors as always, presentation is key in this round. Each dish should reflect your personal story, and you will be judged accordingly. Good luck, contestants. Your time starts . . . right now."

Pete buckled down over the rock of unease centered firmly in his stomach. He hadn't come this far to lose out because of his past. Hell, he'd paid for those years in spades—no way was he going to give those bitter memories a piece of him now, no matter what the challenge requirements might be. The only Christmas he wanted to remember was this one, punctuated by the sweet taste of victory.

He stabbed a hand through his hair, forcing himself to think as he skimmed a glance over the crowd.

Lucas's tentative stare from the spectator's section zapped him with all the subtlety of jumper cables on a tapped-out battery. For a split second, Pete's focus did a complete free fall, but then the kid lifted a hand in a silent wave, and the hope on his face locked Pete's determination back into place.

He could either crush this event, or let it crush him, and the latter just wasn't an option. After all, he was only presenting to three judges. He could say just enough to get by without spilling his guts, even if it did skirt the presentation requirements a little. Then he'd let his kickass cookie lead him right to the finals.

So he could donate the prize money to School Days when he won the whole damned thing.

For sixty minutes, Pete worked with laserlike precision, finessing each ingredient to suit the recipe forming in his head. His formal training kicked into gear, melding flavors to create a flawless profile. Toasted hazelnuts met heady brown sugar in the food processor while jewel-toned raspberries deepened and mellowed over low heat. Pete knocked out each task with meticulous care, and by the time the clock hit zero, he was absolutely certain he'd advance. He'd thrown every skill he had into his dish, from the complex flavors to the artful balance of colors and textures on the plate.

"Competitors!" Chase's voice quieted the murmuring crowd. "Since we've asked you for something personal in this round, we'd like to take it a step further."

Pete resisted the urge to wince. He should've known better than to think they'd actually do this straight up. Not that it mattered. He had perfection on his plate, and nothing could throw him off his game now.

"Rather than keep your presentations behind closed doors like last round, we've decided to do them right here, in front of your fellow contestants *and* our public audience."

The cameraman by Pete's station panned over the crowd while he silently clutched. How the hell was he supposed to bolster his reputation by airing out his dirty laundry in front of everyone? Three judges, he could've managed. An entire audience, plus the whole story going on the Internet?

Not a chance. He needed a backup plan. Like yesterday.

"We've drawn numbers to determine presentation order. Today's first contestant is Lily Callahan."

Pete's pulse logjammed in his veins as Lily stepped for-

ward, nodding to Chase and the judges with an unreadable expression.

"The cookie I made today is an eggnog snickerdoodle,
combining two of my favorites from childhood. I wanted
to play up both classic sweet flavors with some depth and
sophistication, so I added nutmeg and a little bit of bour-
bon to the mix. Kind of like sugar and spice, all grown
up."

Laughter rippled from the judges' table as Lily continued. "This cookie reminds me of my tenth Christmas,
when all I wanted was an Easy-Bake Oven." Her voice
wavered with just a hint of emotion, but she kept going.
"I come from a big family, and money was tight, so I
didn't get my hopes up. Still, I wished for that oven, so I
could learn how to bake cookies just like my mom. She is
truly an inspiration to me, and I wanted to be like her in
every sense of the word, especially when I was ten.

"My mom knew how much I wanted the oven even
though I tried to hide it, so she and my dad worked extra
shifts to have enough money to splurge. When I saw it under the tree, it was a dream come true, not just because I
got what'd I'd wished for, but because it taught me that
anything is possible, even for a little girl from the poor side
of town." Lily paused, her matter-of-fact demeanor falling
away to reveal raw emotion that took a potshot at Pete's
sternum as she finished.

"It was then that I knew in my heart I was a baker. I
broke in that Easy-Bake Oven by making snickerdoodles
on Christmas morning, which we all enjoyed with eggnog. While I promise my recipe has been refined over the
years, this cookie, and the flavors in it, really represent the
season for me. I hope you enjoy it."

Lily stepped back to her station while the judges tasted
and took notes, and in that moment, Pete knew he was

screwed. Sure, he could make up some easy-breezy fabrication involving Christmases by the fire and a bunch of other things that had never happened, but no way could he pull off a presentation like Lily's, packed with enough emotional punch to put tears in Chef di Matisse's eyes. Whatever he came up with, especially on the fly, wouldn't be enough.

For a brief second, Pete considered just letting the truth out. But blabbing about his difficult past wouldn't just expose him, and his sister had been through enough already. Ava had come here five years ago to forget, and he'd come to Pine Mountain to look out for her. He couldn't risk the possibility of her having to relive those memories because he'd dragged them all over the Internet for a contest win.

His fellow contestants presented their cookies one by one, many of them with heartfelt stories like Lily's, until finally, he was the last chef standing.

"Our final presentation is from Pete Mancuso," Chase said from the podium, and an event staffer came forward to gather the plates from Pete's station. There, on three tiny white dishes, were his perfectly constructed desserts, showcasing a flawless flavor profile and impeccable skill under a damn-near ridiculous time constraint.

And each one of them held a story he couldn't tell. So instead, Pete did what he always did.

He leveled his cocky smile at the judges, broadcasting the very confidence that had been stamped out of him all his life.

"The cookie I've made for you is a raspberry-acai and chocolate linzer. I softened the tartness of the fruit filling with honey and rose water, and added a swirl of bittersweet ganache to play against the sweetness of the traditional Linzer base." Pete filled the expectant pause with a nod toward the judges. "Please enjoy."

Three sets of eyebrows lifted in plain surprise. "It's such

a beautifully executed cookie, Chef. Don't you want to say anything else about it?" Chef di Matisse looked at him expectantly.

But Pete just shook his head, throwing every ounce of confidence he could work up into his words. "No, Chef. I think this cookie speaks for itself."

With that, he returned to his station. He'd taken plenty of risks in his life—hell, he thrived on it—and they always paid off. So what if he bent the rules a little with presentation? He'd put a work of art on that plate, and the food was all that mattered.

Finally, after a stretch of time that felt better measured by millennia than minutes, Chase stepped back up to the podium. "Well. Once again, our judges were faced with difficult decisions, and once again, mere points have been the deciding factor. You've all worked hard, but only ten of you can proceed to the final round, to be held on Christmas Eve."

Chase began to read the finalist's names, and Pete's chest tightened at Lily's ultra-serious expression from a few stations over. He sent his gaze to the audience, searching for an impartial face to latch on to in order to keep him steady.

Lucas's hopeful stare met him like a punch in the gut. This move would work, he told himself with silent, steely resolve. It had to.

Pete couldn't fail this kid. He knew all too sharply how much the disappointment hurt. But for the first time, his confidence felt flat, like a cake baked at the wrong temperature, never quite making it to where it should be.

Finally, Chase called Lily's name, but Pete's relief was short-lived as the list continued to dwindle.

"Ladies and gentlemen, we have one last spot, and with it, one last chance to win ten thousand dollars. It was an extremely close call, but in the end, once again, only one point made the difference." Chase's eyes skimmed the contestants, and Pete was certain his chest would implode from his heart's feeble efforts to keep up. Finally, Chase said, "Our last finalist in this year's Pine Mountain Christmas Cookie Competition is . . ."

Chapter 10

"**I** cannot believe you did that, you unbelievable jackass."
Lily propped herself up on one elbow, her hair spilling down her bare back as she fixed Pete with the mother of all stern looks.

Too bad for her, he wasn't buying it. Especially since she was still flushed and sweaty from the orgasm he'd given her barely ten minutes ago.

"If I'm not mistaken, you threw yourself at *me* in celebration the minute I got here." He gave up a lazy smile, and Lily's cheeks flushed just enough to make him want a repeat performance of that orgasm-giving thing.

"Not *that*. I meant what you pulled with the judges today. Do you have any idea how close you came to not making the final round?"

Pete shifted to face her, still tangled in the bed sheets. "Haven't we covered this territory?" he asked, skimming his fingers over the slope of her shoulder. "Points aren't cumulative, remember?"

She huffed out an exasperated breath. "Still! It was a massive unnecessary risk. Did you even look at your scores?" She gestured to the folder he'd tossed on the desk in her suite upon arrival, and his gut knotted in unease.

"I was a little distracted," he said, hoping she'd drop it. Not a chance. "But you're not now." Lily grabbed her bathrobe from the chair next to the bed and slipped it on, making a beeline for the folder.

"Come on, Blondie." Pete raked a gaze over her, and goddamn she was beautiful, even wrapped in all that terry cloth. "You distracted me when I walked in the door. It wouldn't really be fair if I didn't distract you back." All it would take was one very strategic tug and about ten seconds, and he could have her naked. Again.

"Using my propensity to follow the rules against me is a low blow," she said, and despite the huskiness in her voice that told him she was thinking about the distraction he could provide, Lily stood firm. "I want to know why you didn't say anything to the judges today."

He blew out a breath, lifting his shoulders in a shrug like nothing doing. "Guess I just wanted to make a statement."

"But if that were true, you would've done exactly that. Only you didn't."

Of all the women in Pine Mountain, Pete had to go and fall for the most direct.

Lily's expression softened, and she sat down next to him on the bed. "Look, I was twenty feet away and I could see that those linzer cookies were the most incredible thing anyone made today. I get that you're not a rules kind of guy." She paused, as if the mere thought of it was total lunacy. "But you were a shoo-in for the final round, right up until you opened your mouth. Or more to the point, didn't. Even for you, it was over the top, and you can't pull that kind of stuff now that Conrad Le Clerc is in the picture."

Her words shot through him like ice water in August. "What?"

She blinked, clearly confused. "Conrad Le Clerc is judging the final round, along with Martin, Olivia, and Chef di Matisse. Didn't you read anything in your folder?"

Christ, that folder was going to be the end of him. "No,

I didn't." Pete pushed up to take the offered papers, shoving his score sheet to the back of the pile as he read. Sure enough, Conrad Le Clerc was listed as the special guest judge for all three courses of the final round on Christmas Eve.

"Looks like they've upped our PR spots too," he said, although it was an understatement. According to the sheet in his hand, they'd actually doubled.

"Yeah, I guess the people at *Delectable* came through with that online spread. But that's good for you, right? I mean, you want to win for the exposure."

Pete flipped his folder closed with a snap. "Sure."

But just like last night, Lily looked right past his no-big-deal smokescreen. She slid the folder from his grasp, her fingers lingering on his wrist. "What's going on, Pete?"

His instinct screamed at him to shut up, but something even deeper overrode it and guided the words right out. "If I win the competition, I'm going to donate the money to School Days."

Lily's lips fell into a perfect pink O. "You're . . . what?"

"I just decided last night, but I'm sure. Those kids like Lucas deserve a good place, a safe place, to go. And for some of them, it might be the only place they can turn. So . . . yeah. If I win, I'm giving them the money."

"But I don't understand. That should've been all the more reason to do what the judges asked today, yet you still took the risk. Why would you do that?"

The tension in his chest coiled and redoubled. "It's complicated. There are things . . . in my past . . . that aren't like yours." Pete stumbled, the words crowding his mouth, and their bitter taste was an all-too-stark reminder that he'd never once spoken about this to anyone other than his sister.

But for the first time in his life, he trusted someone else enough to let it out.

"I know you think I had a charmed upbringing, but I didn't. My parents are alcoholics, and I'm not talking about the harmless-drunk kind. While there was no shortage of love in your house growing up, there was no shortage of mean in mine."

Lily's eyes rounded, dark blue with surprise. "Did they hit you?"

Pete grabbed onto a shaky breath. "Sometimes. But mostly they were happy to yell. And while I learned to expect it, the yelling actually hurt worse."

"Pete, I'm so sorry. I can't even imagine how hard that must've been." Lily wrapped her hand around his. Funny how such a benign gesture could feel so good.

"As bad as it was for me, it was even worse for my younger sister, Ava. She never really grew a thick skin like I did, so I had to be strong for us both."

Lily's fingers tightened, but he barreled on, just wanting to get the words out. "I figured the best way to do that was to prove our parents wrong. Every time they went on a bender and said Ava and I were worthless, I just told them we weren't. I got cockier and cockier, until that bravado became a part of me. It wasn't because I believed I was good enough, but because otherwise, Ava wouldn't believe *she* was. And I couldn't let them crush her. Not even when I turned eighteen and my father threw me out."

"Oh, God." Lily's whisper rode out on a tremble. "That's where the bittersweet came from. Today, in your cookie. You meant it as both sides of your family."

Damn, she could see right through him. "Yeah. Linzers are Ava's favorite, so the whole thing just made sense."

"Did you stay in Philadelphia to look after her, even when you were in culinary school?"

"Until she went to college, yeah. Once she graduated, she decided to leave the city once and for all, to start a new life away from our parents. Her college roommate is from Riverside, so she came out here. But it was really hard on Ava after all the abuse we'd been through. To be honest, I didn't know if she'd make it at first."

"So you moved out here, too, even though you work all the way in the city," Lily finished, and the raw emotion in her gaze was as palpable as a touch.

Pete nodded. "We've stuck together all our lives, and as far as I'm concerned, Ava's my only family. I love her." His voice went rough, but Lily had asked him a question at the start of this, and it needed answering. "It's why I couldn't dredge up all those memories on film, no matter what the judges asked for. I didn't want to hurt her, and I've been pulling off this hotshot act my entire life. I thought my confidence would carry me today like it always has, but the truth is, it's only a cover. Deep down, I'm just a fraud."

"No, you're not." Lily shifted next to him, moving so close he could see the tears glittering in her eyes, and Christ, would she ever stop flooring him with that purely honest expression?

"You're not a fraud for believing in yourself. You are an amazing man." She cupped his face, her mouth like a gift on his. "Amazing."

Emotion he'd been fighting for far too long roiled up, tightening his words to a whisper. "How can you be so sure?"

Lily simply looked at him. "What you put on the plate today—and why you did what you did—proves it. We might've only spent a week together, but some things get into your bones the minute you see them. And what I know in my bones is that you are not a fraud."

And as Lily gathered him close and showed him exactly how worthy she thought he was, Pete knew deep in his marrow he was falling in love with her.

★   ★   ★

The next four days brought some of the most intense hours Lily had ever spent in the kitchen. Rather ironic, really, that the corresponding nights were also the most intense she'd ever spent in the bedroom.

She'd say it was complicated, but it felt too damned good to be anything other than right.

"Hey." Pete sat down next to her on one of the plush couches in the resort lobby, handing her a Styrofoam to-go cup. "I thought you might like an after-dinner pick-me-up."

She murmured her approval. God, he was spoiling her rotten with his coffee-making skills. But this was the last free night they had between now and the final round, and Lily needed caffeine if she wanted to make the best of it.

She took a sip of her heaven in a cup and nodded down at the notes in her lap. "I was going to go through some recipes tonight, kind of fine-tune things before we get really crazy with PR. What do you say?"

"We're already crazy with PR. I say we skip work and take a breather." Pete gave up a mischievous grin and swung his gaze around the room in mock stealth. "You know, where no camera crews will find us."

Ever since the finalists had been announced, Chase had the resort's tech staff working double time to keep up with the crew from *Delectable*. Between both sets of cameras, numerous interviews, and grueling kitchen sessions complete with visits from each judge, neither of them could sneeze without four different media personnel offering a chorus of "God bless you."

"But the camera *loves* you, Chef Mancuso," Lily laughed, mimicking the magazine reporter in charge of *Delectable*'s online spread. "You are just so *dynamic* and *handsome*."

"No way. You're the fan favorite." Pete nudged her with one jeans-clad knee. "I thought people were going to crash the resort's website with all those requests for your snickerdoodle recipe."

Lily shrugged, although she couldn't contain the smile poking at the corners of her lips. "I just wish I'd realized there was flour on my face *before* I went up to present those to the judges."

She and Pete had finally broken down and watched all the spotlights together last night after Chase described the number of hits on the resort's website as "practically viral." As much fun as Lily poked at the swoony reporter, she had to admit the woman was right about Pete. Each clip showed him clearly in his element, making even the most intricate pastry techniques look like a kindergartener could pull them off without a hitch. His talent was obvious, and his sly charm was as plain on film as it was in person.

And Lily was falling head over kitchen clogs in love with him.

"Very funny." The sexy rumble of Pete's laughter delivered her from her thoughts with a clunk. "But I'm ready for a break. Let's forget work for one night and do something fun."

She paused. They really had been going full tilt. "What'd you have in mind?"

"You, me, a bunch of movies from the hotel's pay-per-view menu, and not a cookie or camera all night. Whaddaya think?"

"I think that sounds great." Lily pushed to her feet, tucking her recipes into her bag as they headed past the merrily twinkling tree. After all, who was she to say no to such well laid plans? They could always catch up on work tomorrow.

They rounded the corner by the elevators, a little girl tugging her mom's hand as she led the woman toward the

Christmas tree with clear excitement, and Lily stopped short. "Oh, crap. Can you give me a couple minutes? I totally forgot to call home, and I need to talk to my mom about Christmas Eve."

Pete's dark brows knit together. "Call me crazy, but I'm pretty sure you have plans on Christmas Eve. Gigantic cookie competition, ten thousand dollars. Ring any bells?"

"Of course. But the final round is open to the public just like the last one was." Lily let out a chuckle, realizing the source of his confusion. "You skipped reading the memos in the folder again, didn't you?"

But rather than crack a smile, Pete just looked at her. "So your mom is coming to watch the final round?"

Oh, hell. She'd felt so easy and happy and good about the night in front of her that the words had just flown out. "Ah. Well, it's on Christmas Eve. We usually spend that time together, so yes. My parents are coming."

"It's nice that they support you like that." Although the words were genuine enough, the tightness beneath gave Pete away.

Her heart shifted hard against her breastbone, but it wasn't enough to stamp out her candor. She cared about him too much to pull punches, anyway. "Have you thought about asking Ava to come?"

Cue the cocky smile, and God, it made Lily's chest ache that much harder. "Nah. She spends the holidays with her roommate's family, since I usually work and all. I don't want to mess with that."

"Are you sure? I mean, you deserve some support too."

He shook his head, but the torn emotion in his eyes defied everything coming out of his mouth. "It's all good, Blondie. I'm okay on my own. Plus, you'll be there."

But as the elevator dinged to end the conversation, Lily was already formulating a plan that would make Pete's Christmas worlds different from any of the ones in his past.

Chapter 11

Lily's eyes blinked open before daybreak on Christmas Eve morning, the serene quiet of her hotel suite doing nothing to calm her. But that jangle of nerves would only throw her off her game, both on the contest floor and afterward. The logical thing would be to just forget it and focus on each task as it came.

Right. And then she could go bench press a Buick. Oh, God, this day had the potential to blow up in her face on so many levels. Taking risks was just not her forte. Taking risks with someone she cared for deeply? Had to be the worst plan ever.

"Hey." Pete curled an arm around her, tantalizingly warm from the bed sheets. "It's really early. You should try to get some more sleep."

"You're up," she pointed out, and he sent a chuckle into her hair as he fitted her tight to his side and kissed the crown of her head.

"Yeah. I'm just thinking about today, I guess." Silence filtered between them, measured only by the pull and release of their breath. "I don't want to compete against you."

"Oh." The straightforward words caught Lily off guard. "I know, but we have to. Only one of us can win."

Pete's arm tightened around the back of her ribcage. "I

know, but it doesn't mean I have to like it. I want to win the money for School Days. If I'd had a place like that, who knows how different my life would've turned out? But if I beat you, I'll feel like I'm stealing your dream."

Lily's heart locked in her throat. "You can't think of it like that, Pete. It'll wreck your concentration, and you're going to need all you can get. I know how much you want to help those kids."

"I do, but . . ." His heart sped up beneath the hand Lily had splayed over his chest. "I love you, Lily. I know it's crazy, but I don't care. If I've learned anything over the last couple of weeks, it's that sometimes, honesty really is the best policy, so yeah. I love you, and I don't want you to lose your chance at having your own bakery."

The words wrapped around her heart with an even combination of shock and pure rightness, and Lily pushed up to look at him through the soft, predawn shadows. "Just because you're pursuing your own dream doesn't mean you're stealing mine. Even if you beat me today, I'm still going to have my own bakery someday." She paused, a tiny smile sliding over her lips. "Don't misunderstand me. I'm still going to do all that I can to win. But if that doesn't happen, it's okay. Because no matter what, I'm in love with you, too."

"God, we're a hell of a pair, aren't we?" Pete reached up to ghost a hand over her cheek, and she smiled into the warmth of his palm.

"I guess you were right. Fate had plans for us after all." Lily's mind shifted back to the phone call she'd made a few days ago, and the knot of nerves reappeared in her belly. "Just promise me something."

"What?"

"Don't be afraid to show people who you are. Especially not today."

He went rigid beside her. "You know it's more complicated than that."

But Lily couldn't relent now. "I'm not talking about
getting all personal in front of the cameras. I'm talking
about you really believing in yourself. You're such a good
person, real and honest and truly talented. Just . . . don't
be scared to let that show."

"God, I love you," Pete whispered.

Lily thought of the contest, and more important, who
would be in the audience today to watch it.

She just hoped Pete still felt that way when the timer hit
zero.

Having a camera crew shadow your every move on one
of the biggest mornings of your life was conducive to a lot
of things. Unfortunately for Lily, calmness wasn't one of
them. Even the thought of her teeny-tiny kitchen at home
was less stressful than this.

"Good morning, contestants, and welcome to the final
round of Pine Mountain's Christmas Cookie Competition." Although Chase addressed the small group of chefs
in a private meeting room, away from the public, both sets
of cameras still blinked as merrily as Christmas lights as
they panned from face to face.

"There are a few things to address before we head to
the competition floor. Obviously, you all know this is an
open round, and I'm excited to say, we've got a full house.
You'll each be completing three courses today, to be made
simultaneously within the allotted time. Each contestant
will serve all three cookies before the next person presents. There will be more on the specific requirements
once you're all in the kitchen, but as usual, you'll have a
planning period and then you'll be given time to bake and
plate."

Chase wished them all luck, and before Lily could manage an exhale of any value, they were excused to the competition floor.

"Good luck, Blondie." The corners of Pete's mouth kicked up into the confident grin Lily had grown to love, and she had no choice but to smile back.

"I believe in hard work, not luck, remember?"

"And you're still going to need both," he teased as they crossed the threshold of the double doors and entered the kitchen.

The roar of applause was loud enough to send a deep shard of surprise through Lily's chest, and she felt her lips part despite her efforts to stay cool. Holy *crap*, there were tons of people in here, all cheering and clapping and holding up signs. Her muscles squeezed tight over her heart at the sight of her parents, both with tears shining in their eyes as they frantically waved. Their presence soothed her adrenaline-fueled jitters, and she let the comfort of it surround her.

But then she saw Pete, his eyes locked on a pretty brunette across from his station. His face was absolutely blank as he made eye contact with the woman, a flare of emotion Lily couldn't pin down passing between them.

When he swung his gaze from the woman to her, all of Lily's calm vanished.

Oh, God. She'd risked too much with that phone call to Riverside.

"Hello, and Merry Christmas!" Chase's voice boomed over the microphone, stealing Lily's focus by default. "Welcome to the final round of Pine Mountain's Cookie Contest. Today, each of our chefs will be working their hardest to earn the top spot in our competition, and with it, a ten-thousand-dollar prize."

He went on to graciously thank the contest sponsors,

including *Delectable* magazine, and introduce Martin, Olivia, and Chef di Matisse to the crowd. Conrad Le Clerc received a healthy dose of applause from the spectators as well, and Lily braced herself against the counter as Chase shifted gears. She absolutely meant what she'd said to Pete about fulfilling her dream someday.

Of course, if she won this contest, someday would come a hell of a lot sooner, and seeing the pride on her parents' faces right there in front of her only made her realize all the more how deeply she wanted it.

Despite who she was competing against.

"All right, contestants! The moment you've all been waiting for has arrived."

As usual, resort management had been bank-vault secretive about the parameters for the round, and Lily's skin prickled with anticipation as Chase finally went for the reveal.

"As chefs and professional bakers, you've all had unique journeys to get where you are. For today's final round, we're giving you a chance to honor the people in your lives who have marked your career path as well as shaped you personally. Each of you will choose three holiday-themed cookies to represent the three people or groups of people who have influenced you the most. You will be judged on concept, flavor, plating and presentation, and the contestant with the best overall score will win."

Lily's pulse hammered in her veins, and she forced herself to steadiness as her mind began whirring with potential recipes.

"You will have forty-five minutes to plan your three courses, and three hours to complete them. Choose wisely, chefs. We are looking for the best Christmas cookie out there, and your time to plan starts . . . right now."

For a sliver of a second, Lily paused, her eyes locking on

Pete's across the expanse of the kitchen. His expression was indecipherable, and she took it in with a pang before the flash of the time clock jerked her back to reality.

She needed a plan. *Now.*

Lily kicked her brain into gear, methodically running through flavor profiles. She made a master list, complete with an overarching theme at the top and separate columns for different recipes and flavors, taking care not to choose anything too similar or strange. Her outline came together step by meticulous step, precise ingredients placed by recipe ideas and checked, then double-checked against the whole.

Yeah, she thought as her ideas threaded together and strengthened into a game plan. This was really viable, nothing too risky. This was . . .

Wait.

An idea threw itself front and center, refusing to budge from Lily's brain. Okay, so it was the total opposite of anything she had on her list, and the best strategy was to dismiss it entirely. Everything else fit the theme, and this idea . . . well, it was the boldest, most outwardly brash thing Lily had ever come up with.

"Five minutes, competitors!" Chase's voice rang out. If Lily was going to take this monstrous leap of faith, she'd need every nanosecond of those five minutes to make it fly.

She didn't even hesitate before her pencil started to move across the page.

No two ways about it. Pete was hosed. How the hell something as cut and dried as winning a cookie competition had managed to become an emotional cyclone was beyond him.

Might have something to do with the fact in addition to wanting to donate his winnings to a program that desperately needed it, Pete was in love with his competition.

And oh, by the way, it looked like said competition had somehow managed to not just find his sister, but make sure Ava had a front row seat as Pete was asked to bare his shitty past in cookie form.

He'd always been able to spot Ava's tells from a mile and a half out, and the way her eyes kept darting from his to Lily's was a dead giveaway that the two had spoken at the very least. Christ, the last thing he needed was for Ava to see this disaster of epic proportions. All the sugar in the world couldn't coat his past. Giving up a kidney might be easier than admitting it out loud, not to mention baking cookies to go with it.

But then Ava's gaze landed on his and held. She pinned him with a bold-as-hell stare and mouthed, *win this.*

All of a sudden, everything clicked into place. By the time Ava sent her glance back toward Lily one final time, Pete got the message as if Ava was shouting it in his ear.

It was time to show everyone who he really was.

The ideas slid together seamlessly in his head, and by the time Chase gave the five-minute warning, then called time on the planning period, Pete had an organized strategy. He stood at his station, palms on the stainless steel, waiting for the call to begin baking. When it came, he was calm and ready, his training and skills kicking into gear and his bravado leading the way.

Ironic how much more it helped when you really believed it.

Pete threw a cocky grin at the camera by his side as he flung himself into action, moving with confidence to the pantry to get his *mise en place* situated. Butter came out of the lowboy to soften, pecans went into the oven until they released their familiar, sweet earthy scent, and sugar became caramel, each move more vital and perfect than the one before it.

Whenever Pete felt the pinch of time falling off the

clock, all he had to do was think of Ava, or Lucas, or most of all, Lily, and his focus settled back into place as if it had never strayed. Ingredients became bases, bases became foundations for more complex layers, until finally, all the components turned into a translation of his life through food. But rather than wanting to shove it away, the dishes forming in front of him strengthened Pete's resolve.

He'd saved the best for last, of course, and he glanced over at Lily's station as he moved to put his final dish together. Despite her lightning-fast movements, she looked as composed as she had a few hours ago, and her ability to spin such focus out of the passion he knew lay underneath made him love her all the more.

This last dish might not be the fanciest thing he'd ever come up with, or the flashiest risk he'd ever taken, but it was the most pure thing Pete had ever made, hands down.

"Contestants! You have ten minutes!"

As Pete grabbed a stack of plates from the rack in the pantry, he knew this story needed to be told, even if it meant losing the competition.

He was done keeping it inside.

Chapter 12

"**T**ime!"

Pete held his hands up and took a step back from his station in the standard response to Chase's call. He looked down at the plates on the counter, his pulse taking on a different brand of holy-shit as each one registered.

No going back now.

"And now, we'll begin our presentations." Chase gestured to the contestant at the very end of the row, and Pete made an attempt at actual, honest-to-goodness breath. He found some sense of normalcy by the time the third contestant went, but then Chase called Lily's name, and Pete was right back at ground zero with his nerves.

"My first dish is a red velvet and cream cheese petit-four, with a raspberry jam glaze for just a touch of tartness to keep the other elements in check." She gestured to the plates in front of the judges with a tiny smile. "I chose to make petit-fours to honor the inspiration I get from pastry chefs and other bakers. When I was a girl, I always wanted to attend Sunday tea at L'Orangerie so I could have the petit-fours. The way something so intricate and wonderful fits into one tiny bite reminds me that big dreams fit in small packages. Knowing that there are people out there who love baking as much as I do is a huge inspiration to me. Please enjoy."

After taking his bite, Conrad Le Clerc's faintly accented voice lilted over the crowd. "So tell me, Ms. Callahan. Did you ever come to see me at L'Orangerie?"

Lily's cheeks flushed, and Pete's heart twisted in his chest. "No, Chef. I wanted to, but . . . well, we didn't have a lot of means when I was growing up."

"Well, with petit-fours like this, you have given me a run for my money. These are lovely."

Lily murmured her polite thanks, but the emotion she felt at the compliment was obvious. The staff brought out her next dish, and she continued. "This next dish is a twist on a Christmas classic. What you have in front of you is a cookie I like to call Not Your Grandmother's Fruitcake. I took a traditional fruitcake base and turned it into a drop cookie, lightening the texture yet keeping the candied fruit and nuts for that flavor we all expect from the dish. To give it a complex, grown-up finish, there's a powdered sugar and aged rum glaze on top."

Pete watched the judges as they tasted. Both Olivia and Martin were unable to hide their impressed glances, and even though Chef di Matisse asked several pointed questions about the execution of the dish, Pete could see the enjoyment on her face as well.

"Can you tell us who inspired this dish?" she asked, and the smile that lit Lily's face was sweet enough to make him ache.

"I've lived in Pine Mountain my whole life, and for me, this place—and the people in it—are honored classics. It's my biggest dream to open a bakery here, in the community that has influenced me and my career. I see cookies like these in the bakery window in my mind's eye, every Christmas."

Pete felt renewed unease at competing against Lily, but it didn't have time to linger before Chase said, "And your last dish?"

Lily turned her gaze over her shoulder to land squarely on Pete's for a split second before she turned back to the judges and spoke. "My last dish is a bit more daring than the other two, but it's one that, for me, defines risk. I've only recently realized that sometimes, it's just as important to follow your heart as it is to follow your plans."

"That's a bit of a different philosophy than anything we've seen from you so far, Ms. Callahan." There was no masking the surprise in Chef di Matisse's voice. "Let's see if it pays off."

But Lily didn't backpedal. "My final dish is a Double Chocolate and Lemon Sable cookie. I used a bittersweet and dark chocolate shortbread base, then added another pop of flavor by adding lemon extract to the dough. The candied lemon peel on top ties in with the flavors in the base to bring both elements together with added kick. I wanted to bring together two ingredients that are strong in their own way to show that sometimes, opposites really can attract. Just like me and the person who inspired this cookie."

The judges thanked Lily, and she returned to her station. Throwing in-your-face flavors out there when she'd stuck with such classics until now was a risk of epic proportions, especially for by-the-book Lily. But even with everything right out in front of her on the line, she'd chosen the risk.

And he loved her enough to return the favor.

"Our next presenter is Pete Mancuso." Chase looked at him expectantly, and Pete stepped forward with a new brand of confidence, one he felt not just on the surface, but in his bones.

"Good afternoon. In thinking about my journey as a chef, it's impossible not to focus on my personal journey as well. The three cookies I've made today represent the people in my life who have inspired me to be true to myself no matter what, both in the kitchen and out."

He gestured to the red earthenware plates being passed to the judges, each one carefully chosen and even more carefully put together for presentation. "My first offering is a Christmas favorite. It's an almond-vanilla sugar cookie with royal icing."

"The detail work is stunning," Olivia murmured, eyes wide over the snowflake-shaped cookie on her plate. "I almost don't want to eat it."

Pete's smile grew. Despite the urge to rush, he'd taken some painstaking time to get the lacy pattern of icing just right over each cookie. "Thank you. I made these cookies for my sister, Ava, who came here today to surprise me. While we didn't have the easiest childhood, we always had each other. I chose the snowflake shape because she's one of a kind."

Pete chanced a look past the judges, surprised to find Ava's eyes not full of tears, but brimming with pride and strength as she grinned from ear to ear.

"I agree, the presentation is beautiful." Chef di Matisse followed her compliment with a few questions about the flavors he'd chosen, but overall, her response buoyed his fortitude as he continued with the next dish.

"My second offering is a best-of-both-worlds cookie, based on the age-old argument of chewy versus crispy." He scanned the audience, pausing until he caught Lucas's surprised expression in the crowd. "I'd always thought it had to be one or the other, but a friend of mine showed me that sometimes, you can like both. That open-mindedness means a lot to me, and I chose to honor it with this cookie.

"It's a chewy oatmeal cookie, with currants and white chocolate chunks to really add some texture to the base and give it a festive appearance. On top, you'll find a toasted oat base to add that crispy layer that balances the whole thing out."

"The play of the currants and white chocolate is surprising. Not to mention delicious." Martin nodded his approval. "Well done, Chef."

"Thank you."

With a deep breath, he turned to the judges to present his last dish.

"My third cookie is one that I wouldn't have chosen even a few weeks ago, but I believe it's a perfect example of how something simple and honest can be one of life's sweetest surprises. I've taken a brown sugar base, enhanced the flavor with some fresh vanilla, and topped it with homemade caramel and finely chopped pecans."

"Oh!" Chef di Matisse's mouth curled into a smile. "You've made a Blondie."

Pete nodded, and God, he'd never been so certain about the pure goodness of a dish in his life. "Yes, Chef. The vitality of the flavors in this Blondie remind me of the person who inspired it, and how much she means to me. Please enjoy."

"This is not necessarily a dish that speaks of Christmas." Conrad Le Clerc looked at Pete over the tops of his wire-rimmed glasses. It hadn't escaped Pete's notice that the renowned pastry chef had remained essentially mum throughout his entire presentation, and he swallowed hard before replying.

"Perhaps not, Chef. But I felt it was the truest embodiment of my life right now."

A smile twitched on the old man's lips. "It is quite possibly the best Blondie I've ever had. Bravo, Chef."

"It's an honor, thank you."

Pete made his way back to his station on rubbery legs, and time fast-forwarded through the remaining few contestants until finally, Chase stood before them with his standard happy-host smile.

"As usual, our chefs have made this decision incredibly

difficult for our judges. Each of you has brought talent together with art to tell ten very different, very wonderful life stories. Sadly, only one of you can take home our top prize of ten thousand dollars. Today's winner has shown not just creativity and skill in execution, but a broad range in both flavor and presentation. The winner of this year's Pine Mountain Christmas Cookie Competition is . . ."

Chapter 13

"**C**hef Pete Mancuso!"

The breath pasted to Lily's lungs expanded with a dizzying whoosh, and it snuffed out the slight pang of disappointment at not hearing her own name. Even though it probably broke four different sets of contest protocol, she ran over to Pete's station before Chase was even done with his follow-up. Pete turned toward her, his expression a mixture of pure shock and growing joy, and she threw her arms around him.

"Oh my God, you did it! You won the money for School Days!" Lily pushed up on her toes, completely unconcerned that there were no less than two dozen cameras clicking around them, and planted her mouth right on his.

They parted, Pete still clearly mired in disbelief. "I thought . . . God, Lily, I thought you were going to beat me. That chocolate sable was a brilliant risk."

She shook her head, tears blurring her eyes as she kissed him again. He deserved this, and he'd beaten her fair and square. "It was *your* risk that really paid off. Congratulations."

"But, your bakery . . ."

"Will happen someday regardless." Lily smiled despite the disappointment welling in her chest at the mention of her bakery. She would come to terms with waiting longer for her dream later. Tonight was for celebrating, not sadness.

On the fringes of her awareness, Lily heard Chase finish his wrap-up, thanking the judges and the sponsors, but it was the sound of a feminine throat being cleared that had both her and Pete turning toward the stands.

"There's going to be no living with you now, is there?" The pretty brunette crossed her arms over her chest, but her smile canceled out the toughness in her stance.

"Hey, Ava." Pete let go of Lily to loop his arms around his sister in a tight hug. "It means a lot to me that you came."

"Thanks to Lily." Ava fixed her with a warm glance before returning her eyes to her brother. "I can't believe you didn't even tell me you entered! It's a *huge* deal."

"I know. I just . . . the holidays are hard enough for us. I didn't want to bring back bad memories."

Ava sighed, the sound a total contrast with the chaotic buzz of the crowd now filling the kitchen. "Thank you for looking out for me. But I'm tougher than you think." She smiled at Lily. "And thank you for hitting up the Pine Mountain grapevine to find my number. It seems you two are, um, quite well acquainted."

Lily's cheeks prickled with heat that had nothing to do with the elevated temperature in the room. "I take it you watched the clips online."

"Are you kidding? It was the first thing I did after you called." Ava nodded her head to the growing crowd behind them. "And speaking of which, it looks like you're going to be busy for a while. How about we catch dinner later?"

Lily's head sprang up, and she caught sight of her parents smiling down from the stands. "Actually, I'd love it if you'd both join my family's Christmas celebration. As long as, ah, you're okay with that."

"I am very okay with that." Pete wrapped an arm around her, and it felt better than all the past Christmases combined. "It's about time Ava and I started some new family traditions."

"Pardon me." A gentle voice at Lily's elbow had her turning toward the judge's stand. "I don't mean to interrupt."

"Oh! Mr. Alexander." Lily smiled at the judge. "You're not interrupting at all."

"Yes, well. I was wondering if I could have a word with the two of you."

Lily exchanged a look with Pete while Ava waved a silent good-bye-for-now and slipped through the crowd.

"Sure," he said, and Lily nodded.

"First off, congratulations to you both. It was truly thrilling to watch you compete."

"Thank you," Lily said, trying to keep her curiosity to a dull roar while Pete looked as though he felt the same.

"I'm not sure if you're aware of this, but I'm the silent owner of several bakeries along the Blue Ridge. One of the reasons I offered to judge this contest was to test the market in Pine Mountain."

Lily's heart kicked against her ribs, but she managed a polite, "I see."

"Frankly, Ms. Callahan, your desire to run a bakery interests me a great deal. With talent like yours, I'd be very open to an investment opportunity." He looked from her to Pete. "I realize you'll both probably get a lot of offers, but you're an incredible team. I'd be willing to make it worth your while to open a bakery here in Pine Mountain with me as a silent partner. Are you interested?"

Lily's breath hitched. If the way Conrad Le Clerc had salivated over that Blondie was any indication, all Pete had to do was say the word and his dream job would become a reality. She couldn't ask him to do this, no matter what she wanted.

"I am, yes, but—"

"*We* are," Pete said, looking at her with a slow, sexy grin. "As long as you're up for a partnership, that is."

"Pete." Lily angled herself toward him, and Martin stepped back to let them confer more privately. "You could have that job at L'Orangerie, and you know it."

He laughed and wrapped an arm around her. "Probably. But I don't care. I want this. I want *you*."

Her heart fluttered. "Are you sure?"

"Positive. There's nowhere else I'd rather be than with you, Blondie."

It was all Lily could do to keep her laughter from overflowing. She turned back toward Martin with an ear-to-ear grin. "What's the sugar without the spice? Count us in, Mr. Alexander."

"Together."

Want to get sweet in the kitchen? Kimberly Kincaid says these Blondies are sure to please!

PETE MANCUSO'S BLONDIES

1 cup pecans, roughly chopped
1½ cups all-purpose flour
1 teaspoon salt
2 teaspoons baking powder
¾ cup (1½ sticks) unsalted butter, melted
2 cups light brown sugar (packed)
2 eggs, slightly beaten
2 teaspoons pure vanilla extract
1½ cups (okay to eyeball this) store-bought caramel
    topping
1½ cups thin twisty pretzels, broken into pieces

Preheat oven to 325°F.

Prepare a 9 x 13-inch baking pan by lining it with parchment paper and spraying with cooking spray, leaving some overhang on either side. Set pan aside. Spread pecans in a single layer on a cookie sheet. Bake until just fragrant, about 4 to 5 minutes (this releases lots of flavor—don't be tempted to skip this step!) Remove and cool.

Increase oven temperature to 350°F.

Sift flour, baking powder, and salt together into a small bowl and set aside. Using a mixer, combine melted butter and brown sugar until it resembles wet sand (I promise it will taste better than that). Making sure the mixture has cooled from melting the butter, slowly incorporate eggs and vanilla. Mix well. Add flour mixture in small increments, scraping down sides as needed. This mixture will be thick. Your mixer may protest a little. That's okay!

Stir in pecans by hand and spread mixture in prepared pan with an offset spatula (or you can put a little cooking spray on your hands and press it into place). Bake for 20 to 25 minutes, until the top is golden brown. A cake tester should come up essentially clean, with maybe a crumb or two. These are meant to be slightly gooey in the middle. Cool in the pan on a wire rack for 10 minutes. Lift out of pan to cool completely. Remove and discard parchment.

Once cool, carefully slide the blondie sheet back into the 9 x 13 pan. Top with caramel topping and refrigerate 30 minutes, until set. Just before serving, top with pretzel bits. Slice into bars and serve to the one you love!

Makes approximately 3 dozen bars.

EPILOGUE

January 1

The evening air was crisp, with a light breeze whispering the promise of more snow. The air inside the community center was significantly more heated. Every man, woman, and child in Pine Mountain had jammed inside the big, red-brick building for the second time in a little more than two weeks. But this time, it wasn't about bidding on Christmas cookies. Tonight, it was about what the Christmas cookies had done for the community center. And a few firemen calendars. And a philanthropic gesture or two . . .

Clara spotted Abby near the back of the crowd, just inside the doors. "Oh good, I'm so glad you're here. We've been worried about you! When did you finally get your power back on?"

Abby's cheeks were a little pink, but it was the twinkle in her eyes that had Clara suspecting it wasn't the cold winter chill that had put it there. "I'm . . . not entirely sure what day that was."

Clara's gaze narrowed. "Oh . . . really."

"I'm sorry, I know I should have called, or . . . or something. I was a little distracted."

"Right! With the holidays and your business. I wasn't thinking. How is it going?"

"Well, anatomically correct men definitely had something to do with the distraction. Man, actually." Her blush deepened and awareness dawned for Clara.

She playfully swatted at her friend. "You . . . you gingerbread maker. Here Lily and I were worried that you'd frozen to death in your cabin. Will was offering to send half the fire department up there."

Now Abby arched a brow. "Will? And who might that be?"

"Oh, well, I kind of almost burned down my house. The morning after the cookie swap actually. And . . . an old friend offered me a place to stay."

"An old . . . friend. I see." Abby's lips twitched, but the twinkle in her eyes held nothing back.

"So, who's the anatomically correct guy?" Clara demanded, steering the topic back to Abby. "And, more important, *where's* the guy?"

"He's heading up to the stage. There."

Clara looked at where she was pointing and—"Isn't that the guy who crashed the cookie swap? The guy who paid—" She broke off, gasped. "*No!* He's the guy! The guy who paid all that money, for *your* cookies. How did you—and where did you—I mean, he took off out of here like a bat out of hell."

"And he crashed said batmobile halfway up the mountain. I . . . found him. And helped him." At Clara's look of unmitigated glee, Abby nudged her friend in the side. "Sort of like how your *old friend* helped you. I'm guessing."

Now it was Clara who felt the heat climb in her cheeks. "Maybe."

"And where is this old friend?"

Clara nodded toward the stage at the front of the room. "Oh, he's up there, too."

"Up . . ." Abby turned to look at the stage. "There?

Which one? Oh, look! There's Lily and Pete! I wasn't sure she'd be able to talk him into being here." She quickly turned to Clara. "Oh. Yeah. Pete. And Lily. Awkward. Did you hear, I mean, have you talked to Lily?"

"Yes, and don't worry. It's fine. Surprising," she added, which didn't begin to cover it, "but fine." Not the part where Pete had fallen for Lily, but that her workaholic, career focused friend had fallen right back. Watching Lily now, up on stage, tucked under the arm of Pete Mancuso, Clara noticed the way they looked at each other. It was a look she now recognized, and understood. Intimately. "Well. I'll be damned." They'd fallen all the way. She grinned, truly happy for both of them.

"He beat her, you know," Abby said. "In the cookie contest, I mean. Won the whole dang thing. That's why he's here."

"Oh, I'm thinking she won a pretty nice prize herself."

"True," Abby said, her happy sigh echoing Clara's.

Hearing that, Clara glanced down at Abby and her eyes widened a bit. It looked like maybe Abby understood that look now, too. Interesting. And awesome.

"Hey, I saw your cookie column in the paper," Abby commented as the crowd on the stage continued to assemble. Every year on New Year's Day, Pine Mountain hosted a community Giving Back Brunch, where various local individuals or businesses helped to launch the new year by making charitable donations and contributions. "I haven't had the chance to read all of them," Abby went on, "but I loved the direction you took. I bet your editor is thrilled."

"Well, she was. I actually kind of quit. The day after Christmas."

Abby's mouth dropped open. "You *what?*"

"The column was only supposed to run until then, but it did pretty well with readers and Fran wanted to make it permanent. But, to be honest, I didn't want to get stuck again doing something I'm really not cut out for. Will gave me an idea about approaching another paper with my story ideas. So . . . I did."

"We only have one paper."

"Well, Bealetown has one, too. And it turns out their editor was really interested in my sample stories."

"Sample stories? When did you have time to write sample stories?"

"Once I got the cookie column slant figured out, we were able to get them done pretty quickly."

Abby grinned. "We?"

"I baked. He kept his kitchen from going up in flames. Anyway, I ended up writing a story about the new tri-county forensic lab and a side story about one of the cold cases they think they'll be able to finally close that involves several of the local families. I want to write stories about what's happening in the community, both bigger picture, and smaller, more intimate stories. Anyway, the Bealetown editor offered me a job, starting tomorrow, actually."

"That's . . . incredible!"

Clara looked back at the stage in time to see Abby's man—"What's his name?"

"Whose name?"

"Your anatomically correct, real-live man?"

Abby laughed. And blushed a little. "Lander. Lander Reynolds."

"Why is he up on stage?"

"I'll tell you if you tell me which one is Will."

"Well . . . he's the guy holding the big oversized check."

Abby's mouth dropped open and she turned to Clara. "The guy wearing only a fireman's hat and uniform pants?"

"Technically, he's not really a fireman anymore." Like that made all the difference. "In fact, he's going to head up that forensic lab I wrote the story about. We . . . we went to college together."

Abby's eyes goggled. "He's *that* Will? He was on the cover of that calendar. You never said he looked like that."

"He didn't. Back then. And you know he's on the calendar cover because . . . ?"

"Well, maybe it's possible I saw one. Somewhere. Oh, right, I bought one." She gave Clara a sheepish smile. "It was for a good cause."

Clara laughed. "That's what Will keeps telling himself. He will be so glad when this is over."

They watched as first the fire department presented their check to the children's hospital charity, whose main business offices happened to be in Pine Mountain.

Then Lander stepped up and announced a new annual college scholarship sponsored by his family's bank, Philadelphia Capital, for seniors graduating from the local high school. He mentioned how grateful he was for the town's warm welcome—at which Clara nudged Abby and whispered, "And how warm was it?"

Abby nudged back, but her smile said it all, as Lander went on to explain that he wanted to become an integral part of helping the town grow, seeing as he was now a resident. At which point Clara hugged Abby, then whispered, "I want all the details. Every crumb."

"I'll share if you will. Does he dress like that when you're baking?"

Clara snicker-snorted, drawing a few glances and a fresh peal of laughter from Abby.

Then it was finally Pete's turn. He stepped up and donated his winnings from the resort cookie contest to Marianna, the community director, for use in the center's School Days program for the town's underprivileged kids. He tried to quickly duck back in line, but Marianna grabbed him, and her heartfelt hug of thanks was felt by every person in the room. Pete seemed momentarily stunned, then hugged her back, and the cheers grew louder.

"Lily said he wanted to make the contribution anonymous, but she convinced him that it was a good thing, letting other locals know how easy it is to share, to give back, and that it would spread more goodwill than simply sending a check in the mail. Lander and I had pretty much the same conversation."

"Good for both of you. And good for both of them."

All three men actually looked like they'd rather be almost anywhere else, and Clara had no doubt they'd all have preferred to make their contributions in a far less public fashion. But looking around at all the smiling faces, seeing everyone clapping, cheering them, she knew it was important to give folks a chance to come together, celebrate the good things together, and be inspired to create more of those occasions. It was why the town held the annual brunch in the first place.

As Marianna made her closing speech, still wiping tears from her eyes, Abby linked her arm through Clara's and pressed her head briefly against Clara's shoulder. "This might have been the best Christmas ever."

Clara thought about the amazing changes that had happened for all three of them since the time, just a few weeks earlier, when they'd all been standing in that same exact spot. She squeezed Abby's arm and grinned. "Santa works in mysterious ways."

Lily popped through the crowd just then and pulled them both into a group hug. "Happy New Year!"

Pete, Lander, and Will emerged through the crowd and smiled as introductions were made.

Pete took Lily's hand just as Lander found Abby's. Will smiled at Clara, then, still half-dressed, stepped behind her and grinned sheepishly as he wove his arms around her waist.

Clara covered his hands with her own, and smiled as her gaze connected with Lily's and Abby's. They each busted out in grins at the same time.

"Happy best year!" Clara announced.

"I'll raise a cookie to that!" Lily said.

"Mine come already raised," Abby added, making the three women laugh, and their men look a tad adorably uncomfortable.

"Yeah, well, I think I'll stick to supplying the milk," Clara said.

Everyone laughed as Lily and Abby both quickly chimed, "Here, here!"

"Play to your strengths," Will murmured in her ear, as conversation broke out amongst the other four.

She squeezed his hands and leaned back against him. "You know, I think we all finally have."

Eager to get back to Pine Mountain? Bellamy Blake doesn't know it, but she's heading that way, and into the arms of sexy mechanic Shane Griffin. Read on for a taste of *Turn Up the Heat* by Kimberly Kincaid, coming in March.

The contract on Bellamy Blake's desk was a doorstop waiting to happen. She flipped through the pages absently, rolling her eyes at the legalese. Hell, it could be *Portuguese* as far as she was concerned. Being a real estate analyst for the second largest bank in Philadelphia had sounded so much better when she'd started, fresh out of graduate school. After three years, an endless supply of doorstops and a boss who made Attila the Hun look like a lap dog, the whole thing had lost most of its luster.

Bellamy sank back in her sleek leather desk chair and stared at the waste of foliage that was her current contract, trying to ignore the headache forming behind her eyes. Still, the doorstop-slash-contract wasn't going to negotiate itself. It was time to buck up and take one for Team Paycheck, headache be damned.

Bellamy had no sooner waded to her knees in fine print when the phone on her desk rang. She was so grateful for the distraction that she didn't even check the caller ID before she scooped the phone to her ear. Maybe it would be a cheesy office supply salesman with a well-rehearsed spiel on the virtues of buying toner cartridges in bulk. That would be good for at least twenty minutes of distraction.

This had to be an all-time low.

"Bellamy Blake," she murmured, pushing her blond curls over her shoulder to tuck the phone to her ear.

"I cannot *believe* you didn't tell us you're moving to San Diego, you hideous bitch!"

Bellamy sat back, unfazed at her best friend Holly's theatrics, and grinned. This was even better than the toner guy. "Slow down there, Encyclopedia Dramatica. What are you talking about?" she laughed. "And by the way, hello is usually customary for the whole phone-greeting thing. Just so you know."

"Screw hello! You're *moving*?! If you told Jenna and the two of you kept it from me because you knew I'd freak out, I'm killing you both!" Holly wailed. Man, her flair for the old melodrama was on fire today.

"Are you out of your mind? I just reupped the lease on my condo. Why would I . . . oh! Hold on, my cell phone is ringing." Bellamy paused to dig through her purse. "You know how my boss is. If I let her go to voicemail even once, she'll light that thing up like Times Square on New Year's Eve until I answer."

"Boss, schmoss! For once, the Wicked Witch can wait!"

The caller ID made Bellamy sag with relief. "Oh, it's Jenna! Hang on." She slid her cell phone under her other ear and tipped her head toward it.

"Hey, Jenna, let me call you back. I've got Holly on the other line, and she's ranting about—"

"California? God, Bellamy! Did Derek propose or something to get you to go? Why didn't you say anything?"

Didn't anyone stick with a good old-fashioned *hello* anymore? And what was with the idea of her moving across the country?

"Okay, remind me not to sample whatever Kool-Aid you and Holly have obviously been sharing. I'm not moving to California, and I'm *definitely* not getting married.

What the hell is going on?" If her friends wanted to pull one over on her in the practical joke department, they needed to work on their skills, big time.

"You're getting *married*?" Holly's screech from the forgotten office phone rivaled that of a tornado warning going full bore, grabbing Bellamy's attention.

She fumbled as she scooped the other receiver back to her ear. "No! Jesus, Holly. I just said I'm *not* getting married!" Bellamy huffed, starting to get exasperated.

"I'm Jenna, not Holly," her other best friend replied from the cell phone, confused.

Bellamy released a heavy sigh. "Holly's on my office phone, and I've got one of you on each ear, even though you're both insane. Look, if this is some kind of sick candid camera thing that you guys are planning to throw on YouTube, so help me . . ."

"Bellamy, are you watching Derek's newscast?"

Whoa. What was with Jenna's talking-down-a-suicide-jumper voice? She only reserved that for Holly when she was going full-tilt, so something must really be up. Bellamy paused.

"Just because he's my boyfriend doesn't mean I watch all of his newscasts, Jenna. I'm at work, and my boss just dropped a couple hundred pages worth of a contract on my desk." Bellamy's stomach shifted uncomfortably. "Why?"

"Oh my freaking God. You don't know," Holly breathed.

Bellamy pressed her office phone to her ear, feeling like a human Ping-Pong ball. "Don't know what, Holly? Come on, you guys. What's going on?"

"Derek's moving to San Diego," they replied, in stereo.

Bellamy's brows knit together in confusion, and her first impulse was to laugh, although it came out more like a nervous croak. "That's impossible. I think he'd have told me if he was moving across the country." It wasn't as if San

Diego was a hop, skip and jump from Derek's upscale Philadelphia brownstone. It was on another coast, for God's sake.

"Uh, sweetie, maybe you should call him," Holly offered.

The croak made a repeat performance. "Okay, first of all, that's going to be kind of hard seeing as how both of my phones are tied up at the moment. Secondly, he's clearly on the air right now, saying something that's making the both of you lose your marbles." Ugh, what was that tightness in her chest? Who'd have thought that turkey and Swiss could give a girl heartburn like this.

"Google him, or grab the live stream from the Internet or something," Holly tried again. "Because I'm telling you, I'm not making this up."

Far be it for Bellamy to be a spoilsport, especially if it would put an end to this weird little charade. "You want me to Google my boyfriend to prove that you're playing a practical joke on me? Okay, fine. Whatever blows your skirt up," she laughed.

Bellamy no sooner had her hands over her keyboard when Jenna's voice cut through the phone line attached to Bellamy's other ear in a panic. "Wait, did Holly tell you to . . . wait! Bellamy, don't—"

Too late.

Bellamy's heart did the pitter-patter-holy-shit in her chest as her eyes focused on Channel Eight's home page. The headline ANCHORMAN DEREK PATTERSON BIDS PHILADELPHIA A FOND FAREWELL splashed over a handsome headshot that was all too familiar.

Her boyfriend was moving to California, and he hadn't told her a damned thing.

And don't miss Donna Kauffman's new series, *The Bachelors of Blueberry Cove,* **coming next month.**

PELICAN POINT

"Humor, heart, and characters you wish lived
next door."
—Mariah Stewart

Blueberry Cove, Maine, is as small-town as small towns get. More than a little quirky, it has sheltered generations of families. But there's always room for a new face . . .

Fixing things has always been Alex McFarland's greatest gift and keenest pleasure. But with her own life thoroughly broken, she's signed on to renovate the dilapidated Pelican Point lighthouse, hoping to reconnect with herself. The last thing she expects is to find herself falling in love—with the glorious coastline, with age-old secrets and welcome-home smiles . . . with rugged Logan McCrae, the man she just might be able to build new hopes on.

DIY is so much better with two . . .